The Element of Surprise

Ashuan Envy 1

Janna Ruth

First published in New Zealand in 2025

Copyright © 2025 by Janna Ruth

67 Montgomery Avenue

Wellington 6012

New Zealand

www.janna-ruth.com

ISBN-13: 978-1-0670398-0-6 (Epub)

ISBN-13: 978-1-0670398-1-3 (Paperback)

The Ashuan Series

Ashuan Greed

A Drop of Magic
A River of Magic
A Spring of Magic

Ashuan Lust

Hell Hath no Fury
Hell Hath no Ambition
Hell Hath no Passion

Ashuan Envy

The Element of Surprise
The Element of Jealousy (coming early 2026)
The Element of Hope (coming mid 2026)

.

Other series

Parisian Ghosts

Ghosts of the Catacombs
Ghosts of the Crusade
Ghosts of the Resistance
Ghosts of the Opera
Ghosts of the Provence

Ghosts of the World Fair
Ghosts of the Monarchy (coming August 2025)
Ghosts of the Empire (coming October 2025)
Ghosts of the Revolution (coming January 2026)

Spirit Seeker

A Force of Nature
Natural Enemies
Back to Nature
Against Human Nature
Natural Disaster

ASHUAN ENVY BOOK 1

THE ELEMENT OF SURPRISE

JANNA RUTH

For all the everyday heroes who lead with empathy and hope.

Recap: Ashuan Lust

Here are a couple of things to remember about what happened in Ashuan Lust:

- Matt's mother, the Archdemon of Lust, incited a battle between her three sons, Balthasar, Caspar, and of course, Matt, making them believe they'd be succeeding her. In truth, she was looking for a new mate. Matt and his friends survived various attacks by his brothers, but were eventually lured to Hell when his mother kidnapped Samantha.

- During the rescue mission, Matt killed his brother Caspar, Samantha's emblem of power awakened, and Balthasar ultimately deposed of his mother and became the new Archdemon of Lust. It was then revealed, he'd been working with Chay all along.

- Matt and Samantha went through a lot during Ashuan Lust. After Matt apologised for the crimes he committed in Ashuan Greed, their relationship was slowly mending until they could no longer deny their love and finally got together in the finale.

- Samantha had an especially hard time. She was often targeted by Matt's brothers and later his mother. At the same time, her parents' marriage was falling apart and resulted not just in a divorce but her mother and sister moving away.

- Fabian was mostly concerned with his mother, who suffered

from burnout. He put a lot of effort into keeping his mother's shop open while juggling finals at school. He started the season dating Lucille, but the relationship fizzled out fast, and he got together with Ophelia, a young girl he'd rescued from an Ishtar cult.

- Jan initially worked at the youth hostel, but eventually lost his job and got kicked out of home. He then moved into the Blackstone House, a run-down, cursed property and made it his own. He continued learning about his healing powers and began training as a paramedic.

- Lucille had a lot of romantic drama, dating first Fabian and then young reporter Philipp. Neither was meant to last. Meanwhile, her parents adopted a boy, Pascal, who she despised at first, but later learnt had telekinetic powers and needed her.

- Rachel learnt the truth about her parents' break-up only to see them get back together again when her father temporarily moved to Greenvalley. She acquired a ghost companion named Hugo von Hohenstetten and later developed a crush on hospital technician Adam Black. Although he moved back to New Zealand, Rachel decided to give their relationship a chance.

- Apart from Jan, the friends graduated with their class, making plans for their future studies. Fabian's became almost immediately derailed when the university rejected him prematurely. At the end of Ashuan Lust, he instead received a mysterious letter from the Citadel of Magic.

And that's what you missed on Ashuan Lust.

A note about sensitive topics

There is a lot of magic and paranormal creatures in this series that create all kinds of magical drama. Some of it is action-packed, some of it is funny, and some of it can cut a bit deeper than you might expect. If you don't like spoilers and you're cool with everything, skip this note and start the book. If you want to be prepared, read on. I'm writing this because reading should be fun, not bear nasty surprises.

Our heroes are entering a new phase in their life. Some of them stay in Greenvalley, while others study at exotic places such as the Citadel of Magic and the University of Fader. These places often have different sensibilities and deal with different magics, among them a secret necromancy club that performs human and animal experiments as well as dealing with fresh organs.

In Fader, our heroes are dragged into a terror attack on the parliament, complete with lockdown, police crackdown, and assassins.

In another adventure, they're forced to deal with a vengeful god that initiates a purge-like situation.

But Greenvalley isn't safe either, and in one instance, they encounter a type of monster that literally eats the flesh of living people.

Lastly, the stakes are high as always and not everyone will make it out alive of this book. In fact, the death at the end of the book might be one of the hardest I've ever written into Ashuan (and I've already written it three times).

While our heroes live in a dangerous world, it's also a beautiful one.
For every dark place there is light and humour, and—of course—magic.
Lots and lots of magic.

Have fun with *Ashuan Envy*!

Love, Janna

Part 1
Water & Fire

Fabian

The letter sat on his desk, judging him silently.

We are pleased to offer you a place at the Citadel of Magic...

Fabian glared at it from his bed. By now, the letter should've been riddled with holes or at least soggy, but the paper had resisted his feelings on the matter for three months and it wasn't going to start disintegrating now. So much for his famed elemental magic.

His decision changed every day. Some days, he felt intrigued, and since nothing else had come up, he thought about giving it a shot. Other days, he hated the letter and all it stood for with unbridled passion. The reason nothing else had come up was precisely because the Citadel of Magic wanted him: they'd messed with his mundane university applications, the rejection letters coming hard and fast. Now autumn had arrived and all his friends were off to university—or continuing their professional training, in Jan's case—while he had no plan and no prospects. Maybe once the offer had finally lapsed, they'd give up trying to recruit him.

The door opened and his girlfriend slipped in. Ophelia dropped her school bag and immediately slung her arms around his neck, snuggling against him. "Stop staring at it!"

Fabian forced himself to look away and kiss her. "Sorry." For a few precious moments, he forgot all about the letter.

"Don't be sorry." Ophelia sounded amused. "It's a big decision. One you really need to make, though. The semester starts on Monday."

That was only three days away. Fabian groaned and let himself fall backwards onto the bed.

Ophelia immediately climbed him and started to kiss his neck.

He buried a hand in her long black hair, welcoming the distracting attention, but the image of the letter had burnt itself into his retina. "I don't wanna go." Today's mood was definitely a no-go.

"Then tell them that. You have to reach out eventually."

"I can't."

The letter had explained acceptance would be registered by a drop of blood on the enrolment form, which gave Fabian the creeps, but there'd been no instruction about what to do if he wanted to refuse, nor had there been a return address or any contact information.

"You can reach us in the usual way," was a useless instruction if one didn't know what the usual way was.

"Have you asked Samantha yet?" Ophelia sat back up. Her hands splayed on his chest, she regarded him with mild annoyance.

"Nope," Fabian admitted.

While his friends had been there when he'd received the letter, it'd also happened in the aftermath of Samantha being kidnapped and their near-disastrous attempt to free her. He doubted anyone even remembered. Much less Samantha.

Ophelia sighed. "Fabian, please. I don't know enough about the magical world to help you. If it were me—"

"—you'd take it in a heartbeat."

She didn't even look ashamed. "If only they offered Snake Whispering or Shadow Wielding."

Who knew what they did? Was the Citadel full of elemental mages? Or did they teach other magical disciplines, too? To find out, Fabian would have to attend, which brought him back to the letter.

"Screw this." He put his hands on Ophelia's hips and began stroking upwards.

Ophelia grinned. "Gladly."

The next day, they met with their friends at a café near Greenvalley University. The campus was preparing for the onslaught of students hitting it in a week. For now, it was still blissfully empty, and the café had sufficient space for their rather large group. When Fabian and Ophelia arrived, Matt and Samantha were already there, unable to refrain from touching or kissing each other for even a minute. Robert and Anne arrived soon after, followed by Jan, who groaned when he saw them.

"What's he doing here?" Jan asked Anne.

"I thought this was an open invite," Robert said.

Jan raised an eyebrow. "Just like when you thought my birthday was an open invite?" They'd celebrated Jan's 21st a month ago at the town's only club.

Robert grins. "That was a great party."

"To which you weren't invited."

Anne just shrugged, unwilling to take sides between her brother and her dorky boyfriend.

The tension dissolved with the arrival of Rachel and Lucille. Lucille had missed the party after travelling all summer. Now her skin was tan, but her hair was much shorter, falling only to her shoulders and newly strawberry blonde.

"That's pretty," Samantha said as Lucille greeted everyone, kissing cheeks. "Planned or accident?"

"Planned," Lucille said. "I thought, new phase, new look." She glanced over at the university. "I can't wait to get started."

"Same!" Samantha's eyes were gleaming.

She'd always been studious, and Fabian knew she'd thrive here, blossoming under the academic challenges and opportunities. It reminded him, though, how she'd be doing it without him. For the first time in their lives, Samantha would be going somewhere he couldn't follow, and it scared him. Even if he took up the citadel's offer, how was he going to survive without his best friend constantly on his case?

"Happy belated birthday," Lucille said to Jan, then grabbed something from her bag. "Hope this is alright."

Without opening it, Jan joked, "If it isn't, I can probably sell it to help pay off my car."

Lucille slapped him on the shoulder. "You know, I didn't miss that at all in Palau."

"How was it?" Ophelia asked.

"Oh, it was amazing. Clear waters for miles, green forests, warm weather, and some seriously hot guys. On the other hand, there was little else to do than dive and flirt."

"I wouldn't mind that," Matt said. He turned to Samantha. "Flirt a little with my eyes, dive deep..." As Samantha burst into giggles, he kissed her.

Anne covered her eyes while Jan groaned and Ophelia sneaked an arm around Fabian's back with a big grin. As for Fabian, he was just glad his best friend had finally found the love and commitment she deserved.

Lucille's face mirrored his feelings. She clapped her hands. "Well, Palau was great, but we all want to know what New Zealand was like?" She grinned at Rachel.

Judging by Rachel's eye roll, she'd already told Lucille all there was to know. "Fine. New Zealand was mind-blowing. It's a breathtaking country full of natural wonders."

"And human wonders?" Lucille batted her eyes.

Rachel's cheeks flushed. "I had a very good-looking guide who really made me feel welcome. He showed me not just the natural wonders—" she paused while Robert excused himself to go to the bathroom "—but the magical ones, too."

Samantha pulled away from Matt. "What?"

"Adam's a witch," Lucille said, eyes glistening. She cleared her throat. "Sorry, didn't want to steal your thunder."

If Rachel was annoyed, she didn't show it. "Well, he can weave magic like you, Sam. Apparently, his mum taught him. It was part of the reason he'd applied for the position in Greenvalley. However, what may be more exciting—"

"More exciting than him being one of us?" Lucille asked.

"Oh, he's much more than that," Rachel said, sounding a little smug. "His father, Geoffrey Black, is a world traveller. He's never home because he holds a seat at the Interglobal Parliament in Fader."

"No way!" Matt exclaimed. "For Ashuan?"

Fabian looked back and forth between them. "Wait, what are we talking about?"

"The Interglobal Parliament," Matt said, in a reverent tone. "They basically rule all the worlds in the Interglobal Union. Fader... you know, where I'll be studying from next week on."

"Oh, the other world."

Fabian still struggled with the concept of other worlds. Travelling to Hell was one thing—humanity had known about Heaven and Hell for millennia. But the fact completely other worlds existed, enough of them to form a common parliament, freaked him out.

Matt nodded. "They're only the most important, most influential, and most powerful political body in the Abstract Space, but no biggie. And Adam's father has a seat?" he asked Rachel, who nodded.

"For Ashuan."

Matt frowned. "Really? But Ashuan hasn't been integrated into the Interglobal Community yet. I'm sure Chay would've mentioned it if it had. He's been an adviser to the parliament for two hundred years or so."

"Well, why don't we ask him on Monday?" Rachel said. "We're still meeting Chay in Fader, right? I told Adam to be there." Rachel had a secret little smile Fabian had never seen on her before. "It's much cheaper than flights."

"Didn't you just see each other three days ago?" Lucille asked with unveiled glee. She didn't even wait for her to answer before squealing and throwing her arms around her neck. "I'm so happy for you!"

Jan rolled his eyes, but he seemed more amused than cranky. "Speaking of Monday—I got pulled into a shift, so I can't come."

"Monday!" Robert returned just at that moment. "I'll see you at the hospital!"

"Why?" Jan frowned. "Are you finally getting brain surgery?"

Anne shot him a dark glare, but then she cleared her throat. "I was trying to tell you this before, but well Robert signed up for a free social year and—"

"I'm helping at the hospital," Robert said, with unbridled enthusiasm. "Isn't that great? We're gonna be colleagues!"

"Yay me," Jan said, drily. "I'll have to ask for some extra tours."

"Are the rest of you coming?" Samantha asked.

Ophelia moaned. "Well, Anne and I have school. Otherwise, totally." She looked at Fabian. "You've got to tell me all about it!"

Fabian rubbed his neck. "Sure, I…" If he took the offer, he'd have school on Monday, too. "Um, I might… I don't know."

"Oh, please." Samantha made big puppy eyes. "It's not dangerous. We're just gonna go to the park and visit the market."

"And tour parliament," Rachel added. "Adam's father invited us."

Lucille gasped. "Oh, he's my favourite boyfriend of yours ever."

"Ouch." Fabian winced. To his knowledge, Rachel's only other boyfriend had been him. It hadn't been a great relationship, but it hadn't been that bad.

Lucille poked her tongue out at him and grinned while the conversation moved on. Fabian leant back and listened, his thoughts still with the damned letter in his room. Apart from Ophelia, who gave him a knowing smile and rubbed his leg, no one even noticed him withdrawing.

The goodbyes seemed to last forever, but slowly everyone filed out. Fabian had his arm around Ophelia's shoulders and was about to leave, too, when Samantha popped up beside him.

"Hey, we barely had a chance to talk. I was thinking about visiting my grandma. Would you like to come? You know, just the two of us?"

Irritated, Fabian stared. "What about Matt?"

"I already sent him home." She looked past him at Ophelia. "Sorry, I don't want to steal him or anything. If you have plans—"

"No." Ophelia ducked out from under Fabian's arm and clapped his chest. "He's all yours."

Fabian frowned. "What's happening?"

"You go with Sam," Ophelia said, nodding. "You're best friends, right? You haven't caught up in ages, and I still have homework. This

is good." It came across as a bit too desperate. "You can talk about...
stuff."

When he finally got her meaning, Fabian almost groaned. "Yeah.
Stuff."

"I love stuff." Samantha giggled, before taking Fabian's arm and
leading him away. Once they were out of earshot, she dropped the mask.
"Seriously, tell me about the 'stuff'. What's going on with you? You
were awfully quiet."

"That's just because Lucille was so loud." Fabian sighed. "Fine. You
probably don't remember, but I got this letter—"

"Of course, I remember. The Citadel of Magic invited you to study
Elemental Magic."

Fabian stared at her. "You remember? But you never said anything."

Snorting, Samantha rolled her eyes. "Of course not. I've known you
long enough to know I need to let you work magical things out for
yourself. Are you going?"

"I don't know. But I have to decide before Monday."

"Left it to the last minute, I see." She chuckled as they turned onto
the forest path. "What's holding you back? Because for the record, I'd
kill to study magic. It beats Chemistry by far."

"You don't want to study Chemistry?"

For years, Samantha had been planning her university life out. It was
supposed to be a fresh start away from the Elite Clique and all the petty
ostracising she'd experienced, while Fabian had always dreamt of a time
when he was finally free of school itself.

Since then, their lives had completely changed. Now it revolved
around magic, other worlds, and looming prophecies. It didn't surprise
him at all that studying Chemistry felt like a step back in comparison.

Samantha shook her head. "I do. It's not my first choice, but I feel this
obligation to Greenvalley and I love chemistry. I'm looking forward to
all the practicals and topics we didn't even touch in school. There's this
class—" She stopped herself. "Nice try. Now, tell me about the Citadel.
Why don't you want to go?"

"I don't know. It feels like a trap."

She raised an eyebrow. "A trap?"

Fabian nodded. "Yeah. They're not exactly trustworthy, meddling with my applications and so on. I feel like I'm being pushed into going there. What if it's all a trap?"

"What if they really, really want you?"

He snorted. "Why would they want me?"

"Oh, you know. You're just one of the most powerful elemental mages in existence," Samantha said with a teasing smile. "This could be a good thing."

Fabian shook his head. "You don't know if I'm powerful. We don't know any other elemental mages."

"True, but how likely is it any others have taken it up with demons and lived to tell the tale? More than once?"

In Hell, Fabian had faced down four demons of the Black Guard, killers through and through. It had almost cost him his life, but in the end he'd prevailed.

"Without Jan, I would've been dead."

"Aren't you curious about the other elemental mages?" Samantha asked a little softer. "I can't wait to meet Adam and talk magic weaving with him. Yours is so different. You constantly have to balance your feelings with the power behind it. I know you've struggled. Wouldn't it be nice to meet people who've been through the same?"

Fabian bit his lip, letting her words sink in. "I guess."

She smiled. "Now, while you were wrestling with this, I started my own inquiries."

"Of course you did." If there was one thing he knew about Samantha, it was that she did her research.

"Grandma knows about this Citadel, and she said an invitation is pretty special." Ahead of them, Elda's little hut came into view. Samantha bounced up the stairs and rang the doorbell. "You should feel honoured."

The door opened, and Elda greeted them with a smile. "Oh, hello. That's a pleasant surprise. Is it just the two of you? Well, come on in. I've just finished a load of baking."

Fabian hugged the older woman, who was like a grandmother to him, eagerly sniffing the air. "Your walnut ones? Yummy."

"Fabi's ready to hear about the Citadel," Samantha announced as they shuffled into the library and sat in the comfy armchairs by the window.

Elda vanished for a moment, only to return with a pot of tea, three cups, and oven-warm cookies. "So, have you finally come to terms with the idea of studying magic?" she asked.

Fabian reached for a cookie and sank deeper into his chair. "Not really. I can't imagine what there is to learn. I can control water... more or less." He bit into the cookie and sighed. Elda's walnut cookies were the perfect mixture of nutty and sugary. "These are so good."

"Thank you." Elda settled in the chair opposite and sipped at her teacup. "Well, there's always more to learn. As for the Citadel of Magic, it's a unique organisation. A global society of magic users in a secret place. However, they're incredibly selective, relying almost completely on legacy students. You're basically the first person I know who's been invited without prior ties."

His mouth full of cookie, Fabian mumbled, "Why me?" He nodded at Samantha. "Why not Sam?" The way she sat on the edge of her seat told him how much she envied him the offer.

"Because witches like Samantha are as common as the stars. Sorry, sweetie. You're no doubt very talented but just imagine how many witches live in the Harz region alone. Besides, the Citadel is notoriously opposed to witches."

"Opposed?" Samantha's shoulders dropped by a margin.

Elda shrugged. "Your grandfather used to rant about it. They were too haughty, living in their castle in the clouds, while witches took care of their communities. They wouldn't be the first to dismiss our work."

Fabian sat up to grab another cookie. "Elitist, classicist, maybe magicist... if that's a word. Sounds like just the place for me."

"Oh, I'm sure things have changed. I mean, this was fifty years ago. It was a different time." Elda smiled. "This right here could be a sign they're committed to changing. At the very least, you should check it out."

He glanced over at Samantha, who was biting her lip. Her eyes betrayed a profound hunger. While she'd never force him to make a choice, Fabian couldn't help but feel like he owed it to her—and maybe all the witches in his life—to accept.

"You mentioned a secret place. Is it really secret? The letter only said to use the magical rivers to carry me to the Citadel."

"That's specific." Samantha snorted. "How are you supposed to know where to get out?"

"Well, I..." Samantha had never travelled on the magical rivers, unlike Fabian. "I think I saw it when we... you know. An old castle surrounded by snow."

Elda nodded. "That fits what I've heard about the Citadel. I always assumed it was up north, in one of the Scandinavian countries, or maybe Canada."

"Does that mean the classes will be in English?"

"Within a global mage community?" Elda chuckled. "I'm pretty sure they figured out a language spell that allows everyone to speak in their native language and be understood."

Now that was the sort of magic Fabian could get behind. "Got to admit, that sounds pretty cool."

"Very," Samantha said.

"Wish we'd had that during our exams." It would've lessened his anxiety a lot.

Samantha snorted. "That would be called 'cheating'." Finally, she scooted backwards and fully sunk into the armchair. "I wish I could go."

"Don't worry, darling. You'll have other tasks ahead of you."

"Magical ones?"

Elda chuckled. "Of course. I think it's time for you and Lucille to formally join the Harzer witches at Walpurgis. One of you will become the Greenvalley Witch in the not-so-far future."

Immediately, Samantha sat up straight again. "Don't say that, Grandma!"

"What? That I'm ready to retire and enjoy the years I've got left in quiet service?"

"You can retire as much as you want, but those years better be a couple of decades."

Fabian nodded. "Yes, don't you dare die on us." He'd already seen too much death in the last two years.

"Well, I'll see what I can do." Elda winked. "I wouldn't want to miss any of your journeys. You've already achieved so much more than Cecille and I could've ever dreamt of."

The words sank into Fabian's stomach and settled there, weighing on him. This offer wasn't just about him but all those who'd come before him. All the witches who'd been excluded. He finally saw the letter for what it was: a chance. A chance to be a little more than he was. Maybe a chance to change the broken world they lived in for the better. For those unheard and cast aside. Those who'd never had a chance like this.

"Guess I can't come to Fader on Monday."

Samantha grinned at him. "Fader isn't running away." She reached for his hand. "You're gonna do amazing."

He wasn't so sure about that, but he was willing to give it a try.

Rachel

Dark smoke was rising from the mountain towering over the lush tropical island below Rachel. She was sitting on a cloud, a little confused and intrigued by where the dreamworld had taken her. The vibrant green of the vegetation, white beaches, and glistening waves made her think she was somewhere in the tropics. Several small villages flanked the side of the mountain. Not a mountain, Rachel thought. An active volcano.

He will step out of the shadows as dark as the night.

She searched for the speaker, but the words seem to bloom in her head as she watched the volcano rumble underneath her.

He'll serve envy, jealous of the light.

Shadows crept across the volcano's slopes, which convulsed under them like an animal in pain. Glowing red lava bubbled to the top, eerily blood-like.

His shadow will devour Ashuan...

Darkness encroached the mountain, squeezing the life out of it until, at last, it exploded. Rocks and ashes were flung high in the air, the plume quickly covering the sky, suffocating the life below. The forests burnt and civilisation withered, until all that remained was a thick layer of ash.

...leaving nothing but blight.

The ash rose. It crawled in through her nose and her ears, corroding and burning. When Rachel tried to scream, she could only cough instead. The fire was inside her, quickly dissolving her body as the light dimmed. Just before she lost sight of it all, a winged figure appeared. It was the last thing she saw before the darkness claimed her, leaving her with nothing but pain.

As soon as Rachel woke, she scribbled down the lines of the prophecy she'd heard. When she'd been younger, she'd often forgotten her dreams as soon as she'd opened her eyes, but now she was more aware. As excruciating as it'd been, Rachel remembered every second. And it hadn't been good. None of it. Compared to other prophecies, it had also been terrifyingly specific.

"The end of the world. What better way to start university?"

"What was that, Miss Rachel?" Her loyal ghost, Hugo, floated to her side.

She sank back on her bed. "I'm pretty sure I had a prophetic dream. Something about a volcanic eruption caused by shadow magic, ending with the death of everything living on Ashuan."

"That sounds like a dream to me," Hugo said with a heavy frown. "Or rather, a nightmare."

"Believe me, I know the difference. This was a vision. Unfortunately, it didn't come with a countdown." The future she'd seen could come about tomorrow, next week, or next century. "As if one world-ending prophecy wasn't enough."

Unfortunately, this one hadn't included any hope of fighting the imminent apocalypse. Unless that mysterious figure right at the end would save them. It had been too dark to see them clearly. The only thing she knew was their wings hadn't been the bat-shaped ones of demons, but rather more like a bird. Or an angel. She'd never asked Matt if angels existed.

Just then, her phone beeped, and the instant smile on her face wiped the dark wisps of doom away. "Adam."

She reached for her phone while Hugo groaned, and scrolled through the messages Adam had left her overnight. The time difference between New Zealand and Germany was exactly twelve hours now they'd switched from summer to winter time. They only had those hours in the early morning or late evening when they were both awake, and nearly no time for them to be asleep simultaneously.

Eagerly, Rachel hit the call button and sighed happily when Adam's face appeared on her screen. She loved everything about it. The deep chocolate eyes, the dark brown curls, and the dimples when he smiled. It was strange to see the light from his window when her world was still dark.

"You're up early."

From his position, she could see he was in his workshop, where he tinkered with discarded broken machines.

"Couldn't sleep."

He winced. "Bad dreams?"

"You could say that." She sighed. "I'll tell you later. You're going to come later, right?" She'd only just realised that for him it'd be close to midnight when they met in Fader. Apparently, the interglobal capital was more aligned with her side of the globe than Adam's.

He gave her a thumbs up. "I've stocked up on Pepsi and had a nap earlier. I can't wait to see you again."

"Me, too." And just like that, the prophecy was merely a nag at the back of her mind. "It's been too long."

"Way too long."

In the corner, Hugo harrumphed. "He's not the one who was left alone for three months."

Rachel giggled. "Oh, I can't wait for you to come back to Greenvalley."

"I'm working on it. I've got a call with the hospital later this week. At 1am." As so often, institutions seemed entirely oblivious to big time differences. "They liked my work, so fingers crossed, we can work something out so I can get on that visa application."

"Well, if they don't take you, I'll set Jan on them."

Adam laughed. It was a deep, open laugh that felt like thunder rolling down her spine. Rachel loved it. After a lifetime of loud and shrill emotions while guarding her own, she appreciated the ease with which he loved and laughed. "Is he coming? I might instruct him to drop my name occasionally. 'You know, I miss that Adam guy. He always got the machines working again'."

"Yeah, because you cheated." Rachel giggled.

"Hey, I'm using the tools in my arsenal to save lives." After his mother had died in hospital due to a faulty machine, Adam had dedicated his magic and work to making sure it never happened to anyone else.

"I know. But no, Jan's got to work. I think he's sitting in on actual rides now and has a twelve-hour shift or something." She hadn't exactly listened to Jan's explanation, her thoughts with Adam, as they so often were these days.

They talked for an hour or two while the sky outside brightened, just as his grew darker. When she finally heard her parents stir, she managed to tear herself away, knowing they'd see each other again in a few hours. With a happy sigh, she remained on the bed, pressing the phone to her chest. It wasn't until Hugo cleared his throat Rachel remembered she wasn't alone.

She sat up and wagged her finger at him. "Don't. I know you're going to try to talk sense into me. I had sense for the longest time. I get to be silly."

"As long as you know how silly you are. There was a rather urgent prophecy."

"Not urgent. Just a prophecy." She swung her legs out of the bed and started dressing. "And I haven't forgotten, but I can't be all doom and gloom."

Hugo floated past as if she'd personally insulted him. She shook her head and let it go. Ever since she'd shown interest in Adam, Hugo had acted erratically. No matter how many times she told him he was irreplaceable, he wouldn't warm to her relationship. As if he really thought he'd have a shot, incorporeal as he was.

When she came downstairs, her father was already setting the breakfast table. "Ready for your day trip?"

She'd told her parents she was going to Hanover to catch some obscure exhibition she and her friends were interested in. "Almost. Just need to pack a drink." For a moment, she thought about packing lunch but then decided against it. They were going to visit a local market, after all.

"Well, while you're here, there's something I... or rather we need to tell you about."

Rachel returned with her water bottle and stuffed it into her backpack. "Sounds serious."

"It's not serious serious, but as you know my sabbatical is coming to an end, so I had to think about what's going to come next. I've got a faculty waiting for my return in LA, you know."

"You're going back." Just as they'd started to resemble a little family again, her father was breaking them apart once more. She sat, looking at him unimpressed. "When?"

"Next month."

"Awesome."

Mick winced. "Don't be like that. I really enjoyed this last year. Greenvalley is very charming, but it's not exactly a vibrant city. It's starting to feel quite small."

"I know your home is in LA, at your university, not here with Mum and me."

The grimace only deepened. "Actually, Annette and I talked about going together."

"What?"

He grinned sheepishly. "We want to give it another try."

"You two. In LA? What about me? I'm starting university next week, here in Greenvalley." And even if she weren't, this was her home, where her friends were and her destiny lay. "Adam's trying to get here."

Mick reached for her hand, but she quickly stowed it under her table. He sighed. "I'm excited for all of this. You're embarking on new adventures, living your own life now."

"You don't want me to come," she realised. Why was she even shocked? Her parents had never cared to include her in anything.

"It's not that," Mick said quickly. "If you want to come, we'll make it work. I'll help you get a place at one of the universities nearby. I just didn't think you'd be interested. Your life is here, and you haven't needed us for a long time." Each word was like a stab to her heart. "Now, don't you worry, Bug. I want you to concentrate on your studies, so you'll keep the house, and I'll make sure you have enough to cover groceries and everything else."

Rachel bit her lip, trying her hardest not to give him a piece of her mind. The old bitter taste of disappointment swirled in her mouth, creeping down her throat. Living alone wouldn't bother her at all. She'd practically done it for years. "Well, sounds like you've thoroughly planned it all out already. Great." She got up. "I believe it's time for me to go."

"Rachel—"

"Just text me before you leave. Or not."

"You didn't even eat breakfast." But he gave up quickly. "We'll talk about it when you're back. With your mum."

"Great."

She strode through the living room and into the hall, fighting back tears as she put on her shoes. Angrily, she wiped her eyes. Her parents didn't deserve her tears. They never had. Still frustrated, she nearly tore the door out of its hinges, only to stop short in front of Chay.

The honey-haired half-demon gave her a lop-sided smile. "Good morning, Rachel. I believe you've had a dream you wanted to discuss."

Her heart sank. If Chay turned up on her doorstep first thing in the morning, the prophecy was more dire than she'd thought. "How much time do we have?"

"At least a couple of months, maybe even a year." He winced. "Not exactly long to prepare, so let's compare notes. Maybe we can figure out how to stop this in its tracks."

With a sigh, she joined him, closing the door behind her. This was exactly why she'd never even think of leaving Greenvalley.

Matt

"Time to get up!"

The call rang through the house. Matt growled and buried his nose deeper into Samantha's black hair.

A knock on the door was next. "Someone needs to go with Crumbs," Jan said, the annoyance thick in his voice. "You've got classes, Matt, and Neve will turn him into a Crumbs-popsicle if he pees on the carpet again."

Matt groaned, while the steps behind the door retreated downstairs. "I hate him."

"No, you don't." Samantha turned in his arms, a lazy grin on her lips. "You just hate leaving the bed you share with me."

He ran his hands over her body and pressed her to his chest. "Damn right, I do." He pressed his lips to her neck and kissed her favourite spot until she gasped.

"Yes, Neve, Matt has agreed..." Jan called from downstairs.

Rolling his eyes, Matt let go of Samantha and swung his legs over the edge of the bed.

During the summer, they'd renovated the entire floor, putting down linoleum and painting the walls in a pastel green. Plants were lined up under the windows and along the workspace on the eastern side of the house; there was a spiral staircase, hung with fairy lights, that led to the little tower on top of the house, where Samantha kept her witch books, herbs, and the cauldron; while a Japanese folding screen separated the new double bed they'd bought from the rest of the room. To their left was the upstairs bathroom, which was still an ongoing project.

Matt saw all this, but the one thing he didn't see were the clothes he'd been wearing the previous night. "My things?"

"Check the door."

Matt got up, giving Samantha a perfect view of his naked backside. Opening the door a fraction, he glanced outside. Sure enough, a pile of clothes lay in front of the door. Jan must've carried them upstairs earlier.

"Huh."

He opened the door a little wider and dragged them inside with his foot, then began to dress in fresh clothes from the wardrobe. By the time he was ready, Samantha had fallen asleep again. Matt watched as the morning light danced on her cheeks and caught in her hair, making it shimmer like obsidian. Her shoulders were exposed, and he caught a hint of her curves under the blanket, causing his pants to tighten.

Even after three months, he still hadn't had his fill of her. He tiptoed back to the bed and bent over carefully. Her eyelashes fluttered slightly under his breath, like black butterflies. Her lips parted and Matt was drawn to them. Running his tongue over them, he could still taste the sweetness of their night's lovemaking.

As Samantha stirred, he whispered, "Wake up, Sleeping Beauty." Then he remembered how the fairy tale ended and used his lips to get the message across.

Samantha turned and stretched her arms above her head. The blanket dropped even further. Matt resisted putting his hands on her only with great restrain. Groaning, he withdrew and returned to the wardrobe.

Picking the first two pieces of lingerie, he held them up. "Do you want to entice me with the black or the red tonight?"

She laughed and threw a pillow at him. "Black."

Grinning, he dropped the lingerie on the bed. "What else do you want to wear, or are you keeping it nice and airy?" The thought excited him a little too much, and he straightened his pants.

"While I walk through Fader?" Samantha asked, in mock outrage. "Give me a pair of jeans and the green tunic."

There was another knock on the door and Matt heard Crumbs' claws scratching over the boards in the hallway. "I'm coming!" Just not the way he wanted to. He threw Samantha's clothes over. "I'm out with Crumbs, okay?"

She reached out for him and he came to her willingly, stealing another long kiss, provoking Jan to knock again.

Jan was waiting for him downstairs with Crumbs. The dog bounded up the steps, nearly making Matt tumble down in his joy.

"I'm not the one going to university," Jan bleated.

"There's still two hours until then," Matt said.

Jan snorted. "Not a lot of time, thinking how long it takes the two of you to get out of bed…"

Matt grabbed Crumbs' leash and slipped into his shoes. "Yes, Mum."

"I'm not—"

With a grin, Matt closed the door. This right here was his life now, and he couldn't be any happier.

The first sight of Fader was staggering. The group had met up with Chay, who'd transported them through the rivers of magic. According to him, the interglobal community's defences prevented them from simply teleporting there. They'd arrived in an enormous plaza surrounded by stony gates, each filled with a silver curtain of magic.

Matt had barely set a foot on the ground before he was directed to join a queue that stretched across half of the plaza. It was moving at a steady speed, but every second someone new stepped through the gates. The waiting crowd was as varied as grains of sand on a beach. He saw humans in all shapes and sizes, as well as elves, dwarves, and creatures he had no name for.

His friends joined him, looking around curiously. The city itself was blocked by a wall. Beyond it, Matt saw a multitude of roofs rising as far as he could see.

"Chay?" An official in purple garb approached the group, frowning slightly. "What are you doing in line?"

"Introducing these four to the wonders of Fader and the interglobal community."

The official snorted. "Come on. I'll get you registered."

They bypassed the queue, much to the dismay of the travellers still waiting.

Matt couldn't help notice how many seemed to recognise Chay. "Preferential treatment," he teased, clicking his tongue.

Chay shot him a withering look. "Be glad for it. It usually takes an hour to get to registration if you're a first timer." He told the official, "Homeworld's Ashuan."

"Ashuan, Ashuan..." The official frowned as he led them to a multi-coloured column. "Are they part of the union?" When Chay shook his head, he smiled. "Ah, that explains it. One of the late ones, then. Is it world-changing business?" He seemed to be eager for the latest political gossip.

"Not yet. For now"—Chay clapped Matt's shoulder—"we've got a new student. He's a half-demon like me. My protégé."

"Lucky man. I take it you're vouching for him, then?"

"With my life."

Matt wasn't quite sure if Chay was literally putting his life on the line for him, but it was better to be safe than sorry. With the conflict around his mother's abdication settled, studying in Fader should be a breeze.

The official waved him forward to step into the column. "This will scan your magical signature and save it for the gates. Next time you arrive, you can step through without being held up."

"Fascinating," Samantha mumbled.

Matt smiled as he stepped into the column, knowing Samantha would interrogate Chay about the magic involved. The column barely made him feel anything. Within half a minute he was done and free to go.

He was waiting on the other side when he noticed a commotion. A man had passed the silver gates, which had promptly turned violet and frozen him in place. Two officials approached, released him, and led him to a closed structure on the far side.

"What's the deal with him?" Matt asked.

"Oh, he must have a no-entry status or only with limitations," Chay said.

"And the curtain knows?" Lucille asked.

The official grinned. "The curtain is pure magic. It knows." He let Rachel and Samantha through, then nodded at Chay. "Good luck in there."

"Say hi to your husband for me."

Together, they stepped through the gate on the other side, arriving in an alley as wide as their school grounds. The street was split into several lanes by flowering trees, giving it the appearance of a promenade. Fountains propelled water high into the air, where it morphed into fluttering birds before settling back into the basin. Vendors were grilling meat in their flame-bearing hands, while others displayed breathtaking cutting art as they split multiple fruit with one slice of magic, making the food look like flowers. Floating carriages waited in a line, eagerly waving new arrivals to them. Most of the travellers chose to walk, apart from some important-looking delegation, who were whisked away in one of the carriages, travelling a metre above their heads.

Samantha spun around, laughing. "Is everything magic here?"

"A lot of it," Chay said, with a smile. "People from all worlds come here, bringing their magical talents. The art district alone would take a month to explore and a year to catch all performances."

"It's a massive city," Lucille exclaimed. "I've been to New York and Tokyo, but this tops them all while retaining a medieval charm. Has it always been so big?"

Chay shook his head. "Not at all. It exploded in the last hundred and fifty years with the parliament gathering more support. When I first started, it was much smaller. Still the biggest city I'd ever seen, but smaller than this."

"Started?" Rachel asked. "I thought this was your home?"

"Home world. Fader is the capital of the Eastlands. I was born in the High North, which is... well, north of here."

Matt snickered. "Yeah, where's it's really cold."

Chay didn't talk often about his beginnings. In fact, Matt knew annoyingly little about his friend's heritage, but he had occasionally regaled him with stories from his childhood. They usually involved snow.

"We do have summers."

"Yes. Every five years."

Chay rolled his eyes. "You wouldn't last five hours at the Ice Lakes."

"Ice Lakes?" Lucille asked, her eyes glistening. "That sounds pretty. Are you going to show us one day? Your homeland sounds perfect for a winter holiday."

Matt had seen Chay's face darken whenever he mentioned his home, and he'd learnt long ago not to push, so was surprised when he said, "That's highly unlikely. The borders were closed over two hundred years ago."

"Completely?" Lucille looked as if the idea of a country completely locking down was unthinkable.

"They've been at war for even longer. It's all the North has known for centuries."

"Did you fight in the war?" Samantha asked softly.

A pained expression flashed across Chay's face. "Let's talk about it another time. There's more than enough to see in Fader, and Matt here has to get to class. Come, the university isn't far."

Samantha searched Matt's gaze. He shrugged. All that had been new to him, too. The Chay he knew had always been a diplomat, trusted adviser to the interglobal community, and saviour of worlds. Those things were all true in Fader. Even here on the streets, random people recognised Chay and pointed him out to their acquaintances.

"Is this a normal day in Fader for you?"

"I usually jump straight to the parliament or whoever I want to see to avoid the attention."

"Sorry." Still, Matt couldn't help laughing at his friend's discomfort.

A few moments later, the laughter stuck in his throat when they rounded a corner to see a giant golden palace rising across from an extensive park. Countless people were headed towards it, chatting and buzzing with energy. Matt shuddered as a snow drift moved past him, apparently also heading for class.

"This is... big." If Matt had to take a guess, all of Hell could've attended and still not filled the seats.

Chay chuckled. "The interglobal society currently includes seventy-two worlds, not counting the ones Lukrya is in contact with that haven't officially joined yet, like Ashuan and Hescaryn. Therefore, lots and lots of students."

"Admission must be extremely selective," Lucille said, unveiled awe in her voice.

Samantha's eyes were full of longing. "Just imagine all that knowledge."

Slightly embarrassed, Matt rubbed the back of his head. "It's apparently easy when you know a valued alumnus." Or an interglobal celebrity. "Someone to measure up to."

Chay patted his shoulder. "You've got this."

"Did you see that in my future, or are you just saying that because you're my friend?"

Matt was starting to feel sick. He didn't deserve this spot. Someone like Samantha did. Someone who would thrive here.

Just then, she stepped in front of him. "Don't worry, Matt. Some might have more experience, but I've heard it all evens out within a semester. I don't think this university is any different in that regard. And you're smart. You've already done it once. Coming to Ashuan, entering Year Twelve without any prior schooling... I know you had private tutors, but they weren't specialised in Ashuan and you still had a really good average at the end. This isn't your first rodeo."

He couldn't help but smile. He loved this woman so much. "Thank you." Samantha was absolutely right. He'd already jumped into a different world and quickly integrated himself. His Geography major had basically been World Studies for beginners. "Are you okay with me going?"

"Absolutely. But I do expect you to share all your notes, textbooks, and homework with me."

Matt burst out laughing. "I'll make sure to be extra meticulous."

Grinning, Samantha threaded her arms through his and pulled him in for a kiss. "Go get them."

With one last wave, the group left him in front of the university to continue their sightseeing. Matt faced the golden palace again, squared his shoulders, and joined the mass of students.

Fabian

Snow-laden fir trees covered dramatic cliffs and slopes beneath a clear blue sky. Tucked within the mountain's nooks and crannies stood a citadel of immense age, its weathered grey rock clinging to the ground, vines claiming its turrets. The courtyard lay silent as a grave, without any sentries standing watch, other than a flock of crows searching for hidden treasures.

Fabian arrived, huffing. He'd overslept and had been held up by both his cat—who'd thrown up on the carpet—and his need to gather the courage to travel through the rivers of magic by himself. Last time he'd attempted it, he'd landed in the Dûr Lôrac in Hell. In comparison, this trip had been ridiculously easy, as if the magic had already known where he'd wanted to go. Unfortunately, that wasn't the case now he'd finally arrived at the Citadel.

He barely had time to take in the scenery as he ran toward the wooden gates at the end of the courtyard. Stumbling up the stairs, he entered a polished hallway lined with statues and hung with portraits of, what he assumed were, famous mages and headmasters. If the Citadel even had a headmaster. The only thing missing was a sign telling him how to get to registration or his classes... or anywhere.

Time already running out, Fabian ran up the stairs and followed a dark red carpet. Rooms lined both sides yet most doors remained locked, while the few open were vacant. He checked his watch to make sure it was Monday. Maybe he'd got the date wrong and everyone was still enjoying their break. Then again, they had to have someone take care of the grounds.

After wandering without much success, he arrived at a crossing. Unsure which hallway to try next, Fabian closed his eyes and raised his arm to let it sway. In the rivers, the magic had helped. Maybe it could help him here, too. His arm swung left, and he wasted no time following, bursting through a door.

His feet came to a skidding stop as he stared down a deep chasm. The walls were made of jagged, grey stone, offering little-to-no purchase, nothing but darkness looming below. Snowflakes whirled between the sides, trundling down until they were lost in the deep.

Heart pounding and gasping for breath, Fabian stumbled backwards until he hit the wall. Just as he thought he'd made it to safety, the wall gave way, and he fell into the darkness. Groaning, he rubbed his back and crouched to catch his breath, only to find two yellow eyes staring at him.

Fabian gulped. "Um... hi."

The responding hiss made him gulp.

Slowly, his eyes adjusted, revealing a terrifying sight. In front of him sat a mangy creature—half cat, half woman. She was mostly humanoid and thankfully wore clothes, but under her long stringy hair a pair of tattered, almost-rotten, cat ears rose. Her fingers ended in claws and her skin was of a wax-like quality where it wasn't covered in isolated clumps of fur. She looked as if she hadn't eaten in days, which would explain her hungry eyes.

Fabian raised his arms, shakily forming a delta with his fingers. "I'm warning you—I'm a mage."

The cat-woman chuckled, the sound a raspy rattle, as if someone had shaken a bag of marbles. "Everyone here is a mage."

Fabian swallowed. "Fair enough. I just—" It only occurred to him then the creature had spoken to him. Like her body, her voice was a mixture of woman and cat: melodic but with a whine to it. "Are you a student?"

"Not anymore." She shook her head. "But you're one."

"I'm one," he repeated, still not sure what to make of this unlikely encounter.

She smiled, exposing two rather long teeth. "I'm Clio. I've been waiting for you."

"For me? You're not going to eat me, are you?" They always wanted to eat him.

She laughed again. "I no longer need food."

Fabian gave her body another look. In his opinion, she needed it much more than him, but he wasn't going to disagree with a cat-lady.

"You're the one who'll save us."

He blinked. "What?" Surely, she was mistaken. He wasn't here to save anyone, just go to school and learn about his magic.

"But first, you'll have to find the way."

A perfect reminder of his priorities. Fabian scrambled to his feet. "Finding the way sounds good. I'm expected at the welcoming ceremony. You don't happen to know where that's supposed to take place?"

Clio cocked her head, reminding him starkly of his own cat when she silently judged him. Then she turned around and ran on all fours into the darkness. Fabian hesitated for a moment but decided he had very little to lose—apart from maybe his life if she chose to eat him after all—and followed.

Two turns later, he burst through a tapestry into another light corridor. At the end, a large double-winged door labelled, 'Grand Hall' appeared.

Clio smiled. "That's where you have to go. See you later."

And with that, she vanished back into the secret passageway, her half-rotten tail smacking Fabian's leg. The encounter had left him extremely confused, but lacking time to dissect it, he shrugged and hurried towards the door. Carefully, he opened it and peeked inside. When he saw rows and rows of students listening to a grey-haired professor at the front, he let out a sigh of relief.

As quietly as possible, he slipped into an empty back-row chair.

"...discipline and order. Any violation of the Citadel's principles will be severely punished. If you're unsure whether something's allowed, better not to do it. Or at least check your student guide first." The professor nodded and Fabian felt as if he'd already failed. "And now I want to introduce you to the Director of Studies, Professor Takuna."

He rejoined the row of seated professors and a Japanese man took his spot at the podium. Unlike the previous speaker, he had a few smiles for the students, who greeted him with lacklustre applause.

"It's good to see so many of you here on this glorious day. Most of you are well-known to us. We taught your parents and your grandparents and turned your older siblings into talented mages. But a few of you are first-generation mages who've received the honour of joining our exalted ranks. You were chosen for the immense talent you've already displayed."

Fabian sank deeper into his seat, not feeling particularly talented.

"The Citadel of Magic is more than a place to study. We're a community. A family. Our students and professors hail from all corners of the world, we teach over thirty different paths of magic, and we support each other, learn from each other, and inspire each other. Our community is growing through you. What you give us, we'll return tenfold. Now..." He paused, his voice rising, as if something exciting was about to happen. Some students glanced about or exchanged whispers. "I have some special news for you. This year, we're honoured to welcome four exceptional students to our ranks. For nearly forty years, the Citadel has been lacking an elemental mage. Now there are four, one of each element." He smiled ominously. "We expect great things from them."

As applause resounded throughout the hall, Fabian deflated even further into his chair. They were the first in forty years? How was that possible? Was elemental magic really that rare? Then why had it picked him?

"But enough of the speeches. Let's start this new year with a feast. Welcome to the Citadel of Magic!"

Once again, the students clapped wildly, the applause only rising, when the back wall of the hall disintegrated and revealed a huge dining hall, each table loaded with food.

Slowly, Fabian rose from his chair with the rest of the student body, looking around uncertainly. In front of him, a blond woman spun around and grinned.

"There you are. I was wondering when you'd finally get here."

Fabian stared, sure he must be dreaming. "Shayna?"

Samantha

After dropping Matt off, Chay led the group through the streets of Fader, searching for the park, where Rachel said Adam was supposed to meet them. Progress was slow as each turn revealed fresh sights. Sometimes, it was a street performer, showing wondrous tricks of magic; other times, the magic was much more mundane, woven into the city's very being. They passed a house with broken shingles being repaired by an army of hammers and tools Samantha couldn't recognise, no workers in sight; a wind blowing through the streets picked up all the litter and bundled it up, shrinking it until nothing remained; and a mural walked with them for two blocks.

"I love it here," Samantha exclaimed.

Lucille nodded. "Same!"

In front of them, Chay chuckled while Rachel seemed to have no time to look at all the wonders, constantly pushing him to walk faster. When at last they reached a blooming park, she finally seemed to relax.

All around them, orange flowers covered the trees. The wind blew through the petals, making them dance like fire sparks. Sandy pathways led through the park, while the grass invited visitors to sit. Diplomats strolled past, engrossed in serious conversation, and parents took their young ones for a walk. Students gathered under the trees, and a group of people played music together.

Then suddenly, Rachel let out a cry—"Adam!"—and ran towards a young man on a bench. Samantha had never seen him before, but with his typical Ashuan clothes, he stood out like a sore thumb.

Rachel threw herself into his arms, and he whirled her around with a big grin before he stooped and kissed her.

"Young love," Lucille sighed.

Samantha eyed her, amused. "You know Rachel is six months older than you?"

"Five. And in terms of relationships, I'm basically a granny."

Samantha burst out laughing, then linked their arms. "Come on, Grandma, let's introduce ourselves."

"He's surprisingly handsome," Lucille said as they approached the couple.

He probably was, with his dark complexion, brown locks, and intricate tattoos peeking out from under his sleeve, but he was no Matt. Still, Samantha couldn't help but warn, "Do not interfere."

"Please. I'm a girls' girl. After Hugo, I was just doubting Rachel's taste. The main thing is she's happy."

Rachel let go of her boyfriend and grinned at them. "So, this is Adam. And these are my friends, Samantha, Lucille, and Chay. We left Matt and Fabian at school, and Jan has to work."

Adam smiled, exposing adorable dimples. "It's great to finally meet you in the flesh. Rachel's told me so much about you and your adventures."

Samantha and Lucille shared a look. Rachel wasn't exactly known to be a chatterbox. Lucille stepped forward and gave Adam a big hug, kissing his cheeks. "Well, it's nice to meet you. Welcome to the family."

"And you," he asked Chay. "You're not the Chay, are you?"

"I'm afraid I am."

Astounded, Samantha regarded Adam. "You've heard of him?"

"My father talks non-stop about 'Chay this', 'Chay that'. He really admires you."

Chay clearly hadn't expected this random guy from Ashuan to know him, much less his father. "And your father is?"

"Geoffrey Black. He works at the Interglobal Parliament for the Citadel of Magic."

"You know the Citadel, too?" Samantha asked before Chay had a chance to reply. "Fabian just started there."

"Good for him." Adam rubbed the back of his neck. "Hope he likes it more than me. When they invited me, I couldn't run the other way fast enough."

Samantha wanted to ask more, but this time Chay interrupted her. "Geoffrey, yes, of course, I know Geoffrey. He's a great mediator in complex situations. Being Ashuan's only envoy has placed him in a neutral position. Just recently he helped quell a conflict between the Phalesian and Iperanian delegations."

Despite the glowing words from Chay, Adam looked less than enthused. "Yeah, I'm sure he's good at his job."

"So, you're magically talented, too, right?" Lucille asked. "Weaving magic, like Samantha? Why such a mundane job in Ashuan when you probably could've had an internship here? Maybe even visit the university?"

"Because, unlike my father, I like Ashuan," he said, in a terse voice

No one really knew what to say. Rachel rubbed Adam's arm and smiled at him.

Chay cleared his throat. "Now that we're complete, shall we head to the market?"

"Yes!" Lucille said, with such gratefulness, Samantha had to giggle. Regardless of the world, as long as Lucille could shop, everything was fine.

When Chay had mentioned there was a market, Samantha had imagined a street or perhaps a plaza. Instead, they were looking at an entire district. If she had to describe it, she would've said it was a cross between an oriental bazaar and medieval farmer's market. A vast variety of goods exceeding her wildest dreams was displayed under colourful awnings, protecting them from the sun. There was food, livestock, cloth, and trinkets, and then there was magic. One stall was filled with tiny machines all tinkering away on their own, another sold spells, the next miracle healing.

"We should stock the Magic Circle with this stuff," Lucille said. "We'd go viral in a month."

"Way too much attention."

They'd be hounded by all the wrong customers. The last thing Greenvalley needed were more magic tourists to poison the spring.

Behind them, Adam bought Rachel a sort of fried bread that immediately had her moan, "This is delicious!"

"It's the magically stirred cream on top," Adam said, with a laugh. "My favourite."

Samantha couldn't help smiling. She just wished Matt was here to share the experience with her. They hadn't been apart this long since they'd returned home.

"Oh, this looks good."

Behind a row of food sellers sat a large pavilion filled from top to bottom with plants, making it impossible to tell which ones were for sale and which were part of the decor. Without waiting for the others to agree, Samantha pulled Lucille towards it. As soon as they stepped inside, the air changed to a refreshing, slightly humid breeze. Almost as if they'd walked into a forest.

"Now this, I could live in."

Lucille laughed. "How about Matt? Would he join you?"

"He goes wherever I go," she joked. "But I don't see why not. He doesn't really seem to care too much about his surroundings as long as I'm happy." She'd made almost all the design decisions in their room, and he'd immediately agreed.

"Aww, he only cares about you. That's sweet. So, how's living together?"

Samantha grinned. "Exciting."

"Uh!" Lucille gasped. "Oh, I see. Yeah, I guess that's an advantage."

"But really, he's super sweet, and he helps with everything. It's not even a question. He just takes care of whatever needs to be done, whether that's cleaning or fixing stuff."

After living with her father for almost twenty years, Samantha had always assumed men needed to be told about household tasks, as if they were completely blind to them. Jan certainly needed nudging, though a plan had improved things a lot. Matt, however, was different. It was one of the few advantages of his upbringing in a different world.

"As if he couldn't get any dreamier." Lucille hugged her. "I'm glad the two of you are happy. You deserve it."

Some would say they were moving too fast, but after what they'd been through in the Residence of Lust, Samantha couldn't imagine ever being parted. Life was too short anyway. At least, hers was.

She paused to watch a swarm of butterflies flutter between the orchids in the pavilion and sighed. One day she'd have to bring Matt back here for longer. Maybe she'd visit when he had a break in his schedule or at the weekend.

They exited the pavilion into a quieter part of the market filled with little booths. Almost immediately, a woman clad in multicoloured swaths of cloth approached. "Two Yaren for your future?"

Samantha glanced back at Chay who frowned but didn't step in. Lucille took care of the transaction, exchanging green shimmering stones. As usual, she had no concept of price and value.

The woman took Lucille's hand and studied it for a minute. She nodded to herself and said, "You've a year of love ahead of you, but you'll have to decide what's more important: the cause or your love."

Lucille shrugged. "Love sounds good."

Samantha giggled. She had no idea if the woman was any good at divination but she was damn good at figuring out the one thing Lucille loved even more than shopping.

She let go of Lucille's hand and took Samantha's. Almost immediately, she startled. "Oh, you don't know this yet, but in half a year, your child will enter the world."

All merriness vanished from Samantha's face and her hand dropped like dead weight.

"In half a year?" Lucille asked. Her voice was tinny in Samantha's ears. "But that would mean she'd already be... Oh." She turned. "Sam?"

Samantha was still staring ahead, not really seeing or hearing anything. If she was pregnant... If it had happened three months ago... Suddenly she felt sick to the bone. "No, no."

"Would you like to have your future told?" the diviner asked someone else. "I can do special couple—"

"I think you've said enough already," Chay said, in a calm but authoritative voice.

"Yes, yes, excuse me, Seer. I don't want to step on any toes." Her head bowed, the woman backed away and vanished into a booth.

Lucille waved her hand in front of Samantha's face. "Was she the real deal or just your typical fair diviner?" she asked Chay.

"I suppose we'll see what the future brings."

His non-answer broke the spell on Samantha, and she whimpered. It couldn't be true. It simply wasn't allowed to be. If it had really happened three months ago, then Matt... He wasn't the only one she'd slept with during that period.

Matt

Over a thousand students were taking World Studies alongside Matt. They all came together in a giant auditorium which, despite its size, was able to magically project the lecturer's voice to the students, regardless of distance. The entry-level lecture was about the history of World Studies, interglobal rules, and exploration of new worlds. It was accompanied by an exercise that simulated a model exploration, but unlike their main lecture they would be magically assigned into smaller groups of thirty.

There were a few other lectures they had to take as a full cohort, such as 'Worlds of the Interglobal Community I' and 'Famous World Explorers', while the rest of the course was split by interest, with classes such as 'Political Systems', 'Plant Life', 'Magic Properties', and 'Philosophy'. In their first two years, they had to pick and pass at least sixteen courses from a pool of fifty. In their third year, they'd explore hand-picked model worlds, an offer that changed depending on which lecturers were available.

As overwhelming as it all sounded, Matt was eager. His whole life, he'd focused solely on two realms. He'd known about the others, but Chay had never taken him anywhere. Now his horizon wasn't just widened, it had exploded, dropped off, and left him in a whole other universe. There was so much to learn, far more than anyone could in a lifetime—unless, of course, that someone had demon blood. If he remembered correctly, Chay had studied for three decades, if not longer, and taught a couple more. For the first time, Matt understood why he'd choose to spend his eternity this way, unlike full demons who had little interest in progress, too engrossed in the constant battle of dominance and sin.

The lecture ended and the room began to empty. Even with twelve exits, it was an excruciatingly slow process, but the schedule accommodated for it.

When Matt passed the front dais, the professor called out, "Matt Traidous? Or do you prefer Melchior?"

Frowning, he stepped aside to let the other students passed. "You know me?" The last thing he'd expected was someone picking him out from a crowd of over a thousand.

"Please. Chay told us about you. It was a glowing recommendation, impossible to ignore."

Matt's cheeks flushed as the weight of Chay's shadow settled on his shoulders once more. "Oh, um, Matt is fine."

"Did you know that many of the worlds we study today have been explored and connected with the interglobal community through Chay's work?" The pressure on Matt's shoulders increased. "It's been over a hundred years since he was a student here, but his contribution to our field has been so immense, they named an entire wing after him. It'll be interesting to see what your contribution will be."

Matt swallowed hard. "Um..."

The professor laughed. "Not in the first semester, of course. But if you ever need some help, don't be afraid to reach out. Now, I don't want to keep you from your lunch break. Be quick or you'll be out of a seat."

"Thanks, I guess."

Feeling a bit light-headed, he turned and found himself face to face with a sensual young woman. She had pitch-black hair and golden eyes, with skin scaled like a snake. He wouldn't have been surprised if her tongue was forked, too.

"Can I help you?"

She crossed her arms in front of her chest and gave him an incredibly inquisitive look, as if searching for something. "Chay's protégé. That's the kind of pressure I could live without."

"So, you know him, too?" Did anyone in Fader not?

"Who doesn't? But I guess I know him personally after he spent some time with my tribe a few years ago. It's what inspired me to study here." She flicked her tongue over her lip. It wasn't forked but it was a good bit longer than a human's. "I'm Vydra."

"Matt."

He wasn't quite sure what to make of her, mostly because he knew absolutely nothing about her species. He couldn't even tell whether she was trying to decide whether she wanted to sleep with him or kill him. If she was anything like a demon, it'd be both.

"Relax," Vydra said. "I'm not here to start drama. Any friend of... Chay's is a friend of mine." The smile that followed was an honest one. "Shall we get food?"

He shrugged, deciding to take a chance. "Sure, why not? You know where the hall is?"

She laughed. "The hall? There's about twenty different ones. Any specific taste?"

"I wouldn't know. This is my first time in Fader."

"Mine, too. My plan was to go to a different hall each day, bar the ones too far away. Shall we start with the one closest to the library? I think our next class is over there."

"Sure. Let's do that."

In less than five minutes, they were getting along like old friends, and Matt was glad he had someone to share this big new experience with.

Fabian

Fabian's brain simply refused to accept Shayna's presence in a place like this. She wasn't a mage. She didn't even believe in magic. Perhaps she had a doppelgänger, some sort of magical twin... but then again she'd talked to him exactly like the Shayna he knew.

He must've been staring slack-jawed for minutes, only pulled back by her giggling, "You should see your face."

"What are you doing here?"

Part of the reason for starting university had been to escape the Elite Clique. There'd been a good chance some of them would attend Greenvalley University, but here? This made no sense.

"Studying," Shayna said, coquettishly, before shuffling out of her row to stop holding everything up.

Fabian followed her example, still too stunned to think for himself.

On the way towards the hall, a table had appeared, laden with personalised study guides. Judging by the line, they were expected to pick one up before filling their bellies ahead of their first class.

"I'm a freshman just like you," Shayna said, as they got into line. "More than that, I'm one of the infamous elemental mages." She rolled her eyes and snorted. "My element is fire."

"What? But how? I don't... You don't seem surprised about me being here."

She grimaced. "Please, I've known about you for two years or so."

He'd barely discovered his magic two years ago. "And you never said anything?"

"It's not like we were friends."

Fabian didn't quite see the obstacle, but Shayna clearly seemed to assume it was perfectly normal behaviour.

"Sure... So, you've been able to wield magic all this time?"

Her best friends had been the ringleaders of Samantha's incessant mobbing. For years, she'd suffered from the ridicule thrown at her, just because she openly believed in magic. The fact one of them had been a mage herself all this time didn't really compute.

"Well," Shayna said, dialling back her usual cheekiness a bit, "it took me a while to make the connection. Let's just say there's been one fire too many in my life. The first time it happened I caused a forest fire when I went camping with my family. Terrible experience, only made worse once I realised I was the one who'd caused it. The worst one was the fire at Lucille's fashion show. Luckily, you were there." She grinned. "That's when I found out you were like me."

When she batted her eyelashes at him, Fabian nearly groaned. He finally understood why she'd been low-key obsessed with him towards the end of her school career. It seemed to have been an awkward attempt to get closer to him, without ever actually committing.

"You should've said something. You could've helped us."

"I did help. Back when that cult was in town and you met your lovely and totally-not-evil girlfriend, I started a fire to distract everyone and allow them to flee." She turned to introduce herself to the professor handing out study guides. "Shayna Richards, Elemental Magic."

The distractingly beautiful woman's eyes lit up. "Miss Richards, what a pleasure to meet you. We can't wait to see what you'll surprise us with."

Even though it wasn't directed at him, Fabian felt himself shrink under the pressure. While Shayna smiled and nodded through an onslaught of expectations, someone grabbed his arm and pulled him from the queue and into a corner.

"They can't see you," a now familiar cat-like voice said.

"Clio." Fabian sighed. "How am I supposed to study without being seen?"

"Seeing isn't necessarily seeing."

His brain hurt just trying to decipher what she meant. "I suppose you don't want me to attract any attention? I just don't see how picking up my study guide like everyone else in this room would." If anything, the opposite was the case.

"You're not like everybody else."

"True. I'm the only one without a study guide."

To his surprise, Clio produced a study guide with his name printed on it, the cover slightly scratched. "Now you've got one."

Fabian took the little book and stared at it, still wrapping his head around the whole situation. "Did you steal this?"

But when he looked up, she'd already vanished. Shayna reappeared at his side. "There you are. You could've saved me from that woman."

"Sorry," he said absentmindedly, still trying to find Clio in the crowd.

"Who are you looking for?"

He stopped. "Doesn't matter. Shall we get food?"

"Is that a date?"

This time, he did groan. "You gonna be like this every day now?"

She laughed and hooked her arm through his. "I just can't resist that sweet blush. Come on."

They walked towards the hall and were surprised when they were properly seated by a host. Naturally, it was a table at the top of the hall, and it was on a freaking dais, so anyone could watch them, as if they were zoo animals.

"I want to go home," Fabian muttered.

Three figures had already been seated around the table, among them the serious professor who'd been talking when Fabian had entered the lecture hall. He was a tall Black man with short-cropped grey hair and an immaculately cut suit. Next to him sat a young woman with an angular face, East-Asian features, and long brown hair. She positively preened in her chair, as if all the attention wasn't just welcomed but expected. It stood in stark contrast to the last figure at the table, a blond, white boy in a worn-down hoodie who seemed too young to be of university age. He had his shoulders drawn up and his eyes on his plate, chewing for ages on one bite.

The professor nodded as they approached. "Ms Richards, Mr Bendtfeld. Please take a seat and have some food. I'm Professor Terian, your lecturer for Elemental Magic."

Fabian swallowed as he took his seat beside Shayna. Luckily, the two remaining chairs had been next to each other, since the other students seemed dramatically opposed to a friendly chat. The food, however, was a delicious spread, which he was grateful for since he'd had to miss breakfast.

"Ms Richards is our fire mage, and Mr Bendtfeld controls water," Professor Terian explained. "They're both from Germany." He gave them the slightest of smiles. "Now, this is Camdyn Winter, an air mage from Ireland, and Kaia Takuna, one of the Citadel's own, who's our earth mage, of course."

"The director's daughter?" Shayna asked, eyebrows rising.

Kaia gave her a shark-like smile. "How wonderful, you're capable of simple deduction. I'll have you know I had to delay my studies for a year to wait for you."

"Kaia, please." Professor Terian shook his head. "While you're eating, let me tell you a bit about your studies. Your primary subject will be Elemental Magic, which will be exclusively taught by me, so we're going to spend a lot of time together. Apart from that, you'll also be instructed in Magic Theory and Citadel History with the other freshmen."

"I've already completed those," Kaia said, further alienating herself from the group. "Had to pass the time somehow."

"Too bad your presence wasn't deemed important enough to be taught ahead of our arrival," Shayna said, with a lovely smile.

Fabian choked on his food.

As expected, Kaia huffed, but before she could lash out again, Professor Terian cleared his throat. "There was a reason for the delay. Elemental mages are incredibly rare. To have four of them roughly the same age, one for each element, has only happened twice before. There are certain advantages of training a full cohort. I expect you to be a close-knit team by the end of your studies."

Now it was Kaia who looked as if she was choking. Shayna's eyes widened and she half-snorted. Fabian glanced at Camdyn, searching for a glimmer of hope, but the boy remained with his head down, every inch of him screaming he didn't want to be there.

"During your course, we'll study elementary theory and practise magic," Professor Terian continued, as if he hadn't just caused a silent war. "I expect active participation, initiative, and independent training outside school hours. You'll be tested throughout the school year on both theory and practical magic. And you'll have to pass on your own and as a team."

Fabian exchanged a look with Shayna. Suddenly, he was glad to have her here. At least they could face the Citadel and their classmates together. Beyond that, he saw little hope of succeeding.

Lucille

Chay had kept the most exciting part of the tour for last. Fader was a miraculous city full of magic, but the one thing that truly fascinated Lucille was the Interglobal Parliament. She wondered when it had started and what its function was among the worlds. What laws were necessary to keep the worlds of Abstract Space from starting an Interglobal War? Did they regulate trade? Magic?

Parliament convened within a colossal dome, though the upper portion floated in the air above the city. Lucille craned her neck, trying to see what was on top of the platform, but the air seemed thicker around it, shielding it from the viewers outside.

"What's up there?"

"That," Chay explained, "is where parliament sits. It's floating to show off the power of the Interglobal Community, and as part of the safety measures. Even I can't jump up there. I have to take an elevator that only works for cleared personnel."

"They do that with magical webs, right?" Lucille said, looking at Samantha, but her friend was chewing her lip and lost in thought, likely still worrying about the diviner's ominous message.

"Indeed," Chay said. "Very complex webs crafted by a small army of witches."

He led them up a wide staircase. At the top, they found similar gates to those they'd encountered on arrival. Chay registered their names, and they stepped through the curtains into a marble-clad foyer. The first thing Lucille noticed were the words on the walls. When she tried to read a portion, the letters shimmered and changed form until the text was easily readable: ...agree to uphold the constitution in good faith or risk a twenty-five-year long ban...

"Is this...?"

"The interglobal constitution, yes. It starts over there." He pointed at glittering gold letters further up the wall.

"Amazing."

Lucille could've spent hours in this room alone, but her friends pulled her down a corridor lined with breathtaking paintings. Each collage showcased different regions, each more captivating than the one before. It took her four paintings to realise they all displayed the current members of the Interglobal Union. After five more, she came to a muted painting in black and white. Its design was futuristic, entirely devoid of natural elements.

"Is there really a black-and-white world?"

Chay stopped to look, waving to a passing woman. "Oh, no, that's Zyrdan. They were banned eighteen years ago for attacking another world. The interglobal community doesn't take lightly to imperialistic ventures."

"Ha, now I get why Ashuan isn't a part yet."

"It's also why Fader, or rather the Eastlands, refuse to allow representatives of their neighbouring countries to speak in parliament."

"They refuse?"

Chay nodded. "Lukrya, that's the name of the whole world, might be the centre of the interglobal community, but it's far from united. The Eastlands do more trade with the Surkryan countries than their fellow Norkryan neighbours, and far more trade with other worlds. As much as I adore the Interglobal Union, the Eastlands are quite enjoying their diplomatic monopoly. By now, they're far more advanced than their neighbours, who, I guess you could say, still have medieval-like structures."

"And that hasn't got them banned?"

He shook his head. "One of the most important rights is that each world governs itself and no other can intervene or influence them. It's to protect the cultural identity and political and magical ecosystem of each."

"Makes sense. I bet that also avoids a lot of conflicts." Lucille had initially thought of the Interglobal Union as a similar arrangement as the European Union, but there seemed much less governance. "So, what do they do?"

"Well, they have a defence pact, which I helped formulate." Chay raised his hand to a passing legislator. "Essentially, if one world gets attacked, the others rise to defend it, like in Zyrdan's case." He pointed at the muted painting. "Then there's interglobal trade and an exchange of knowledge, especially regarding magic. There are a few who want a tighter-knit community, the so-called Old Worlder."

"Old Worlder?" Lucille was soaking up every piece of knowledge like a sponge.

He greeted yet another person and nodded. "Long—very long—ago, all the worlds were one: the Old World."

"Oh, the one Draken broke, the guy we're supposed to face, eventually."

"Ssh." Chay lowered his voice. "Don't mention that here, or these people will try to pin you down and hold you here. For your protection and training, officially, but really to control and use you. Technically, Kairos broke the world with Matt's sword, but if he hadn't, Draken's magic would've consumed everything."

It was slowly coming back to her. When she'd first read the book Chay had written, much of what she knew was history had read like a fantasy novel, which had never been her favourite genre. It hadn't helped that it'd digressed into specific details, historical documents, and lore from a time hardly anyone remembered. It was as much a research journal as it was a historical account.

Still, she'd retained the basic strokes of the story: Draken had led a conquest through the entire Old World, seeking the Towers of Magic—the very origins of each type of magic—to drain them completely. His greed had known no bounds, and with each tower he'd conquered, he'd become more unstoppable. The world had seemed doomed. But a small group of heroes had set out to stop him. They'd found the Emblems of Magic, one of which Lucille now carried, and together, they'd formed the Circle of Magic, empowering the youngest of them, Matt's soul ancestor Kairos, to face Draken in battle. Many sacrifices were made—almost all had died on the mission—but in the end, Kairos bested Draken. Only, it'd been too late. The magic had been about to be unleashed, so Kairos had struck it, and in the process, the world had broken into many smaller worlds.

How that fitted with what she'd learnt at school about the creation of the solar system and her own planet, Lucille didn't know. Magic, she assumed. Samantha may have known, but it wasn't the kind of discourse Lucille enjoyed. She found the present moment, specifically this intriguing union of worlds, far more compelling.

They continued and made it to an airy plaza with an indoor garden and beautiful fountain of colourful magic. Tourists and legislators alike filled the plaza, clustering in small groups. Quite a few of them noticed Chay and greeted him.

Lucille laughed softly. "Does everyone know you?"

"I occasionally work for the parliament, if that's what you mean. Often as an ambassador in a new world... like Ashuan."

"That's so cool. Honestly, that's exactly the kind of job I'd love to have one day."

Chay chuckled softly. "Maybe you will."

"Is that a promise?" Lucille asked, hoping she'd read his vague answer correctly. If so, she was excited for the future. She looked for Samantha but found her still worrying herself sick.

Meanwhile, Adam and Rachel had approached a middle-aged man with short brown hair with silvering sides. He looked rather impatient and barked almost immediately, "You were supposed to meet me ten minutes ago."

"Sorry," Adam said, nonchalantly. "We got held up at the market. Dad, this is Rachel. She spent the winter in New Zealand, but you missed her."

"The win... Yes, your winter, my summer." Rachel smiled shyly. "Hi."

"Hi," Adam's father said, "I'm Geoffrey." Then he turned to his son. "Listen, we'll have to do the restaurant another time. Some important work came in and I only have a few minutes."

Lucille's heart went out to Adam as his face soured. How often had she heard the same words from her father?

But before Adam could get another word in, Geoffrey noticed Chay. "Chay! Just the man we need." He disregarded Adam immediately. "Could I possibly steal you away? There's a very delicate issue that could use some of your special insight."

Chay sighed. "Well, if it's urgent, I guess I can spare some time." He glanced at the others. "Have a look around. I'll join you soon."

Adam stared at his father's back as he hurried down a corridor with Chay, his jaw shaking slightly. Quietly, Rachel slipped her hand into his and squeezed it.

"I'm sorry," she whispered.

Lucille felt sorry for him, too. "I guess he's got a lot of work today?"

"You mean every day." Adam turned abruptly and marched back the way they'd come.

"I know exactly how you feel. My father's the same."

"That's true," Rachel said. "He is."

Adam snorted. "Oh, yeah? Did he also emigrate to avoid you?"

"He didn't flee from you," Rachel said gently, clearly knowing more about the situation.

"Well, that's how it feels."

"Why do you think he fled?" Samantha asked, for once trying to participate, though her fingers were already back at her mouth.

Adam paused and sighed. "My mother died six years ago. At that point, Dad had already been working in Fader and gone for longer and longer periods. She was in a coma for a while, which meant he couldn't do anything, anyway. His words, not mine. I had to repeat an entire year of school because I spent nearly every moment at her side. When she died, he was gone, too. He waited until I'd finished school, then he officially emigrated to Lukrya. Since then I've only seen him once or twice a year, if I put some effort into it. I mean I get it... and then again, I don't."

Rachel squeezed his hand again while Lucille restrained herself from giving him a hug. He looked like he needed it, and she couldn't help wondering if her father would've left, too, if she'd been a bit older. But no, his coping mechanism had involved Linda.

"When my mother died, my father quickly remarried so some other woman could take care of me. The first thing she did was send me to boarding school."

"Ouch." Somehow, the similarity made Adam laugh. "You get it then."

"Oh, yes. I mean, we're good now, or... sort of good. Or maybe I'm just too old to care."

"There's definitely an element of that. I mean I wish—"

Suddenly, an alarm blared. The employees returned to their offices or wherever they were needed to be, while confusion spread among the tourists.

"Shall we leave?" Rachel asked.

Adam frowned. "I don't know. Can we?"

Security arrived and began to usher people towards the exit, but instead of letting them out, they told them to enter investigation rooms.

"Investigation?" Lucille asked, already feeling wrongfully accused.

The nearest security woman nodded sharply. "Simple protocol. The web picked up someone with bad intentions. But don't worry—we'll find them quickly."

Lucille startled as the door was closed behind them. In her opinion, someone with bad intentions sounded like magical short code for a bomb threat.

Fabian

After the welcome feast, Professor Terian escorted the elemental mages to their classroom located in one of the many towers of the citadel. For four people, it was a surprisingly large room and completely circular. Four desks had been pushed to the side, leaving the centre empty. Long windows granted them a breathtaking view of the mountainside, snow swirling in the sky. The floor was bare stone, and Fabian felt the cold seep into his shoes. As beautiful as the Citadel was, it could certainly benefit from heating.

Professor Terian waved them inside. While he grabbed some utensils from a nearby shelf, he said, "Please gather around and form a circle."

They shuffled into place awkwardly, keeping more distance from each other than necessary. Kaia held her chin high, as if she physically had to look down on everyone.

Professor Terian returned with three bowls, one containing water, one filled with soil, and one with coals, and arranged them in the middle. He joined their circle. "Okay, who wants to demonstrate their element first?"

Fabian stared at his feet, but Kaia immediately stepped forward. "I will."

She stood above her designated bowl and held her hands above the soil. Like a puppeteer, she moved her fingers, pulling the earth up and slowly shaping it into an impressive little figurine.

"Very good," Professor Terian said. "Excellent control there."

With a smug smile, Kaia returned to her spot, leaving her figurine to crumble in her wake. Shayna snorted softly, clearly unimpressed. Fabian wasn't quite sure. Kaia's attitude grated on him but he had to admit she was talented. He doubted he could form water into a specific shape.

"Maybe Mr Winter next?" Professor Terian nodded encouragingly at the boy.

Camdyn, who'd hidden his hands in his hoodie, looked absolutely terrified. He stepped forward, shoulders drawn up, and stared at a point in the air. Facing away, he couldn't see Kaia's pitying, condescending look.

"Use your hands to guide the magic," Professor Terian said gently. "While elemental magic often responds to our emotions, we can also guide it through our arms and hands."

Watching Camdyn was painful. For fifteen minutes, he focused on a random point in the air, unsure of how to move his hands and letting them droop further with every passing minute. Not even a breeze rose.

"Maybe if we open a window," Fabian suggested. There was enough wind outside.

But Professor Terian shook his head. "No, this time, I want to see where everyone's at so I can adjust your individual pathways. Keep trying. Maybe recall a specific emotion that summoned wind before?"

"How do you know he's an elemental mage?" Kaia chimed in. "Has he ever done it before?"

"I assure you every one of you has been vetted. Camdyn is a wind mage."

Fabian pitied the boy even more. Camdyn seemed to try hard, his focus never wavering, but he wasn't deaf, and Kaia's stupid comments had done nothing but make his movements even more choppy.

"It always helps me to form my fingers—" Fabian was about to shape his fingers into a delta, but Camdyn suddenly let his arms drop completely and marched back into the circle.

"I'm done."

Professor Terian sighed. "That was a good try, Mr Winter. We'll help you unlock your magic in no time. Ms Richards. Please use the bowl to keep your fire contained."

"Good idea." Shayna stepped forward and took a stand near the bowl with the coals.

Fabian pressed his lips together, watching her with apprehension. Part of him expected her to fail and reveal it had all been a big joke. Instead, the coals began to glow a soft orange. A small flame ignited, flickered, and puffed out again. With a cheerful smile, Shayna took a step back. She really was an elemental mage.

"That's some good control," Professor Terian praised. "You'll see. In half a year, you'll be able to easily control a fire filling the whole bowl. Now, Mr Bendtfeld. If you please."

With a sigh, Fabian stepped forward as Shayna returned to her spot. "What do you want me to do?" Usually, he shot demons in the eyes with a hard jet stream rather than splash around with bowls of water.

Professor Terian smiled. "Surprise us."

Fabian winced at the non-answer. He faced the bowl. Since no one else had used the delta technique, he refrained and willed the water to rise in the bowl. It quickly reached the rim, then rose into the air in a bulbous column.

Across from him, Kaia gasped as the water easily reached Fabian's height. Assuming he'd done enough, he took a step back. Immediately, the water collapsed back into the bowl, splashing them. He gritted his teeth, while the other students jumped back, shrieking.

Only Professor Terian remained in place, his suit pants wet now, and an eyebrow raised disparagingly. "You certainly have talent, but your control needs work."

"You—" Fabian bit his tongue before he could argue the Professor hadn't told him to do anything specific, but the accident had occurred because he hadn't thought about it, so the comment was probably fair. "Of course, Professor."

Professor Terian returned the bowls to the shelf using a floating spell. "Calling your element can be exhausting, so why don't you all take fifteen and then we continue? Meanwhile, I'll get your textbooks."

Camdyn fled the room almost on Professor Terian's heels, leaving Fabian and Shayna alone with Kaia, who had her arms crossed. She regarded them with open hostility.

Shayna ignored her and said to Fabian, "That was an impressive display. I'm sure you could've done even more."

"Please," Kaia said, unable to stay out of the conversation, "the only thing impressive about it was how bad it was. When they said I'd finally get some classmates, I'd expected them to be on my level."

"Your level?" Shayna said. "You mean those few crumbs? Your pretty little figurine collapsed almost immediately."

Kaia leant forward, sneering at her. "That's because I withdrew my magic. It was planned that way, and I don't remember getting dirt on you, unlike some water mage. It was certainly better than your cute little flame."

"At least, it was cute," Shayna said with a shrug and smile. "Can't say the same for you. Right, Fabian?"

Fabian stared at her. "Um... I need some fresh air." He was certainly not going to be dragged into a catfight.

He fled and took a deep breath, only to notice Camdyn sitting next to the door, hugging his legs. Trying for some levity, he quipped, "Phew, it's getting hot in there. Apparently, none of us are up to Kaia's standard, and Shayna's not having it..."

Camdyn startled and looked up at him, eyes wide. They were a clear blue. A smattering of freckles surrounded his nose, the kind of unobtrusive, cute ones, not like Fabian's full-face of blotches. He couldn't be more than sixteen, a year younger than Fabian had been when his magic had come through.

"Hey, don't worry about the exercise. Two years ago, I was in the same place. Sometimes, the water came; sometimes, it didn't. And sometimes it came in full force. Like just now, basically."

"Just leave me alone." Camdyn scrambled up and hurried away.

With a sigh, Fabian strolled down the corridor in the opposite direction. So far, the Citadel wasn't off to a successful start. He'd embarrassed himself in front of the entire class and had immediately lost the approval of his professor. Strength didn't seem to matter as much as excellent control did.

Water arced between his hands, sparkling in the sunlight. Why couldn't he have shown them something like this instead? Though, Kaia would've likely still found a way to disparage him. She oozed privilege and stood for everything Elda had said about the Citadel. So much for times having changed.

Camdyn, on the other hand, didn't even want to be here, and in Fabian's opinion he was way too young. Why did the Citadel call them in now, rather than wait until they'd all come of age? The boy could've hardly discovered his powers.

And then there was Shayna Richards. In high school, she'd run with the it crowd, though she'd left the Elite Clique at the end of the year. She always seemed to be making fun of him, and he could never tell if she was flirting or just getting a kick out of pretending to do so. They hadn't been friends—far from it—but now they'd have to see each other every single day. The thought filled him with dread. At the same time, he welcomed the familiar face. She could be the one thing that'd keep him sane. Or drive him insane.

Fabian wandered the corridors, lost in thought, when he suddenly remembered the time. "Shit!" He hadn't checked when Professor Terian had left the room and now had no idea whether it'd already been fifteen minutes or fewer. Worse than that, he promptly got lost trying to retrace his steps.

Why did the Citadel have to have so many corridors and stairs and balconies? Fabian strode down the corridor, but everywhere he looked, the place looked unfamiliar.

Just then, he saw a familiar tail vanishing around a corner. "Clio?"

He hurried after her. For a moment, he wondered if he'd had the wrong cat-woman—who knew how many there were—but then Clio paused and cocked her head like a cat. "You."

"Yes, me. I'm Fabian, by the way." Last time, he'd failed to introduce himself, but then he remembered the issue with the study guide. "Which you obviously knew. Um, do you happen to know how I can get back to the Elemental Magic classroom? Quickly, if possible?"

She obviously knew all the secret passages. Sure enough, she slipped past the tapestry of a woman tending to a giant wheel. Fabian followed. "Thank you."

Only five metres behind the tapestry was a door. Stepping through the door, Fabian's hope of returning to the classroom was dashed when only darkness greeted him. "Are you sure this is—"

A paw covered his mouth and Clio's yellow eyes appeared in front of him. She hissed, which he took as a plea to be quiet. She pointed at a rectangle of light a few metres ahead. The light was flickering, illuminating a grate. She stood next to the rectangle and pointed downwards.

Fabian highly doubted he'd switched floors without knowing but couldn't help but throw a glance down. What he saw immediately brought up bile. He covered his mouth and backed away before looking down again, more carefully.

A ladder was attached to the grate, leading into some kind of dungeon. A fire was burning next to a table with a corpse. He knew it was a corpse, because the chest had been opened and the ribs cracked to reveal the heart. Fresh blood was dripping on the ground next to the table. A student—at least she looked young enough to be a student—dressed in a black robe reached into the body and cut the heart from its veins. She lifted it in the air and moved it to a nearby table, where a younger student stood, looking nervous. Four other figures in black robes stood around him, keeping him from bolting.

The older student placed the heart into his shaky waiting hands and painted something on his forehead with her bloody fingers. Initially surprised by its weight, the young student paused, concentrating. After a moment, the heart pulsed again, prompting smiles and nods from the other students.

Tasting vomit in his throat, Fabian walked backwards until he bumped into the door. If Clio was still there, he didn't see her. Not that it mattered. He pushed through the door, stumbled past the tapestry, found the nearest window, and threw up into the chasm below.

Rachel

Despite already questioning them, security kept the group in the investigation room. The tourists had formed clusters, continuing their interrupted conversations or enjoying the supplied food. Adam paced, his displeasure growing with each minute. Rachel had tried to talk him through it, but this was something he had to go through alone. Meanwhile, Samantha was having a nervous breakdown, not because of the security threat, but because of her dumb prophecy.

"Of course I didn't have access to my contraception, but I went to the gynaecologist straight after our return and... my period is regular, I don't feel sick or anything..." Samantha buried her face in her hands. "I don't want to be pregnant, not from that. Not..."

Rachel wondered if letting her know about her dream prophecy would lift her spirits. After all, if the world ended, she wouldn't have to worry about an unwanted pregnancy.

Lucille was rubbing her back. "If you really were pregnant, I'm sure Chay would've said something and not some random palm reader who's looking to make a quick buck."

"Chay also didn't say anything when I was about to be kidnapped," Samantha said tensely. "He might be able to see the future, but he does very little to change it."

Far from it, Rachel thought. No one tried harder to change the future than Chay, but there was a problem with it... "The future can't be changed. When I have a vision and it's not a straight-up warning, there's nothing I can change either." She bit her lip, wondering if the dream she'd had was a warning or vision.

"Isn't it kind of useless, then?" Samantha asked, tears in her eyes.

Rachel felt the sting but shrugged it off. "Well, it's not about changing the future, but changing some of the details." Like the fact it would hit their world.

"Well, I'd like to have the details of my pregnancy changed."

"You're not pregnant," Lucille said determinedly. When Samantha looked up at her, bottom lip quivering, Lucille sighed. "Look. As soon as we're back home, you're going to walk into a pharmacy, pick up a test or three, and get some answers. There's nothing we can do right now."

"Yeah, but when are we gonna get back home?" Tears were streaming down Samantha's face. Lucille immediately pulled her close and hugged her tight.

"My father will be here any minute. I asked them to inform him," Adam said. "He... and there he is." He let out a tremendous sigh of relief.

The door opened, and Geoffrey strode in, looking confused. "Adam?"

"There you are. Do you have any idea what's going on?"

"That's classified information. Need-to-know basis only."

Adam groaned. "Fine. Whatever. Can you get us out at least? It's getting late and—"

"You know I can't do that."

"Why not?"

Geoffrey rolled his eyes. "Because they're still investigating. No one can leave until security has given clearance."

Adam stared at him. "And there's nothing you can do about that?"

"I don't have the authority to do anything and I won't." A little softer, he added, "I can't believe you'd ask me to use my influence to get preferential treatment for you and your friends."

Adam's face stiffened, and he bit his lip. "That was silly of me. Agreed."

His father completely missed the sarcasm and nodded. "Good. I'm glad you've come to your senses. Now let me return to work, please."

"Of course. Sorry."

"I'm sure it won't take much longer." Geoffrey hastened out of the room while Adam clenched his fists, barely able to control his features.

After a moment, he turned and found a gentle smile for them. "It was worth a try. Sorry I can't get you out earlier."

Samantha had dried her tears, slowly coming to her senses. "Thanks for trying. I appreciate it." She frowned. "What's that woman doing?"

Rachel looked over her shoulder. A bronze-skinned woman was inching towards the door that'd been left ajar by Geoffrey's indignant exit. She peered outside, and suddenly she was gone. "Where did she go?"

"Trying to find a restroom?" Adam asked.

Samantha stood. "I don't like this."

Rachel agreed. "Neither do I."

With a mischievous smile, Lucille rose. "Let's investigate."

The woman was gone once they stepped outside, so they agreed to split up. Lucille and Samantha went one way, while Adam and Rachel headed the other way. It wasn't long until they saw the woman ahead. She heard their steps, threw a glance over her shoulder, and started running.

"Hey!" Rachel called.

She and Adam hurried after her, but the woman was faster.

"Let me try something," Adam said, stopping.

He raised his hands and started weaving. The woman stumbled and fell to the ground. Rachel ran to her, but only a moment later, a deafening alarm began blaring. Behind her, Adam screamed.

She spun around and found him collapsed on the ground, covering his ears. "Adam!"

She was almost at his side when security officers arrived one by one, surrounding them. Startled, she raised her hands, but the officers mostly ignored her. Instead, they dragged Adam up and pressed him against the wall.

"He didn't do anything!" Rachel shrieked, terrified by how quickly the situation had turned against them.

"There was a woman..." Adam tried to say, but one of the officers cut him off.

"Save it for the inspector!"

Rachel looked over her shoulder, not surprised when she found the woman gone. Panic was threatening to overcome her. "What are you going to do with him?" She desperately wanted to help Adam, but all she could do was dream.

"Block his magic," the commanding officer said, before barking, "Hers too."

He pulled out a black metal strip. While his colleagues held Adam's arms, he hit his wrists with the strip. Upon impact, it wrapped itself around Adam's wrists and fused with its own end. He gasped. Before Rachel could comprehend what had happened, an officer pulled her hands down and struck her wrists with another metal strip. A chill spread from her wrists, travelling up her veins until it seized her heart and her head, leaving her reeling.

"We didn't do anything," she cried.

Hasty steps sounded through the corridor. "What's happening here?"

Suddenly, Chay was there, Samantha and Lucille behind him. Lucille raised her hands, but Chay stopped her. "No spells. The security system is running on an anti-magic setting."

"Noted," Adam whimpered. He was incredibly pale and a little green, appearing on the verge of vomiting on his captor's shoes.

The officer turned to Chay. "Lord Chay, you're familiar with the suspects?"

"Very. And they're not suspects. Release them."

Rachel's eyes widened. Not only had the officer called him a lord, but Chay had the audacity to demand their release. Did he really have that kind of power?

"He used magic," the officer protested.

Chay sighed. "For what reason?"

Adam swallowed. "We followed a woman. She was acting suspicious, sneaking out of the room. When she heard us coming, she started running. I tried to stop her... with magic." He rolled his eyes a little, as if he couldn't believe he'd been stupid enough to try it.

"And where is she now?"

"Escaped," Rachel said, sharply. "Because these..." She bit her tongue, reigning her anger in. The security officers were just doing their job. "She managed to escape when the system struck Adam."

Chay cocked his head. "Will you release them now?"

"You believe them?" the captain asked, incredulous.

With a heavy sigh, Chay stepped forward, holding up his bare hand. In front of the captain's eyes, he put the hand on Adam's cheek, then swiftly removed it as if he'd been burnt.

"Care—"

An explosion shook the walls, and the world tilted upside down.

Matt

"Tadaa!" Matt spread his arms as they entered a copper dome and shelves of books rose in front of them. "Found the library."

Next to him, Vydra giggled. "Wow, I don't think I've ever seen this many books in one place."

Matt had seen his fair share of libraries, but none this big. "Same here."

The foyer was full of lockers for the students to stow their bags, as well as at least a dozen checkouts for the lending and returning of books. Once they were past them, they entered a maze of shelves several metres high. It was so big the corridors had street names. At each end, a bust of a famous poet or philosopher stood, their works displayed below. A small army of ladders served librarians and students, and when Matt looked up, he found more galleries.

"Okay, I definitely have to bring Samantha here."

"Samantha?" Vydra asked, suddenly alert.

"My girlfriend," Matt explained, unable to fight the smile that stretched his lips. After all that pining and yearning, it felt good to call her his girlfriend. "We're exclusive," he said equally proud. It was the first relationship of its kind.

Vydra snorted. "Of course you are. So, where is this Samantha now?"

"Oh, she's in town. Chay is showing her and some of my other friends all the sights of Fader. Her classes are starting next week, so she won't be able to come to Fader as often as she likes."

"Are you gonna be apart for the entire term?" Vydra asked, incredulous.

Matt shook his head and grinned. "Half-demon, remember? I can be at her side in an instant."

"Must be nice," she sighed. "I had to find a place to stay in the city. The nearest gate to my village is four hours away. Certainly not something I want to do every week, much less every day."

"Excuse me?" They were approached by a tall, bronze-skinned man with fine-cut features. His long brown hair was bound by a leather band in the nape of his neck and he was wearing a fitted tunic with an elegant brocade robe on top of it. A large signet ring on his right hand displayed two coiled snakes, biting each other. "Merik an Derendi of Phalos. I couldn't help but overhear your conversation. You're a half-demon?"

Matt frowned slightly. "Don't worry. I'm not gonna kill anyone."

Merik burst into laughter, earning himself some evil glares from the librarians. "Good to know. Though you might change your mind once you start 'Worlds of the Interglobal Community'. One world every week, and each week, you have to hand in an essay."

"You're a World Studies student?"

"Fifth semester. I'm specialising in species research. I've read about demons, but I don't think I've ever met one, not even a half-demon. I thought you guys were mostly in Hescaryn and Ashuan."

"Well, I live in Ashuan."

Merik's eyes widened. "No way! Okay, I've got so many questions. First up, what's your name?" he said, with a charming smile and out-stretched hand.

"I'd better leave you to it," Vydra said softly, and slipped away.

He was a bit sorry to see Vydra go, but Merik had such a captivating aura of grandeur, it was hard to ignore him. He chuckled. "It's Matt... Traidous."

"Matt Traidous of Ashuan," Merik repeated, licking his lips as if he could taste the name.

"Well, actually of Hescaryn... Though I guess, in that case, it would be Melchior of the House of Lust."

Merik grinned. "Yeah, I can see that working out for you. Do you need to get out a book or can I invite you for a phai outside? It's a hot drink. Very energising."

"I was just getting the lay of the land. Make sure I know where everything is."

"Look, Matt... or Melchior." He put an arm around Matt's shoulders and turned him around. "If you need any help, just come to me. I know the library like the back of my hand. If you want, I can even lend you my notes."

Slightly overwhelmed, Matt nodded. "That would be incredibly helpful. I feel like I'm already lost, and we've only had three lectures so far."

Merik laughed again. "Oh, believe me, I know the feeling." He raised a hand to a mean-looking librarian. "We're leaving, don't worry." To Matt he whispered, "They're quite strict with their rules, though how anyone can study in silence in the main room when hordes of students are trampling through, moving ladders, and throwing books around, I don't know. The best spots are at the back and on the third floor."

"Thanks." That was actually helpful to know.

Merik led him past the checkouts. "Told you I know this place. I practically lived here during the first semester. So, tell me: how does a half-demon from Ashuan enrol at the University of Fader?"

"I'm friends with Chay. He's—"

Merik already nodded. "Ah, Lord Chay, of course. The only other half-demon ever heard of in these parts."

"Lord?"

"You weren't aware? He was made an honorary lord ages ago. That means he's got the title and authority but no lands to go with it. Some call him Lord of the Snow Lakes, but I'm pretty sure the High North would take issue with that."

The onslaught of unexpected information had left Matt disoriented. It was like he hardly knew his friend. Chay shared what he shared, and while living in Hescaryn it had never occurred to Matt—or interested him—to ask for more. His time in Ashuan had changed him, and now he felt like a horrible friend.

"He doesn't like talking about his... youth."

"Is that so? I mean, I only know the rumours, of course, but the High North exiled him for a century or so, and he actually first approached the Interglobal Parliament as an emissary of the Middlemark." Merik rolled his eyes. "Okay, fine, I know a bit more. He's been a bit of a special interest for me."

"Because of your focus on different species?"

"Exactly. I find demons awfully interesting. Is it true their society has two governing bodies despite being allergic to rules?"

Matt burst out laughing. "No one said they were effective. But yes, we've got the Small Council and Council of Seven."

"The Seven are the deadly sins, right? What were they?" He frowned as he began counting, "Lust, Greed, Gluttony, Sloth, Pride, Wrath, and... what was the last one?"

"Envy."

"Right, Envy. Of course. Is it true you can petition one of the Archdemons to help you?"

"You mean summon them? Technically, yes. They love corrupting humans, especially if they're willing. Personally, I wouldn't call on Wrath, though. He's just as likely to kill you as he is to help you."

Merik grinned. "I love that! Such a fascinating society. I'm going to petition—not summon—for Hescaryn to be put on the excursion list for us third years."

"You want to kill your classmates?"

Laughing, he clapped his back. "No, no, of course not. The excursions are not a group thing. We have to pick a world from the list, go there for a month—though we can split that into multiple shorter visits—and provide a comprehensive report at the end. And I'd really love for Hescaryn to be mine. No one else would pick it."

"Right..." Matt felt a flutter of excitement about his third-year prospects. The thought of systematically exploring a world unknown to him was thrilling. "How are your survival skills?" He eyed the older student's brocade robe as they stood in line at the café outside the library.

"I'm decent with a sword, not Man of the Dragon level like Chay, but good enough,"—another phrase Matt had never heard—"and I have access to... I think you'd call them watch dogs. Loyal creatures I can summon for certain purposes. They're contained in scrolls..." He shook his head. "It's complicated. Phalesian speciality. Two phais please," he ordered. "Two drops of sugar."

"Drops?" It turned out what Merik had called sugar was more like a syrup, dropped in with a tiny spoon.

"Without the sugar, it's too sour."

Curious, Matt watched the phai being poured. It was a thick golden liquid served in slender cups that looked more like test probes than dishes. When the sugar was dropped in, swirls of red spread through it. He picked up his cup and smelt it, expecting something like coffee. Instead, he was reminded of citrus fruits.

"Is it fruity?"

The place was overflowing with students, but they were in luck and found a recently vacated table. Fascinated, Matt watched the dirty dishes dancing away and into the kitchen.

"The phai? It's made from tree-sap, I think. Something in the swamps of Mynos. That's what makes it so good, you know?"

"What does?"

"The swamps... Oh, right, you've only just arrived here. They're further north from Fader and they're home to the Green Tower of Magic. You know, the fabled origin of green magic."

Matt wished Samantha was here right now. She'd eat that shit up. "I'm only an expert on black magic."

"Don't you have a tower in Hescaryn, too? The Black Tower."

Now that Merik said it, Matt felt like an idiot. "Yes, yes, of course. The Black Tower of Sephira." Sephira had been the capital before Lucin had been built. It was a much darker, secluded place, dominated by a giant black tower which held the key to the Throne of Chaos. "Every Lord of Chaos has to be anointed by the pure black magic in the tower before they can assume the throne. We haven't had one in over a thousand years."

"And you're only a half-demon, rather young, right? No wonder you're starting to forget. So, no one has laid claim to it? No descendant of the last one? Distant relative?"

"Hescaryn doesn't believe in that kind of succession. It's power and power only. Some have tried, but they've all failed. The problem is that the last Lord of Chaos, Mirialle, wasn't killed by demons but in the vampire uprising. Her power was lost."

"And I assume the Council of Seven has got quite comfortable?"

Matt shrugged. "Naturally."

He leant back and took a cautious sip of the phai. As Merik had warned him, it was quite sour, but as soon as he'd swallowed, he felt energy coursing through his veins. He felt alive, as if he'd only been asleep until now. "Wow, this stuff is..."

"The key to surviving university," Merik said, in all seriousness.

Matt laughed.

Three students slipped into the booth behind them. "...still haven't caught the assailant," one exclaimed.

The girl next to him gasped. "Still? They locked down parliament hours ago. Is something horrible going to happen?"

"Hopefully not. I heard Lord Chay was present. Surely, he'll stop whatever's happening."

Parliament was locked down. Chay was present. An assailant...

Matt swallowed, the phai suddenly turning bitter. The parliament had been part of Samantha's itinerary. If they'd been locked inside with an attacker...

"Um... I have to go."

And without waiting for Merik's response, he simply vanished.

Matt reappeared in front of the parliament building. He ignored the shiny dome and stairs, focusing solely on the column of rising smoke.

A crowd had gathered in front, full of concern and sensational curiosity. None of them could get past the line of security guards. Behind the guards, a solid wall blocked off the entrance—magic no doubt.

With little regard for anyone else, Matt pushed to the front of the crowd until he managed to get hold of an officer. "You need to let me in. My girlfriend's inside."

"No one goes in or out. Get back," the officer barked.

For a moment, Matt briefly considered forcing his way through. Sensing it would only worsen the situation, he pulled back and tried to jump. The jump itself worked, but instead of reappearing inside, he slammed into a wall and was thrown back out on the street.

Stunned and a little dizzy, he leant against the wall behind him to catch his breath. Nothing had ever blocked him from a space jump before. Obviously, the Interglobal Parliament was secure against demons. Unfortunately, that meant Samantha was locked inside with whatever madman had tried to blow it up.

"Chay!" he called, quickly drawing blood and smearing a pentahedral star on the wall to strengthen his summons. "Chay, please. Come on, tell me you're not in there."

But he was. Or if not, he'd chosen to ignore Matt, as he so often did.

Despairing, Matt rubbed his face and crouched in front of the wall. He had no choice but to sit this one out and hope Samantha and his friends got out unhurt.

Fabian

Fabian stared at his table, his mind still stuck on the horrifying images he'd seen in the basement. Professor Terian was lecturing, but he didn't hear a single word of it. Had they killed the person right there or had they somehow got hold of a freshly deceased one? No, of course, they'd killed them. Corpses didn't bleed. Who? Who had they killed, and why? What plans did they have for their heart? Were they even students? If so, what magic required bleeding hearts?

He was starting to feel sick again when the class suddenly ended and Professor Terian left the room, Camdyn right on his heels.

"Hey," Shayna spoke to him, her bag already packed. "Did something happen?"

"He probably came face to face with reality," Kaia said. "You don't belong here. The Citadel usually doesn't take run-of-the-mill mages."

"Run-of-the-mill?" Shayna asked, outraged.

Kaia smiled smugly. "You're not Citadel mages. My ancestors were all mages. Our family has spread to very branch of magic. My father is the director of studies, and my mother is the First Councillor. My aunt—"

"Oh, shut up!" Shayna snapped.

"You asked."

"Not about your ancestry. We get it—you're better than us, blah, blah, blah. Now sod off and bother someone who cares."

Kaia left the room in a huff. Shayna rolled her eyes. "Oh dear, it almost makes me wish Cheryl was back in my life. Just because Kaia can move a bit of dirt around and was born in the Citadel." When Fabian didn't react, she waved her hand in front of him. "Are you okay?"

Fabian swallowed hard. "How did we land here?"

She sat on his desk. "Do you mean the Citadel or this wonderful little class?"

"They're experimenting on humans."

"Excuse me?"

He nodded, slowly regaining his cognitive abilities. "I saw it with my own two eyes. Down in the basement. They had a fresh corpse and"—bile rose in his throat—"they were practising magic on it."

"Are you talking about necromancy? Because that can't be true. Terian just told us they banned necromancy two hundred years ago. I think they still teach the theory or you can find information in some books, but practising will get you immediately expelled."

"I saw what I saw." Necromancy. That fit the bill. The heart had started beating again when the young student had touched it.

Shayna bit her lip. "Are you sure... I mean, I believe you, of course, but... If it's true, we'll have to report it."

"To whom? Terian? That guy already hates me." After he'd finally found the classroom again, Professor Terian had lectured him about the importance of punctuality.

"He'll have to accept it if you have proof."

"But I don't."

She hopped off his desk and held up her phone. "Well, then we'll have to get some. Photos, videos. We'll find something incriminating."

"First, we'll have to find the place again."

"I've got time."

He nodded slowly, the beginnings of an action plan forming. "Okay, um, and you're sure it's illegal? The necromancy, I mean?"

"You didn't hear a single word Terian just said, right?" Shayna chuckled softly to herself. "Don't worry, you can copy my notes. But first, let's look for your necromancers." She held her hand out.

He took it and nodded, suddenly determined. "Let's bring those monsters down."

Fabian spent thirty minutes relocating the tapestry depicting a woman and her wheel. He confirmed it by checking the balcony he'd thrown up from. "I swear, I hate this place. A labyrinth would be easier to navigate."

Shayna snickered. "It's day one. Give the Citadel a chance."

"Not when they're teaching necromancy."

Maybe he was a little biased, but he couldn't possibly imagine anything good coming from a discipline that required dead bodies. Especially not if it involved killing them in the first place.

"As I told you, it's forbidden."

"Didn't stop those students." He shuddered, remembering the bleeding, beating heart again. "How do you even get into that?"

Shayna pulled a face. "You're asking the wrong person. I can't even deal with the mouse traps at my parents' bed and breakfast. So, what do we do now?"

"Come with me." He lifted the tapestry and heard Shayna gasp when it revealed a secret passage. "There are tons of them, as if the corridors aren't confusing enough already."

"That's kind of cool," she whispered as she snuck past, pulling out her phone to record.

Fabian led her through the door to the grate on the floor. As before, a fire burnt in the room below, providing light. Other than that, it had been vacated. The corpse had been removed, and no body parts were lying around, dead or alive. The only thing bearing witness to the atrocities were the dark spots on the ground. Blood.

"Well, that's a bit of a bust." Apparently, class was over for the necromancers, too.

Just then, Fabian saw movement. Initially, he believed it was a large cat, but then he recognised Clio scurrying through the room, looking for something. Shayna opened her mouth, but Fabian quickly put his hand over her mouth. He still didn't know what to make of the strange cat-woman. Was she helping him or was she in league with the necromancers? No, if she were, she wouldn't have shown him here. Clio wanted him to find out. But why?

He motioned to Shayna to withdraw, and they both crept backwards. Just as he was about to reach for the door, it swung open. The light blinded him.

"What do we have here?" an icy voice asked.

Before Fabian's eyes adjusted, someone slipped past him, and he suddenly felt an arm around his neck and the cut of a blade on his cheek. "What the hell?"

Next to him, Shayna shrieked, "Don't you dare touch me!" Fire flared and her assailant, the young woman he'd seen before, backed away.

In the flickering light, Fabian saw three people, all of them wearing black robes. One of them had Fabian immobilised, holding a dagger way too close to his eye. His cheek was burning. A drop of blood rolled down his chin.

"Would you look at that?" a guy with a long tooth earring—their leader—said. "You must be the legendary elemental mages."

"Legendary, my ass," the woman said. "That's the puniest flame I've ever seen. Look, it's already flickering. They're not even real mages." She sounded like Kaia.

Just as Fabian was about to call her out, the grate moved, revealing Clio. "Fabian?"

"What are you doing here?" the leader asked coldly. "Snooping around again? I'll have to teach you a lesson."

He pushed his arm up and sliced into his skin. As blood welled up, he spoke in an unfamiliar language full of hisses that crawled over Fabian's skin.

Clio screamed. She curled up on the ground, trying to protect herself from whatever onslaught of cruelty had been flung at her.

"Leave her alone!" Fabian shouted, trying to free himself from the vice grip—to no avail.

The necromancer laughed. "Don't worry about her. She's nothing but a failed experiment. My creature through and through. Right, Clio?"

"Bastard!"

Shayna threw her flame at him, but he easily sidestepped it. Simultaneously, Clio stopped screaming and attacked Shayna. Her claws glinted in the last strokes of the flame.

"Clio, no!" Fabian shouted, but the cat-woman didn't listen to him. She hissed and snarled as she attacked Shayna.

The dagger near his eye was moving closer. Fabian grabbed his captor's wrist and summoned the water to him. Within seconds, he was screaming.

"What the fuck, dude?" The man stumbled away, holding his dehydrated arm, dagger dropping on the floor.

"What are you doing, Flynn?" the woman hissed.

"He... he did something to my arm." Flynn looked at Fabian with sheer horror.

Fabian dashed forwards, threw his arms around Clio and wrenched her away from Shayna. "Clio, stop. We're your friends." She tried to clout him, but he pulled back his head. "It's me, Fabian. Remember?"

Clio paused. "Fabian?"

The necromancer groaned. "You're so weak-willed, Clio. Oh well, this cat isn't a failure." He reached into his bag and dropped a pile of bones on the ground. As he and the woman chanted in their weird language, the bones grew and rose and rearranged themselves until they'd taken the shape of a giant cat.

Fabian swallowed and let go of Clio, who immediately bolted, while Shayna held onto his shoulders and whispered, "What is that?"

By the looks of it, it was a small panther or perhaps a lynx. Fabian backed up a little, slowly raising his hands. The skeleton cat crouched, ready to pounce.

"Go," the necromancer hissed.

The cat jumped, and Fabian let loose. A jet of water hit the collection of bones and scattered them all around the tunnel, then bounced off the wall, drenched the necromancers, and pushed them aside.

"Run!"

Shayna bolted without hesitation, and Fabian followed. Together, they crashed through the tapestry, promptly slipping in a puddle of water caused by his own magic. Fabian gasped and braced himself for the impact before checking on Shayna. In the light, he saw several scratch marks on her face and arms. Otherwise, she looked fine but scared.

Steps thumped behind them, and the three necromancers burst out of the tapestry. All three of them raised knives and cut themselves. Fabian went down, screaming in agony. The pain was like a worm inside of him, eating away at his substance, and it was whispering, Kill the girl.

Shaking, Fabian raised his arm. Shayna was in front of him, screaming her head off. He could shut her up so easily, fill her mouth with water and drown out any noise.

Instead, his arm swung sideways and his water hit the lead necromancer, throwing him down the corridor. He and Shayna collapsed in a heap, making the pain and pressure to ease a little. He recalled the water and split it into two streams, poised to strike the others. No one told him what to do, much less forced him to turn on his friends.

He was just about to let loose when his body was lifted in the air and he lost his balance. His stomach dropped as he did an involuntary flip. Floating upside down, he found himself in some kind of bubble. But he wasn't the only one. He, Shayna, and the two remaining necromancers floated in the air while two professors strode down the corridor.

One of them was their very own professor, Terian, and he had his arms raised, seemingly controlling the bubbles. The other was drenched and seething, but Fabian recognised him, too: the director of studies, Professor Takuna. Kaia's father.

"What in every gods' name is going on here?" he yelled. His voice made the bubble walls shiver.

Behind him, the necromancer's leader grabbed hold of a statue and pulled himself up. "These"—he coughed—"wild mages were trying... We said something stupid, but they attacked. No impulse control whatsoever. It was... wild."

"You lying piece of shit!" Shayna hissed. "Professor Terian, they attacked us. They're necromancers."

"There are no necromancers in this Citadel," Professor Takuna immediately admonished her. "Such an accusation is a serious matter, young woman."

"I saw them," Fabian protested, still struggling to find his balance. "Just check... just..." If this went on any longer, he was going to throw up again.

Just then, the tapestry moved and Clio appeared, a bone in her mouth. She dropped it in front of Professor Takuna's feet and sat back, her rotting tail flipping back and forth. "There's more," she said.

Suddenly, the bubbles burst, and they fell. Fabian cried out seconds before he collapsed on the ground. Glaring, he looked up at his professor, but Terian's face had gone grey.

"Clio?"

Lucille

Coughing, Lucille rose from the rubble. Dust was slowly settling around her, revealing death and destruction. A piece of ceiling had come down, striking two security officers. One was most certainly dead, while the other was screaming, her legs crushed by the rock, not even half a metre from where Rachel was sitting on the ground, stunned.

To her left, Adam, Chay, and the security captain had gone down. Chay's shirt was torn, and he had one wing extended over Adam and the captain to shield them from debris. Nevertheless, Adam was writhing on the ground, groaning in pain. As Lucille watched, the captain tapped the black metal band around his wrists and released him. His left hand immediately flew to his right shoulder and he grimaced.

Next to Lucille, Samantha stumbled to her feet, a dusty trail of blood running down the side of her face, her eyes wide. "What just happened?"

"Explosion. It's not going to be the only one," Chay said. He held Adam's hand. "Sorry about this." Gritting his teeth, he placed his other hand on Adam's shoulder, then pulled and twisted. The relief on Adam's face was instant.

The captain released Rachel as he spoke to a green wisp in the air. "Requesting reinforcements. Further explosions to be expected. Need medical assistance in corridor four."

The wisp raced off into the distance.

Chay dusted off his arms and tucked in his wings. "Samantha, Lucille, I need you at the platform." He pointed ahead, then vanished with the captain and two other officers.

Lucille looked at Samantha, still struggling to comprehend the situation. Meanwhile, Rachel ran to Adam and threw her arms around his neck. "Are you okay?"

"Could be better..." He was still massaging his shoulder.

"I'm going to stay with him," Rachel said. "Go stop that madwoman."

Samantha and Lucille glanced at each other, then started running. Thanks to the tour, they knew exactly where to go.

Breathing heavily, they skidded to a stop when the hallway widened into the plaza below the floating parliament. A fight had broken out between two dozen hooded figures and half as many security officers. A few people were already on the ground, dead or injured. Not all of them were fighting, though. Six were standing around the garden, eyes raised at the platform above them, which was leaning precariously.

"They're undoing the floating spell," Samantha called out.

Lucille swallowed, imagining the giant platform coming down on them. Who knew how many important delegates and legislators were currently in danger?

"Can you do it?" Chay asked, appearing next to them.

Samantha started weaving. "I can try."

Two seconds later, one of the enemy witches pointed at Samantha and shouted something in a foreign language. Three magic missiles were instantly aimed at them.

"Scutum Protecto!" Lucille shouted.

Her shield formed less than a second before the missiles hit. The impact nearly threw Lucille to the ground, but Samantha remained upright, weaving intensely. Above them, the tilting of the platform was slowing to a creep.

The triple attack had left the shield weak. Lucille knew she'd have to strengthen the spell or take out the assailants. When she tried to find them, Chay had already killed two. She decided to strengthen her spell instead and protect Samantha while she was dealing with the more important task.

"I can't do it alone," Samantha groaned, the sweat leaving streaks on her dusty face.

"Take my magic then." Lucille held her hand out.

Without even hesitating, Samantha grabbed her wrist and began wrapping her spells around it. Lucille felt a tug in her stomach and her shield flickered.

Meanwhile, Chay had dealt with three other attackers, taking out enough for the tide to turn. Reinforcements arrived a minute later, and a small army of mages began weaving with Samantha, righting the platform and reinforcing the floating spell.

When the dust had settled and all the cloaked figures were either dead or apprehended, Samantha lowered her arms and sunk against Lucille.

Feeling a bit weak as well, Lucille put her arm around her friend and leant on her. "Do you think we've had the full tour now?"

Samantha laughed softly. "You know, I really wanted to see that spell up close."

Lucille giggled. Even to her ears, it sounded slightly insane.

As soon as security gave clearance, the elevator came down, carrying a dozen of whom Lucille assumed were the most important delegates, and Geoffrey Black. A dark-skinned woman with enviable long earrings and a rich robe approached Chay.

"Lord Chay. It's always a pleasure to see you. I suppose we have you to thank for the coordination of a swift response?"

The half-demon turned around. "If you want to thank someone, thank Samantha Kollmer and Lucille de Cerque from Ashuan. Without them, the parliament would've fallen. You'd do well to remember their names."

The woman stared at her so intently Lucille shrivelled a little inside. "Any friend of Chay's is mine. Thank you, ladies. I'll make sure you'll be recognised."

"Adam Black, too," Lucille blurted out. "He tried to stop this from happening in the first place and was injured in the process." The info wasn't so much for her benefit but Geoffrey's, hovering over her shoulder.

All her comment resulted in was the slightest widening of his eyes. What a cold man.

The delegation continued on, speaking to the captain of the security and other officers. Chay followed, offering his insight. He might not have been a member of the parliament, but he clearly held a position of trust among the elected officials.

Samantha leant in. "Call me crazy, but I think Chay knew exactly what he was doing bringing us here today."

"Remember our names," Lucille muttered. "Yeah, I think you're right."

Fabian

Fabian and Shayna were in Terian's office above their elemental magic class. It was a round room full of books and wondrous displays, among them a globe with flowing lines that gleamed in soft green. Once in a while, a spot flared up and faded again. The centrepiece was a large desk. Terian was leaning against it, Clio curled up on top. The professor was stroking her hair lovingly as she purred, deeply satisfied.

It was such a peaceful scene, Fabian felt slightly reconciled with the Citadel.

"She's my niece," Terian said, his voice much gentler. "Eight years ago, she vanished one day after class. She'd only started the month before. We never found out what happened to her."

"What did happen to her?"

"We're unlikely to pinpoint it exactly, but I assume she was operated on. And"—he scratched behind her cat ears—"had her body augmented with these cat appendages. Maybe even a bone or two. The rest is pure necromancy."

"So, you're saying she's not alive?"

Terian watched his niece thoughtfully. "I think, for the most part, she is. Some parts are dead, though, and it's through those they were able to control her." He massaged the bridge of his nose. "I can't believe we've had a group of necromancers practising right under our noses. You did a good thing today, uncovering this travesty. I'm deeply sorry this happened on your first day."

Fabian sank deeper into his chair. "It's been quite the day." He still wasn't convinced the school was really for him, but at least necromancy was truly banned. "Will you be able to heal her?" Right now, Clio seemed content, but the experiments hadn't just changed her body.

Terian sighed. "I'm afraid many of the changes will be permanent. I'll try my best, but I might not be able to do more than make her comfortable and assure she can live in peace."

"And maybe not put freshmen in danger," Shayna muttered. The scratches on her face had been treated, but judging by the way she wriggled her nose, they were itching quite a bit.

Fabian reached out and held her hand before she could pick at her wounds. "She was just trying to finally be free."

When they'd first met, Clio had called him a saviour. This was what she must've meant.

"By leading us right into their lair. Why didn't she ask... you, for example?" Shayna pointed at Terian.

The professor crossed his arms. "The only thing I can think of is a curse that made it impossible for her to talk to any Citadel-born mages. You're the first wild mages we've had in a decade." He nodded at Fabian. "Impressive work, by the way. You were holding back in class. I didn't expect a wild mage to be so proficient already."

Fabian couldn't help himself. "Well, maybe you underestimated us."

Terian chuckled. "Maybe. Now, it's getting quite late. I'm sure you want to go home and have dinner. Since you've already practised your powers, I'll be lenient and forgive homework for today. I just hope you're not planning on uncovering a necromancy conspiracy every day."

"You and me both, Professor."

Shayna giggled. "Let's get you back to your girlfriend. She's probably thinking I've seduced or something."

"You d-d..." Annoyed, Fabian cleared his throat. "She doesn't even know you're here."

"Better tell her, then, before she finds out on her own."

It was like her words had lit a fire under him. He jumped up. "I have to go. See you tomorrow, Professor."

"Maybe you could try to be on time."

Shayna giggled, while Fabian's face flushed like a tomato. He nodded sharply and turned abruptly on his heel.

Ophelia was already waiting in his room. When he opened the door, she threw her hands up. "Finally. You said classes would only go until four."

It was nearly seven. Fabian crawled onto the bed and gave her a quick kiss. "Sorry, it was a big day. We busted a necromancer student association."

"We? Is that part of your class? If so, you've got the best course of study ever."

He chuckled and sunk onto the bed next to her. "No, fortunately, that wasn't part of the course. When I said we..." For a moment, he hesitated. Ophelia had shown her insecurity on the rare occasions she'd noticed Shayna's weird interest. But not telling her wasn't an option. "You won't believe who's my new classmate."

"Who?"

"Shayna Richards."

As predicted, Ophelia's eyes widened and her mouth flew open. "That bitch who was hitting on you at Sam's birthday?"

"She didn't... Yes, that Shayna. Cheryl's friend."

"Oh, Ishtar, you poor guy." She wrapped her arms around him and pressed her body against him, batting her eyes at him. "She can do magic?"

"Apparently, she can control fire. Well, more or less."

"I bet she isn't half as good as you." She held her nose up, prompting Fabian to kiss it. "Also, fire and water don't go together. At all."

He couldn't help but snort. "Look, you've got nothing to worry about. I'm not interested in Shayna, but our class is so small, it's good to have someone on my side. Cause the rest, oh my god. Cheryl is a saint compared to that Kaia! And Camdyn..."

Ophelia cuddled with him as he recounted his first day. Merle entered, hopped onto the bed and curled up on his legs, a complete angel after the disaster this morning. She reminded him of Clio, so he gave her some extra scratches.

"I'm not sure what to think of the Citadel. I really hope today was an exception. Because if I have to battle necromancers and deal with arrogant queen bees every day, I might as well stay in Greenvalley."

"Maybe you should," Ophelia purred. She pulled him in for a long kiss.

But as chaotic and scary as his first day had been, Fabian was determined to return tomorrow. Maybe monster hunting had ruined him, but he was no longer able to imagine a day without magic. And apart from that, a fire had been lit in him. The Citadel hadn't gone with the times at all. He and Shayna—and Camdyn—weren't just some rare wild mages invited to study; they were the only ones. At least half the Citadel, if not all, expected them to fail.

And Fabian was going to prove them wrong.

Rachel

The Interglobal Parliament provided a healer for Adam and he received a formal apology from the security captain. Rachel was sat by his side, holding his hand as he received treatment, when his father entered. Impatiently, he waited for the healer to finish and leave.

"What were you thinking?" Geoffrey snapped, surprising both Rachel and Adam.

"Thinking?" When Geoffrey tapped his foot, short of proclaiming he never thought, Adam hurried to say, "There was no one else. She just walked out of that room."

"Then you could've rung the alarm, told someone. Really, boy, you need to use your head, at least from time to time. You know how to contact security and you know about the no-magic spell."

Adam lowered his head and mumbled, "Sorry", but Rachel felt his hand tighten around hers.

"Well, at least you didn't get too badly injured and your friends made themselves useful." His voice dropped a little, as if he didn't quite know how to say something nice. "You're free to go now."

"Cool," Adam said sullenly, the rejection so visible on his face, it hurt Rachel. "What about you?"

Geoffrey sighed. "I've got a lot of work waiting for me. We have to investigate what happened today and how they were able to smuggle a gate device in. And why, of course. Lots of paperwork, too. It'll take us weeks, maybe even months, to clean up." He nodded at them. "I'll call."

Adam raised an eyebrow, not deigning the promise with an answer.

As Geoffrey rushed out again, Rachel stroked Adam's hand. "Don't listen to him. He—"

Chay appeared in the door. Behind him, Lucille and Samantha peeked inside. "Everyone's free to leave now, so let me bring you back to the portals."

Rachel was relieved to leave parliament behind. So far, she hadn't been too impressed by Fader. Sure, everything was big and colourful and there was magic everywhere, but it was all a bit too showy, and the politics side either bored or infuriated her. Mostly infuriated, since it had turned what had been planned as a fun date into a shit show.

She wasn't the only one feeling that way. Now the attack was over and her skills were no longer required, Samantha was a bundle of nerves again. When they stepped outside and saw Matt waiting impatiently at the bottom of the stairs, she cried out and threw herself into his arms, sobbing.

"Just take her home straight away. The pharmacy closes in ten minutes," Lucille said.

"The pharmacy?"

Rachel didn't blame him for being confused. She hoped Samantha wasn't pregnant, though. Not that she doubted Matt's love for her, but he was still learning what it meant to be human, and throwing a baby into the mix would bring the honeymoon phase to a swift end. Hopefully, he'd step up and prove her wrong, but she wasn't going to hold her breath.

"Be nice," Lucille called, clearly worried about his reaction, too.

Still confused, Matt took the advice and vanished with Samantha in his arms. Chay sighed a little, a habit Rachel had noticed before, almost as if he wasn't a huge fan of the happy couple. Rachel wondered why and whether it had anything to do with last night's dream.

She mulled over Chay's words from this morning.

Something major is going to happen in Ashuan. I don't know if it's the end of the world. It can't be, but I know many people will die if it isn't stopped. There's a prophecy, but I feel like we've only heard half of it.

If the first half brought death and destruction to the world by causing a freaking volcanic eruption, Rachel wasn't sure she wanted to hear the rest.

Look for the signs, Rachel. The shadows and whispers. They're going to make their first move much earlier than we expect.

"How come," Adam mused, dragging Rachel from her thoughts, "Chay, who is the Chay, has time to accompany us back home, while my father can't even spare five minutes?"

She squeezed his hand. "Oh, Adam, parents are... They think we'll be here forever."

"What do you mean?"

Her own brief altercation with her father came to Rachel's mind. "We're their children, so naturally we're always going to be interested in a relationship with them, but what they fail to understand is we're not children any longer. And there's only so much hurt we can take before we realise we don't need them, and we've got our own lives."

"You mean I should stop hoping he'll come around one day?"

Rachel shrugged. "Maybe he will, but what I'm really saying is you shouldn't waste your time on him. Let him come to you if he wants a relationship. You've got your own life to live." She suddenly had an idea, which immediately lifted her spirits. "Hey! Apparently, my parents are planning to move to America."

"Both of them?" Lucille asked, shocked. Clearly, she'd been listening in the whole time and had reached the point where she just had to insert herself.

"Yep. But they're gonna let me have the house. And man, it's a big house." She smiled at Adam. "Why don't you move in once you've got everything sorted?"

Adam stopped short. "You want me to move in?"

"I know it's fast, but you need somewhere to stay and... well, I've got room. We'd be flatmates."

"Oh, but for a real shared flat, you need more than one flatmate," Lucille said, chipper. "I'm in. My parents suck, too."

Rachel stared at her. "I don't have a butler."

Lucille burst out laughing. "That's what makes it so exciting. It's going to be the ultimate university experience."

"Can you cook?"

"No, but I can order takeaways."

"Sold," Adam said, grinning from ear to ear.

Rachel looked at him in surprise, then at Lucille's smug smile, and she finally understood. By offering to move in with her, too, Lucille had made it easier for Adam to accept her premature proposal. Now, instead of living together as a couple, they'd just be roommates who were hooking up. It wasn't much different from what Matt and Samantha were doing with Jan at the Blackstone House.

"The Abandoned Children flat." Lucille painted a picture with her words. "It'll be like family. The real deal."

Rachel smiled. "You're right. After all, family isn't just blood, it's the people you choose to be with."

Adam raised her hand to his mouth and kissed it softly. "And I'd choose you every day."

Samantha

The tears had dried on Samantha's face, but the pain in her stomach continued as she sat on the edge of her bed with Matt and waited for the pregnancy test to deliver the news. Matt had his arm around her, while Samantha was hugging herself, a tight ball of despair. He hadn't asked a single question, just marched into the pharmacy, bought a bunch of pregnancy tests, and helped as much he could.

Still, she feared the result. A baby wasn't part of the plan on a good day. She was just starting university, not even twenty yet, and their relationship was so young still. But that wasn't what truly bothered her about the possibility. It was the fact she couldn't be sure it was Matt's.

Her eyes welled up again, just as the test started to reveal the result.

"Negative," Matt said, only a hint of relief in his voice.

Samantha groaned, the tension leaving her body in one big whoosh as she leant back and dropped into the mattress. Pressing the balls of her hands into her eyes, she took one shuddering breath after the other. "I'm not pregnant."

"That's a good thing, isn't it?" Matt asked, lying next to her, head propped on his hand.

"Yes, Matt, that's a very good thing."

He let out a real sigh of relief. "Good, I wasn't sure... That woman has a lot to answer for!"

Unable to reply, Samantha just waved him off. She didn't care about the soothsayer and her stupid prediction. Not anymore. Even though she was glad the test had been negative, the tears kept flowing.

"Hey." Matt nudged her shoulder with a cautious finger. "Talk to me."

"It's... it's not that. I'm glad. Really glad. Just..."

"You were worried the child would've been one of Melaney's lovers?"

Samantha could only nod, her throat quickly constricting.

Matt laid down next to her and put his arm around her, gently rubbing his thumb across her shoulder. "I'm so sorry, Sam. I should've been there faster."

"It's not your fault."

For the last three months, she'd pushed all memories of her hellish nightmare aside and let Matt sweep her off her feet. Now, it was all coming back. The unwanted feelings, the abuse, the moments she couldn't remember but knew had happened. "You were just as much a victim of your mother as I was."

Melaney had messed with his mind and forced him into submission to feed her sick obsession. Never mind the environment he'd grown up in.

"You don't need to worry about me," Matt said softly. "She hurt you, and if she were still alive, I'd kill her for it, as well as every demon who'd dared to touch you."

Samantha couldn't help but roll her eyes. It was such a Matt thing to say. But the words had the expected effect. "You'd kill for me. Amazing."

"I'd do anything for you," Matt said. He leant down and kissed her other shoulder. The touch of his lips left a burning imprint. "Any sacrifice, physical, mental, or moral. You're all that matters to me. Not our friends, not the world, not Chay's plans. You. You're everything." He followed each sentence with a kiss on her skin.

The flow of tears stopped as desire bloomed in her body. With a sudden need, Samantha grabbed his shirt and pulled him on top of her. "Make me forget their touch."

Matt's lazy grin almost made her lose her mind. "Your wish is my command." He lowered his mouth on hers.

Within seconds, Matt made her forget the pregnancy scare, her nightmares, and anything bad that had ever happened to her.

Part 2

Song & Death

Lucille

The day Lucille's life would change forever had finally come. She stepped out of the car and looked at the blocky buildings of the Green-valley University campus. In a town marked by whimsical, traditional Fachwerk houses, the modern angles and amount of glass were staggering. Sunlight glinted in the windows, promising a bright future.

It was here Lucille would make connections that would benefit her all her life, and where she might meet her one true love. So many new experiences were waiting for her—lectures instead of classes, and a library that even surpassed the one at home. She'd dig deep into the history of the world and deepen her understanding of long-dead languages to reveal their secrets. But most importantly, she'd make a ton of new friends, attend some wicked parties, and flirt.

"Is that driver going to move in with us, too?" Rachel called. She and Samantha were standing near the entrance, snickering.

Lucille tossed her hair in mock derision, but her shorter hair refused the dramatics. "I'll cope without."

Samantha burst out laughing. "We'll see about that."

"I'll whip her into shape," Rachel said, scaring Lucille.

"When are your parents moving out?"

"End of the month, I think. Right now, the house is a mess. Boxes everywhere."

Samantha held up her hand to quiet them. "Let's take this in for one moment. From today on, we're university students."

Excitement spread from Lucille's hair to her toes. "I know," she giggled.

"Every day just maths, maths, maths," Rachel said with a deep, contented sigh.

Lucille shuddered. "Not for me."

Rachel turned up her nose. "You keep your dusty books and dead languages, and I'll stick to my flawless, logical numbers."

"You're in a good mood," Lucille commented, noting Rachel was exceptionally talkative and assertive today.

Her friend blushed. "Adam gave me a pep-talk this morning."

"Good man." Lucille wondered if Adam had given her a little more than that but knew better than to ask.

"Okay, then." Samantha checked the time. "I have to go to the end of campus. I'll see you two at lunch in the hall?" Monday was only one of two days in the week when they had a long enough lunch break at the same time. "Got some new plans to show you." She was already walking backwards, a smile tugging at her lips.

"Can't wait."

Lucille and Samantha had been working on a secret project for a while now. Together, they were trying to rebuild the magical barrier their grandmothers had once erected around Greenvalley, before Malcolm had torn it down. Restoring it would make their town a little safer—or so they hoped.

Rachel nodded and walked off in a different direction, leaving Lucille alone. It suddenly dawned on her that while her friends were at the same university, their subjects didn't have the slightest overlap. They were all starting afresh.

Lucille swallowed heavily. Last time she'd started a new school, the town had been overrun by mindless zombies, and she'd found out she was a witch. As happy as she was about it now, it'd been a shock to the system. What if today was equally daunting? What if she didn't find any friends? What if she hated her course?

She shook her head. She had this. If she could battle demons, she could battle first day jitters. At the very least, she was still in her hometown, not halfway across the world, as her father would've preferred. It was going to be okay.

Three hours later, Lucille was buzzing. All three classes had been exactly what she'd wanted them to be: interesting and demanding. Within minutes of each lecture it'd become clear that this was no longer school. For each hour they spent in class, they were expected to spend another hour, if not more, at home. The reading list alone would keep her busy for the rest of the semester. It was a lot, but Lucille was highly motivated. As long as the monsters left her alone, she'd get it done.

"That web had better work," she told Samantha as she met up with her friends the hall, picking out her lunch from the buffet. "I don't have time for monster hunting."

Samantha laughed. "I don't know. A monster hunt might be a welcome distraction once in a while."

"Unless the world is ending," Rachel muttered.

Lucille and Samantha stared at her. "Was maths that bad?"

"Oh no, maths was amazing. I only understood half of it."

"And that's a good thing?" Lucille asked.

"Of course. It'll be fun figuring it out. I bet in a month today's lesson will look like kindergarten maths."

"If you say so." Lucille rolled her eyes. "I'll pay today. We have to celebrate, after all." She looked around at the food options and immediately regretted her words—nothing appealed.

Not wanting to be rude, Lucille went straight to the salad bar. Her first instinct was to tell the cook at the mansion to pack her a lunch, but she quickly stopped that train of thought. This was her new life now. No cooks, no chauffeurs, no etiquette. A life of freedom. And grumbling stomachs. Still, she kept her word, and paid for Samantha's and Rachel's trays, which were laden with lunch, extra rolls, and even a slice of cake from the dessert bar.

"You're not hungry?" Samantha asked.

"First day jitters."

Rachel snorted, and they searched for a space to sit. Most of the tables in the hall were long enough to sit thirty people, and they were bustling with activity. Some people were eating, others did their homework or reading, but most hung out, either catching up after the summer or introducing themselves after their first class together.

"Over there!" Samantha pointed out a gap between a larger and a smaller group, big enough for them to squeeze in and leave some space on either side. They had to shuffle a bit to get to their seats.

"Definitely a busy time," Lucille said, nearly knocking her tray into the head of one of the guys to their left.

During their meal, Lucille observed the other students. At least half of the group to her left had colourful hair, and they were constantly bursting into laughter, as if they were stand-up comedians. On her right was the smaller group, made up of a girl with ash-blond hair and two guys, one of whom looked quite cute. At least until he opened his mouth.

"I don't know how you do it, Tony," he said to the girl. "Freshmen are the worst. They changed our course pathworks and now we have two with them. There's gonna be so much moaning when Ludwig gets started for real."

Lucille's ears perked up. She'd just left a lecture held by a Professor Ludwig. Had that boy been in her class? And did she have to worry about the class now? The professor had sounded strict but not unreasonable.

"That'll be a rude awakening," the guy opposite him said. He had a mouth too wide to be pretty but lent itself naturally to grinning.

"At least we don't have to try to teach them something," the original guy said, only to lead into the segue, "like Miss TA over here."

Tony, as he'd called her, burst out laughing. "Believe it or not, Dennis, I'm looking forward to it. But then again, I don't study boring dusty history like you two idiots."

So, they were on her course. The guys at least.

Dennis shook his head. "I don't understand you. Don't you know all freshmen are monsters?" He leant forward and gesticulated with his apple. "As soon as they find out you're happy to answer questions, they'll tear you apart. They're like bloodhounds."

Lucille couldn't help herself snorting. When Dennis turned around, frowning, Lucille shrugged and quipped, "Don't worry, no one will ever ask you."

The other guy grinned again. "You're freshmen, right? Of course you are."

"Don't listen to Dennis," Tony said. "He was the worst of them."

"Which means I know what I'm talking about," Dennis said, the beginnings of a grin on his face.

His ability to laugh about himself endeared him a little to Lucille. Now he was looking at her, he really was cute. He had ruffled light-brown hair that looked impossibly soft and hazel eyes to die for.

"Oh, hey," Tony suddenly called out, pointing at Samantha. "You're one of the chem students, aren't you?" She grabbed her tray and changed seats. "I think you're in my Wednesday lab. I'm Antonia—Tony."

Samantha excitedly shook her offered hand. "I can't wait to get started on the labs. If it has a working Bunsen burner, I'll be in heaven."

"You went to Greenvalley High, right?" Antonia laughed. "I remember the shoddy equipment. It's probably still the same."

"I don't think it's changed since the nineties."

"Well," the guy with the wide grin said, "I'm Jakob, and I hate chemistry."

"Hi, Jakob," Lucille and Dennis said simultaneously. They looked at each other and laughed.

Jakob grimaced. "Third-year History."

"Same here," Dennis said, "and my name's Dennis."

"What a coincidence," said Lucille and batted her eyes. "I'm just starting History. I'll be the one with the annoying questions. Lucille de... Lucille."

Dennis ran a hand through his hair and made a big show of a sigh. "I guess I'll have to get over myself and try to answer them, then."

The flirty answer was on Lucille's lips, but she decided to leave it at a promising smile. This conversation was the perfect antidote to the lacklustre lunch options. Her university experience was looking up again.

Jan

If Jan had to pick one place in the universe he'd never wanted to set foot in, Caspar's private rooms would be at the top of the list. As he followed Matt and Balthasar through the Residence, he half-expected the General of Terror to jump out from behind a curtain and murder him in cold blood. At the very least, he expected his rooms to be booby-trapped to the ceiling.

Instead, they were surprisingly spartan—no curtain in sight. Apart from a few weapons in a stand and that terrible armour in a corner, there wasn't much that screamed Caspar. He had a simple bed—single—a set of drawers, two chairs, and a giant table with a complex, three-dimensional map carved into it.

"The Council is stable for now," Balthasar said.

Balthasar and Matt had been comparing notes ever since they'd arrived at the residence. Jan didn't quite trust the peace. Last year, Balthasar had attacked either Greenvalley or his group of friends. Now he was the generous, wise older brother, freely offering his insight.

Balthasar grabbed some books from a pile and dumped them into Jan's arms, never even looking at him. "They left me in charge of the Small Council, not that I'm complaining. They're all busy with the Muhrren riots."

"Muhrren riots?" Matt asked, grabbing another book to dump into Jan's arms.

"Nothing of note." Balthasar waved a hand. "Sandor will take the Black Guard there, execute a few leaders, and assume control. All in the name of the Seven, of course."

"You mistrust the new General of Horrors?" Matt asked.

Balthasar shrugged. "He's not Caspar. Not that I ever trusted Caspar, but at least he wasn't one of Hel's creatures. Mistrusting Hel is how you survive the Council of Seven."

Jan had trouble following the conversation. His one experience with Hell had been the day he'd spent with Fabian trying to escape the Dûr Lôrac and find his little sister. All he gathered was that Caspar had already been replaced and Balthasar didn't like the new guy. Considering he'd tried to kill the previous one, Jan decided not to remember the name. The other one, however...

"Who's Hel?"

"Pride," Matt said without a moment's hesitation. "I thought Volac—Wrath—was commanding the Black Guard."

"Don't ask me how Hel managed to convince him of her candidate. Those two never see eye-to-eye. With luck, he'll rip our new general apart next week. I should probably look into backing my own candidates."

Matt snorted. "You don't need the Black Guard. If you're still Head of the Small Council, you've got the entire Army of Death under your thumb. And you're the Archdemon of Lust. What else do you want?"

"It's less about want and more about enjoying the intellectual challenge. Besides, as you just said, the Black Guard is traditionally led by the House of Wrath. Now Hel has her claws in him, and I'd like to know why. Pride isn't like most of the other sins. Wrath can barely lead a conversation without losing his temper, Sloth hardly ever bothers following the conversation, Envy only sees things he can't have, and Greed... Actually, Greed's a bit weird right now." Balthasar waved it off and continued before they could ask questions. "But Pride... Sure, she's arrogant as heck, but Hel's an incredibly capable stateswoman. She's held her seat for thousands of years, longer than anyone else. That woman knows how to play the rest of them like a fiddle. Plus, she hates Chay."

"She hates Chay?" Matt asked, as if the concept were unfathomable.

Balthasar nodded. He flicked through the rest of the books, tossing most of them aside. "It's because he's half-demon and she's too proud to accept his help. Thinks he's butting in where he doesn't belong. Thing is, Chay's wary of her, too, and I'm starting to think he's right." He dumped the remaining books into Jan's arms before looking through a rack of scrolls.

Jan staggered slightly. Not all the books were big tomes but it was quite the pile now. For someone who despised his healing powers and reportedly used them once every ten years or less, Caspar had a lot of books on healing.

"What about the others? Aren't you wary of all of them?" Matt asked, opening drawers.

"Volac is easy to control. You just have to make sure he has a target—that's preferably not you—to let out all that wrath. Iyaga, though..." He pulled a face. "I don't know why she's the Archdemon of Greed, but she likes me. Got her with the whole 'we're both pretty new at this' angle. Moloch is a complete riddle to me, and as for Yash, I don't think she even knows what's going on. Now Pyke... Historically, he's an easy target, but I don't know if it's because our paths have rarely crossed or because something's changed, but he's got this glint in his eyes. As if he knows something the rest of us don't."

"I'm sure you'll figure it out. An intellectual challenge, right?" Matt turned to Jan. "You need help with that?"

Jan bit his lip before he snapped, "I'm good, but if there are any more, I'll need a cart." The thought of reading all the books frightened him. He only noticed then that he was actually able to read them. "How come all of these books are in German?"

"They're not." Balthasar picked up the top book and ran his finger over a rune on the spine. "Caspar just slapped translation runes on them. Lazy bastard." He threw the book back on the pile.

"You mean all these books..." Jan stared at the pile in awe. Some of the tomes didn't even look like paper, and yet he could read them as easily as a comic book. "That's actually pretty cool."

"Yes, yes. Caspar loved his runes." Balthasar grabbed a bag and stuffed it with scrolls, then hung it over Jan's head as if he were part of the furnishings.

Matt opened another drawer. "You know what? I think I'll take these runes home for Samantha, if you don't mind."

Balthasar made an inviting gesture. "Take whatever you want, Melchior. It's either you or the next vulture."

"Vulture?"

"He's dead," Balthasar explained. "His stuff is free to whoever claims it first. Obviously, I control access to the residence, but if one of my lovers wants to claim that ugly helmet for roleplay, I don't mind. This room will be picked clean in a few months. Not that there's much here to begin with."

Jan saw Matt swallowing and concentrating a little too hard on packing up the runes. He didn't know everything that'd happened in the residence, but he'd heard from Lucille that Matt had killed his brother. Good riddance, in Jan's opinion, but the once ice-cold half-demon who'd taken nearly a year to take responsibility for Daniel's murder seemed to have regrets.

"Do you want to check Menuha's rooms?" Balthasar asked.

Matt shook his head. "There's just human trinkets there. If I wanted that I'd just have to walk into the nearest dollar shop." He finished packing the runes and grabbed half of Jan's books, lightening his load. "Let's go."

Jan followed him to the front of the residence, only to run into him when Matt suddenly stopped. "What are you doing?"

"Is she talking to a shadow?" Matt said, squinting across the square of residences.

"Who?" There were several demons around.

"Alecia." Matt clicked his tongue. "On the left. She's the premiere disciple of Envy."

Jan looked across and found a honey-haired woman rolling her eyes at something the man next to her had said. Only, there was no man, just the thick shadow of one.

Just then, the demon's gaze met theirs, and she frowned. Turning on her heel, she vanished inside what Jan assumed was the Residence of Envy. The shadow man lingered, and even though he had no eyes, Jan felt as if he was staring right through him.

"Let's just jump home," he whispered.

"Agreed."

A second later, they were gone.

Shayna

The classroom was so quiet Shayna felt as if she could hear the snow falling outside. They were sitting on silky pillows in a circle, trying to meditate. Shayna had never been one for meditation—that had always been Jennifer's shtick. Every time she tried, she quickly grew bored and started fiddling with her skirt. If she'd had matches, she might have started a fire. Funnily enough, that would've been appropriate for today's exercise.

While they were all trying to relax on the pillows and listen inside, Professor Terian was walking around with slow soft steps. He spoke in his deep, sonorous voice, "Elemental magic is more than a source of power. It's a part of you. Only when you accept and respect it as such will you gain an understanding of the full scope of your potential. You are limitless. Relax and feel the magic flowing through you."

"If I relax any more, I'm gonna fall asleep," Fabian whispered.

Shayna couldn't help herself and giggled, earning an angry hiss from Kaia.

"If you think my lessons are superfluous, please leave," Professor Terian said sternly.

Even Camdyn joined in as they all said in unison, "Apologies, Professor."

"Become one with your magic," he continued. "Close off all other thoughts. Stop thinking altogether."

"My natural talent," Fabian muttered under his breath.

"True," Shayna shot back, her lips curling into a smile.

One of the reasons she'd accepted the Citadel's invitation had been her hope of Fabian attending, too. With him at her side, she felt like she could finally lean into the magic she'd hidden inside for so long. But she hadn't counted on him being so hilarious while doing it.

Professor Terian came to a stop between the two and cleared his throat. "Relax!" he said, sharply and not meditative at all.

Shayna and Fabian both burst into giggles. She quickly covered her mouth and opened her eyes, glancing at him. "I'm so sorry."

"Yeah, me, too," Fabian muttered.

The professor glared, then swiftly strode to his desk. "Maybe some time in detention will help you relax better. You're both to stay after class."

Fabian opened his mouth to protest but closed it quickly. Meanwhile, Kaia was giving them a smug look, as if she'd punished them personally.

Shayna stuck out her tongue, causing Kaia to turn her nose up and close her eyes again. Rolling her eyes, Shayna returned to the exercise. She couldn't feel any magic flowing through her body, not even heat, and now she was in trouble with a professor for the first time in her life. With Fabian in the same boat, she wasn't too mad about it.

"Scrubbing!" Fabian complained as he furiously scrubbed the walls of the basement he and Shayna had found themselves in. "What happened to a good old essay or destroying documents by hand?"

Shayna knelt next to him, attacking a stubborn patch of dirt. Her clothes were half-soaked with dirty water and her fingers felt as if they were waterlogged. Even Fabian's presence couldn't help her enjoy this punishment. "I guess mages are a bit behind the times. We should probably be glad they're not hanging us upside down from the ceiling."

"Don't give them ideas!" Fabian complained.

"You don't really believe that, do you?"

He shrugged and wiped his cheek. "It's only been a week since we busted the necromancer club. Who knows what else happens in these walls? I don't like this place."

That was a shame, because Shayna loved it, secret necromancer cults and all. She never would've admitted it, but attending a magic school had been at the top of her wish list when she'd been much younger. "What about classes?"

"Honestly, I'm not feeling them yet. The history, sure, that's interesting, but the magic stuff?" He imitated Professor Terian's voice, "Relax!" Snorting, he continued, "Imagine standing in front of a demon and relaxing. I'd be dead faster than I could even think 'relaxation'."

Shayna giggled. Unlike her, Fabian had plenty of hands-on experience when it came to using his element in battle. He'd handed the necromancers their asses a week ago. In comparison, her fire powers were laughable. If she didn't set something flammable on fire, the best she could hope for was replacing a torch.

"I don't think Terian is thinking about the practical application."

"Well, he should. That's the only reason I'm here: to get better and more capable at defending those I love."

"And here I thought you were here for me," Shayna quipped.

As expected, Fabian's cheeks flushed delightfully red. "Why would you think...?" He caught himself. "You're messing with me."

"Always." She chuckled and moved to another spot so she could turn her back on him. "You're so easy to tease, you know?"

Fabian sighed. "I wish you'd stop. Ophelia's already giving me enough shit about attending the same school as you."

"Oh no, what's the little cultist baby worried about? Is she afraid I might steal you away?" When he was silent, Shayna threw a glance over her shoulder. "She is worried about it. Okay, let's get this clear." She stood up and held out her sponge, dripping water all over the floor. "I love teasing you. I think it's adorable how quickly your ears flush, but I'm not planning on getting between you and your girlfriend. You're happy with her, right?"

"Absolutely. I love her." There was no hesitation this time.

Shayna's cheeks strained a little as she barely avoided a grimace. "That's fantastic. So, she's got nothing to worry about then. Or do you want me to ignore you all semester long? Is that what she wants? Don't talk to me or something silly?"

Fabian rubbed his neck, clearly uncomfortable. "That would be ridiculous and boring."

"Lonely," Shayna added.

"Right. With Kaia being so anti outsiders and Camdyn never opening his mouth, the last thing I need is to keep my distance from you."

"Then don't."

Fabian took a deep breath. "You're only doing this because it's fun, right?"

Shayna nodded, hoping he'd stop forcing an answer soon.

"Then you're right. She's got nothing to worry about."

"Yeah, unless you fall for me, of course." She bit her wicked tongue, but his beet-red face was worth it.

Scrubbing the basement took them nearly two hours. At the end, they were so exhausted they could've easily completed Professor Terian's exercise. Instead, they dragged their feet home, barely exchanging another word. Shayna watched Fabian drudge towards his home near the forest, while she hopped on the bus that took her to the bed and breakfast her parents ran, near the Witches' Hump.

"There you are!" her mother greeted her from the reception desk. "Where the hell have you been?"

Shayna slumped into one of the armchairs. "I had classes. I told you I can't be home early all the time."

During the long summer break her mother had come to rely on her help. It was a family business, one she was expected to take over eventually. Unfortunately, Shayna couldn't think of anything more boring.

"I don't understand why you have to go to university when you could've taken hospitality classes at the Polytech. And don't sit down!

The restaurant needs to be set up. Come on, get started. The first guests will be down in forty-five minutes."

With a massive sigh, Shayna pushed herself up again. She dropped her bag behind the counter. "Why can't you just hire more people?"

"Oh? Are you made of money now?"

Shayna rolled her eyes and entered the little restaurant to the left of the entrance. It had a bar and fourteen tables, all of which had to be covered with tablecloths and set for the evening rush. She started with the linens, making quick process of it, wondering what she'd need hospitality school for. She'd done this since she'd been old enough to hold the cutlery tray.

On the other side of the room was the massive fireplace that gave the restaurant the proper Harz feeling. Shayna knelt, stacked some wood and held out her hands. Relax. When nothing happened, she simply grabbed one of the logs and forced her fire into it. It flickered alive and Shayna put it back, never once feeling the burn. It was the only advantage of being a fire mage. Fire rarely hurt her. At least not in such a short time.

One day, she'd have to come clean to her parents and admit she wasn't doing a business class at university. She wondered if Fabian's parents knew, but then she remembered his mother led the local witch shop, so he'd probably drunk magic with his breast milk. Maybe that was the reason for his massive talent. Parental support and constant demon attacks.

Cheryl had always laughed at him and called him a dweeb and coward, but Shayna had known better. Fabian risked his life regularly to defend the town. He was brave—braver than her—and she admired his quiet strength. Most importantly, she loved how it'd never made him cocky or mean. His battle against the necromancers had shown her how easily he could've taken revenge on Cheryl or Alan, but he never had—well, almost never.

She giggled as she remembered his water dragging Alan into the lake and dunking his face repeatedly. Alan needed the occasional knock on his head to remind him he was just as awkward as every other teen. If not in high school, he would find out at police school.

Thinking of Alan reminded her all her friends were gone. Cheryl had left Greenvalley with Ani for a year of work and travel in Australia—or probably more drink and travel, if Shayna knew anything about them. Jennifer had followed Bjorn to study in Munich, Alan went to police school in Aschersleben, and Cian was studying Chemistry in Bielefeld. She still talked to the latter two, but it wasn't the same.

As sad as it was, the Citadel of Magic was Shayna's highlight of the day. She could do without a Cheryl 2.0 earth mage, and whatever was going on with little Camdyn, but spending all day with Fabian was fun. And learning about magic made it a million times better. Like spitting in Cheryl's smug face.

Shayna yawned as she stood and started setting tables. She was just about to place two glasses when the most ear-splitting, screeching song rose. The glasses shattered on the ground as Shayna pressed her hands on her ears, but the song wormed itself into her brain.

Just as quick as it'd started, it stopped. Her hands shook and her breath caught in her throat. Sweat was running down her neck.

"What are you doing, child?" Her mother was in the room, sighing over the broken glass.

"Sorry." Still stunned, Shayna stooped and started picking up the larger pieces. "What was that music?"

The mellow oldies station her mother loved so much was playing in the background, but it was so soft Shayna barely registered it most of the time.

"Music?" Her mother grabbed a brush and dustpan. "What are you talking about? We don't have an endless supply of glasses, you know." She looked over her shoulder as the door swung open and shut on a customer. "Especially not if we have to repair the door."

"Why would we have to repair the door?" Shayna asked.

She watched the customer walk past the window. Her smooth motion made it seem like she was floating. She had the weirdest style: nearly chalk-white skin and long raven-black hair that fell to the ground. Shayna couldn't see her eyes, but she saw her lips moving, as if she was talking to herself.

Her mother brushed the shards together. "Well, with the door opening and shutting on its own, what else are we supposed to do?"

"On its..." Shayna stared as the woman vanished out of sight.

Not talking to herself.

Singing.

Samantha

As if the first week at university wasn't busy enough, Samantha had loaded her plate even further by trying to rebuild the magical barrier Malcolm had broken when he'd entered Greenvalley. She'd studied the spells all summer and developed her own web, which would take things a little further. It didn't simply lock out anything non-human, which would inadvertently backfire on Matt or Chay, as well as other harmless creatures living in the area. Instead, it would identify the threat, read their intent, and only shut out those that wished the human population harm.

She and Lucille had invited her grandmother over for any last insights. Earlier, Matt and Jan had gone to pick up Caspar's books on healing, and now the table was covered in tomes, scrolls, and boxes of runes. Now, Jan was lying on the couch with a book in his hand instead of his phone.

"I never thought I'd see the day you discovered reading," Lucille quipped.

Jan flipped her off and turned the page.

Samantha smoothly blocked his rude gesture from her grandmother and invited her into the study instead. "Sorry about that. I didn't expect them to return with quite so much material."

Though she knew a little about Caspar's true motivations, she'd been surprised to see he'd been quite the scholar. For someone who'd claimed to run on brute strength alone, he'd had an impressive private library, all made accessible by his runes. Samantha was grateful Matt had thought to bring them for her. Binding magic to tiny shapes was a fascinating concept. Finding out what each meant and how they could be used or even replicated would be a fun project. Right after she'd finished this one.

"The biggest change to your old web is that ours will be connected to a computer."

"A computer?" Elda asked in wonder. "You're not using this AI stuff, are you?"

"More like MI, but that's not the point." The idea had come to Samantha when she'd heard about Adam's magical experiments with technology. Usually, technology had an adverse effect on magic, but he'd managed to tie them together. After seeking his advice Samantha had done it, too. "The computer will analyse the magic and tell us what kind of monsters are currently residing in Greenvalley. As long as we've got it in our database, this should work fine."

Her grandmother was still frowning. "Interesting. But you know you need quite a large number of base points?"

Lucille nodded and pointed at the map currently covering the desk. "Already ahead of you. They can't be further apart than one-and-a-half kilometres, so we made a plan before we went out in the field." She showed Elda the dots Rachel had plotted to assure complete coverage. "We've already placed the first forty or something."

Placing a base point was a lot like planting a tree. You had to dig a little hole, weave a tight anchor web and place it in the hole, then cover it with soil, and water it with magic from the rivers. Once they were all placed, it'd be easy to connect them.

Elda studied the placement for a long time. "I'm impressed, girls, though I think it covers a bit too much ground. You've even included the Witch's Hump and part of the forest."

"The forest is important because that's where the spring of magic is. And if there are monsters on the hill, I want to know about it. But that's why instead of a ring, we turned the web into a fully functioning dome, which isn't just supported by the outside posts but a number of inside anchors. Rachel made the calculations."

"Hmm, looks like you've thought of everything." Elda smiled. "Look at you two, already stepping up to your duty of being the next Green-valley Witch."

Lucille scratched the back of her head. "You mean Samantha? Because I'm like Cecille and nearly blind to the rivers of magic."

Elda took her arm and smiled. "Maybe there's more than one way to be the Greenvalley Witch. Just look at what you've done. The world is changing and a new generation will take over. Eventually," she added for Samantha's benefit.

"Eventually!" Samantha repeated forcefully. Her grandmother would live a long, happy life—and no monsters would attack her house in the forest.

Matt strolled in, nibbling on a carrot he'd snuck from the kitchen. "Hey, darling." He kissed Samantha's cheek and put his free arm around her. "Are you almost done?" A little belatedly, he nodded at Lucille and Elda.

"Almost. Matt will help me get the last anchors set," Samantha explained, before putting her hand on Matt's chest and grinning up at him. "It's much faster than driving or hiking from spot to spot."

"I live to serve... you," Matt said, and the look in his eyes promised so much more than just a few space jumps around town.

"And that's our cue to go back to the living room and have some coffee," Lucille said, loudly. "Make sure you're done fast. Remember, we're going bowling tonight. Don't be late."

Samantha rolled her eyes. If everything went smoothly, they'd place all the remaining posts and test the extent of Matt's servitude before they had to be at the bowling lane.

Jan

Jan's paramedic training had moved onto the stage where he had to take shifts at the hospital. Most of the time that meant riding in an ambulance with two seniors, but when there were no calls to attend to, he was expected to pick up the slack at the hospital. At night, though, there was barely anything to do, so instead he sat in a corridor, his eyes glued to one of Caspar's books.

It surprised him how much he was devouring the text. He'd never been a big reader and could count the number of books he'd read as a teenager that'd had more text than pictures on one hand, but there was something about these that completely drew him in.

This one was all about something called 'the thread of life'. He'd skipped most of the introduction, which had been all about mytho-logical depictions of life as a thread, but the actual application of the knowledge fascinated him. It was almost like a healing shortcut. Held correctly, one could strengthen—or weaken—the thread, repair weak spots, and even use it to encourage the production of blood and other internal defence strategies.

A good healer, the book said, always kept an eye on the thread of life while they applied healing to affected body parts. This way, they could see if the patient was at risk of a heart attack or stroke. In a way, it was like a magical defibrillator.

Just then, an alarm blared in one of the patient rooms and a red light flashed above the door. Jan expected the nurses to come running, but the hallway remained empty.

With a few seconds' delay, Jan threw his book down and scrambled to his feet. "Nurse!" he called out, as if the alarm wasn't loud enough.

Not waiting for a response this time, Jan dashed into the room to assess the situation. An older man was lying next to his bed, seemingly unconscious. His lines and monitors had been either ripped off or torn out when he'd fallen.

Jan knelt next to him and felt for his pulse, a simple move he'd already internalised over the last six months. When he found none, he flipped the man on his back and started chest compressions, calling for the nurse again.

"Hey, don't die on me," he muttered before sinking his magic into the old man, trying to figure out what'd happened. "Where's your thread of life? There!" He found a thread so thin it could easily snap in half any minute. And it was dim, not the bright golden light a healthy one would've indicated. Jan poured his entire energy into strengthening the thread, just as he'd read in the book. "That's good. Become nice and strong."

Under his guidance, the thread thickened and began to glow again. Jan opened his eyes and stopped compressions to feel the man's pulse again. It was even and strong. A few seconds later, the man came to, looking confused.

A nurse came running in, pushing a crash cart. Her eyes were wild as she knelt next to Jan. "What happened?"

"Hi," Jan said, catching himself smiling at her.

She was one of his favourites. Her name was Sandra, and she was only a little older than him, with long, curly dark hair, which she always wore tied back in a ponytail or messy bun.

Jan cleared his throat. "I found him on the floor unconscious. Heart attack, I assume. A few chest compressions, and he was back to normal. Sorry, the alarm was blaring and I—"

Sandra mumbled something under her breath as she assessed the patient.

"What?"

"Smoke break," she admitted, with a heavy sigh. "I know one of us should've stayed at the station, but..." She turned to the older man and helped him sit up. "Mr Knaus, what are you doing to us?"

Another nurse entered, looking just as panicked, though this one was a lot older. "The doctor's coming."

"Well, he's a little too late," Sandra said. "Our little trainee's already taken care of the worst. Looks like they're teaching you the good stuff." She smiled, and Jan struggled to fight his grin. If only she knew about the magic.

The other nurse helped her with the patient and together, they pulled him up and helped him to the bed. "Mr Knaus, where were you off to?"

"A woman visited me in my room. She... sang." The older man was looking a bit confused. Not that Jan blamed him. He'd nearly died.

"I was sitting outside the whole time," Jan explained. "There was no one."

"She came through the wall."

"Right," the older nurse said. "Well, if you see that woman again, you just tell us, okay? Just use the call button. No reason to get out of bed."

They were settling him as the doctor arrived. "Not dying, that's good. What do we have here?" she asked.

"Mr Knaus had a fall," Sandra said. "His heart stopped for a moment, but Mr Kerscher was quick to bring him back." She elegantly avoided the delay in response time from the nurses.

Jan could've ratted her out, but that wasn't who he was. "Yes, sorry if I overstepped."

The doctor snorted. "Overstepped? You saved this man's life. Good work. Now, Mr Knaus..." She turned her attention to the patient while the older nurse assisted her.

Jan and Sandra left the room. He picked up his book from the floor, brushing dust off.

"You just saved our lives in there," Sandra whispered. "And Mr Knaus' on top. Thanks for not telling on us."

Jan shrugged. "Look, I've messed up so many times in my life. I'm the last person to judge anyone."

"It won't happen again, promise." She nodded at his book. "Were you reading in the hall?" When he nodded, she smiled. "Silly boy. You can sit in the nurses' station with us. Come on, I'll make you coffee."

"Can't say no to that."

A life saved and a coffee invitation from the prettiest nurse in the hospital. The night was off to a great start.

Lucille

For a Monday night, the bowling hall was surprisingly busy. It might've been the happy hour at the bar or the two-for-one deal they had on the games, but Lucille was surprised to see it so packed. An even bigger surprise was who was sharing their table and the lane next to hers.

"And she's stalking us," Jakob said, with a wide grin. "That's a new low, even for a freshman."

"What do you mean, stalking us?" Dennis said. "She's clearly only here for me."

Lucille pushed her hands on her hips and cocked an eyebrow, but she couldn't fight off her big smile. "You wish. Now scoot over and let me steal some of your fries."

Fabian and Ophelia were at the bar ordering drinks and snacks, while Matt and Samantha were running late, as predicted. If they were having fun, Lucille deserved some, too, even though Rachel rolled her eyes.

With an adorable grin, Dennis moved over and held the basket of fries out. "Be my guest." He was with Jakob and Antonia, both of whom had their significant others with them.

Lucille realised he was in exactly the same position she was: the only single in a group of coupled-up friends. She took a fry with two pointy fingers and slowly placed it between her lips. Judging by Dennis' intensifying gaze, it was working.

"Sorry we're late," Samantha said, pulling Matt behind her. "Did you start already?"

"No, Fabian and Lia are still getting food. Have you finished your... homework?"

"Almost," Samantha said, without missing a beat. "Just need to draw the final conclusion." She and Matt sat next to Rachel and changed their shoes.

Lucille had brought her own. It wasn't like she went bowling often, but the thought of wearing ill-fitting shoes a hundred people had worn before her was too disgusting. It was bad enough she had to worry about her acrylic nails.

Samantha waved at Antonia, and they all introduced each other while they waited for Fabian and Ophelia to join them.

"Incoming!" Fabian was holding three baskets of fries and two pairs of nachos, while Ophelia was balancing a tray of drinks. "Sorry, I spelt your name out," he told Lucille, "but they made a mess of it."

A glance at the points' table made Lucille groan. "Guess I'm Lucy tonight."

"Can I call you Lucy?" Dennis asked, leaning in.

Lucille leant over, her face almost close enough to kiss him. "Over my dead body, Denny."

"'Kay, Lucy."

She jabbed him in his side and scooted closer to Rachel, who had her eyebrow raised. "Don't look at me like that. You've got a boyfriend."

"Who's 18,000 kilometres away?"

"Oh, is your boyfriend in Australia?" Antonia asked.

As Rachel leant forward to answer, Lucille seized the chance to speak to Samantha. "So, all that's left is activating the web?"

Samantha nodded. "I thought you'd want to do it together."

"Now?" Lucille couldn't wait to step into her grandmother's footsteps and cast the biggest spell Cecille had ever woven with Elda.

They held hands behind Rachel's back, and Samantha led her through the final weave. Within half a minute, they were done.

"All finished."

Giddily, Lucille leant back and watched Dennis bowl a perfect strike. Now the magical bit was over, she could concentrate on the pretty parts of life, such as the lines of his back or his perfect grin as he returned to his seat.

They were on their second game when Samantha stepped up to the lane. Lucille had lost the first game terribly—Fabian had won easily—and was on her second drink, more interested in flirting than whatever her point score was.

"...I'm not stuck up," she complained, laughing. Dennis had just found out her last name. "I just like pretty things. Clothes, make-up, boys."

He wriggled his eyebrows. "Do I make the cut?"

Lucille pressed her index finger and thumb together. "By a hair's width."

Dennis opened his mouth in a mock gasp, and she started giggling, just as Samantha dropped the bowling ball.

The loud thump made Lucille jump and sent her heart pounding. Worried, she looked at Samantha, who had both hands pressed over her ears. When she noticed the attention of the entire hall on her, Samantha quickly pushed the ball into the side railing and returned to her seat, where Matt enclosed her in his arms and Fabian leant in.

Since there were more than enough people caring for her friend, Lucille put her hand on Dennis' leg. "You were going to show me how it's really done."

It was the oldest trick in the book, but Lucille relished the idea of Dennis' touch. She'd be surprised if she didn't get a kiss out of him by the end of the night.

Dennis jumped up immediately. "You're in the hands of a master," he said, waggling his eyebrows again.

"Didn't Antonia win your last round?" Lucille teased. Nevertheless, she took his hand and pulled him up with her.

She grabbed her favourite ball, the only one that didn't make her fingers hurt, and stepped up to the lane.

Dennis adjusted her stance before pressing his body against hers so he could mimic the movement of her arms. "Now, look at the pins... gentle... and go!"

Following his lead, she let go of the bowling ball. It started well, but the ball soon went off course and only took one pin with it. "Hands of a master, huh?"

His hands were resting on her hips. "I never said what kind of master."

Laughing, Lucille turned in his grip and put her arms around his neck. "What—" Her gaze caught Samantha looking absolutely distraught in Matt's arms. "Um, why don't you do bowl the second one for me?" She let go and strode over to her friends. "What's going on?"

"A sudden headache," Matt explained. "She heard a high note, but none of us did. I'm going to take her home." The look he gave Lucille told her this was much more than a headache.

"Okay, let me know if you find... the cause."

"Will do."

As she watched Matt and Samantha pack up their stuff, Dennis snuck up behind her, slipping his hands around her waist again. "Saved your shot. You got a spare."

"That's nice." Lucille patted his hands and sat, grabbing her drink. Not even a minute later, her phone buzzed.

We've got banshees in Greenvalley.

"Everything okay?" Dennis asked, trying to catch a glimpse of the text, while he put his chin on her shoulder.

Lucille quickly held the phone away from him. "Hey, that's private."

"Just kidding..." Dennis said, his gaze falling on her lips. "Do you want to take a walk after the game? We could get another drink or..."

"That's a lovely idea," Lucille said, leaning back. "But I'm pretty knackered, so rain check? It's been a long day."

"Of course." He let go and gave her some space.

Lucille smiled while cursing herself. The evening had gone so well. The flirting, especially, had been exhilarating, but there was such a big part of her she'd have to explain to him. Dennis didn't know anything about magic. Chances were, he'd run the other way. But even if he didn't, the thought of walking him through all of that tired her out before she'd even attempted it. And once she had, he'd still be a guy with no magic.

As irrational as it was, the excitement of flirting was already fading.

Matt

Ever since the bowling hall, Samantha had been in pain, complaining of a headache. Despite that, she was in front of the new computer, scanning the output. Matt knew he couldn't tear her away from a research project, so he went to the kitchen and made her one of her special herbal teas. The one against small ailments.

When he brought the pot upstairs, he found Samantha massaging her temples and moaning softly. "Hey, everything okay?"

"Absolutely not," Samantha said. "Something's wrong with the web. It was supposed to alert me, not give me headaches from hell."

Matt put the tea in front of her and gently took over massaging duties. "But there's a monster."

"Banshees." Samantha pointed at the screen. It had pulled up a scanned page from one of Samantha's monster manuals. Three ghostly women stood in a circle, their eyes black, mouths opened wide. "That part works perfectly."

"Are Ashuan banshees different? In Hescaryn they're not really dangerous. I mean, yes, they may appear before someone dies, but they don't cause them."

Samantha leant back and sipped her tea. "That's true here, too, with one exception: the cry of a banshee is strong enough to kill someone with a blossoming, underdeveloped magic ability. Children particularly. It's the primary cause of sudden infant death syndrome."

"I didn't know that. If that's the case, it's too late, though, right? They've already set foot in Greenvalley, so if anyone's dead, it already happened. Banshees don't stay long. They'll be gone soon."

"I hope so. This frequency is making me sick."

Matt bent forward and placed a kiss on her head. "How about I run you a bath while you have another read, and then you go to sleep, while I do some more research?" He knew better than to tear her away from the computer now.

She tipped her head back and smiled up at him. "You know, you're really good at this relationship thing."

He winked and whispered, "I did a lot of research."

Research was about the only thing Matt did these days. Chay had warned him World Studies would be an intense course, but he'd failed to mention just how intense it would be. Within a week, Matt had made the library his new home. He sat at one of the tables in the quiet space upstairs, using three books and two scrolls for his latest essay.

"'The Backbone of the State' by Aeneus Ceceran. That doesn't sound particularly entertaining."

Matt startled at the voice, blotching his essay. "Merik!"

A librarian hushed them and the older student rolled his eyes.

Raising his hand in apology, Matt lowered his voice. "What are you doing here?"

"Correct me if I'm mistaken," Merik said, with faux dramatics, "but I was told the library would be open for all students, not just first years, though they're undoubtedly the most hard-working." He sat at the table, grinning. "You look like you need a break."

Matt yawned. He'd been researching banshees until two in the morning last night, then come to school an hour early, and spent his entire lunch break in the library. "When I was doing politics back in Ashuan, it was all quite clear. A little bit of Weimar Republic here, a little bit of threshold countries there. Now, I'm supposed to compare the constitutional monarchy of a world with little magic with the democracy of a high-magic world, draw conclusions to the Great

Summer Revolution five hundred years ago, and put it all into the context of interglobalisation." Tired, he put his head on Ceceran's tome.

"Ah, yes, I remember that unit. I recommend 'Politics and Morals in the Age of Reason' by Berestli. Ceceran is too heavy for this topic."

"Heavy is an understatement," Matt muttered, head still on the book.

Merik added his own work material to the chaos on the table. "You don't happen to have finished Soil Analysis already? This is my third attempt at this course and I never seem to get it right."

"It must be somewhere over there." Soil Analysis had been a fun exercise. All the practical exercises had been so far. He sat up and rubbed his temples, while Merik searched his notes. "Did you just come here to copy my homework?"

"Not just. What's your relationship to Vydra?"

"We're classmates, still getting to know each other." Matt shrugged.

He liked Vydra. She had a quiet confidence and an aura of self-reliance, like a peer, but they'd only known each other for a week, so Matt was reserving his judgement.

Merik raised an eyebrow. "That's all?"

"Believe me, there's only one woman I'm interested in."

A few years ago, he probably would've slept with Vydra, then dropped her like all the others, but those times were behind him.

"Samantha," Merik said, with a chuckle. "You mentioned her. Once or twice. You should introduce me to her one day, so I can get to know the woman who turned a half-demon of the House of Lust monogamous."

"As long as you keep your fingers away from her," Matt warned.

Merik grinned. "What do you think of me? I know how to behave myself in the vicinity of a lady. I had an excellent education in manners."

"Not excellent enough," a sharp voice said behind them. They both looked up to see the librarian standing there, angrily tapping a scroll. "Otherwise you wouldn't disturb the rest of the library. Hold your private conversations outside."

Once he'd vanished between the shelves again, Matt grinned. "So much for your courtly education."

Merik snorted and leant back, as if he owned the library. Maybe he did, Matt thought. From what little he knew of his friend, Merik was a son of the Grand Bardir of Phalos, a part political, part religious position. His family—and by extension world—was not only well-represented at the Interglobal Parliament, but rich. Rich enough to donate to the University of Fader.

With a sigh, Matt rested his head on the book again. He was trying to remember what he was going to do next, but his eyes kept drooping.

"Did your beloved keep you awake too long or did Ceceran put you to sleep?"

"Neither," Matt mumbled. "We've caught ourselves some banshees at home, and I spent half the night figuring out how to make them go away."

He'd almost stayed home today when Samantha had been even worse in the morning, but she'd made him go to university and promised to skip her first lecture to rest a little longer.

"Banshees?" Merik whistled softly. "You live in the most fascinating place."

Matt mumbled something about Greenvalley attracting monsters, but no intelligible words came out.

Merik clapped his back. "Tell you what, my friend. I actually know a few tricks to keep monsters away. How about I go home with you today? You can introduce me to your quaint little town, and I'll make sure you don't fall asleep on the way there. Come on, I'll shout you a phai."

Fabian

Though Fabian still wasn't a huge fan of the Citadel, he was settling in well. Having Shayna around made it so easy. Their interactions at school had been few and far in between, with half of them happening while Cheryl was leading another attack. Now, their common situation and past helped them bond quickly. In a way, they were pushed together. Camdyn was a real loner, constantly surrounded by a repelling aura, while Kaia ditched them the moment she got out of the classroom to hang with her Citadel friends. It could've been terrible, but Fabian quite enjoyed spending time with Shayna. She was confident, quick-witted, and funny. And she didn't mind listening to him talk about his friends and family.

Another plus for the Citadel was the delicious food. Apparently, there was a course on food magic, and the students regularly outdid themselves, drawing inspiration from all corners of the world. Today's lunch was Korean barbecue with a variety of sauces that made Fabian moan.

"So, good?" Shayna asked before taking a bite. "Oh, yes, I could definitely Harry and Sally that."

"Hmm?"

She waved him off. "One of the old movies my mum likes. You'd only blush if I told you about the scene." The mention alone brought heat to his cheeks.

The Citadel had about two to three hundred active students, but there were many more who lived at the Citadel temporarily or permanently. Still, Camdyn had managed to find a small table just for himself.

He stuck his fork in the food again and again, without ever lifting it to his mouth.

"I wonder what his deal is," Fabian said. If not even the food could excite Camdyn, the situation was dire. "He's really smart, but I haven't seen him wielding any kind of air magic."

Shayna looked over her shoulder. "Maybe he's too young. The fires didn't start until I was sixteen."

"Seventeen for me... but then again, how do they know?"

"Maybe the divination department?" Shayna shrugged. "Honestly, I'm convinced the only reason he can't do magic is because he doesn't want to."

"You mean he's blocking himself?" It wasn't that long ago when Fabian had wanted nothing to do with his magic. "That never worked for me."

Grinning, Shayna laced her hands under her chin and leant forward. "Maybe you secretly wanted it after all."

"Oh, yeah? You a psychologist now?" He laughed, but the laughter died when his gaze fell on Kaia. "Well, I'd rather hear nothing from Camdyn than another word from Kaia."

Their earth classmate was sitting with a group of friends, laughing loudly. Though she never even glanced over, Fabian couldn't shake the feeling she was laughing about them.

"Ignore her. She's just scared we might show her up. Bested by wild mages is little Kaia's worst nightmare." Shayna raised her finger. "Rule number one: most people are insecure. Whether they lash out or withdraw, it's always insecurity. Like your little girlfriend."

"What's wrong with Lia?"

Shayna rolled her eyes. "Nothing. It's just the way she clings to you the moment you step foot in Greenvalley."

"She doesn't! Besides, we're in a relationship. Isn't it normal to spend as much time as possible with each other?" They only saw each other in the evenings now.

"If you were dating me, you'd know that amount of clinginess is not normal."

Fabian snorted. "I've had other relationships."

"Oh, yes, three years with your twin sister."

His mouth dropped open. "Sam is not my sister!"

"But she might as well be," Shayna said, without missing a beat. "And sorry, but that's what it looked like to me. And then your relationship with Rachel? I don't think many people even picked up on that. Definitely no clinginess there, I'll give you that. Then Lucille... what was that?"

"A summer fling."

"Ah, that makes sense."

He snorted again and crossed his arms. "Because she's out of my league?"

Shayna grimaced and waved him off. "Nonsense. That's something Cheryl would say. No, it's just... you've always just dated within your friend group. Hence the whole sibling vibe."

Fabian leant back, trying to process what she was saying. "None of them are related to me."

"The point is, you've never been in a normal relationship. I don't believe in friends to lovers. It's just incestuous."

"Didn't you date Cian in ninth grade?"

"Yeah, how do you think I know this stuff? That said, Cian and I were barely friends before that. The attraction was there from the beginning, then we had our fling, then we realised we were better off as friends. Anyway, Ophelia is hot. Also, incredibly needy."

"So, what's your insecurity for you to not just judge all my girlfriends but actually keep up with them?"

Shayna's grin widened. "You're a quick learner," she said, sounding impressed. "I guess my insecurity is I don't seem to be your type."

"You're totally—" Fabian closed his mouth before he said something he hadn't even thought about. "Wait... you said you weren't interested in me."

She snapped her fingers and leant back. "And there we have it. My daily dose of making you blush."

Fabian covered his cheeks, as if that would do him any good. He couldn't tell if he was really blushing, but now that he thought about it, he felt the heat rising. Annoyed, he dug into his food. "You're terrible."

"Aww, that's what Cian and Alan always say. They hate me."

Even though he tried, Fabian couldn't help but chuckle.

They were on their way home, chatting and discussing Kaia's latest antics in class—she'd thrown a fuss when Professor Terian had ranked Fabian first in raw potential—when they stepped out of the portal and found Ophelia waiting impatiently.

"Lia."

Ophelia threw Shayna an evil glare before focusing on Fabian. "I knew it."

"Knew what?"

"Clingy," Shayna whispered. She stepped forward and tried to walk past.

Ophelia pointed at her. "You're always with her now?"

Fabian rubbed his temples, trying to banish Shayna's voice from his head. "I'm with her because we go to school together. We're just on our way back."

"Lia," Shayna said, "he loves you. You've got nothing to be afraid of. I'm not gonna steal him." She bit her lip, as if desperately trying to keep another quip in. And Fabian knew exactly what she'd say.

Unfortunately, so did Ophelia. "You think you could if you wanted to?"

"Right now, I'd worry more about driving him away, sweetie."

"I'm not your sweetie!" Ophelia said. She raised her hands, about to call her shadows.

Fabian dashed forward and caught her arm. "Lia, don't." He was still struggling to understand why the situation was escalating so quickly. Hadn't he just told her he wasn't interested in Shayna?

Insecurity, Shayna had said. She'd hit the nail on its head.

Fabian knew how tough life had been for Ophelia and how much she needed to feel loved and valued. He'd vowed to be there for her, but now he wondered if maybe he'd been there for her a little too much, quickly becoming the only reliable pillar in her life. As much as he loved her, it was a scary thought—if he couldn't even spend time with a classmate at school, he had to set some boundaries fast.

When Ophelia glared at him, there were tears in her eyes. "You're choosing her?"

"I'm not choosing anyone," Fabian said, aghast. "Lia, Shayna and I are just friends."

"You weren't friends last week."

"Classmates, then." He looked up at Shayna, who was slowly backing away, looking like she wanted nothing to do with his mess.

Ophelia tore her arm free. "Then choose now. Her or me."

"What the—?"

Suddenly, Shayna screamed, pressing her hands to her ears. A moment later, her eyes rolled back in her head, and she collapsed.

Samantha

The shrill song of the banshees tormented Samantha further by the hour. Though she'd skipped her first lecture—much to her chagrin—her headache had only got worse. Now, she was trying to get some quiet time before her afternoon lab, occupying one of the beanbags in the library with an Irish folklore book that included a huge chapter on banshees. Unfortunately, the migraine made it impossible to concentrate.

She'd read the same paragraph for a third time when Lucille arrived. She dragged another bean bag over and unceremoniously dumped herself into it. "I think I'm broken."

"Welcome to the club."

"What? What's happening with you?"

"The banshee problem. They're in my head constantly."

Lucille reached out and massaged her shoulder a little. "Sorry, how did they get in? I thought the web worked?"

"It is working. My theory is they—" Samantha rubbed her temple as a particularly loud shriek stabbed her in the head. When the pain had abated a little, she sighed. "My theory is they were inside Greenvalley before we cast the web, and now they're trapped, getting louder and more deadly by the minute."

"So, we undo the web."

"I tried that." She whimpered as the singing rose again. "But so long as the banshees are trapped in it, I can't touch the magic."

Lucille fell back with a groan. "So, we can only undo the web once the banshees are gone, and the banshee will only go once we undo the web. Damn. Can we fight them?"

"That's what I'm checking, but so far, no luck. Banshees are heralds of death. They're apparitions, not... I don't even know if it's possible to kill them. It's kind of paradox."

Something rustled behind them. Then Dennis pushed his hands into Lucille's beanbag, smiling upside down at her. "What's a paradox?"

Lucille forced a laugh. "That the library is such a popular meeting place," she said quickly, "when it's supposed to be where people go to learn quietly."

"It's the location. Did you know it's also a popular couples' spot? I could show you around?"

"Can you now?"

Samantha wasn't sure, but she thought Lucille sounded nervous.

Dennis grinned. "It's good you know an older, experienced student."

Suddenly, Lucille sat up straight, barely avoiding a collision with Dennis and practically turning her back on him. "Tempting, but I've got a lot of homework to catch up on. Maybe another time."

If Dennis was surprised, he didn't show it. Instead, he joked, "Students who are actually learning in the library. Must be freshmen season."

Forcing another laugh, Lucille waved at him. "I'll see you in class tomorrow."

"See you then, Lucy."

As soon as he was gone, the smile slipped off Lucille's face.

Samantha raised an eyebrow at her. "What was that?"

"I told you," Lucille moaned, sinking back again. "I'm broken. Dennis is... He's sweet and funny. He seems to be everything I want from a university relationship. You know, someone fun and exciting."

"But?"

"He doesn't know anything about magic. If I really want a relationship with him, I'll have to tell him I'm a witch, explain all the magic in Greenvalley, hope he doesn't freak out about the monsters... It's just so complicated."

Lucille's problem only made Samantha's head hurt more. "How do you know he's not secretly a mage, too?"

"Do you think so?"

"Honestly?" Samantha shrugged. "No, he seems like a normal dude."

"Exactly. And I've dated normal guys... I want more. Or maybe I just don't want to start from zero every single time."

"But isn't that always the case in a new relationship?"

Lucille sank even deeper. "You don't get it. Matt is half-demon. You two have always been able to match each other's intellect. Remember when he was genuinely interested in the magic plant book you were reading?"

It took Samantha a moment to recall that particular memory. Back then, she'd still been wary about sharing her witch activities. But Matt had never laughed at her. With no concept of what was cool or not, he'd simply respected her interests.

"Rachel got so lucky," Lucille moaned. "She falls in love with the one guy who's secretly a magic weaver and whose father is an interglobal ambassador and friends with Chay. No explanation needed, instant understanding."

"Is it really the lack of understanding or that dating a normal guy bores you?" Samantha massaged her temples again, trying to breathe through the next onslaught.

Pouting, Lucille crossed her arms. "I just want love. Real, sweep-me-off-my-feet love. And Dennis... he's just not it."

Samantha smiled softly. "Maybe that's a sign. You don't have to rush into anything if you're not feeling it."

"But this is a new chapter of my life."

"Then maybe not dating is the way to go?"

Lucille's eyes widened. "You're right. I don't need a man. I'm an independent woman and I can make the most out of university, not wait around for Mr Right."

Samantha had trouble following her friend's sudden mood swing and simply nodded along. Right now, she had bigger problems. Such as the trapped banshees in her head.

Jan

Jan jumped out of the rig and rattled off the vital information for the patient he'd just helped transport to the hospital. A car had swerved off the road to avoid hitting a deer and tumbled down the side of the road. Trees had stopped it from sliding all the way into the river, but they'd had to wait for the fire department to retrieve the driver before the paramedics had been able to swoop in. By that time, the patient had already lost a lot of blood. Thanks to Jan strengthening his thread of life, he was still alive.

"Go wash up and find something to eat before we head out again," his instructor told Jan once they'd successfully handed the man over to hospital personnel.

Jan looked at his hands and found them stained with blood. It was a sight he'd gotten used to by now. He and the other trainee, André, went to the nearest bathroom to wash themselves.

"Did you really save someone's life last night?" André asked as he scrubbed his hands.

"We saved someone's life just now."

André rolled his neck. "That was under supervision. I heard you did it all by yourself. Brought someone back from the dead?"

Jan shrugged, fighting the urge to grin. "It was just luck I got there quickly. Anyone could've done it."

André snorted, and they left the bathroom again, if not clean, then a lot cleaner. "If you say so."

A pair of nurses—one of them Sandra—crossed their way. She smiled when she saw him. "Hi Jan."

"Um, hello."

The nurses giggled and vanished behind a corner. This time, Jan couldn't stop his smile, but when he turned around to André, his colleague glared. "What's the matter with you?"

"That nurse never talks to any of us. They're all so snotty."

"Sandra?"

"And you're on a first name basis now."

Jan frowned. "Yeah, it's called having a good rapport with colleagues, you know?" Snotty was really the last thing he'd call any of the nurses. His mother would've seen to that.

"Kerscher?" The doctor from last night approached. "Do you have a few minutes?"

"Um, sure." Jan exchanged a look with André. "What's this about?"

She waved him along. "Come with me."

"Do you need more help?" André asked, eager to jump in.

"No, no, just Kerscher."

Jan shrugged and followed the doctor to a well-known room. It was the same one he'd saved the patient in last night.

"Mr Knaus has been asking for you," the doctor said and beckoned him inside. The old man was sitting upright and smiling at him. "Mr Knaus, here's the young paramedic who looked after you last night—Mr Kerscher."

"I heard you saved my life," he said, chipper. "Thank you for that, young man."

Slightly embarrassed, Jan rubbed his neck. "Um, it's my job..." He side-eyed the doctor and amended his words. "I mean, being first on scene, that's my job, um I—"

"Well, I'm glad you were here. You—" Suddenly, the old man grimaced in pain. At first it looked as if he was about to cover his ears but then he clutched his chest instead. "I—"

"Mr Knaus?" The doctor stepped forward, quickly assessing the situation. A second later, she pressed the emergency button. "Get the crash cart," she said, but Jan jumped forward to grab Mr Knaus' hand instead and search for the thread of life. "Crash cart," she repeated. "Now!"

"Sorry," Jan hurried out of the room, only to see Sandra already rolling the cart towards them.

He stumbled back to let her past, then approached the patient again and stepped in to do chest compressions while the doctor prepared more dire measures. Knowing he'd only have seconds before the defibrillator took over, Jan sank his magic into the patient. Like before, the thread of life appeared pale and thin in front of him, but just as he was about to touch it, it snapped apart.

"Step back!"

Jan raised his hands in shock, while the doctor applied the first shock. They all stared at the monitor. Nothing.

The ripped ends taunted Jan. He wanted nothing more than to jump back in and try to reattach them—if that was even possible—but all he could do was watch as the doctor tried to save Mr Knaus' life, until at last, she stopped and pronounced him dead.

"Time of death: 2:38 pm." She put the defibrillator away and sighed. "I've never seen anything like this. He was here for a routine surgery tomorrow. And his stats…" She shook her head, "Sorry, Kerscher. We did what we could." She asked Sandra to get his emergency contact details so she could inform the family.

As Jan and Sandra stepped outside, the nurse reached out and rubbed his arm. "You win some, you lose some, huh?"

"Yeah." His mind was still stuck on the snapped thread. Such a crude representation of human life. So fast to end.

By the time Jan finished his shift, he'd seen three more people die. The nurses blamed it on a full moon, but that was still half a week away. He arrived home to find Samantha and Lucille in the living room, looking agitated.

"They're getting stronger every minute," Samantha said, clutching her coffee cup.

"The banshees?" Jan asked, remembering the group note. "I thought they'd be gone by now."

Samantha groaned. "They can't. They're stuck in the web."

Jan had no idea what she was talking about, but the wheels of his mind were turning. "Can they kill people? Like... people at the hospital?"

"Only those with latent magical potential." Samantha covered her ears and winced. "And me, apparently... or, at least, I might consider death if this goes on any longer."

The ears. Mr Knaus had tried to cover his ears. "Shit. That explains why we lost four people today. Healthy people... I mean, not healthy, but they all had a sudden heart attack. The woman in the café wasn't even a patient." She'd simply dropped dead while waiting for her coffee.

Lucille and Samantha exchanged a worried glance. "What if it's not just getting louder but stronger, attacking more and more people, even those with minuscule magic?"

"There's something else I've got to tell you." Jan sat down. "It's something I learnt from Caspar's books. Every person has a thread of life. It's like a cheat code. Instead of healing the actual wound or illness, you apply the magic straight to the thread. It worked wonders last night, but today... it just ripped." He couldn't get the frayed ends out of his head. "There was nothing I could do."

"It's the banshees," Samantha said, massaging her temples. "Their song is like a death spell. I don't think you can heal it."

"Come on, let me have a look at that." Jan scooted over and put his hands on Samantha's head. The pain hit him almost immediately. "How can you even think?"

She only grimaced, and he pushed past the pain to find her thread. From what he could tell, it was still strong and bright, but black slime was coating and encroaching on it. He tried to remove some of it, only to be stabbed by more searing pain.

Samantha whimpered. "We need to do something."

"Why can't you just turn the web off?"

Lucille sighed. "We tried. It won't work so long as the banshees are trapped in it. We need to remove them first."

"Okay, how do we kill them?"

"We can't," Samantha whined. "They're immune to magic and invincible. They're not mortal."

Jan leant back, defeated. "So, what? We just sit here, waiting until their song is loud enough to kill anyone with magic powers in Greenvalley?"

"Yeah, including us," Samantha said bitterly.

"There must be something we can do!"

"What about evacuating the town?" Lucille asked. "The web doesn't prevent humans from coming or going. So, if everyone just left..."

Jan snorted. "How are you going to get everyone to leave? We don't even know who might be affected or not."

"We know someone," Samantha said softly. Her eyes widened suddenly. "Anne."

Jan's heart sank immediately. "Oh no, don't tell me she's next."

"That, too, but she's blessed by Hanna, the Goddess of Life. Song of death, goddess of life. She might be able to help us."

"That's genius." Lucille nodded. "Let's get Anne here."

Even though he wasn't happy about it, Jan pulled out his phone. Whether she could help or not, he wanted Anne around so he could monitor her. He'd drive her out of the city himself if she showed any sign of dying.

Lucille

While they waited, Lucille called Albert and asked him to keep an eye on Pascal. Her little brother had more than latent magical talent, but with the song getting louder, he'd also be at risk. She wished Albert would just take him and leave the city until they'd figured out a viable solution, but Pascal had a full social calendar and Linda still didn't know about his telekinesis.

Anne arrived, and Neve flew down the stairs, squealing with joy. "Snowball fight."

"Later, okay?" Anne said. She turned her attention to her brother and friends. "You said you needed my help?"

Jan had been hunched over Caspar's books, while Samantha was lying on the couch with a cold flannel on her forehead.

"Do you hear a song?" Jan asked.

"Funny you should ask. I've had the most annoying tone ringing in my ear all day long, and I feel like it's getting louder."

Jan punched the table. "Damn!"

Anne looked immediately worried. "What's going on?"

"We've got a problem with a pair of banshees—maybe more," Lucille explained. "They're harbingers of death, so we thought we could counter them with life magic. Maybe a prayer?"

"Uh... I could try." Anne seemed completely overwhelmed. "I'm still a novice and I don't actually know anything about proper prayers."

The door opened and Matt arrived, a stranger in tow. And what a stranger he was. Lucille bit her lip as she took in his tall, confident stature and exquisite bone structure. His bronze skin was a shade darker than Matt's and his amber eyes looked nearly golden. His clothes—a form-fitting silken tunic and rich velvet robe—immediately identified him as a stranger to Ashuan.

"Full house, huh?" Matt wondered aloud. His gaze fell on Samantha. "Sam?" He rushed to her side, leaving his guest to fend for himself.

If he felt self-conscious at all, the beautiful stranger didn't show it. Instead, he bowed to Lucille. "Merik an Derendi of Phalos. I'm one of Matt's senior class-men."

"Enchanté," Lucille mumbled. "I mean, nice to meet you. What brings you to Ashuan?"

"Can we discuss that later?" Jan interrupted. "Sorry, Merik, but this is a bad time. Anne, what do you need?"

Confused, Anne tore her gaze from Merik. "I... I don't know. I told you, I've got nothing to go on. In the demon temple, they gave each of us a plant pot..."

"How about the garden, then?" Jan got up and took his sister outside.

"Sorry," Lucille said to Merik, feeling like a bad hostess, though this wasn't even her home. "Things are always a little chaotic in Greenvalley. I'm Lucille... de Cerque."

"Is there anything I can help with?"

"Maybe. Do you know how to kill or get rid of banshees?"

Merik cocked his head. "I'm afraid I'm not familiar with that word. What are they?"

While Lucille gave him a crash course in banshees and their current problem, Jan and Anne returned.

"Anything?" Jan asked.

Matt had helped Samantha sit up. She looked incredibly pale. "No, it's just getting worse."

"Sorry, I wish I was better help," Anne mumbled.

"What about an anti-magic web?" Matt mused. "To neutralise the magic." He gently nudged Samantha. "It's your speciality."

Samantha grimaced. "Worth a try, but it's a big city." She took a deep breath and started weaving. A few weaves in, she cried out and covered her ears, then tried again. A tear ran down her cheek. "I can't concentrate."

"Have you tried banning them?" Merik asked.

"To where?" Lucille asked. "Ireland? I mean, what I'm trying to say is they're native to Ashuan."

"No, no, I mean banning them into an object. Usually, it's a scroll. We have a few of them in the Phalesian Archives."

Lucille had a million questions, but she whittled it down to the one that mattered most: "Do you know how to do that?"

"Unfortunately, I don't possess that kind of talent. I was hoping one of you did. Matt said you're all extremely talented, especially for someone from Ashuan."

"Talented my ass," Jan grumbled, putting his jacket on. "I'm going back to the hospital to try to do what I can. Threads of life shouldn't rip like that. Maybe I can figure out how to put tape around them or something."

"You're not making any sense," Lucille said.

Jan rolled his eyes. "I'm trying to save people's lives. Keep me posted, okay?" His gaze fell on Anne. "Matt... can you do me a solid and take Anne away from here if she shows any sign of... weakening?"

"Sure." Matt looked at Samantha. "Maybe I should take you away from Ashuan, too."

But Samantha shook her head. "No. This is my mess. I need to find a solution. I'll look into banishing circles. It's a good idea."

When Jan had gone and Matt had helped Samantha up to her private library, Merik scratched his forehead. "Is there always so much drama here?"

Apologetically, Lucille smiled. "Welcome to Greenvalley!"

Fabian

Within seconds, Fabian was at Shayna's side. "Shayna, what's going on?"

She was curled up on the ground, holding her head, crying. "Make it stop! Please, make it stop."

Fabian put his hands under her and hauled her into his arms. "It's going to be okay. Don't worry." He was only a few metres from the gate, behind which help was waiting.

"She's just pretending," Ophelia said when he shifted Shayna's weight and she put her arms around him. "It's such a cheap trick."

"Don't be ridiculous," Fabian snapped. There was no pretending in the rapid breathing and cold sweat that had broken out all over her. "She needs medical help."

"Then call an ambulance. You don't need to take her to another world."

"The Citadel's in our world." After a week, Fabian felt fairly confident with the short trip on the rivers. More confident than leading an ambulance to the spring of magic.

Ophelia huffed. "And they've got better doctors there?"

"This isn't a normal illness. She was fine just moments ago." Step by step, Fabian carried Shayna towards the gate.

"A little too well," Ophelia argued.

He had no idea why she was so against him helping Shayna. "It's probably Samantha's banshees. You read the group text. They go after anyone with magic ability."

For some reason, that made Ophelia smile. "Oh, is she too weak to withstand them? That makes sense."

"How can you be so mean right now?" Fabian asked, exasperated. Shayna was getting heavy in his arms, especially since she was writhing in pain.

"Because it's a trick! I know you, Fabian. A girl plays damsel in distress and you're at her beck and call."

"Just put me down," Shayna whispered. "I can make it there without your help."

"You heard her," Ophelia said. "You don't have to play the hero."

"I'm not playing hero!" Fabian bellowed, at the end of his wits. "Now, are you gonna help or are you just gonna stand there and prattle on?"

Ophelia had tears in her eyes when she ran past him and blocked the gate with outstretched arms. "Her or me."

"If you think I'm going to let someone die just so you don't have to be jealous, you don't know me at all." And with that, he barrelled past her and seized the rivers of magic.

Fabian stumbled into the courtyard of the Citadel, nearly dropping Shayna. He carried her to a bench and was just about to get help when he noticed her breathing was normalising and colour was returning to her face. "Better?"

Shayna nodded, still too shaken to speak.

Fabian sat down next to her and rubbed her back. "Sorry about that."

"Don't be," she whispered. "And thanks for choosing my life."

He snorted. "Ophelia had no right demanding I choose."

"I told you. She's afraid of losing you."

"That may be but it doesn't make it right." He still couldn't believe Ophelia would argue in a life-or-death situation like that. "Perhaps she did just lose me."

Shayna softly patted his thigh. "Give her some grace. I... I know I haven't been nice to her, calling her your cultist girlfriend and so on. She went through hell with that cult, and you helped her get out. It's no wonder she loves you so much. You're probably the only person she has, and now you're no longer at school and she only sees you in the evening, and probably not even every day. It's a big change and you're well past the honeymoon phase. I get it, you know? The only question you should ask yourself is whether she's worth fighting for or if you want to cut her loose."

"I don't want to cut her loose." That sounded awful.

"But?"

Fabian rubbed his face, feeling the pressure of Ophelia's needs battling with his love for her. "I love her. She's important to me. And yes, right now she's a bit clingy, probably because of what you've just said. I just don't know how to make her less insecure. I've already told her she's got nothing to worry about, and I make sure I see her every day and send her little messages throughout the day, but I'm starting to think the only thing that would truly make her happy would be me quitting the Citadel."

"It's not the Citadel," Shayna said, leaning back. "It's me. The only thing that would make her happy would be for you to cut me out of your life again, pretend I don't exist, and never mention me, much less save my life. We can go home at separate times."

"Sure, that would work," Fabian said bitterly. "Until the next girl she feels threatened by comes along."

Shayna chuckled softly. "You're just too friendly and kind. Easy to fall in love with."

"Well, I'd like to stay kind," Fabian said, sullenly.

Saying it out loud made him realise he wasn't at fault. He'd done nothing to make Ophelia jealous. And ignoring Shayna when half the class already pretended they didn't exist was out of the question. This wasn't something he could fix by giving up more and more. But it was something he wanted to fix.

"She's worth it."

Shayna nodded, her smile tinged with sadness. "I knew you'd say that."

Matt

For the time being, headphones seemed to be working for Samantha. At least, it helped her study her books. Still, Matt saw the tension in her shoulders and heard the occasional sharp gasp. His girlfriend was suffering, and there was nothing he could do about it.

"I've got something!" Anne hopped up, holding one of Caspar's books. "It's called the Song of Life and... it has no words."

"So, is it just a melody?" Lucille asked. "I'm sure there are apps we can use to play it for us." Apart from Samantha, none of them were musically talented.

Anne shook her head. "It's not that either."

Frustrated, Matt plucked the book out of her hands and studied the page before passing it to Samantha. "'The murmur of a brook, the morning chorus, the wind in the leaves'? What kind of song is that?"

"Magic," Samantha said, after a single look. "It's a magical song."

"Can you sing it?"

"With death in my ears? Doubtful."

"That's it!" Lucille clapped her hands, looking excited. She'd been sitting next to Merik, who'd offered to stay and help. "I don't know why we didn't think of it before. We have to stop Samantha from hearing the banshees. If she's deaf, they don't stand a chance. Sam can sing the song, and we can finally put an end to this."

Matt massaged his temples, trying to stay calm. "You want to make my girlfriend deaf?"

"Only temporarily, of course. Let me check my spell list."

Matt nearly punched her, but he managed to turn away and shake out his fist instead. His gaze fell on Samantha. "I'm not going to risk you going permanently deaf just to save this town."

"I have to do it. Besides, I think I know how." Stubborn as always Samantha gave the book back to Anne and went to the boxes with Caspar's runes. A moment later, she held one up. It consisted of three sticks, one of which was bent into an arc. "Deafness."

"That's Caspar's," Matt pointed out, as if it wasn't obvious to everyone.

Samantha frowned. "And?"

"I don't trust him. Everything he cared about was how to hurt people. This will hurt you."

Her face softened. "That wasn't all he cared about."

Matt felt the anger rise again, but underneath it was something else. A feeling he knew way too well by now—guilt.

It made no sense at all. Caspar had attacked him. He'd tried to kill him—and he'd died with Jeyne's name on his lips. His one true love. Samantha's ancestor. "What if it's permanent?"

"It's a rune, Matt. Runes are meant to be broken when they've served their purpose."

"Have you ever done rune magic? Do you know how to break them?" Right now, it looked easy enough to snap, but Matt had no idea how that changed when its magic was released.

"This song is the best chance we have right now," Samantha pleaded. "So, what if I go deaf?"

He couldn't believe what he was hearing. Just then, Anne pressed her hands on her ears and swayed on the spot. At the same time, Samantha screamed and fell to her knees, tears streaming down her face. Panicked, Matt looked back and forth between the two of them.

"Go, go, you promised Jan!" Samantha shouted.

Matt hated it, but while Samantha was in a lot of pain, she didn't seem close to death, unlike Anne, whose eyes were rolling back. Matt jumped forward, caught her before she hit the ground, and took her to Fader.

It took an hour to get Anne properly settled and make sure she was safe, with no Chay around to jump the line. When Matt finally returned, he found the house empty, apart from Neve.

"Where did everyone go?"

Neve was pouting on the banister, which she'd turned extra slippery. "No one wants to play with Neve. Play with banshee instead."

"Did they mention where?" When Neve's face darkened, he nearly wrung her neck. "Neve, I'll play with you the whole weekend. Just tell me where Samantha is."

Her eyes lit up and she pointed towards the table. Matt strode over and found a map and note. "They're near the Magic Circle," he read. "Get ready for an epic snowball fight."

Before Neve could reply, he'd already jumped away.

Matt stumbled out behind the Magic Circle and ran up the street, looking up and down until he found the group. Lucille, Samantha, and Merik stood in front of three hollow-eyed women in rags with flowing black hair. The banshees.

Now that he'd come face to face with them, Matt heard their horrible cries. Both Merik and Lucille had their ears covered, but Samantha stood there, completely unbothered, the bent shape of a rune glowing on her forehead. Caspar's rune.

"What did you do?" Matt snapped at Lucille.

She rolled her eyes. "There was no other choice. She..." Her phone rang. "That's Albert." Her face was turning white as she took the call. "Al—Is it Pascal?" Her wide gaze met Matt's, pleading with him.

Matt looked at the banshees and his girlfriend, who stood before them unafraid, opening her mouth, ready to sing. In a few moments, it might all be over.

In a few moments, Pascal might already be dead. Matt had to trust Samantha knew what she was doing.

"I'm going to get him. Just take care of Sam!"

Samantha

It wasn't just one banshee but three of them, and they were even more terrible than Samantha had expected. At first glance, they looked like pale women in grey rags, their long black hair unkempt and tangled. But the truly horrifying thing about them were their faces. Instead of eyes, they had two dark hollows, with black veins spreading over their sunken cheeks. And then there were their mouths, black gaping holes covering a third of their faces, perpetually open in a scream. A scream Samantha no longer heard but felt in every fibre of her body.

The pain in her head had subsided, but her entire being was fraying at the seams. It wasn't just a song of death, it was a spell that ate into her magic, and she knew if she didn't stop it right now, it would be the end of her.

Her fingers tightened around the copied instructions for the song of life. She'd never attempted to sing magic, but something about looking at the individual spell parts made sense, almost as if she could hear the music just by looking at it.

A drop of blood fell on the page. Startled, Samantha wiped her nose. Her hand came away bloody, but there was more. The veins under her skin were darkening, just like the banshees'. The rune of deafness had given her a false sense of security. Time was running out faster than she thought.

Samantha stuffed the page into her back pocket and raised her hands, as if to play an invisible harp. She opened her mouth and sang the first note when all three banshees faced and screamed at her. The scream was like a physical shove, picking her off the ground and throwing her onto the street.

Lucille stepped in, weaving a spell around her, a look of panic on her face. Samantha couldn't hear the spell but she saw the shield forming around her. Merik handed Lucille something that looked like an empty scroll. Apparently, they were trying to ban the banshees, after all.

Her friend had just started to incant something when she suddenly dropped the scroll and covered her ears, screaming. The wind picked up the paper and sent it flying. Merik jumped after it, but the song assaulted him, too, and he crumpled not too far from Lucille.

Desperate, Samantha brushed off the road rash and stumbled back to her feet. Her entire body felt the scream of death worming its way into her soul. Despite that, she raised her hands again and forced the first notes out.

The wonderful tranquil sound of a brook tumbling over stones broke from her mouth, the memory of it strong enough to hear it in her mind. She weaved in the song of birds wooing each other and added the pop of opening buds. Laughter bubbled from her lips, mixing with the sounds of melting ice and grass breaking the soil, rain falling onto leaves, thunder rumbling in the distance, the flutter of wings. She didn't need the page to tell her what elements to add to her melody. It all came from her heart, healing the cracks on her skin as sunlight hit the banshees.

They continued screaming, their death notes attacking the song, trying to bring dissonance into it. Samantha felt the icy touch of winter, the hot humidity of rotting leaves. But all that was life, too, and she countered them by growing mushrooms in the soil and placing animal traces in the snow.

Life and death battled for dominance inside her. She could feel the decay of time, the end of her life, but it wasn't now. Now, she lived with her senses and her heart wide open, drinking in the magical world around her.

The screams ebbed away as the power of the banshees waned. One by one, the three women closed their mouths, staring, as if in mourning for all that has escaped the grasp of death—for now at least.

Then, their bodies liquefied. The three banshees wound around each other, screaming in horror. Samantha followed the trail of their spirits as they were sucked into the empty scroll, quickly filling it with mysterious symbols. She half-expected Merik or Lucille to have achieved it but instead, she found Robert.

"Robert?"

He said something, but the rune on her forehead prevented her from hearing him. He wasn't speaking to her, anyway. His eyes—much harder than she'd ever seen them before—were focused on the banshees. Only when every trace of them had been inscribed onto the scroll did Robert blink. He looked at the scroll in his hands, then at Samantha and Lucille. His eyes widened, as if in panic.

The scroll dropped to the ground as he bolted. Lucille ran after him but stopped soon enough. She picked up the scroll and opened her mouth, but Merik stepped in and shook his head. Samantha had no idea what they were talking about, but the scroll changed hands yet again, and Lucille came to her, saying something. Still deaf, Samantha didn't understand a single word.

Lucille rolled her eyes and quickly typed a note on her phone: Let's go back to the house and break the rune.

Breaking the rune was a little more complicated than Samantha had anticipated. Because it'd melted into her skin, she couldn't just snap it in half. But Lucille found a description and shoved Caspar's book into Samantha's hand to read for herself. Sitting in front of the mirror, Samantha redrew the shape with her finger, concentrating on breaking it.

Nothing happened.

She did it a second and a third time, while Matt arrived with Anne and immediately started berating Lucille. Samantha watched them in the mirror as tears formed in her eyes. She didn't want to be deaf. Not permanently.

Just then, on her fourth attempt, the rune crumbled and fell from her skin.

"...so reckless. What if she never hears again? I could've evacuated her!" Matt shouted.

Samantha gasped. More tears flowed down her face, but this time, they were from relief. "I can hear you."

In an instant, Matt was behind her, slinging his arms around her and pressing his cheek against hers. "You're alive and well."

Samantha held his arms and nodded shakily. "Yes, the Song of Life worked... and Robert."

"Robert?"

"Oh, yes." Lucille crossed her arms. "Where did he come from? I mean, I know he always turns up at the most inopportune moments but today was... strangely opportune. He banished the banshees."

They all turned to Anne, who looked like a deer in headlights. "Robert doesn't believe in magic. He... Are you sure that was him?"

"Actually, no," Lucille said. "I mean, yes, it was Robert, but he looked as if he was possessed. That wasn't his usual awkward self. He was confident and commanding."

"He had to be," Merik chimed in. "It's the only way to banish a creature."

Anne laughed nervously. "Robert isn't commanding. Like never. He's such a sweetheart."

"Well, something happened to him today," Samantha said, not quite sure what she'd witnessed. "Maybe you could carefully probe him. Try to ask him what happened."

With a sigh, Anne nodded. "Of course. I'll ask him. Maybe something did possess him."

"Or maybe Greenvalley has a lot more magically talented people than we knew," Lucille mused.

Samantha knew she was thinking of Dennis, hoping he'd magically reveal himself, but what was an opportunity for Lucille was a source of anguish for Samantha. How many people had died in the last two days because of her failing web?

Matt's arms around her tightened, as if he could tell what was going on in her head. He kissed her on the temple and stood. "Now, I love a good debrief, but I'm desperate for some rest, and so is Sam. Merik, I—"

His friend raised his hands. "Don't worry about me. I'll see myself out." He waved the scroll. "I'll make sure this goes in the sealed section of the Phalesian Archives to keep it safe. We'll have to do this again, maybe at a quieter time?"

Next to him, Lucille laughed. "If you think Greenvalley is ever quiet, I'd hate to disappoint you. It's not a week if we aren't in mortal danger."

"And yet, you survive and thrive," Merik said.

Was Samantha mistaken or was there an undeniable spark between them? Poor Dennis might never get the chance to prove himself.

They filed out of the house, with Anne promising to talk to Robert. When the door was shut, Matt swivelled Samantha's chair around and crouched in front of her. "Talk to me."

Tears filled her eyes again. "It's all my fault. Everyone who died over the last twenty-four hours died because of me," she whispered. "I was trying to keep the town safe, not—"

Matt held her hands. "You didn't invite the banshees."

"No, but I held them here. I made them stronger, more potent."

"You don't know that." When she wanted to protest, Matt shook his head. "And if it's true, then it was an accident. It doesn't negate the fact those banshees had no business being in town. What brought them here? They're not local and they're not aggressive, web or no web. This isn't on you. Besides, you saved everyone, too."

"Well, Robert did."

Matt grimaced. "Bullshit. He banished them after you neutralised them—if that was even him. You fought and defeated them in spite of all the pain they caused you. As for those who died... Were they really affected by the banshees or did they just happen to die? I think we've got a pretty good handle on who has magic powers in Greenvalley and who doesn't."

"Like Robert?" Samantha mused. "Or Shayna?" It had been the biggest shock when Fabian had told her about his new classmate.

"What's the point of this speculation, Sam? You did a good thing. As soon as you noticed something had gone wrong, you went above and beyond to fix it. I evacuated the people we did know about. As for everyone else? Was there anyone who died outside the hospital last night?"

"Are you saying the banshee victims were already sick?"

Matt nodded softly. "I believe so. Remember, the banshees are har-binger of death, not death itself."

Shuddering, Samantha let go of the heavy weight on her shoulders. Matt was right. A lot of factors had played into today's strategy, and there was no proof her web had killed anyone. Just lingering doubt.

Unfortunately, the prolonged scream of the banshees had unravelled most of her work. One day, she'd redo it—after making sure nothing was trapped inside—but for now it was enough to serve as a warning system.

"Caspar's stuff really helped us today," she said, desperate to change the topic.

It wasn't just the rune she'd used to temporarily block out sound. The Song of Life had been from one of his healing books, which had also helped Jan make new leeway.

Matt sighed. "Just imagine the wasted potential. He could've done so much good."

Samantha cocked her head. Caspar's healing powers hadn't exactly been in demand in Hell, and she doubted he or any other demon had ever been interested in 'doing good', as Matt had put it. No, this was about something else. Something Matt had managed to hide from her until now.

"He chose differently."

"I know." Matt buried his face in her knees.

Smiling, Samantha pulled her hands free from his grip and placed them on his head. "He didn't leave you any choice."

"I know," Matt repeated, his voice a little hoarse.

Instead of pushing, she gently ran her fingers through his hair. They both had blood on their hands. Such was the nature of their circumstances, their destiny. It would be impossible to get through this without some regrettable mistakes, not when the powers they fought had no such qualms.

All they could do was the very best they could.

Lucille

"The banishment was a pretty good idea," Lucille said to Merik outside the Blackstone House. Anne had left quickly, worrying about Robert, but Lucille had yet to call her ride. "We got lucky Robert was able to do it, but the idea was solid."

"What's the deal with him?" Merik asked, looking a little overwhelmed—not that Lucille blamed him. He'd been baptised by fire in Greenvalley.

She shrugged. "I don't know. He's a former classmate, usually quite annoying—oh, and Anne's boyfriend, though what she sees in him, I don't know. He's a bit hard to read, to be honest. Like, he always seems to be around when something happens, but he's such an awkward guy, and I could've sworn he had no magic. Anyone in this town but him."

"There's quite a lot of magic in this town. When I learnt about Ashuan in school, I thought it was a very... magic-deficient world. I mean, no world is truly without magic, but Ashuan seemed particularly bland. I always assumed that was the reason why everyone knew about it but no one bothered to reach out and include it in the Interglobal Community. Well, until recently."

"Until recently?"

Merik shrugged. "Recent in political terms. Ashuan has a seat in the Interglobal Parliament, which doesn't quite make sense to me, but here we are. Maybe I simply misjudged."

"You're talking about Geoffrey Black?"

"You know him?" Merik sounded surprised.

"Well, not really. I've only met him once. A friend of mine is dating his son, and we happened to visit him in Fader during that horrible attack on parliament."

Merik's eyes widened. "You were there?"

Lucille nodded and laughed. "Honestly, not the best day to be introduced to interglobal politics."

"It's a cursed territory." When she frowned, Merik explained, "Complicated and full of traps and pitfalls."

"Oh, yes, I suppose so. Quite impressive, though. We actually ended up helping out security. Or mostly, Samantha did. I just protected her while she held up the floating spell. We even got honorary tokens for it."

"That was you?" Merik laughed softly. "I did hear about an Ashuan intervention, but again, I couldn't make sense of it." He turned the ring on his hand and looked back at the house. "She's quite powerful, isn't she?"

Lucille playfully put a hand on his arm. "She's not the only one."

He looked at her, his golden eyes drinking her in. "Tell me more," he demanded in a low voice that raced down her spine, filling her with excitement.

She licked her lip and jerked her chin a little. "Why don't we continue this somewhere more comfortable?"

Merik slipped an arm around her, pressing her body against his. "I thought you'd never ask."

Fabian

Fabian half-expected Ophelia to be waiting at the gate, but when he arrived, she was nowhere to be seen. A barrage of group chat messages assaulted him instead. Cell phone reception at the Citadel of Magic was spotty at best, which made it extra hard to stay in touch with his girlfriend throughout the day.

From the texts, he gathered Greenvalley was safe again, and the threat had been neutralised. He quickly popped back to the Citadel to tell Shayna she could go home, but she'd decided to take advantage of the Citadel's hospitality and spend the night there. For a moment, Fabian was tempted to do the same, but something called him back.

An hour later, he was in front of Ophelia's shared living space. It was already past curfew, but that mattered little to the teenager who opened the door and bid him inside. They all knew him well by now.

"She's already asleep," the young guy said. "Said she had a headache."

Panic spiked in Fabian. Had Ophelia succumbed to the banshees while he'd been busy saving Shayna?

"Thanks," he said and knocked on the door. "Lia?"

When she didn't answer, he quietly pressed down the handle and pushed. His heart was racing, expecting to see her collapsed on the floor. Instead, he found her curled up in bed, staring into the darkness.

"Lia?" Fabian crouched in front of the bed and ran his hand through her dark locks. "I'm here."

Her eyes focused on him. "Are you really?"

"I'm sorry. Today was intense. Did the banshees get to you, too?"

"A little," she whispered.

It was blatantly obvious she was playing it down, probably so she wouldn't seem as weak as Shayna—if one could call it weak to be struck down by a harbinger of death. "I'm sorry I wasn't there."

"It's okay. I didn't need help."

"Oh, Lia."

She sat up in bed, her dark eyes haunting him. "Is she alive?" When he nodded, Ophelia let out a sigh of relief. "Good. I... I don't know what came over me. I don't want her dead."

"That's good to know," Fabian said softly. "You scared me out there."

Tears were rolling down her cheek. "I'm scared all the time." She flew into his arms, sobbing. "You're the best thing that's ever happened to me, but she's... she's much prettier than me and older and wittier, and now she's got the same kind of magic like you, not my tainted scary one."

"You think fire isn't scary?"

"Are you afraid of her?"

Fabian slipped his arms around her waist and pulled her closer. "No, but I'm not afraid of you either."

"Liar. You don't like my snakes."

The two pet snakes in the terrarium had been rather unsettling initially, but he'd gotten used to them. "Avo and Cado? Are you kidding me? I love those guys. They look a lot scarier than they are. Like you."

Ophelia couldn't help but snort amusedly. "You think I look scary?" she asked, a little snotty-nosed.

Fabian rubbed her lower back, his hand slowly dipping lower. "You're a badass, Lia, strong, unafraid, and you are, by far, the sexiest woman I've ever seen, and I know Matt's family."

She preened like a cat in his embrace. With a wicked smile, she slid forward and wrapped her legs around his body, cradling his head. "Monsters don't scare me but you do. I mean, losing you."

"You're not going to lose me, Lia. I love you, snakes, shadows, and all. But you need to loosen your grip a little. Didn't you want me to embrace my magic and go the Citadel?"

"Of course."

"Well, Shayna's been a great friend, and I like hanging out with her during class. That's... I don't want to change that," Fabian admitted. "But that's all it is. We're classmates and friends. Two fish out of water in a rather hostile environment. Don't make me choose between the two of you."

Ophelia gave him a brief nod, still sniffing a little, while her fingers buried into his hair. "You still think I'm sexier than her, right?"

"By miles."

She laughed and kissed him on the lips. "It hurts seeing you with her, but I know that's a me problem. I'll work on it. I promise."

"Come here." He pulled her closer until she slipped from the bed into his lap, laughing. Then he kissed her until there was no doubt left about who he came home to.

Alecia

The Residence of Envy was changing. Each day, it was a little darker than before, prompting Alecia to sneak more and more mage lights in. Every so often, she'd find them smashed and extinguished. The work of the Shadow.

It was grating on her how quickly he'd curried Pyke's favour. Officially, he hadn't replaced her as the First Disciple. Unofficially, though…

"What are you doing?"

As so often, she found the Shadow in Pyke's mirror room. The mirror room was the heart of the residence. It was filled with all kinds of mirrors: big and small, narrow and wide, round and bent, all of them enchanted. They didn't reflect the viewers' image but showed what he wanted to see instead.

Pyke used them to spy on his enemies—of which there were many. They fed his envy, and with it his power. But it wasn't Pyke who'd taken up residence in the mirror room, but the Shadow. And as so often, he was watching a little town in Ashuan.

"Seen anything interesting?"

Alecia sat on a chaise lounge in the middle of the room, which gave her the perfect angle to see past him into the mirror. Or at least, it would've, if the mirror hadn't darkened immediately, covered in his signature shadows.

"They withstood the banshees," the Shadow whispered.

The initial pang of jealousy at having her viewing denied was replaced by smugness. "Of course they did."

After seeing the humans fight in the Residence of Lust a few months ago, Alecia doubted something as weak as a banshee would hurt them, whether they'd been corrupted by the Shadow or not.

"This place," the Shadow continued, as if she'd never said anything. "Greenvalley. It's full of magic."

"Malcolm thought so, too," she said, pretending to be bored. "He attempted to bring it to Hescaryn but was stopped by the same humans who'll foil all your plans."

That particular nugget had been quite the surprise. They hadn't just facilitated Melaney's fall, but killed Malcolm, too. Naturally, she'd had to dig deeper after that.

The Shadow crept closer. "You think they can stop me? The one who'll bring doom to their world?"

Alecia yawned. Grandstanding had never impressed her. "I hope the banshees weren't part of that plan, because if so, my dear shady friend, you're not going to bring much doom to anything, much less their world. Maybe next time you should go yourself."

"You don't like me," the Shadow said, looming over her. "You detest my presence."

"Whatever gave me away?" Alecia put a hand to her chest and blinked.

"Are you jealous?"

She laughed in his shadowy face. "If I weren't jealous, I'd be in the wrong house. Now, as for you." She stood up in a languid movement and walked to the mirror, elegantly bypassing him. With a flick of her hand, she pulled the image of Greenvalley back, staring at Lucille, who was in the company of a tall, golden stranger. The sweet yearning of envy hit her as she watched them kiss. The Shadow hissed behind her, which might have been him clearing his non-existent throat. "As I was saying, they'll crush you under their feet."

The six of them and their friends were Alecia's juiciest secret. She'd gone into the Residence of Lust to find out what plan Melaney was hatching and had stumbled over Chay's grand plan instead.

She'd been wary of Chay ever since he'd entered Hescaryn and quickly garnered the favour of the Council of Seven. In her opinion, they'd relied too much on him and his visions. Sure, they flung the usual abuse at him and threatened to kill him at least twice per session, but they called him back, again and again. Alecia had always wondered why he heeded their call. Unlike other demons, he'd figured out how to block the summons. And yet, when the Seven called, he came.

Now she finally knew why. The Seven didn't control him—he controlled them. Or at least, he tried to. Lust and Greed were already his, and now Alecia had to decide whether Envy should stand against him or with him. It all depended on what version of the story she fed Pyke. That of the half-demon overreaching, trying to manipulate the most powerful demons in Hescaryn? Or that of the clever seer, shepherding the destined Six to prepare for the War of Worlds, trying to lay Hell at their feet. If Pyke learnt of their identity, he'd want to get his hands on them. As devoted as Alecia was to her lord, envy kept the secret inside. It was hers and hers alone. For now, she held all the power in her hand.

So long as the Shadow didn't cross her plans with his ridiculous scheme.

"It is I who will crush them," the Shadow hissed. "And I've already made my next move."

Curious, Alecia followed him into the audience chamber of the residence. Hidden in the shadows created by her hated companion, a man knelt in front of the throne. When he raised his head, Alecia gasped.

"Lord Pyke," he said, in a melodic voice used to command. "My name is Merik an Derendi of Phalos, and I've come to ask for your favour."

Part 3

Madness & Devotion

Rachel

The dreamworld was uncharacteristically dark these days. Rachel knew it was due to the prophecy looming over her, though she couldn't tell if her dreams reflected the impending doom in the web of fate or her fear of it.

She missed hanging out with Nico—or rather the dreamer behind his face. Without him, the dreamworld felt vast and full of hidden traps. Especially now the Dark One had cast his shadow upon it. Rachel hugged herself and sought out the only other dreamer in her vicinity: her mother.

Soon, she'd be far away, and though their relationship had never been close, Rachel was sorry to see her go. There was still so much left unspoken; so many questions left unanswered.

"Why did you never leave the meadow?" Rachel asked.

The meadow was her base in the dreamworld, the place from where she embarked to other dreams. It was also the only location besides her nightmares where she found her mother. It always struck her how different Annette looked here. It wasn't just that she was thirty years younger and had brown plaits instead of her crazy, colourful hair-do—she looked so peaceful here, unharmed by the shards of her adult life.

"Why would I leave?" Annette asked. She was seated, weaving a wreath from dream flowers. "The world out there... it's scary."

Rachel sat next to her. "Scary, yes, but also full of wonders. You can dream anything."

Annette squinted at the darkness. "It's cold out there."

"Cold?" Rachel followed her gaze. Something was slithering through the grass. At first, she thought it was a snake but then she saw long shadows.

She jumped up and willed them away from her meadow. She might as well have willed the stars to stop shining. The shadows encroached on her, then swept around her to crawl all over her mother. Not knowing what to do, Rachel could only stare as they crawled into Annette's open mouth and darkened her eyes.

Annette rose and said in an eerie voice, "He'll step out of the shadows, as dark as the night."

Rachel groaned. "Not this again."

"He'll serve Envy, jealous of the light."

"Yes, yes, I know, but what am I supposed to do?"

Her mother was relentless. "His shadows will devour the earth, leaving nothing but blight."

Suddenly, there were screams around them. Fire exploded into the sky, and Rachel threw herself into the meadow, taking her mother down with her.

"There's more," her mother gasped, but her voice and eyes were normal again. "I... what's happening?"

"Just the end of the world, you know?" Rachel whimpered. "Mum, I'm—" When she looked around, her mother was gone. "Scared," she whispered.

Rachel woke and immediately threw her blanket aside to get up and pace. "Chay," she muttered. "Chay. Come on. I need you."

"A bad dream?" Hugo asked, looking worried.

"A bad vision. The world is ending, and I don't know how to stop it." Her voice was shaking. She felt like she was losing the plot. "I don't even know if anyone can stop it."

"There must be a way."

Rachel whirled around. "Chay!"

The half-demon had appeared in her room, looking as if she'd dragged him out of bed. "Sorry, I came as fast as I could. Did you glean any more information from the dream?"

She shook her head. "No, just darkness and fire. The same three lines." Then her eyes widened. "My mother. She said... she said there was more, but I don't know if she meant more terrible things or more—"

"Prophecy." Chay nodded. Deep in thought, he walked around Rachel's room. "It feels incomplete, I agree. It's the only thing that gives me hope."

"When are we going to tell the others?" When Rachel had first dreamed of the prophecy, Chay had bade her keep it secret. At least for the moment. There wasn't anything they could do until they had more information, he'd said. "I... I don't want to deal with this on my own. It's too much."

Chay smiled with compassion. "I know, and I'm sorry. You're right. We should inform the others, get more eyes and ears on it."

Rachel bit her lip. She'd only just realised how many horrible visions Chay usually saw. He had no one to share them with as he tried to prevent the worst. How many worlds had he seen ending in his life? How few had he been able to save?

"I don't know how to do it."

He knew exactly what she meant. "The secret's fairly simple, I'm afraid—there's no way I can't do it. What good is it to see the future if you don't act on it?"

It wasn't the same as changing the future or preventing a vision from coming true, but Rachel took it. The alternative was too shocking to consider.

"So, we're going to tell them?"

"Yes. I have an idea how we can find out more about this prophecy. Just give me a chance to put plans into motion. Meet me with the others at Balthasar's in a few hours."

"At Balthasar's?" Rachel asked, horrified, but Chay had already gone. "Sure, let's skip the apocalypse and go straight to Hell."

"I don't like this, Rachel," Hugo said, his face full of worry.

She sighed. "Well, I didn't ask for this." Just as her life was finally looking up, the world had decided to end. "Maybe we should just move to Hell."

It all ended up there anyway.

Jan

"I'm coming!" Jan called, grabbing yesterday's pullover and throwing it on. He was still half asleep, but the doorbell was relentless. It wasn't even five in the morning yet. "You've got to be kidding me." With a fake smile, he ripped the door open. "This'd better be an emergency."

He almost recoiled when he saw the figure on his doorstep. It was a man in his forties, maybe even fifties, and there was nothing to distinguish him from a drunk homeless guy, down to the run-down clothes, patchy stubble, and overwhelming stench.

"Stop staring and let me inside. It's cold out here," the stranger said, his voice gruff.

"Who are you?"

He grunted and pushed past Jan. Rubbing his hands, he took a good look around the foyer. "Could be warmer. Now, come on. I need some food, and if you got a drink or two, I wouldn't say no to that, either."

"Um, this isn't a homeless shelter or food bank," Jan said, irritated. "Get out before I throw you out."

The man hardly even flinched. "Nah, believe me, I don't want this any more than you do."

Jan crossed his arms and glared at the invader. "Oh, yeah? What are you doing here, then? What do you want?"

"Food and drink, just as I said. I've come a long way."

"Yeah, no. Look, I'll call you a taxi but I'm sure as hell not giving you a drink."

"Stop acting as if it's such an unreasonable thing to ask for," the man muttered.

Before Jan could question him further, he heard footsteps. Matt and Samantha were coming down. While Matt hadn't bothered dressing, parading around in pyjama shorts, Samantha clutched a robe around her shoulders.

"What's going on?" she asked. "Who's that?"

"Feel free to ask him. He's not making any sense to me," Jan said, frustrated.

The stranger regarded the newcomers suspiciously and cocked his head. "Chay's boy, I assume?"

Apprehensively, Jan took a step back. Random drunkards didn't know Chay. There seemed to be more to this man than he'd initially thought.

"You…" Matt's eyes widened. "You're the healer, aren't you? Leandres." He slipped an arm around Samantha. "Could you start breakfast, maybe make some coffee?"

Samantha gave him a long look, but then nodded. "Sure, but I want an explanation."

The old man followed Samantha as she moved into the kitchen, claiming the couch in the living room as if it'd always belonged to him. Jan stared at him, bewildered, before asking Matt, "You know this guy?"

"That's Leandres, the experienced healer Chay promised to find for you. He must've agreed to teach you."

This morning was getting stranger and stranger. "He's supposed to be my mentor?"

Jan had all but forgotten about the whole teacher business. When he'd received healing in Hanna's temple, the healer had been shocked to hear he'd been self-taught. Looking at this dirty old man, who was emptying all kinds of trash from the pockets of his coat, Jan thought he was doing perfectly fine with Caspar's books and paramedic training.

"He's supposed to be one of the best," Matt said, though he didn't sound convinced.

"He's a homeless bum with a drinking problem," Jan protested.

Matt shrugged. "Well, now he has a home, I suppose."

"You want to let him live in our house? My house?" Jan corrected quickly.

"It's the price for his lessons: a bed and food."

Jan snorted. "I'm not going to supply his drink."

Meanwhile, Leandres had found a dead grasshopper in his pocket. He looked at it, shrugged, and popped it into his mouth. The crunch made Jan and Matt shudder.

"Lovely," Jan said, bile creeping up his throat. "Just lovely."

It wasn't even seven yet when the doorbell rang again. Tired, Jan rubbed his face and opened it to reveal Lucille, Fabian, Ophelia, Anne, and Rachel. "More guests. Yeah. Are we celebrating something?"

Rachel sighed heavily. "Not really. I had a vision."

"Wonderful." This day just kept getting worse. "Come in. Now, don't be scared. This is Leandres, my new healing mentor." He made a sweeping bow towards the living room.

Leandres had moved from the couch to the dining table, where he was stuffing himself with the warmed bread rolls and waffles Samantha had made. A bag of lollies—courtesy of Neve—lay untouched, while the snow witch painted ice flowers on the windows. Samantha and Matt were both staring at Leandres in various shades of disgust, while Crumbs sat next to him, eagerly lapping up the scraps that fell down to the ground.

"How wonderful," Lucille said, with practised politeness. "Nice to meet you, Master Leandres. I'm a friend of Jan's, Lucille."

The healer grunted then belched, causing Lucille's fake friendliness to wither faster than a rose in a drought.

Matt nodded towards the kitchen. "Let's talk in there."

They shuffled into the small kitchen. Jan closed the door behind him and hissed, "This is so not on. I don't want him living here. I don't even know if I want him as a teacher."

"Just trust Chay," Matt repeated, like a broken record. "If he says Leandres is the best mentor for you, then he is."

"Speaking of Chay," Rachel said before Jan could protest. "he wants us to meet him at the Residence of Lust in an hour or two. We've both had the same prophetic dreams lately. Full of darkness and fire—a lot of doom and gloom."

Fabian cleared his throat, already paling. "But that's not the prophecy, right? Just the setting."

Rachel took out her notebook while Samantha passed cups of coffee around. "He'll step out of the shadows, as dark as the night. He'll serve Envy, jealous of the light. His shadows will devour the earth, leaving nothing but blight." She looked up at Fabian. "Yeah, I don't think it's just the setting. Chay believes our world is ending."

"Awesome," Jan said. "If the world's ending, there's no point in me starting this weird mentorship." Maybe it wasn't the appropriate reaction, but Leandres had riled him up too much to care.

"Do we know which world is ending?" Ophelia asked. "It's not necessarily ours, right? There could be other earths, right?"

Next to her, Fabian had buried his face in his hands, processing the chilling news with his usual despair.

"It's ours. Trust me. However, before you all lose your mind,"—even Rachel looked like she was losing it—"there's reason to believe we don't have the whole prophecy yet. Chay said he had an idea how to find the rest. That's why he wants to meet us in Hell."

"Yes, let's go to Hell," Jan exclaimed. "We might die, but at least I can ask Chay what the hell he was thinking sending me that!" He pointed at the door, only to notice it had opened.

Leandres stood there, pile of empty plates in his hand. "Just dropping these off." His gaze met Jan's as he put them on the counter. "And you're staying here. It's time we got started." Without waiting for an answer, he shuffled back out, closing the door behind him.

"I don't get a say in this?" Jan asked his friends, wondering why this was happening.

Samantha grimaced. "Honestly, I'd rather not have him stay here alone."

"We've got Neve." Jan rolled his eyes and sighed. "Fine. I'll stay with Mr Grumpy and see if he's really as good as Chay says he is. Maybe it's the wrong guy. Please ask Chay if he meant this Leandres."

Matt put a hand on his shoulder. "I'll make sure to ask."

"And about this whole world-ending business..."

Jan looked around the group. They all were a little pale. Fabian was crouching on the floor, still running his hands over his face, and Anne had tears in her eyes as she bit her lip. It was slowly sinking in this wasn't just an empty threat. They were really looking at the apocalypse.

"Let's just find a way to stop it."

Chay

There was no manual on how to save a world. Not even when you could see the future. For Chay, it was both a puzzle and dance on the wire. Whenever he touched another living being, he saw their life flash in front of his eyes. If he was lucky, he saw them shrivel and wither as their life stretched as far as it would go. But no matter if their lives were short or long, they always ended suddenly when death came calling. The visions came fast, like gut punches. He saw flashes of interactions, big moments, and great emotions. Those were the puzzle pieces he had to fit together.

The wire part came from his own role in the future. Chay never saw himself, never knew what his future held. He was the hole in the fabric of fate, and it was up to him to guess where his action was needed and when to step back and let destiny unfold. In Fader, they called him the saviour of worlds, but many times, his contributions were minuscule compared to the actual players. He wasn't the hero, just a voice in the background, gentle guidance, never knowing whether he got it right until the future had become the past.

This newest of visions had thrown a massive spanner in his plans. The Six were already destined to heartbreak and challenges far beyond humanly possible. And now their world was ending? He had to help them but he couldn't let the bigger picture out of sight—the pieces he moved now could block others from being moved later; potentially vital ones. Or he could use the immediate threat in his larger picture.

And there was one that was proving increasingly stubborn.

"Balthasar, I need her!" Chay followed the new archdemon through his residence. "Without Iyaga, the Council of Seven will never bend their knees. Volac and Hel are unapproachable, Moloch has ignored my pleas for a private meeting, and Yash has slept through them. As for Pyke..." Plenty of visions lately revolved around the Archdemon of Envy. "I have other plans for him."

"Charming," Balthasar said, his voice dripping with acid. "Does Pyke know of these plans?"

Chay snorted. "Of course not." He had yet to find an in with the Archdemon, but if he played his cards right...

Balthasar whirled around, glaring. "Am I supposed to feel honoured?"

His fury was a terrible thing but Chay didn't even flinch. "I don't care how you feel. You owe me." A deal was a deal, and theirs had been made in blood.

"Not that!"

Chay rolled his eyes. "You're already sleeping with her. What's so difficult about having a conversation outside of bed?" Annoyed, he threw his hands in the air. "Teach her greed in your bed, for all I care."

"I can't. That woman doesn't have an inkling of it in her blood."

"And that's why I need you. You've got more than enough for both of you."

Someone cleared their throat behind him. Matt. "I don't want to disturb you, but it's getting cold."

"Your kids are here," Balthasar snarled, pointing at the visitors from Ashuan.

True to her word, Rachel had brought almost all of them. Only Jan was missing, but then again, Chay had always known he would be.

"They're not my children," he said, massaging the root of his nose.

"If I didn't know any better," Lucille said to Samantha, not even trying to keep her voice low, "I'd say they're having marital issues."

Chay felt his lips twitch. His and Balthasar's relationship was unique. They respected each other beyond a dragon's doubt, but Balthasar was demon through and through and could only be trusted to serve himself. He'd simply decided long ago that currying Chay's favour was serving him the best. That didn't mean he was always happy about what he proposed.

"Rachel said something about a prophecy," Matt said, his arms crossed with faux nonchalance. "You've had an idea?"

"Oh yes," Balthasar hissed, "Tell us the great secrets of the future... Oh wait, you never do that."

The barbs were getting to Chay. Telling someone their future had never once worked in his favour. "You want to know your future? You're all going to die. Sooner or later. Happy now?"

"Cool, cool," Fabian said, his expression as if the world had already ended. "That clears it all up."

Chay cursed himself. Despite being one of the most powerful mages, the boy had no confidence. His approach had to be different. "You're not gonna... I mean, you're human, so death is a given..." He was off his game today, thanks to Balthasar.

"Just tell us our world isn't ending, please." Fabian's entire body was begging him, from his eyes and shaky voice to the tension in his limbs.

What could he tell him to lead him back to the path he was supposed to be on?

"Is Ashuan the next world to face its end?" Matt asked.

Unlike Fabian, he demanded an answer. Chay knew he was losing his influence on him. It was a natural process, one necessary for their survival, but it hurt nonetheless. Matt had looked up to him for so long, oblivious to his long list of failures.

Fortunately, the way he'd phrased his question had opened another option for Chay. "I highly doubt it. Ylvadin is breaking apart as we speak. It'll only last another week or so. Ashuan has more time."

"That's great for us," Fabian said, his eyes wide with fear. "So, it's true? We're facing the apocalypse?"

"One apocalypse. It's not Ashuan's first. And it won't be its last."

"So helpful, as usual," Balthasar said, bitterness lacing his words. He was in a terribly foul mood today, further complicating Chay's plan.

He had to move fast before it all broke apart. "The good thing is we've received a prophecy—or part of one. In order to stop the apocalypse, we'll have to get the lines interpreted. And completed."

Rachel nodded. "How do we do that?"

"Someone spoke this prophecy. You'll have to find them and make sure you get a complete copy." They were almost there. Just a tiny push more.

"And where would we find them?" Leave it to Samantha for some much-needed pragmatism. That girl was always pro-active, never satisfied with leaving things to fate. Chay wished it mattered.

"Prophecies are spoken by prophets. I'd recommend starting at the Serathon temple in Ylvadin. They've stored thousands of prophecies there."

Matt frowned. "Ylvadin? The world you said was breaking apart?"

Chay couldn't help but smile as the puzzle pieces fell into place. "There's still time."

"This is madness," Fabian complained, just as Chay knew he would. "What if that world ends while we're there?"

Next to him, Samantha's eyes hardened. "We have to find out what's going to happen to our world so we can stop it from happening, and if that's our best chance..."

"...and Chay says we've got time," Matt continued.

Little, but time, nonetheless.

"I'd love the chance to visit a temple," Anne chimed in. She was new to the group, and Chay didn't quite know how she fit into the grand scheme of things yet.

As usual, Lucille took charge. "Then that's what we're going to do. We'll go to Ylvadin and save our prophecy before it vanishes with the rest."

Chay winced at the stark reminder of all those visions of the future vanishing in a matter of days. There was nothing he could do to save them all.

"I'll come with you."

Balthasar snorted. "Trying to grab some more prophecies for yourself?"

It was time for the last puzzle piece to move into place. "You and Iyaga will join us, too."

For once, he'd managed to surprise the demon. Balthasar's mouth dropped open, and he huffed, "Excuse me?"

"You owe me."

Balthasar shut his mouth again and glowered, but he no longer protested. The final piece had been placed. Now it was up to the future to reveal to Chay whether he'd chosen the right path.

Lucille

Travelling had always been a special interest of Lucille's. She'd been to London, Tokyo, and New York, gone skiing in the most stunning mountain regions, and scuba diving on tropical islands. She'd thought she'd seen it all, and in less than twenty years of her life. And then she'd learnt about other worlds. Last year, she'd first set stepped into Hell—though dangerous, it had been strangely beautiful—and just a few weeks ago, she'd visited the bustling centre of the interglobal community. Now, she was taking her first steps in yet another world, and once again, it was unlike anything she'd ever seen.

If there was one word to describe Ylvadin, it would be 'dramatic'. Spires of snow-covered rock rose all around them, some so high, their tops were in the clouds. Some had steps hewn into the stone, circling upwards, while tenuous bridges swung in the wind. Birds circled the spires, their screams filling the air. Small villages were nestled in between, tucked away under the snow, but if there were any people, they seemed to prefer to stay inside.

Chay led the group to the outskirts of a village at the foot of a winding path that led up to a cloud-covered spire. "Serathon's temple is up there."

"Oh dear." As much as she appreciated the view, Lucille had hoped to avoid climbing one of the spires. "Is it safe?"

"It's part of the pilgrimage," Chay said. "But don't worry, you and I, and... those two"—he looked back at Balthasar and Iyaga, who clung to her lover, looking up at him with adoring eyes—"will stay down here."

"What? Why?"

"Yes, why?" Matt asked, frowning.

"Because he's got some secret agenda, of course," Balthasar said, bitingly. "Like always." He looked at Iyaga. "We should just leave."

The new Archdemon of Greed was disturbingly unlike Malcolm. From what Lucille had gathered, the magic they'd freed by killing Malcolm had sought her out, raising her from an obscure life without any ambitions. She had long blond hair and ice-blue eyes just a little too large for her face, giving her a perpetual look of wonder and innocence. Lucille knew better than to trust her, but as she continued to be nothing but nice and courteous, her resolve wavered. If anything, she reminded her of Menuha.

Iyaga looked around in awe, her hand still pressed to Balthasar's chest. "Oh, please let's stay a while. It's so beautiful." She gazed upwards. "And so open and wide."

"That's just the sky," Balthasar muttered, less enthused. Nevertheless, he kept one arm around her waist and didn't seem to mind her affections. The only one he glared at was Chay. "Fine, we'll stay. Might as well test out the bed here."

Iyaga let out an excited squeal as Balthasar took her hand. He pulled her towards the little house at the edge of the village Chay had rented. From the looks of it, it wasn't big enough for more than one bedroom.

Lucille dreaded having to listen to the two archdemons making out while she waited for the others. "Do I really have to stay here?"

Chay gave her a pitying look. "Unfortunately, yes. Balthasar is right. I have a plan in mind, and for it to work, I need you to stay here while the others visit the temple." He turned to the group. "A word of caution: Serathon might be the God of Knowledge and Devotion, but he's also the God of Madness, and they say he prefers the two in balance."

"This is getting better and better," Fabian muttered.

"You'll only have erratic access to your magic," Chay continued. "Don't rely on it. And remember, Ylvadin is close to a collapse. The temple might not be safe."

Fabian snorted. "And here I thought the end of a world was a picnic in the park."

"Relax," Samantha said. "We're visiting a temple, not a battlefield."

"Can we go?" Anne asked, sounding more eager than afraid. "I'm cold and it's a long way up."

Chay's gaze locked with Matt's. "Remember the rules of interglobal hospitality I taught you. Don't offend anyone and respect their ways. Be careful on your way up. The steps will be icy, but there's a guiding rope in the rock face."

Matt looked amused. "Yes, Dad. Anything else or can we get on with it?"

"Get on with it," Chay said, despite looking as if he had a million more things to say.

"See you later."

"See you tomorrow."

Matt's confidence faltered. "See you"—he sighed—"tomorrow." He re-arranged his backpack and started walking. The others fell in line behind him.

"Tomorrow?" Fabian asked, sounding horrified. "Why aren't we returning today?"

Ophelia linked her arm with his and smiled up at him. "You'll find out."

Soon, their chatter was lost in the wind.

Lucille braced herself against the cold as she watched her friends start their ascent. Part of her was glad she was spared climbing an icy spire into breathtaking heights but, then again, the alternative wasn't looking too rosy.

"We have to share the house with them for a full night?"

Chay's lips twitched. "You wouldn't believe how many times I've had to endure something like that to save a world. Let's go inside and see if they've got the fire started anywhere other than the bedroom."

With one last longing look at her friends, Lucille followed him.

Matt

After two hours of careful climbing, the group had made it to the top of the spire. Matt's fingers tingled as they stepped into the entry hall of the Serathon temple. He'd put his jacket around Samantha, not that it'd helped much. Her cheeks and nose were bright red from the cold, and snow was melting in her dark locks. It reminded him of a winter night two years ago, when he'd first felt this sublime tug in his stomach. All he wanted to do was take her hands and warm them against his stomach as he'd done back then.

Unfortunately, now was not the time or place. Two priests were already heading towards them. Their heads were shaven on both sides and they were dressed in light-blue robes knotted over their left shoulder. A dark blue sash denoted their rank, even though they bowed deferentially to them.

"Welcome to the halls of Serathon. May he imbue you with devotion and keep the madness away a little longer," they said, in well-practised unison.

"We're most grateful for the warm welcome in your halls," Matt said, speaking the words Chay had taught him so many years ago. "We approach this temple to dare a glimpse of the future, in the hope Serathon will guide our ways."

He earned a couple of confused looks from his friends but ignored them. Nervous, he bowed deep and gestured to the others to follow his lead.

The priests rose again, benevolent smiles on their faces. "You're most welcome in our library. But first, let us warm and feed you."

"It would be a great pleasure and an even greater honour," Matt replied, grateful for them bringing it up on their own.

As the priests invited them to an adjoining chamber, Samantha nudged him. "Where did all that come from?" she asked, waving her finger in front of his face and grinning.

Matt felt himself blush. "Chay drilled it into me when we talked about temple customs: make sure everyone eats and drinks something, so we're protected by the laws of hospitality."

"Do we need protection?" Fabian asked, swallowing hard.

"He's the God of Devotion and Madness, so let's be careful."

Fabian closed his eyes and inhaled sharply through his nose. Thankfully, after that, he managed to keep the panic at bay and control his features.

Fire basins were burning in the room, eliciting a few gasps of relief. Two novices awaited them. One held a basket of bread while the other had a pitcher of water.

The priests watched them eat and drink. When they were done, the one on the left pointed to the novice holding the food. "Finn will take care of you throughout your visit," he said, then turned on his heel and left, his partner and the other novice following him.

Matt smiled at the fifteen-year-old, sandy-haired boy they left behind. "Well, then. It's just you and us, I guess. Can you tell us where we can find the library of prophecies?"

Finn's grey eyes widened. He shook his head and put a finger to his lips.

"Vow of silence, I see." That made things a lot more complicated.

"Can you show us?" Samantha asked, friendly as ever.

The boy nodded and led them down a dark corridor.

"Why would he take a vow of silence?" Anne asked. While Fabian and Ophelia hung back, she seemed interested in the temple proceedings.

"It's probably a punishment for misbehaviour." When the boy's ears turned red, Matt smirked. "Told you."

Finn led them to a room at the end of the corridor. It was uncharacteristically wide, seeming to curve around the entire temple. Matt assumed it had something to do with the priests surrounding themselves with their god's knowledge.

Flickering mage lights illuminated rows of shelves filled with scrolls, each sealed with a tag. Presumably, they all included a prophecy. If the library really stretched around the temple, there must've been thousands, if not tens of thousands. But the most curious sight wasn't the scrolls, but the row of desks ahead. At each, a person sat, their legs chained to the desk. Despite their predicament, they were writing furiously.

Matt was about to ask one for directions when a priest stepped in his way. The dark colour of his sash gave him away as one of the higher priests, perhaps the High Priest himself.

"How may I help you, pilgrim?" He shot a quick glare at Finn, who seemed to shrink a little, before smiling wanly at the group again.

Matt had a dozen questions, but this was a world of no concern for him, and he knew better than to interfere with their culture. "We received a prophecy but believe it incomplete. We hoped it'd been spoken in this temple." He looked past the priest and shrugged. "Or written, I suppose."

The priest moved fluidly to block his view again. "You may write it down over there." He pointed to a lectern near the door which had a stack of paper and old-fashioned quill at the ready. "One of our prophets will look at it."

Rachel shrugged and made her way over to the lectern to write down the remnants.

"Why are they chained to the desk?" Anne asked, her curiosity getting the better of her.

Finn hissed at her, then quickly clamped his mouth shut, flushing red under his fingers.

The priest grimaced. "You made a vow to Serathon, Finn." The boy hung his head. "As for the prophets: they are of no concern to you." Despite his smile, there was a sharpness to his voice. "Finn will take care of you while you wait." He glared at the boy again. "Have rooms prepared, and for the love of Serathon, keep your vow this time."

With burning red ears, Finn bowed, nearly kissing the floor in the process.

Anne looked as if she was about to step in. Not wanting to risk her actions aggravating the situation, Matt grabbed her arm and shook his head. With a small sigh, Anne deflated, and they followed the boy from the room.

"That was strange," Samantha whispered.

Matt nodded. He suddenly had a good idea why Chay hadn't accompanied them. "Looks like we're staying the night."

Small surprise there.

The rest of the day passed in boredom. Their room was sparse but sufficient, and Finn provided them with whatever they asked for—apart from any prophecies. Several times he looked as if he was about to say something, but then seemed to remember his vow before he broke it. Matt passed the time by telling Anne all he knew about temple customs, pulling from the depth of his studies. Samantha leant against him, dozing a little, while Rachel, Fabian, and Ophelia chatted about Fabian's new school.

When night fell, no priest had come. Finn brought them dinner, then cleared the plates and dimmed the lights.

"This is going well," Fabian said.

Matt grinned and put a finger to his lips. For thirty minutes, he kept everyone quiet. When they didn't hear anything outside the door, he opened it and checked. The corridor was empty.

"Who wants to go on a midnight library date?"

"Sounds perfect," Samantha said, and gave his cheek a little kiss.

"Finally," Ophelia exclaimed. "I was about to go crazy."

They slipped out in the darkness. Everything was going well until they reached the end of the corridor. There, Finn sat slumped against the wall, half-asleep. When he heard their steps, his eyes flew open and he opened his mouth.

"Vow of silence," Matt reminded him.

He closed his mouth again but glared, then clenched his fist to knock it into the wall.

Ophelia snatched it out of the air and grinned. "Relax, Finny, we're just stretching our legs a little."

"Don't worry," Samantha said, a little kinder. "We're not here to start any trouble. We just want to know what's about to happen to our world."

Finn tore his hand free and crossed his arms, clearly intent in blocking their way. Matt shared a glance with Fabian over the boy's head, then they both grabbed one arm each and simply dragged him along.

"Maybe we should go back," Anne said.

"Don't be ridiculous." Ophelia linked her arm with hers. "We're just going to look at some scrolls."

Meanwhile, Samantha and Rachel had reached the library without attracting any further attention. They opened the door and waved everyone inside. "No priests, but they're still here," Samantha whispered.

Sure enough, the chained prophets were still sitting at the table. Most of them were resting their heads and slept while sitting, but one at the end of the table was still writing furiously by the light of a candle.

He looked up and Matt tensed, but instead of ringing the alarm, the prophet just stared. Then his lips moved. "...nothing but blight."

"That's our prophecy," Rachel exclaimed.

The prophet nodded once, his eyes suddenly glassy. "...the power to avert the doom. He'll have to spread his wings to escape the tomb. Above the flaming mountain, his hope will loom."

"Is that part of ours?" Fabian asked.

Rachel cocked her head. "Flaming mountain fits the volcanic eruption I saw. Could you repeat that?"

The man stared into nothingness, unmoving.

"You can't force prophecies!"

It took Matt a moment to realise the bright voice belonged to the temple novice. He clicked his tongue. "What will the priests say when they hear you broke your vow?"

Finn nearly bit his tongue off struggling between his duty to defend the temple and vow he'd made. To make things easier, Matt took off his belt and gagged him, while Fabian held his arms. "There, now you can deepen your devotion."

"Don't lose your pants," Samantha commented with a smirk, before taking Rachel's arm. "Come on, let's check the prophecies. He must've spoken the prophecy earlier for you to hear it in your dream, so it's already written down somewhere."

"Spread his wings, escape the tomb," Rachel repeated under her breath.

Anne threw a worried glance at Finn, then quickly followed the other girls.

Meanwhile, Ophelia waved her hand in front of the prophet. He didn't blink, staring right through her. Suddenly, the flame flickered, and he seemed to return to his previous state. "And so, it begins."

"What begins?" Fabian asked.

With Fabian's attention elsewhere, Finn freed himself from his grip, stumbled back, and ripped the belt off. Matt lunged at him, just as the boy's scream echoed through the halls. A moment later, Matt had knocked him out, but it was too late. He heard urgent steps in the corridor.

"Sam!" He dashed behind the shelves just as the door opened and a group of spear-bearing priests entered the library.

Samantha was at the end of a shelf with Rachel and Anne, arms full of prophecies. She shared a glance with Matt and pushed the scrolls into Anne's grip. "Quick, hide!"

Rachel and Anne ran deeper into the room while Samantha stepped towards Matt. "Let's hold them back."

He would've preferred for her to hide, too, but he knew no one else he'd rather have at his side. Determined, he reached for his sword, only for his hand to come up empty. "What...?" That had never happened before.

"Limited magic," Samantha reminded him.

"What now?"

Samantha drew her Torakh and nodded towards one of the tall mage light candelabras on the wall. "That could make a fine weapon."

"Love you." He kissed her cheek and grabbed the candelabra just in time to block the first attack.

The spear head didn't impress him—it was too round and thick to stab anything. But then, a narrow depression in the head lit up in red from the bottom to the tip, along with a crackling noise.

Matt ducked and swiped the candelabra at the priest's feet. The electric jolt from the spear hit the shelf instead, leaving a scorch mark, and the priest fell on his back. Eager to pin him down, Matt drove the candelabra into the stone. Its tips found grooves on the floor, barely missing the man's neck. The make-shift weapon shook from the impact, but not as much as the priest's throat. Matt was just about to retrieve his weapon when Samantha screamed behind him.

Panicked, he whirled around, only to see her crumpled on the floor, a priest standing over her. He raised his hand, ready to release his deadly energy, when something hard hit the small of his back. Electricity raced up and down his spine, and Matt blacked out.

Jan

While the others were off on fun adventures, Jan was stuck at home with his so-called mentor. After his extensive breakfast, he finally exhibited some signs of being a healer and asked Jan to show him the herbal beds. Over the summer, Samantha had grown plenty of herbs in the garden, but now autumn was knocking on the door, they looked a little sad.

"Is that all?" Leandres grumbled.

"Yep. And you can thank Sam for it. She's the garden witch in the house."

The old man side-eyed him. "Maybe I should teach her, then."

"Fine with me, but she can't heal." At least not without her flowers.

Leandres pulled a face. "So, you think just because you know some magic tricks you don't have to bother with the craft?"

"I'm training full-time to be a paramedic. I think that's plenty of craft, don't you?"

"Not in the slightest." Leandres shook his head and wiped his nose. "All you'll learn there is how to patch them up long enough for a real healer to take over."

Jan groaned. "Sure. But I can't study medicine. I don't have the right qualifications." And there was no way in hell he'd be able to go back to school, somehow pass with top marks, and get into medical school.

Leandres waved him off. "Modern bullshit. I'll teach you everything you need to know. Starting with how to grow the right herbs."

"And if I'm not interested?" Jan was still struggling to understand why he needed a mentor when he'd be doing just fine. Especially now he had Caspar's collection to draw from.

"I was told you're in dire need of a teacher. So, I'll stay right here until I deem your education finished."

"Right here? In the garden? Because I don't have room in the house." That wasn't quite true. There was still a guest room on his level—one he was reluctant to give to someone as unsavoury as Leandres.

Just then, Neve flew out of the house and hugged Jan's neck. While it'd had a nice cooling effect in summer, it was way too cold now. "Leandres can sleep in Neve's room."

Shuddering, Jan extricated himself from Neve's icy embrace. "Neve, your room..." The little snow witch had claimed the cellar, turning it into a winter wonderland. Jan smiled, an idea crossing his mind. "Actually, that's perfect. Yes, you can sleep in Neve's room." Leandres wouldn't last a day.

"Very well," the healer said, smiling at Neve. "Thank you, little one."

"Neve made new friend," the little witch told Jan proudly.

He patted her head. "How about you keep your new friend busy? I hear he wants to dig a hole in the garden or something. I have to go to my—apparently—bullshit training."

It was a busy day in the ambulance. As soon as they'd delivered one patient to the hospital, they were called out to the next incident. Between drunk hikers who'd fallen into a ravine, five alerts at the elderly home, and a pile-up on the access road, Jan had little time to think about his new teacher. By the end of his shift in the afternoon, he was bloodied and drained, having barely managed to keep the last patient alive.

Sleepwalking through the hospital, he ran into his fellow trainees. Today had been a theory day, but Jan's teachers and the active paramedics had agreed to cut his theory down to give him more time in the field.

"You look like shit!" Timothy, a tall lanky guy, called out. He held out his hand. "Tough day?"

"Don't you know it? How was... maths?" For a moment, Jan couldn't even remember what class he was supposed to have been in.

Another classmate, Ellie, grinned. "Yeah, you missed a test. Sad times, I know."

"So sad." Jan laughed.

Everyone at the hospital had welcomed him with open arms. Not because of his mother, but because they actually valued him as a colleague. For once, Jan could taste the sweet nectar of success. They all loved him. All but André—or as Jan called him: Mr Sourpuss.

Even now, he glowered at him instead of joining in with friendly banter. "Kinzel wants to see you," he muttered, making it sound as if Jan was in trouble.

"Don't worry," Ellie said. "It's just about the test. I think he's letting you do a take home version."

"Nice."

André snorted. "It's called cheating." He shuffled off, both hands in his pocket.

"Guess it didn't go too well for him?" Jan asked.

Timothy rolled his eyes. "That guy's just eaten alive by jealousy. And Kinzel. Hey, you free now?"

"Almost. I'll just clean up, check what Kinzel wants, and meet you at the bar?"

"You got it." They clasped hands once more, before his classmates left, and Jan headed to the bathrooms.

He was scrubbing his hands when the nearest stall opened and Robert came out. Jan groaned, but then remembered things had changed between them. "What are you doing here?"

Robert stared at him, wide-eyed. For a moment, it looked as if he was about to bolt, but then he headed to the sink to wash his hands. "Nursing school."

"Oh, really? You want to be a nurse?"

A few months ago, the prospect of seeing Robert every day would've annoy Jan, but now he tried to be a little more open. For Anne's sake—and maybe all of theirs, if Robert truly was a mage. He still couldn't believe it, but according to Samantha and Lucille, Robert had banished the banshees into paper, effectively removing them from Greenvalley.

Robert shrugged. "Yeah."

"That's cool." Something was off. Robert usually sought out his presence and babbled without any filter, ignoring all social cues. Now, he didn't even dare look him in the eye. "Soooo, magic, huh?"

"What about it?" Robert asked darkly. Before Jan could answer, he went into deflection mode. "You're still hot on that occultism trend, right?"

Jan frowned. Definitely weird. "Yeah, I guess I am." With a sigh, he considered what it must've been like to Robert. From what Lucille and Samantha had said, he'd looked shocked after the banishment, almost as if he'd had no idea what he'd been doing. "Look, if you're freaked out, that's perfectly normal. Fabian really struggled to come to terms with his powers back then."

"Fabian," Robert said in a strangely high voice. "What's he doing these days?"

The odd behaviour grated on Jan. "He's studying at the Citadel of Magic. He can control water, you know?"

Robert's lips stretched, and it took Jan a moment to identify the grimace as a smile. "You're so funny, Jan. Still a jokester, right?" He clapped Jan's shoulder, ready to leave.

Angrily, Jan caught his wrist. "It's not a joke, Robert." He let go almost immediately. "Fine, if you don't want to deal with your magic, don't. My mistake for thinking you'd be useful for once."

Robert's face fell, and he stared at the floor. "Well, maybe I am useless." Without another word, he slunk out of the bathroom.

Jan barely managed to contain his frustration, grabbing the sink so hard he almost ripped it from the wall. "A fluke," he told his mirror image. "It was just a fluke. Robert's not one of us. We don't need him."

After all, they were the Six, prophesied heroes with plenty of magical talents, even if all Jan could do was put his friends back together again. Though, according to his new teacher, he wasn't even good at that.

By the time Jan arrived back home, it was dark outside. He'd spent the evening at the bar with his classmates, telling tales from the call-outs he'd been on, and doing his make-up test with Ellie's help. It'd been fun, but now his house was strangely empty. Apparently, Matt and Samantha hadn't returned yet. He sent a message to the group chat and watched it remain unanswered. None of them had made it back.

At first, he tried to sleep but worrying about Anne and the others kept him awake. If only he knew where they'd gone. Maybe he could go to Hell and ask Balthasar. Jan snorted. "And what? Heal my way through the demons?"

He rubbed his face. Worrying about his friends wasn't the only thing keeping him awake. When he'd come home, the house had been quiet. Only the dirty plates showed any activity. He'd checked the couch and guest room, but hadn't found Leandres, which meant he'd either left or taken up Neve's ridiculous offer.

With a sigh, Jan got out of his bed again. Repulsive or not, he couldn't let the man freeze.

In order to keep the rest of the house mostly snow-free, he'd agreed to give Neve free rein of the cellar. As soon as Jan stepped on the stairs, the cold seeped into his bare feet and his breath formed little clouds. He rubbed his hands together as he descended into the depths of winter. He was just about to clear his throat when someone grabbed him from behind, putting pressure on his windpipe. His reflexes kicked in and he grabbed the attacker's arm, ready to throw him, but a wave of weakness washed over him.

As suddenly as the attack had started, it stopped. Jan fell to his knees and dropped into the snow. Groaning, he turned, still struggling to understand why he felt as if he'd run a marathon, but his attacker had lost interest. The light flickered on, revealing Neve and a frozen Leandres.

"No one hurts Jan," the little snow witch declared.

He dragged himself up, using the wall for support. "Be a dear and thaw him out. Just the upper body."

Neve looked a bit disappointed but followed his wishes.

As soon as he'd thawed out, Leandres huffed and rubbed his hands together. "You. Why are you sneaking around at night?"

"In my own home?" Jan asked, still dizzy. "I didn't want to be rude and wake you by turning the light on."

Leandres snorted. "What do you want?"

"Look. I'm sorry about earlier. You don't have to sleep down here. We actually have a guest room. It's warmer."

"You feeling bad?"

"Very," Jan admitted. He shook his head, trying to clear it, but to no avail. "What did you do to me?"

Leandres smirked. "Come here." He waited for Jan to drag himself closer before healing him. "Probably not what we should start with, but healing goes both ways."

"Both ways?" Jan's mouth dropped open when he finally understood. "You mean I could kill someone?"

"Oh, absolutely. If you can restart a heart, you can stop it."

"And that's allowed?" Feeling stronger, he backed away. Suddenly, his own powers terrified him.

Leandres looked at him, confused. "Who'd forbid it?"

"Well..." Jan rubbed his neck. Something jogged his mind, some kind of... "An oath. Do no harm or whatever it is."

"You're well in your right to make such a vow. Still, if I'm going to teach you, I'm going to teach you all of it. The good and the bad. You need to know what you're doing—and what you're capable of—before you accidentally do harm."

Jan swallowed hard. "I see. Um... look, I—Neve, you can thaw the rest of him—you don't have to sleep down here."

Once they were free of ice, Leandres shook out his legs. "I don't mind."

"It's freezing cold!"

"What doesn't kill you makes you stronger. Isn't that what you say here?"

"Yeah, but... What if it does kill you?"

Leandres smiled. "Let me worry about myself, boy, and you worry about you. Right now, you should get some sleep. We start early in the morning."

Rachel

At first, Rachel thought it was sheer luck the priests never found her and Anne, but then the shadows around them parted and Ophelia appeared looking scared. Her magic must've helped obscure them.

"They've taken Fabian," she whispered. "He just collapsed. What if he...?" Her eyes filled with tears.

Anne reached out and took her hand. "I'm sure he's fine."

Rachel wasn't quite so sure. Something about this temple had been off from the very beginning. They'd got the prophecy—or at least another part of it—but it might all be in vain if they didn't manage to make it back home.

"We just seem to attract murderous temples," Anne said, her voice on the verge of breaking.

Ophelia winced. "That's gods for you. It always ends in blood and slaughter."

The words shook something loose from Rachel, almost as if they'd been part of a prophecy once, too. "Let's see if we can find where they took the others and get out of here."

Chay had said he'd see them tomorrow. But would he see all of them? Or only Matt?

Concealed in Ophelia's shadows, they snuck to the library entrance. Everything seemed quiet—there were no priests guarding the library, and the prophets were still sleeping. All but one.

"There you are," the man said, looking right at them. "Don't worry, I won't call for the priests."

The girls looked at each other. They'd have to be stupid to believe him. Rachel put a finger to her lips and stepped out of the shadows alone. "Why not?" she said, her voice calm and steady.

The prophet smiled sadly. "We're not exactly friends."

Her gaze fell on his chains. "I can see that."

He followed her line of sight and snorted. "Ah, that. No, I'm afraid that's always been a sign of my servitude for Serathon. It symbolises an anchor against the madness that comes from seeing the future."

Rachel shivered, barely withstanding the urge to hug herself. "So, you're saying you're mad?"

"That's what the priests say, but I'm not the one who lost his way." He gave her another sad smile. "I prophesied the end of this world and what it means for this temple."

"Guess they didn't like the apocalypse?"

"Oh, they didn't mind that. But they hated when I told them not all would be welcomed in Serathon's halls. In fact, very few will be."

"Oh." Rachel didn't know enough about Serathon to grasp the whole meaning, but she gathered it was their version of afterlife reward. "Is Serathon a picky god?"

The prophet chuckled. "You're a funny one. When madness becomes greater than devotion, Serathon will come from his halls and judge his flock. May all the righteous live to see a new day. May all the unbalanced know nothing but decay."

"I assume madness has been ruling this temple for a while?"

"A long while."

"You know, if you want to flee, I could try to pick the lock," Ophelia said, releasing her shadows. "Enrico taught me." She had her arms crossed, as if to protect herself while she divulged this unsavoury talent.

The prophet nodded. "It's not flight I seek, but assistance of the righteous. Please."

"Aren't you afraid?" Anne asked.

"Fear is stronger when the outcome is unknown. I've seen what happens, so I accept my fate with knowledge and devotion."

Ophelia knelt before him and picked the lock. "There, now you can accept your fate standing."

Rachel faced the door and was hit by a sense of foreboding. "Shadows please."

As darkness clad her again, she stepped outside.

Screams echoed through the night, followed by ragged breathing. Somewhere in the distance, weapons rang against each other. But the worst was the sight at her feet: a priest lay face down on the ground, blood pooling around him.

The prophet joined her by her side. "Serathon has arrived. Now, the judgement will begin."

Chay

The clouds had lifted and Chay could see the temple at the top of the spire rising in front of the moon. A reddish moon, fitting for the madness which would unfold. He'd known it'd happen tonight, but he'd hoped he'd be mistaken. As always, the vision had proved true.

"They won't die," he muttered, unable to tear his gaze away.

"You're the one looking out the window, not us," Balthasar said.

Chay hadn't noticed the demon approaching. "They can't," he repeated.

Sometimes, a world was doomed, and there was nothing he could do. That was the case for Ylvadin. Still, he'd brought the Six here. A gamble. They'd featured in no vision he'd received of Serathon's vengeance. Not because they shouldn't be here, but because nothing they would do would affect the fate of this world.

He was relying on his other visions, the ones of later battles and challenges. But fate was poor protection against the randomness of death. Caspar's demise had shown him that. By bringing them here, he might have exposed them to unnecessary risks, ones that didn't just put their lives but those of everyone in jeopardy. If only he could finally learn to trust the future.

"You mean you still need them?" Balthasar needled him relentlessly.

"Let it be," Chay said, with a sigh. He glanced at Lucille and Iyaga at the dinner table, excitedly questioning each other about demon and human life. "She seems nice."

Balthasar snorted. "Nice isn't greedy."

He had a point. "Please. Could you try for me?"

Balthasar pouted, but his usual composure kicked in quickly, and soon, his face gave nothing away. Instead of promising, he left Chay at the window and strolled to the table. He ran his long fingers across Iyaga's neck. The Archdemon of Greed sat up straight, her eyes widening, lips parted.

Chay heard his whisper through the entire room, "Time for dessert."

Judging by Lucille's suddenly tense posture, she could feel the power of Lust in the air. Unfortunately, it was the only sin that unfolded. Balthasar took Iyaga's hand and led her to the bedroom.

Small blessings, Chay thought when he heard Iyaga moaning barely a minute later.

Lucille's expression spoke of her misery. "Do I really have to hear this?"

"I'm so sorry."

She stood up and joined him at the window. Not that the few metres made much difference. "Why does it matter how greedy she is? I like her like this."

"I like her, too. And more importantly, she likes me. Or rather, she likes Balthasar and is following his lead. The problem is, if she doesn't fully embrace her sin, she'll have no standing in the Council of Seven. We need a strong archdemon on our side."

Lucille swallowed. "I'm almost afraid to ask, but why do we need an archdemon?"

"You'll see."

Pouting, she stared out the window. "What's going to happen to Ylvadin? You said the world is ending but there's still time. So why don't we try save it?"

"Believe me, I've tried, but Serathon's influence is too strong. The people here trust him with their life and soul. They believe he'll raise them to his side—the whole 'reward the believers, punish the non-believers' shtick priests love."

"But he won't?"

"Oh, he will. It's just not many stayed true enough in their heart. Frighteningly few will be rewarded—they all think it'll be them, their minds already lost to the madness. But even taking them out of the equation, people will die. All of them. Disregarding a few refugees, Ylvadin will cease to exist."

"Right." Lucille hugged herself, her face more anxious than before. "So, it's judgement day and my friends are right in the middle of the action?"

Chay looked up at the spire again. A dark cloud seemed to have settled around the temple. "They'll survive. They must."

Fabian

Fabian came to, groaning. His entire body felt as if he'd been punched and kicked while on the ground. He turned but his arms protested. He blinked, trying to clear the brain fog, tugging at his arms, but no matter what he tried, they wouldn't move freely.

Suddenly, everything came back to him. The late-night adventure. The priests attacking. Their electric spears.

He struggled to sit up. Something was holding his arms back, severely constricting his movements. After a moment, he recognised the cold bite of metal around his wrists.

"You've got to be kidding me."

Someone had chained him to the wall. Not only that, they'd also removed his clothes, changing him into a long grey shirt. To top things off, he was alone in—what he assumed was—a cell.

Fabian felt a panic attack coming on. He'd lived through a lot of things in his barely even twenty years but chained to the wall in a medieval-like dungeon surely took the cake. What was next? Were they going to torture them?

Just then, he heard a voice crying out in pain.

"Sam!"

The scream had clearly been his best friend. She screamed a second time, only to have her voice cut off. Fabian lurched forward and threw up his meagre dinner.

"I guess—" The boy from last night—Finn—was in the doorway, a tray of food in his hands. He bit his tongue, as if he'd just remembered his vow of silence, but then sighed and set down the tray. "You probably won't need this right now."

"You," Fabian huffed.

"I mean, I'd eat it if I were you. It's probably the last time they'll feed you. Some didn't even want to give you this much. As punishment, of course." Now he'd decided to break his vow the boy's chatter was nearly unstoppable.

Fabian was struggling to make sense of his situation. "Punishment for what? You're the ones who attacked us."

"You broke into the library of prophecies," Finn said.

"Yeah, okay, that was a stupid idea," Fabian admitted, "but that's no reason to murder your guests. I thought we were safe after having some of your food." Hadn't Matt said something about that when he'd urged them to eat and drink upon arrival?

Finn shrugged. "Serathon is the God of Madness. Besides, you're still alive. Can't say the same for everyone."

"Who?" Fabian barked. "Did you kill my friends?" He felt the water rise in him, ready to lash out.

As if he'd sensed it, Finn took a step back. "Not your friends. They're alive. For now. I... You shouldn't have come."

"Yeah, no kidding." What were they thinking, heading into a world about to end? If the people here knew their fate, it was no small wonder they were all going a little crazy. "Can't say I'm a big fan of your god. I've yet to see something good come from madness."

Finn rolled his eyes. "You're as blind as all the non-believers."

"Ah, right. I guess you're simply better than me?"

"Of course. I serve Serathon."

Fabian nearly laughed. It was clear to him the boy didn't have the slightest idea what he was talking about. "And everyone who doesn't serve Serathon is automatically..."

"Doomed," Finn said, with an eagerness that reminded Fabian of a young Samantha.

"Amazing. And you believe that nonsense?"

Finn gasped. "Serathon's teachings aren't nonsense. They're the truth borne from madness. But it's a fine line. Only the most devoted can step into the madness and escape unscathed. You can't fear the unknown.

If you're brave and willing to give Serathon your life and your mind, he'll... he'll..." His righteous outburst stopped. Finn cast his gaze downwards, wringing his hands. "He'll reward me."

"Giving your life, huh?" The speech had left Fabian rather unimpressed. "Are you that eager to die?"

"My life belongs to Serathon," Finn said, though he couldn't quite hide the fear in his voice.

Something else was going on. Something that had put the living fear into the boy. He wasn't just talking about giving his life theoretically, but as if it were a forgone conclusion—and imminent.

"How long has it belonged to Serathon?" Fabian asked, trying to project calm.

"I was given to the temple a few days after I was born."

Fabian couldn't help himself. He felt sorry for the boy. He'd never known anything outside the temple, and had his whole life devoted to a mad god before he was even old enough to speak. "What's going on here, Finn?"

The boy shook, his eyes widening as he struggled to contain his fear. "Serathon's will."

"And that is..."

"Not your concern," Finn snapped. "Now eat your food or don't. I have... duties."

He fled before Fabian could level another question at him. The door slammed shut, and Finn's rapid steps ran down the corridor.

It wasn't long before the screaming started.

Matt

Matt woke up angry. He didn't mind that someone had tried to kill him or injure him, or had even thought chaining him to the wall was a good idea. But they'd separated him from Samantha. They'd dared to lay a hand on Samantha. And now they were screaming outside the walls.

Matt stared into the darkness, letting the anger grow. He tugged hard on his left hand and ripped it from the wall, chain and all. He repeated the gesture with his right, before slamming both wrists against the stone to break the chains. It hurt, but the pain only fuelled him further.

The temple may have blocked most of his magic, but it didn't siphon away his strength. He glared at the locked door and kicked it hard enough to blast it off its hinges. It hit something on the other side—something soft and squishy that groaned. Matt didn't care. He stepped on the door.

Looking around, he found himself in a torch-lit corridor and utter mayhem. A priest jostled past, screaming as if there was no tomorrow. Another was swallowed by shadows, who cut off his legs, then made short work of the rest of him. Matt looked down but, if anything, the shadows seemed to flee from his feet. They weren't interested in him—only the priests.

When he looked up again, he saw two priests enter a room further down, spears in hand. Curious, Matt followed them. He'd hoped to find one of his friends, but an unfamiliar woman huddled in a corner. She wore the same long grey shirt Matt had found himself in.

One of the priests dragged her to her feet. "Your time has come to face Serathon," he said.

The woman looked around wildly. "But I was to be pardoned. I made a deal. I—"

"Sinners won't be pardoned," the other priest said.

While one held her, exposing her neck, the other readied his spear. He was about to stab her when Matt grabbed the end of the blasted weapon, tore it from the priest's hand, broke it on his knee, then broke the priest's neck. The other priest dropped the woman and ran for the door, where a hungry shadow swallowed him whole. Warily, Matt watched the shadows, but as before, they retreated.

The woman fell to her knees, tugging at his shirt. "You saved me. You stopped a great injustice."

"I don't care," Matt growled. "You could've murdered the high priest himself for all I care. Now, run."

Whatever had come over the temple was only going to grow stronger. They had the missing part of the prophecy. Now he had to find his friends—most importantly, Samantha—and get out of here.

The urgency deep in his bones, Matt continued down the corridor, but every cell he came across had already been opened, its inmate killed in cold blood. Panic pumped in his veins as the number of corpses grew—not to mention the actual slaughter going on in the corridor as priests ran for their life. Abruptly, he turned and ran the other way.

On this side, the cells were still locked, and he felt a surge of hope. He kicked them open, confirmed they didn't hold any of his friends, and continued on. The actual prisoners meant little to him, though he was surprised how many the priests had deemed unworthy of freedom and decided to murder.

Faster and faster, he opened cells, his hope fraying with every disappointment, when suddenly—

"Matt?"

Exhausted, he fell to his knees in front of Samantha, crushing her to his chest. She protested feebly at first, but was soon crying with relief.

"I thought—" Matt started.

He let go and quickly freed her from her chains. Unlike him, her skin carried the blemishes of their fight. One arm was cut and bore a burn mark, and her face was bruised where she must've fallen. Like every other prisoner, she was wearing a long shirt—which meant someone had touched and undressed her.

"I'm going to kill them."

Samantha cradled his face, despite the visible pain in her shoulders. "No, no. We have to find the others and get out of here. Please."

Matt took a deep breath, letting the anger evaporate with his breath. When he felt like he was in control of his feelings again, he nodded. "Let's get you out of here."

Rachel

Of all places, the library seemed the safest. Rachel and the others kept the doors closed, hoping the corpse out front would deter any priests from seeking refuge with them. Rachel had read books about the purge and watched it play out on TV, but they'd been fictitious. Why couldn't this world just end peacefully, or if not peacefully then at least without their supreme god killing everyone?

"Your prophecy came true," Anne said to the prophet.

Her voice was shaky, but she seemed to be holding herself together just fine. A few hours with the Hanna priests in Hescaryn had done wonders for her resilience.

The prophet slumped against one of the shelves. "They always do. It's the curse of seeing."

Rachel was sure Chay had said something similar once. "Then what's the point? Why see the future if you can't change it?"

It was a paradox that had gnawed on her for a while. She knew Chay's visions of the future were incomplete—he saw too much too often and had to sift through tons of unimportant detail to get to the vital bits. Rachel had no idea how he did it, but to know whatever he saw would happen exactly the way it did? Why have visions at all?

The prophet smiled. "Why live if you're going to die, anyway? Even with zero chance of survival we cling to life, drinking as much of it as we can before the well dries up. Prophecies are warnings, not instructions. You can't stop the future from happening but you can shape your present."

"Look, as much as I appreciate this philosophy session," Ophelia said, "how are we going to get out? Because everyone's gone mad. Literally. Serathon has turned against his devotees. It's only a matter of time until he comes after us, too."

"You have nothing to fear from Serathon," the priest said.

Rachel crossed her arms. "But we have everything to fear from his priests."

If what they'd seen outside was any indication, the priests had gone just as mad as their god. They could very well decide to kill everyone to curry favour.

"There's a way out," the prophet said. "Follow me."

He led them past the other prophets, all deep in prayer, accepting of the fate they knew was coming. Deeper into the library they went, making Rachel wonder if there was a back door. Instead, the prophet stopped at one of the shelves and pushed it aside, revealing a narrow tunnel.

"It used to be an emergency escape for if the library caught fire. It leads straight back to the entrance hall," he explained.

"But what about the others?"

"Let's just hope they're already there," Ophelia said. "If not, we'll get help. We have two archdemons and a battle-hardened half-demon in the village."

Rachel appreciated her pragmatism. They didn't always see eye to eye—not after her cult had tried to sacrifice Rachel—but she liked that there was no bullshitting with Ophelia. The girl knew how to hold her own in a crisis.

"The important thing is we've got the prophecy," Rachel said. "We need to bring it back to Ashuan. The others..." There was no way Chay would've let them enter this temple if he'd seen them all dying here. "They'll be fine."

They squeezed into the tunnel, Ophelia taking the lead and the prophet bringing up the rear.

"This prophecy of yours," the prophet said quietly. "It's important, isn't it, to willingly enter a world in decline for a fate you can't change."

"You said there was hope," Rachel reminded him. Unlike Chay's visions, the prophecy wasn't as clear-cut about the future. "There might be someone who can stop all this."

"Ah, the boy who'll have to spread his wings. You're right. Your apocalypse isn't guaranteed."

Rachel let out a shaky breath. There was a fighting chance. "How do we know who he is? Will he? I mean, there are eight billion people in our world, roughly half of them male. It could be anyone."

The prophet whistled, as if he couldn't quite imagine that many people in a single world. "Prophecies come to those who need them. This one came to you because it's within your power to find the saviour. You have to look for the signs. It'll all make sense one day."

"One day... You make it sound like we have all the time in the world."

"Compared to Ylvadin, you do. Use it wisely. Never ignore the prophecy."

Rachel sighed. The priests had ignored the prophecy given to them and now they were paying the ultimate price. If only there was a hint as to where they should start looking, instead of more and more riddles.

"We'll cling to life for as long as we can," she whispered.

The prophecy was a problem for tomorrow. Today, they had to survive this apocalypse.

Jan

Jan regretted taking up Leandres' offer of teaching when the old man woke him at four in the morning to set up a new herb garden. Frost covered the leaves and the soil was half frozen as Jan laboured away. Meanwhile, Leandres stood next to him and did nothing but complain.

"It needs to be bigger. Deeper. Just dig, boy."

Despite the chilly morning, Jan was soon covered in sweat, but when the sun finally came up and the frost turned to dew, he was ready to plant the herbs Leandres had gathered overnight.

Jan had never been much of a gardener. He couldn't even keep a pot plant alive. If it'd been up to him, he'd simply have laid some turf and tried not to kill the existing trees. That's why he hadn't really minded when Matt had approached him with his bogus idea of gifting the garden to Samantha. It'd all worked out in the end.

"You need to leave more space between the plants. They need air to breathe."

"Whatever."

The plants looked perfectly fine to Jan. They were going to die in the next frost, anyway. Unless Leandres was planning on teaching him how to heal plants. He half-expected this was nothing but a futile exercise meant to teach him a lesson.

The old man clicked his tongue. "Why can't you be more careful?"

"Because I'm tired," Jan snapped. "And they're just plants." Really not worth getting up several hours before his alarm clock and working himself to the bone over.

"Just plants? These herbs will help you save lives. If you don't treat them with care now, how can you hope to make medicine from them?"

Jan froze. "I thought you didn't care for all this modern medicine stuff."

"Herbal medicines are hardly modern."

"Fair," Jan mumbled. He tried to treat the next plant with more care, but his fingers were stiff and he kept yawning. To keep himself awake, he asked, "So, what exactly will I be learning?" All this had surprisingly little to do with healing magic.

Leandres counted out his answer on his fingers. "I'll teach you everything about healing herbs, mixing all kinds of strengthening potions, diagnostics, aftercare, and of course, healing itself."

The one thing Jan was interested in seemed to be the least of his priorities. Furthermore, the programme sounded daunting. "Um... I guess I should tell you that I'm not particularly good at learning."

"Then you're probably not going to be a particularly good healer, either."

Jan gulped. Motivational speeches truly weren't his mentor's style. "What I was trying to say is I'm more of a practical guy. Like, give me something I can do with my hands, and I'm good. The rest..." He stopped when Leandres stared pointedly at the herbal bed. "Hey, I did a good job here!"

This guy was seriously starting to annoy him. If he wanted to teach an herbal witch, he should've picked one.

Leandres snorted. "You need both if you want to be a successful healer: practical craft and theoretical knowledge."

This was starting to sound a lot worse than redoing his high school diploma and studying medicine. "Okay, but why? Can't you simply heal the thread of life?" Maybe the concept was unknown to Leandres.

"Why take care of the symptoms when you can just grab the defibrillator instead? Honestly, boy, do you use an anvil to hammer in nails, too? Healing is a fine art, not a blunt tool."

Jan didn't particularly care about art or finesse. All he wanted to do was be dependable when disaster struck again. "If the person's alive, who cares?"

"And you?" Leandres prompted. "How many people will you be able to help when your powers are exhausted after healing one?"

That was an aspect Jan hadn't thought about. So far, he'd pushed and pushed, ignoring pain and every other side effect to get the job done. But he remembered bringing Fabian back from the brink of death and how bone-dead tired he'd been after that. If he'd had to care for anyone else then, they would've died. The blunt hammer approach was good in a single emergency, but in every other situation, he wouldn't last the night. And he had a feeling those situations would become more and more frequent.

The next herb he planted, he handled with much more care.

Still, one more thing nagged at him. "How are they going to survive out here? It'll be winter before long."

Leandres gave him a toothy grin. "Good thing you're living with a talented witch, isn't it? Speaking of her, you wouldn't know where she is?"

Where indeed? None of his friends had returned last night. And that could only mean one thing: they were in deep trouble.

Fabian

The prolonged position against the wall was making Fabian's shoulders ache. He had no idea how much time had passed or what was happening behind the walls. The screams had died down, as if everyone else was already dead, only now and then, someone ran past his door or there were distant calls. The silence was almost worse. What if everyone was already dead, and he was doomed to die abandoned and locked away in a cell? He tested the strength of the chains again, but all it did was make his shoulders hurt even more. Maybe if he could get his wrists wet enough...

The door opened, and Finn reappeared. Instead of food, he'd acquired one of the electric spears. He looked over his shoulder, closed the door, and pointing his weapon at Fabian.

While Fabian often erred on the side of caution, he didn't believe he was here to kill him. "Who did you steal that from?"

"Answer my questions or I'll use it on you."

Fabian raised an eyebrow. It didn't sound like he was in any real danger here.

"The priests say it's your fault, so why shouldn't I kill you?"

"Because you know this has nothing to do with me or my friends. Besides, you don't want that."

Finn bristled. "Why not?"

Fabian almost laughed. "Because you're not a crazy killer who mistakes devotion for fanaticism."

Instead of refuting him, Finn said, "How would you know?" His voice dipped slightly, and he took a shaky breath.

"Because if you were, you'd have killed me already." Fabian softened his approach. "And you're fifteen. You've still got your whole life ahead of you."

Finn swallowed and shook his head. "I don't. Everyone's dying. It was prophesied. Serathon is judging us. He'll bring the devoted to his side and drown the rest in darkness. The shadows..." He had to swallow again. "The shadows are leaving me alone. That means I served Serathon true and justly. He'll let me into his halls." He looked up at Fabian, his gaze harsh again. "Answer!"

"Was there a question?"

Fabian mulled his words over. He wasn't a huge fan of religion—in his opinion, it caused more problems than it solved. But his girlfriend was a devoted follower of Ishtar, and though her experience had been abysmal, her faith was unwavering. He wouldn't get through to Finn by telling him to disregard his god, no matter how mad and bloodthirsty they seemed.

"I don't know enough about Serathon to pass judgement. Maybe you're right and he'll welcome you into his halls with open arms. I hope so, but if not... Look, for me, there are too many open questions. I don't believe in life after death, but I do believe in life before death. And if you stay in this temple, in this world, you won't get to live that life. And maybe your god will reward you or maybe he won't. But there's nothing you can do about that. And you'll still never be older than fifteen."

Finn seemed to hang onto his every word. He could see the hunger for life in the boy's eyes, one that had been so limited and constricted until now. His world might have been on fire, but he wasn't ready to go up in flames just yet.

"I don't want to die." His voice was finally breaking. "But what choice do I have? My life belongs to Serathon. Surely, he knows what's best for me? What he wants me to be?"

Fabian wished he knew what to say, but he was out of his depth—just like always. "Maybe... Maybe your god sent us here for that reason?" The thought that some foreign entity had any influence on his life made Fabian's skin crawl, but the boy seemed hooked. "I'm just saying. What if our presence is all part of his plan? Maybe he wants you to come with us and spread his teachings in a better, safer place?"

What Fabian really wanted was to get him out of the obvious death trap he'd found himself in. To leave him here after seeing the innocence in his eyes... Fabian couldn't do it. Not that he was in any position to leave, with his arms chained to the wall.

"How do I know that's what he wants?"

Now that was a question Fabian could answer. "Listen to your heart, Finn. Your god gave you free will, didn't he? What do you think is right?"

The grip on his spear tightened. For a split-second, Fabian worried he'd kill him after all, but then Finn dropped the weapon, tears streaming down his face, and started to unchain him.

A few minutes later, Fabian and Finn came to a skidding stop in the temple's foyer, arriving there at the same time as Matt and Samantha.

Samantha was instantly all over them. "Oh, gosh, you're alive!"

"So are you." They hugged quickly. Fabian pointed at Finn. "He's coming with us."

Matt shrugged. "Sure." He threw Fabian a bundle of clothes.

While Fabian gratefully slipped into the pants, Matt regarded the spear in Finn's hand. "Can you fight with that thing? Because our path might be ... hindered."

He pointed towards the row of priests blocking the way out. Voices raised in prayer, they were pushing every priest who tried to flee back into the shadows.

"Lovely." Fabian sighed.

A fixture on the wall started shaking. Dust shook free. Then the stone itself moved aside, revealing Ophelia's head.

"Lia!" Fabian pulled her out of the hidden pathway. "And there's Rachel and Anne, too." And the priest from the library.

They looked like they'd climbed through a sea of dust covered in cobwebs, but none of them bore any wounds.

Ophelia slung her arms around his waist and hugged him so tight it hurt. "I was so scared about you."

"Same." He kissed her hair, glad no one had died in the madness. At least, so far.

"Everyone's here, good," Matt announced. "Let's get out, then."

"You don't want to leave us so soon, do you?" The High Priest called out, interrupting his prayer.

Matt stepped forward. Despite bearing no weapon, he oozed confidence and danger. "You seem a little busy, so I'm sure you don't mind us taking off and leaving you to it. Happy dying or whatever."

"No one will leave this temple." The High Priest's gaze fell on Finn and the prophet. "And certainly not any of my acolytes or prophets."

Seeing the boy's determination waver, Fabian put a hand on Finn's shoulder. "You're doing the right thing."

The prophet joined Matt, proudly raising his chin. "Let them go. They don't belong here. Their fate will lead them somewhere else."

"Then they shouldn't have come."

Matt clenched his fists and rolled his neck. "Let's stop talking and end this quickly. Preferably before the shadows swallow everything."

"As you wish." The High Priest took a step back and his row of priests advanced. Each bore a spear, their tips crackling. "Serathon, lend us your favour against the unbelievers."

Fabian swallowed but took a fighting stance. While the temple may have been blocking most of his magic, it couldn't completely cut his connection to water. His gaze darted to the basin in front of the giant Serathon statue, and the water rose to his command. He felt it struggle and tugged a little harder, feeding all his fear and anger into it.

The priests had almost reached Matt and the prophet when the entire temple groaned. Fabian looked around. The water splashed back into the basin. As though it was the literal last drop in the barrel, a crack splintered through the podium beneath the basin. Stone gnashed and suddenly, the giant statue tipped forwards.

"Watch out!" Samantha screamed.

Serathon toppled and crashed to the ground. The impact was powerful enough to drive them all to their knees as clouds of dust robbed them of their sight.

Coughing, Fabian scrambled to his feet. "Is everyone okay?"

There were murmurs of assent from just about everyone, but before he could count the voices, he saw the crackle of electricity in the air. He was about to throw himself back on the ground when someone jumped up and blocked the assault.

Finn groaned, the force of the attack driving him back.

Matt stepped in to catch him, then took the spear. "Good job. I'll take over now. Everyone, out! I'll keep the rest busy."

"Rest?" Fabian asked, but then he saw it. The dust had lifted just enough to show the giant statue had taken out most of the priests who'd come at them. Fabian swallowed. "Yeah, I think Serathon's made his will clear."

Coincidence or not, he wasn't going to waste his time debating divine intervention. He helped Ophelia and Anne up, while Rachel was already running towards the door.

"Matt." Samantha looked hesitant to follow suit. There were still a handful of priests, including the High Priest, rising from the dust.

"Go! I can't fight if I have to worry about you!"

"I'll stand with him," the prophet said. "Serathon will judge my worth. No one else."

Samantha sighed, but she nodded, and she, Fabian, and the others followed Rachel.

Matt handed the spear to the prophet and punched the nearest priest in the face. Bones broke as he disarmed him, then used his own weapon against him. One down. Many more to go.

The others ran for the door. Two priests saw them and pivoted into their path. One stabbed his spear at Ophelia, who evaded it, but knocked into Anne, making her stumble and fall. Another saw his chance and grabbed for her, when a shadow opened beneath him and cut off half his leg.

As Finn helped Anne up, Fabian drew on his dwindling water powers to push the first priest away. With sheer luck, he fell right into the next shadow. He turned, eager to see the last of this place, when he noticed Rachel and Samantha struggling with the door.

Rachel let go and faced them, her face ashen. "It won't budge. Serathon's locked the temple down. We'll all be judged now."

Lucille

The snow glistened in the morning sun, while the spires were clad in silvery clouds. It was a beautiful but cold day. Lucille's fingers were freezing as she scooped snow into a bowl for a cup of tea—certainly not the kind of activity she'd ever thought she'd have to do, but at least it was a chance to get out of the house.

Bracing herself, she returned and hung the pot over the fire she'd lit with her magic. Chay was still asleep in the chair by the window, and by the lack of sound from the bedroom, so were the archdemons.

As if the thought had summoned him, the door opened, and Balthasar stepped out, dressed immaculately as always, not a hair out of place. "Good morning."

"Morning. Did you sleep well?" Lucille wanted to slap herself. Why was she asking the Archdemon of Lust about anything sleep related?

His eyes took on a glint that made her feel hotter than the fire in front of her. "Excellently. Are you making tea?"

"We'll see." She would've preferred coffee, but of course they hadn't packed for an overnight trip. Or any kind of trip.

Meanwhile, Balthasar had found Chay asleep. "Would you look at that? Our little house prophet is still wandering the Realm of Dreams."

"Hopefully he doesn't wake up with yet another apocalyptic vision."

Balthasar snorted. "You think he has any other type of dream?" It was a strangely fond sentiment.

Lucille regarded the archdemon a little closer. During the last year, Balthasar had tested and tried to kill them multiple times. Now he had what he wanted, he seemed almost docile. As if all those assaults hadn't been personal, just a necessary consequence.

"May I ask why you let him tell you what to do?"

As expected, he raised an eyebrow. "I'm most certainly not letting him do anything." With another fond look at Chay, he admitted, "I just learnt long ago it'd be beneficial for me to listen to what he says. I wouldn't be the archdemon without his help."

Lucille startled. "What? Are you saying Chay planned this?"

"You'll find out quickly Chay plans everything. If he can. But it's not that easy. Though he can see the future, he can't change it. Neither of us can. Knowing it just allows him—and through him, me—to use events for personal gain. You could compare it to the Ashuan stock market. I can't prevent the stock prices from falling or rising, but knowing it'll happen, I can invest in the right ones."

"You know your way around our stock market?"

"It's an amusing past-time."

"Must be the greed in your blood."

Balthasar grinned. "Possibly." He paused to listen. "Hmm, sounds like the real Miss Greed is awakening."

Iyaga came out of the bedroom, clad in nothing but a sheer robe and leant into Balthasar. He wasted no time and kissed her with unbridled passion.

Lucille coughed. "Tea water."

"Why don't you make us all a cup, darling?" Balthasar said, laughing. He extracted himself from Iyaga and nudged Chay awake.

The half-demon started, eyes wide in confusion. His gaze settled on Balthasar and he relaxed again. "It's you."

"Yep. Also, it's morning, and this world is still in existence."

"I knew it would be," Chay mumbled.

"Could I also have a cup of tea?" Iyaga asked.

Lucille looked at the shelf above her. "Of course, I... Oh, there's only three cups."

"In that case, I'll share with Balthasar." Iyaga threw a smitten look at the other archdemon.

Balthasar grimaced, and Chay raised a hand to his mouth, clearly hiding a chuckle. Lucille was confused.

As soon as Iyaga went outside for her morning toilet, she asked: "Are you sure she's the Archdemon of Greed?" Malcolm wouldn't have been caught dead offering to share anything.

"Positive," Chay said, with a sigh.

Balthasar rolled his eyes and spread his arms, before sarcastically declaring, "Welcome to my world."

Despite the sun standing high in the sky, Lucille's friends still hadn't returned from their mission. She was both bored and worried. Chay was much the same, staring at the spire, as if his will could crumble it.

After breakfast, Balthasar and Iyaga had spent the hours back in bed, much to Lucille's chagrin, but now they were talking and Lucille couldn't help listening.

"Are you finally going to tell me what this is all about?" Iyaga asked.

"You'll have to ask Chay, not me. I'm just passing time."

There were a few more kissing noises, which would fuel Lucille's nightmares for a long time, but this time, Iyaga didn't let herself be distracted so easily. "Why are you always with the Seer?"

"We're partners."

"But why? You're an archdemon," she said it as if Balthasar's choice of partner was beneath him.

"And I won't be archdemon for long if I ignore his visions." He kissed her some more, then said, "These are unique times, which require unique methods. There will be a time when all the deadly sins will have to unite behind one cause. Chay will lead us—in counsel. He's not taking the throne, if you're worried about that," Balthasar said. "I agree with his course of action, so I'm pledging Lust to his cause."

Lucille checked with Chay. The half-demon was clearly listening, too. He gave her a little shrug when he noticed her gaze, seemingly confirming Balthasar's claims.

Interesting, she thought, wondering what use Chay saw in a united Council of Seven.

"If it's for Hescaryn's gain, it'll be my duty to pledge Greed to his cause as well," Iyaga whispered, quickly followed by a moan.

"Are you so keen to give up the power bestowed to you?" Balthasar growled. "Where can I find that Greed you want to share with him?"

"There's only one thing I want," Iyaga said, sounding more forceful than before. "You."

Lucille shared another look with Chay. In her opinion, Iyaga was as far removed from Greed as demonly possible. Had the magic chosen wrongly? Or was it always random? Did it matter? How important was it for Hell's stability to have seven archdemons who truly encapsulated their sins?

Chay jerked his head to the door and stood. "It's time."

Lucille followed him outside, eager to get away from the sounds now coming from the room. "Are you going to tell me why you kept me here?"

"I will, because I need you to do me a little favour."

Half an hour later, Chay and Lucille were outside, watching the spire. Dark clouds had gathered around the top, obscuring the temple. After what Chay had told her, Lucille had been worrying endlessly—grateful she was outside the massacre happening at lofty heights—but worried, all the same.

"Did you see Balthasar?" Iyaga came out, looking around. "He said he was just stepping out quickly?"

"Balthasar?" Lucille asked, her voice a little squeaky. "Um... he went up to the temple. He was wondering what was taking them so long."

Sure enough, they could see Balthasar climbing the spire high above them. A moment later, the clouds swallowed him.

"Without telling me?" Iyaga said, her tone offended.

"He told us he was getting bored. He probably wants to find out what the priests of Serathon get up to in their chambers when their god's not looking."

Iyaga's pretty face distorted in anger. "While I'm right here?"

A shiver ran down Lucille's spine that had nothing to do with the icy air around them. So far, Iyaga had seemed so innocent and lovely, but her ire was a stark reminder there was no such thing as a harmless demon.

"His lust knows no boundaries," Chay said, a note of pity in his voice.

Lucille caught a green shimmer from the corner of the eye. Iyaga was glowing slightly. Her eyes were as unforgiving and sharp as flint. "He's mine. Mine alone." Then she vanished.

A moment later, the real Balthasar stepped out from behind the house where Lucille had hidden his presence with an illusion. "Was there a reason for these theatrics?"

Chay grinned smugly. "We just woke her greed."

Balthasar rolled his eyes. "Great. All she wants is me."

"To think, two years of drama class comes down to this," Lucille sighed. "This had better be worth it." She still didn't understand the importance of Chay's plan or why he seemed so pleased with himself.

"Believe me. If it wasn't utterly necessary, I wouldn't have asked."

Samantha

Samantha tried to unravel the magic that held the doors locked again, but if it was a spell, it was one far beyond her skills. Brute force didn't help, either, not that any of them were strong enough to try.

Unfortunately, Matt was still locked in battle with the priests. He'd managed to acquire one of the spears, but was clearly inexperienced at wielding the weapon. Reflex had him swiping and blocking, when he should've been dodging and stabbing, even using his fist to land a blow instead. Though he was physically stronger, there were too many priests—and the spots of shadow around him continued to grow.

The shadows were both a curse and boon. While they seemed to have it out for the priests, they also slowly swallowed up the entire ground. Soon, there'd be no difference between those who deserved the judgement of Serathon and those who didn't.

On their side of the room, Fabian used what meagre access to water he had to keep the occasional priest gunning for them at bay, while Ophelia—the only one whose powers were unaffected—pushed the shadows away. Finn and Anne knelt next to the door, praying to their respective gods.

Samantha checked with Rachel. Both their powers seemed completely useless in this temple, and with the door closed, there was no hope of help from the outside.

Shaking, Samantha drew her Torakh. "I'm going to help him."

"Sam!" Rachel called, but she didn't let it her stop her as she avoided the patches of black and ran for Matt.

Nearby, the High Priest and the prophet were locked in battle. "I should've had you executed when you first uttered those cursed words," the High Priest drawled.

The prophet pushed back, his spear crackling. "The future can't be changed. Not even by you!"

"We'll see about that."

Samantha jumped back, nearly falling down a black hole when the High Priest charged at the prophet. Pulling back, he stumbled over Serathon's statue and lost his weapon.

A crazy glint entered the High Priest's eyes. "Prepare to meet his madness."

"I'll stand before Serathon with a clean conscience. I don't fear you or anyone."

"Then die!"

Samantha lunged forward, but it was too late. The spear had already embedded itself in the prophet's chest. His body shook in its death throes, making the bile rise in her throat.

The High Priest's gaze fell on her. "You're next, witch."

Fortunately, Serathon had different plans. The shadows crawled out from under the statue, wrapped themselves around the High Priest and dragged him backwards into the pits of darkness where none yearned to follow. His screams echoed in Samantha's ears long after he was gone.

The High Priest had barely vanished before Samantha's attention was drawn to Matt. He was struggling to defend himself against two priests, the spot of unblemished ground he was on growing smaller by the second.

One of his opponents managed to break through his defences and hit the back of his knees, the subsequent electric shock buckling his legs. Somehow, he still managed to use the momentum to drive his spear into the belly of the other man. The one at his back, however, raised his spear above Matt's neck. Without thinking, Samantha drove her Torakh into his side. Blood spurted out, and she let out a scream, quickly taking a step back again.

Matt whirled around, grabbed the priest by the shoulders, and threw him into the shadows. Then he pulled Samantha to his chest and held her, his heart pumping against her cheek. "I told you to go."

"As if I could just leave you," she said, breathless from the blow she'd just dealt.

The shadows closed in around them, cutting off their retreat. Though not a single priest remained alive, the doors were still closed.

"Can't you jump us out of here?"

Matt winced. "If I could, I would've done it the moment they attacked."

"What if Serathon himself has gone mad?" she heard the acolyte ask, fearfully.

Fabian was next to him, arms by his sides, and ghastly pale. "I don't know."

"Please, Hanna," Anne prayed next to him. "Protect our lives."

The doors burst open, nearly sending the group flying into the shadows. Light flooded the hall, blinding them. In the dark, a tall figure with blazing eyes appeared. It wasn't until she spoke Samantha recognised Iyaga.

"Where is Balthasar?"

"Not here?" Matt answered, confused.

He didn't waste another second in scooping Samantha up and balancing on a thin beam of light to carry her out, following the others as they fled.

"I want him." Up close, the archdeacon's skin shimmered an unearthly green.

Balthasar appeared behind her. "I'm right here, gorgeous."

Iyaga spun around, wrapping her arms around him. As soon as she'd claimed him, the green glow vanished and her threatening aura dissipated.

Behind them, the temple groaned and ached. Samantha glanced up. "Let's get out of here while we still can."

They'd barely set foot on the ground below when the temple crumbled, spire and all.

Matt

"I can't believe you sent us there, knowing exactly what was going to happen!" Matt shouted the moment they reached the house at the bottom of the spire, where Lucille and Chay were waiting.

Chay gave him that pitying look he'd perfected so well. "I did what I had to do to ensure you got the prophecy. You did get the prophecy, didn't you?"

Rachel nodded, but Matt wasn't ready to let Chay off the hook so easily. "You risked Sam's life."

"It's kind of hard to separate the two of you." Chay regarded the group.

They were covered in dust and grime. They hadn't truly slept in two days, nor eaten or drunk enough. Instead, they'd been fighting for their life in a godforsaken temple turned bloodbath.

Slowly, though, the rage abated, and Matt saw a little more clearly. "You brought Iyaga along to save us."

"And to waken her greed." Chay nodded, before explaining, "Every archdemon has a power that's larger than life. Your mother could control anyone in the throes of lust."

It was an experience Matt was trying to forget.

"It's the power of greed to hyper-fixate on one thing only. Nothing can stop the archdemon from reaching it. Not even death—or a mad god. That's why I brought both Iyaga and Balthasar."

"I'm impressed," Lucille said, next to them.

If Matt was honest, he was impressed, too. It must've taken meticulous planning. Knowing Chay, it was only one of many objectives he'd pursued today. There were probably half a dozen others at play; little steps of something much bigger.

Chay shrugged. "It was nothing."

"You know, if you wanted a challenge, we're facing an apocalypse in Ashuan," Lucille said, coyly.

"I know, and the end of all worlds." Chay smiled, though it was beginning to look more like a grimace now. "Let's hope I can orchestrate our defences just as well then."

Though Matt still felt slighted, he couldn't help see the bigger picture. Chay rarely did something that didn't serve a bigger purpose. "You know, if you need help..."

"Oh, I'll need a lot. And you'll provide it. You are the Six, after all."

Lucille laughed and shook her head. She hugged Samantha. "I'm so glad you're all back. I wish I could've gone with you."

"Believe me, you don't. It turned into a real bloodbath up there." Samantha shuddered. There was still blood on her shirt from the man she'd stabbed.

"I don't know. Between a bloodbath and listening to Balthasar having sex all night, I'm afraid the former sounds more tempting."

"In that case, I missed my calling," Balthasar said, dryly.

Immediately, Iyaga was all over him. "Absolutely not." The gaze with which she watched him was downright greedy. "How about spending another night? All the nights?"

"You're getting a little too greedy," Balthasar teased her before spreading his arms. "Lust has to satisfy many needs."

Matt rolled his eyes. "Ugh. Keep it in your pants."

Balthasar grinned. "For a short time, at least." He nodded at Chay. "Did you get what you wanted?"

"You did, didn't you?" Chay searched Rachel's gaze. "The prophecy was longer than we thought?"

Rachel took out a piece of paper and handed it to him. "The good news is, it speaks of a saviour who can avert the dark shadow we're facing. The bad news is... I still think we're missing a small part."

"Yeah, the part where it tells us who the saviour is," Fabian complained. Now the danger had passed, he was back to his whiny self.

"Someone with wings," Anne said. "Though maybe that's just metaphorical for coming into his own and freeing himself from whatever's holding him back."

Chay nodded gravely. "You'll learn his identity when the time is right."

Balthasar groaned. "And here we go again with more secrets. Why don't you just tell them who it is?" But before Chay could say anything, Balthasar slipped an arm around Iyaga and they vanished.

Pondering the same question, Matt glared at Chay. "You know, don't you? Why not just tell us?"

"Because of what Anne said: your hero will have to spread his wings. He can't do that if he takes on this responsibility too early. He has to grow into it. I'm sorry. Sometimes, the best course of action is to simply let the future unfold."

Matt wanted to protest, but was reminded of his own torturous part. Chay could've stopped him that New Year's Day. But if he'd spared him the pain, he never would've learnt the lessons he'd so bitterly needed to. He never would've won Samantha's love and come into his own.

"Alright. We've got what we came for, so let's head out before Serathon's madness spreads across the whole world."

"What about me?" the young acolyte spoke up.

Matt still didn't quite understand why he was with them, but Fabian put a hand on Finn's shoulder and smiled. "You're coming with us. I told you: there's nothing left in this world for you, but there's a life waiting outside it."

Chay nodded sagely. "I have a feeling Anne's parents could be convinced to take the boy in."

"My parents?" Anne asked, her eyes wide.

Matt nearly snorted. "You have a feeling, huh?"

Chay raised his hands, washing himself in innocence.

Next to him, Lucille giggled. "Let's take what we can get. Who knows when we might get the next morsel of wisdom?"

One day, Matt would sit Chay down and force him to fully divulge what he knew and his plans for them, but today, he let it slide. In the end, they'd got what they'd come for: a sliver of hope.

They dropped Finn and Anne off at her apartment and agreed to meet soon to analyse the bits of prophecy they'd gathered. Then Matt and Samantha returned home, where they found Jan half-asleep on the couch, buried in scrolls. He woke when Samantha had finished writing the two parts of the prophecy on the whiteboard in the living room. It would be their singular focus in the months to come.

"You're back." Jan rubbed his eyes and put the scrolls aside. "Anne?"

"Safe and sound." Matt sat on the armrest and picked up one of the scrolls, finding it full of drawings of plants. Not exactly the kind of reading he would've expected in Jan's hands. "Things went a little crazy, but she held her own. She might be a little too curious for her own good, but otherwise... no worse than dragging Fabian along."

"Fabian's a very powerful water mage," Samantha said, always quick to defend her best friend.

Matt just grinned. He patted Jan's shoulder. "We got the prophecy, and we got your parents a new son."

"Excuse me?" Jan frowned.

Laughing, Matt explained the situation, ending with, "Your parents actually agreed to house him. You don't mind him getting your room, do you?"

Jan just shrugged. "Not at all. He seems to need a pair of parents, and my parents apparently need a son. I'm happy here."

"Boy!" Leandres' gruff voice called. "Where are you? We've got work to do."

"Okay, mostly happy." Jan pushed himself up and shouted back, "I'm coming." He turned to Samantha with puppy eyes. "You need to tutor me in herbs and stuff. Please."

She laughed. "Sure."

Matt put the scrolls back and walked over, slipping his arms around Samantha. "What do you think? Should I relieve Balthasar from one of his many duties and satisfy you?"

Laughing, she leant into him. "I'd like that much more than if he'd dare touch me. But it has to be in the bath. I desperately need to wash the temple off."

"As you wish," Matt whispered against her neck, loving how she tipped her head back in response.

He still couldn't believe how lucky he'd gotten. Their path to here might have been bumpy and beyond painful, but it had led them to something beautiful. There was no way he'd exchange that for a glimpse of the future.

Rachel

While Rachel had been in Ylvadin, she'd been able to forget about her parents' imminent departure. The weekend after, it became real, as they packed everything into boxes and loaded it into a truck. They'd hired a container, which would eventually deliver their household items and things Annette was taking from her shop to L.A., leaving the house strangely empty.

"Rachel, can you come here?" Annette called.

Rachel had dreaded the call. She was still salty her parents were leaving, whether they continued paying for the house or not. "What is it?"

Annette was on the bed in her otherwise empty bedroom. "I feel like we need to talk."

With a sigh, Rachel sat. "You're leaving. What's there to talk about?"

"You know you're more than welcome to come."

"I don't want that." This was her home. It was where she was needed and where all her friends were, and where Adam would soon be, too.

Annette smiled. "I know. Look, I know I was a horrible mother to you... and Nico." There was still so much pain in her voice whenever she mentioned her dead son.

"Dad wasn't much better."

"That might be the first time I've heard that," Annette said, amused. "I'm sorry. I wish I could turn back time and do better by you."

There had been many times when Rachel had wished for that, if only to see Nico again. "And yet, you're leaving."

"I have to." Annette looked around, seeing things Rachel was blind to. "It all reminds me of him and I... I need a fresh start."

"With the old man."

Her mother laughed. "Don't let him hear that. He's still mad about leaving his thirties behind." She reached out and ran her hand across Rachel's braids. "I'll miss you. My little dreamer."

It was the first time her mother had mentioned the dreams outside of the dreamworld. Suddenly, Rachel hungered for the connection. Annette was the only other dreamer she knew.

"We can still dream together." The time zones would make it more complicated, but it wasn't nearly as bad as what she had with Adam.

"I don't dream anymore. Not on purpose," Annette whispered.

"But why?" Rachel couldn't understand how anyone could not dream.

"Because the dreams demand too much. You can't truly live in both worlds, you know. At least, I couldn't. Promise me you'll be careful." Her hand reached Rachel's cheek.

Rachel was still struggling to process the fact her mother was well aware of what she was doing. When had she stopped actively dreaming? Had it coincided with a major event in her life? Had the price she'd paid for the dreams been her emotional availability?

"The dreamworld is full of hidden abysses," Annette said, deadly serious now. "The deeper you dive in, the harder it'll be to return. You need an anchor, a really strong anchor. Focus on who depends on you: on your friends and Adam. Those people, that's who's important, not that world of dreams and illusions."

Rachel hung onto every word, forgetting to even breathe. She inhaled sharply. Her mother knew so much more than she'd ever let on. It explained everything, but why only divulge it now when Rachel was about to lose her?

"I'll be careful, I promise. Can I still visit you from time to time?" She needed more, so much more.

Annette dropped her hand in her lap and smiled. "Of course. My dreams are always open to you."

Driven by a sudden wave of emotion, Rachel leant over and hugged her mother. To her surprise, Annette returned the gesture without hesitation. They'd never been a family who showed each other a lot of physical affection, not even when Nico was still alive. Now, Rachel regretted all the times they'd chosen to bottle up their pain.

Way too soon, the moment was over, and her father was calling, "It's time to go, Annie."

Rachel and her mother separated and went downstairs. The truck was pulling away; all that was left were their suitcases.

Mick opened his arm, offering another hug. "Don't worry about the house, Bug. I'll pay the rates and put a little more into your bank account, so we have all bases covered. I want you to focus solely on your studies."

And the end of the world, Rachel thought, but just mumbled her thanks.

"This is still cheaper than paying for college in the US."

She laughed and took a step back. "Don't forget about me, okay?"

"Never, Bug." Mick pulled her back and pressed a kiss on her forehead.

Annette took another long moment to look at Rachel, as if memorising every inch of her. "I know I haven't always shown it, but I love you, Rachel."

"I love you too, strange as it is."

Her mother laughed. They hugged again, and when Annette started crying, Rachel felt the tension in her own eyes. She watched from the porch as they loaded their luggage into a taxi. Her father waved once more before he gave Annette a kiss and got in. Annette blew her a kiss, tears still running down her face, then she was gone, too, and Rachel was alone.

"Now, the house is all ours," Hugo said, floating on the doorstep. "It's not exactly proper for an unmarried woman and a man to live together."

"Don't worry. We won't be alone for long."

"You don't mean that scoundrel, Adam, do you?"

Rachel laughed. Hugo's disdain for her boyfriend never failed to amuse her. As if she'd really go for a ghost if Adam wasn't in her heart.

Another fancier car pulled up. Lucille stepped out before her chauffeur could open the door for her.

She saw Rachel and grinned wildly. "I heard there's a free room?"

"If you can manage with just one."

Lucille laughed, and Rachel joined her. She hadn't been sure about this new arrangement, but now she was glad for her friend's presence. It made the empty house a lot less daunting.

Part 4

Claws & Feathers

Rachel

The day had finally come. Rachel was at the small train station in Greenvalley, impatiently waiting for the regional express to arrive. As usual, it was late, and no amount of standing on tiptoes and craning her neck helped it get there sooner. She checked her phone, but there were no messages.

The speakers above crackled alive. "Attention on platform one: the regional express from Hanover is about to arrive. Please stand back."

A wave of giddiness came over Rachel, and her eyes stung, as if she was about to cry. If so, they'd be tears of joy.

The tracks rattled, and soon the whistle of the approaching train sounded. At last, the familiar red nose of the regional express came around the corner. The brakes squealed and fluids hissed, until it came to a stop.

People surged forward, then politely stood to the side to let the passengers disembark first. Rachel was back on her tiptoes, trying to look over everybody's heads.

"Rachel!"

She whipped her head around, and there he was. With a big backpack thrown over his shoulder and smaller one in his hand, Adam grinned at her. She ran to him, barely giving him time to drop the smaller backpack before throwing herself in his arms.

"You made it!"

"Barely," Adam said, laughing.

He stooped to kiss her, and Rachel felt at peace with the world. This right here was why it was worth fighting for Ashuan.

"Did you wait long?" he said, picking his backpack up again and putting an arm around Rachel.

"Since I last saw you." Rachel giggled. Adam made her feel all kinds of things she'd never experienced before. "But no, I've only been waiting about ten minutes. How was your flight?"

He yawned. "Long."

"You could've used the gates. It would've been cheaper and faster."

"But not entirely ethical, never mind the illegal immigration thing." He kissed her cheek. "Maybe when I don't have an official interview."

She slung her arms around him and hugged him tight. "Soon, you'll be here forever."

"If the visa gods smile down on me." He nodded towards the parking lot. "Do you have a car or are we taking the bus?"

"I'm now the proud owner of a car." Rachel snorted. "My mum left hers when she moved to the US. I hardly use it, but it's been coming in handy for weekly groceries. And for picking up overseas boyfriends."

He dropped his backpack again and pulled her into another kiss. "I can't wait to spend the week with you."

Giggling, Rachel took his hand and pulled him towards the small Opel her mother had owned for over ten years. Her parents' departure had upset her at first, but with the prospect of having Adam around whenever she wanted, she was beginning to enjoy her newfound freedom.

Matt

"So, yeah, now we have to find to find some random guy with wings or a huge chip on his shoulder, hoping he'll get his shit together in time to save our world." Matt rolled his eyes. He hated having to trust in fate, rather than getting it done himself.

He was walking down the corridors with Vydra, telling her all about the prophecy and their recent adventure. Last week, the news that Ylvadin had been swallowed by shadows had reached Fader, leaving a vacuum in the Interglobal Parliament, and a scramble to secure any surviving prophecies. It was the most exciting thing that'd happened in a long time, even surpassing the recent attack. Their entire class was suddenly interested and had been hunting for every scrap of knowledge possible, and had spawned hundreds of theories about what had led to the end of the world.

Matt was much less enthused, having seen the end of the world with his own eyes. Or at least, the beginning of it. He didn't see the point in learning about a world that no longer existed. Not when there were more pressing manners, such as the imminent end of his own.

"Just some random guy?" Vydra asked. She was also apparently ignoring the chatter around them. "You don't think it's someone you know?"

"Well, Rachel said something about prophecies always coming to those who need it, so I guess at some point we will. I mean, it could be someone from Greenvalley or maybe from Fabian's Citadel. Heck, it could even be the boy we brought home with us—a little disciple of Serathon."

That was Samantha's preferred theory. To her, it made sense they hadn't just gone to Ylvadin to find the rest of the prophecy but their prophesied hero as well. And after reevaluating his entire life, little Finn certainly had a lot of growing to do. For now, he'd been accompanying Anne to school and settling into a life so far removed from what he'd known, he was bound to struggle. If he really was their prophesied hero, Matt hoped he'd get over it fast.

"You don't think so?" Vydra asked, regarding him with a shrewd look.

"I find it a bit disconcerting to trust the fate of the entire world on a fifteen-year-old."

"Didn't you save your city when you were seventeen?"

"Eighteen, and it was mostly the others. Plus, one archdemon throwing a temper tantrum is hardly comparable to the end of the world." But there were similarities between Ylvadin's end and the prophecy surrounding Ashuan. Just like the former, the latter was threatened to be consumed by shadows. "Maybe Serathon's coming for us now that we've stolen his acolyte."

Vydra bit her thumb, deep in thought. "He shouldn't have any power in Ashuan. No one there prays to him."

"Is that how divine power works?"

She nodded. "According to Marelle's Divine Encyclopaedia, the power of gods is directly proportional to the size of their followers. Or rather, their faith. That's why they call Ashuan the god-forsaken world—you've let go of too many beliefs. Many prior presences have now dwindled completely."

Matt shrugged. He'd never thought much of religion. He knew gods existed and that some, like Hanna, were more prevalent, their belief spreading over multiple worlds, but he'd never pledged his faith to any of them. Not even after learning the original bearers of the two souls who made up his own had ascended to divinity. It was the mortal part that had saved everyone from Draken and broken the world in the process—not the gods.

"I see. Well, we've got one person praying for him in Ashuan now."

What if they'd invited the destruction of their world in? He shook his head. Chay wouldn't have allowed that. And if he had, he was much sicker than Matt had thought, gambling with all their lives.

"One's hardly enough." Vydra tapped her chin. "I think."

They reached one of the study rooms, where Matt immediately saw a familiar face. "Oh, let me introduce you to Merik." The fancy-clad Phalesian noble sat at one of the tables, working on a bunch of scrolls. "He wanted to meet you."

Vydra frowned. "Why?"

"I don't know. Maybe he likes you." When her frown deepened, Matt laughed. "You don't have to do anything you don't want to. If he bothers you—"

"He won't survive." A bit drastic, but Matt respected her for drawing boundaries. Vydra took a deep breath. "Besides, that's rarely what his type wants."

Matt's classes finished early, so he jumped straight to Greenvalley University and caught Samantha as she exited the lecture hall. His lips quirked up when he saw her reading her notes, subconsciously weaving in and out of the crowd. Feeling peevish, he stepped in her way, grinning when she bumped into him.

"Oh, sorry—Matt."

"Didn't your parents teach you not to read while walking?" He kissed her forehead. "Hey, cutie."

She grimaced. "Hey."

Not the enthusiastic greeting he'd expected. "What's wrong?"

As they moved away from the lecture hall, Samantha continued studying her notes. "Nothing, I just have a million things to do."

"Tests coming up?"

"Tests, lab reports, physics prep, prophecies..." She sighed. "What about you?"

"We're good until the end of the semester."

Samantha raised an eyebrow. "What about your essays?"

"If you ignore the essays."

For a few blissful minutes, Matt had been able to forget about the essays he had to write every single week. This week, it was on marriage across different worlds. A topic he hadn't the slightest interest in.

At least that made Samantha smile. "You've got this. And you know I love proofreading, if you need it."

"Only because you also want to study what I'm studying."

She laughed. "True. Your essays are the perfect amount of work I can still fit in, so, make them good."

Matt rolled his eyes. Nevertheless, he put an arm around her, happy to spend time together, even if it meant sharing her with her lecture notes.

They met up with Lucille and her two upper class-men, Dennis and Jakob. Lucille immediately hooked her arm into Samantha's and pulled her away. "There's a wedding happening in the park. Let's watch."

"Didn't you watch from the hall already?" Dennis asked, sounding a little disappointed.

Matt was surprised Lucille wasn't dating him yet, since he was clearly pining for her.

Lucille looked over her shoulder. "I had to concentrate on my test, doofus." She giggled and dragged Samantha along, who'd actually put her notes aside for the moment.

Jakob elbowed Matt. "You're in big trouble now, my friend."

"Why?"

Dennis snorted. "He thinks your girlfriend will be expecting a proposal now."

Matt was more and more confused by the moment. "A proposal?"

"Oh, you know." Jakob grinned from ear to ear. "Swearing eternal love and loyalty, also known as the end of your freedom. Girls dream of that moment from early childhood."

"Don't listen to him," Dennis said. "First off, most of them don't, and secondly, you're barely out of school and far too young to think about marriage."

Matt's head was swimming. Did Samantha really hope they'd get married? Despite his research he was still trying to wrap his head around the concept. It just felt so... pointless. Nevertheless, he followed the girls outside. A small crowd of students had gathered to watch a couple taking pictures under the colourful autumn leaves in the park. Lucille seemed completely in love, while Samantha's gaze was rather sceptical. It gave Matt hope.

"You don't really want this, right?" he asked quietly.

She turned. "What?"

"This whole marriage crap. Eternal love. A binding oath."

Samantha's eyes widened slightly. When she finally spoke, it was slowly, as if she were still putting the sentence together in her head, "You're asking me if I want eternal love?"

"Well, eternity is long. Extremely long."

"Is that so?"

He lowered his voice. "You know what I mean."

The human idea of eternity was limited by their own mortality, but Matt was looking down at hundreds, if not thousands, of years. He couldn't even imagine living that long, much less loving that long.

"Apparently, what I know now is this thing between us is just temporary. Wow."

"Wow?"

"Well, you're expecting it to be over soon. Wow."

Matt felt like he already had one foot in a trap, but he couldn't for the life in him figure out how to pull it out. "I didn't say soon, just that eternity is long. Longer than the average human life—"

"My life expectancy. I understood, no worries."

He let out a sigh of relief. "Good. Then we're on the same page, right? A wedding's not on the cards."

"Matt..." Lucille said, a little strained. Apparently, she'd been listening in.

Samantha had her jaw set and there was the faintest shimmer in her eyes. "Of course. That would be entirely unreasonable. It's all just temporary, anyway. I could practically drop dead tomorrow and then it'd all have been a total waste of your time and energy."

Lucille glared for good measure.

Matt wasn't sure what he'd done to earn this kind of reaction. He'd thought they were on the same page. She was usually so level-headed and logical.

Before he could get to the bottom of it, Robert was running towards them. "Man. Dead. Torn apart. Back there."

"Or you could be torn apart tomorrow," Samantha said pointedly to Matt.

"Is that true?" Dennis asked.

Robert only seemed to notice him then, taking a step back. "Probably not. I mean I... I must've jumped to conclusions. Happens. Bye."

And within seconds, he was gone again.

Matt sighed. "Do you think he'll ever get over it?" Robert had been avoiding them since he'd accidentally helped them ban a monster.

"If there really is a dead guy, probably not," Jakob said, looking a little pale. He swallowed. "What do you think 'torn apart' means?"

Lucille grabbed Dennis' and Jakob's arms. "It's just nonsense. Robert has a horrible taste in humour. Come on, we need to hit the library to study for tomorrow's test." She dragged them with her, throwing a meaningful glance at Matt and Samantha.

Samantha sighed and started walking in the direction Robert had come from. "Let's check it out."

"Hey." Matt hurried after her. "About that marriage thing—"

"Not now. We have a gruesome murder case in the middle of exams' season—that's stressful enough."

Matt knew when he'd been blown off. For some reason, whatever he'd said had caused a rift between them, and if he didn't figure out the root of the problem fast, it would inevitably tear them apart.

But first, they had to deal with the equivalent of human mince.

Lucille

Lucille was on her way home when she saw a familiar figure in front of Rachel's house.

"Merik!" A wide grin slipped onto her face and she fell into his arms. Last time he'd been here, they'd had a rather amorous adventure. Though it'd been little more than a one-night stand, Lucille was happy to see him again. "Is this a booty call?" She didn't mind if it was.

"A what?"

Lucille laughed and waved him off. "Forget it. How did you... First, how did you know I'd be here?"

"I went to your parents' place first, but they told me I'd find you here."

"Oh, have you been waiting for long?" She opened the door.

Merik shook his head. "I'd wait hours in the rain for you."

"That's because you rarely see rain in Phalos. Nothing to do with me."

Despite her joking around, Lucille felt giddy. She'd thought a lot about him in the weeks since, almost asking Matt how she could meet him again, but then the whole thing in Ylvadin had happened and more pressing matters had taken over.

Merik slipped his hand around her hip and pulled her in. "I missed you."

Lucille sighed and stole a kiss. "I missed you, too."

Suddenly eager, she pulled him upstairs and into her new room. Compared to her old one, it was much smaller, but large enough for a bed, her desk, a reasonable selection of her clothes, and a decent-sized bookshelf.

She dropped her bag, cradled Merik's cheeks, and kissed him intensely. He put his arms around her and pressed her to his body with a mixture of confidence and possessiveness that turned her legs to butter. They stumbled backwards until they fell onto the bed.

Around an hour later, they were both lying in bed. Lucille had her head on Merik's chest, absentmindedly stroking his side. "So... did you really just miss me or was there another reason for this surprising—but delightful—visit?"

He laughed softly, his arm across her shoulders. "Both. I'm sorry I couldn't come earlier. I had a lot going on at home, plus a research project that's been taking up most of my time."

"Oh, don't worry. I was pretty busy, too." She smiled up at him, just happy to have him there. "I like this casual thing. It feels... very grown-up."

Merik made it so easy to be with him. He didn't expect any more of her than she was willing to give, and there was something exciting about dating a man from another world.

"I'd love to return the favour one day and visit you." After Fader and Ylvadin, she'd tasted blood and wanted more.

"I mostly live in Fader at the moment, but I can take you to Phalos one day, if you want. Just warning you, though, it's much hotter than here."

"Just like the men." She giggled and rolled onto her back, blissfully staring at the ceiling. "So, what was the other thing?"

Free from her weight, Merik got up and rummaged through his satchel. "I remember you telling me you had an interest in linguistics."

Lucille sat up, sheet wrapped around her. "Interest piqued." She wondered where this was going.

Merik pulled out two scrolls. "This is from my father's private library in Phalos. It's a text in Old Phalesian, which, to my embarrassment, I only have the most rudimentary knowledge of."

"And you think I'll be any better?" Despite her scepticism, she was intrigued, her fingers itching for the ancient-looking scroll. "What makes you think I can decipher it when you can't?"

"For two reasons: first off, you're a witch working with lingual magic. Your magic will aid you in deciphering this. Second, this one is the translation key." He held up a second scroll.

"A key?" She'd expected a whole dictionary, not a meagre scroll.

Merik sat back on the bed, carefully breaking the seal on the first scroll. As he unrolled it, Lucille was immediately drawn to the unfamiliar shapes of the letters. They were reminiscent of Norse runes—if the runes were curved. More importantly, she felt the pull of magic.

He showed her the second scroll, which had a list of symbols matched up with other, even rounder, symbols. Though they looked different, she could see the connection between the letter sets.

"That's New Phalesian, I assume?"

"Correct." He kissed her cheek, rewarding her. "At first glance, you probably think it's a simple decoding task. I promise, I'm not lazy or anything, but the translation requires magic. Old Phalesian was written with magic and will only unlock if you understand the magic in its letters."

She could feel it. She ran her hand across the first scroll, completely in awe. Her fingers itched to get started. "So, what is it?"

"Honestly, for all I know, it could be a cacti cake recipe." Merik rolled his head back and laughed. "Wouldn't that be funny? However, I found it in the historical section of the library, and I'm hoping it has some information about the Black Period—called that because literally nothing survived. Some people think our world ended during that time."

"Wait, what? How could it have ended if you're still here?"

"Not all apocalypses are truly world-ending, often, it's a reset. A cycle. I've come across a lot of similar cultures during my studies. Practically, you have a catastrophic event that wipes out most of the population, leaving only a few chosen ones to rebuild from the ashes. Don't you have anything like that in Ashuan?"

Lucille shook her head, but then she thought again. "Actually, there are some religions with death and rebirth cycles like this." The Norse gods and their Ragnarök came to her mind. In Norse mythology, a pair of humans had survived the literal burning of the world and started anew after the world had been reshaped. "And I guess, if you look into our natural history, there have been several events where most life has been wiped out, only to flourish again afterwards."

"As I said, it's very prevalent. There are legends of a golden age before the Black Period, but so far I've had no luck finding any sources. Hopefully, that'll change now."

Lucille clutched the scroll to her chest. "Leave it with me. I'm very busy at the moment, but I'll do my best to get it back to you soon. Or let you know if I can't do it."

Merik leant forward and kissed her gently. "Lucille de Cerque, you're the best."

Giggling, she put the scrolls aside and pulled him back down between the pillows.

Fabian

Music was playing in the background as Fabian sat on Ophelia's bed and went through his flash cards. Tomorrow, he'd be facing his first big test at the Citadel. Professor Terian had been particularly sparse with details regarding the contents of the test, which made him even more nervous than usual. Elemental magic he could handle, magical history and elemental theory, not so much.

"Did Sam make those for you?" Ophelia asked. She was feeding her pet snakes.

"Hmm?" Fabian looked at the cards. "Oh, those. No, those are Shay—" Too late, he stopped talking. He closed his eyes and took a deep breath. "Sorry."

Ophelia took a moment too long to answer. "She lent you her notes? She must be taking this test a lot less seriously, then."

"No, she—" He sighed again. "You know how badly I do at exams."

"Is it an important one?"

Fabian shrugged. "It's the first, and Terian said it was of utter importance, so, I guess. He's not happy with us. Apparently, we're not learning fast enough or missing something important. Kaia says it's because three of us are wild mages or, in other words, everyone but her is dragging down the average."

Ophelia closed the terrarium and faced him, frowning. "That Kaia girl sounds like a real bitch. Don't you have any nice girls at the Citadel?"

"Really?"

"What?" She batted her eyelashes in innocence.

"Lia, please. We've been through this."

She sighed and came to him, snuggling up to his side. "I just don't like her. She was a good friend of Cheryl's, wasn't she? That doesn't exactly speak to her character. And yes, I know it's impossible to ignore her while you're at the Citadel, and that the two of you knowing each other has made you allies in that stupid class, but Greenvalley is all you have in common, right?"

Fabian didn't quite know what she was trying to get him to say. It was true. He and Shayna were nothing alike. They had different hobbies and liked completely different things. There really was only one thing they bonded over.

"And elemental magic."

It was such a relief to know another elemental mage—who was willing to talk to him. His friends all had magical powers, but they didn't understand what it was like to carry a power that required so much control and could be so destructive at the drop of a hat. While they'd learnt new spells, Fabian had grappled with keeping his emotions contained. Shayna understood that, maybe even more, with her specific element.

Tears formed in Ophelia's eyes. "We've been through so much. You know—and love—me, all of it, even the dark side. I... I don't want to lose you. I can't."

Fabian put an arm around her shoulders and kissed her hair. "I love you, every side of you." Apart from her jealous side, perhaps. "You and I are a couple, whereas Shayna and I go to school together. I know you don't like it, but it's only for a year."

"A year?" Ophelia pulled back, sounding a lot chipper. "It's just a one-year course? I didn't know that. I can do a year." She even smiled.

Though he winced internally, Fabian returned the smile. Truth was, the course was only set for a year, but he doubted that'd be the end of his time at the Citadel. Not when they were all so eager about the prospect of having four elemental mages at the same time.

"Well, maybe it'll be even less if I fail the test tomorrow."

Ophelia put her hand on his, regarding him sternly. "No way. You're going to ace it. You've got Shayna's cards, after all."

He raised an eyebrow at her sudden change of mood, but Ophelia was already hopping off the bed and happily talking to her snakes. It was a pleasant variation from all the tension lately. Chuckling, he returned to his studying.

Fabian convened with Shayna in a study room at the Citadel the following morning, trying to cram as much knowledge into his brain as he could before the test. He'd woken up with a stomach ache and his usual exam jitters. Despite learning intensely for two weeks, he still felt woefully unprepared. And this last-minute session proved it.

"When did the last mage war end?"

"1565?" Fabian asked hopefully.

Shayna winced. "No."

"Earlier or later?"

"Earlier."

The mages had apparently been much more peaceful than anyone else. "1400s?"

"Earlier."

"1300s?"

"1272!" Camdyn barked from behind him. Their classmate was sitting behind them with his much more extensive notes in a large binder.

Shayna rolled her eyes. "Yes, that's correct. Now look at your own notes. Unless you've decided to join in the fun and learn with us?" Her voice only softened at the very end, as if she'd suddenly remembered to be nice.

Camdyn, of course, immediately lowered his head and held up his folder like a shield.

Meanwhile, Kaia approached and sat on their table. She bit into an apple and remarked, "He's desperate to pass, so don't count on it."

Shayna took a deep breath and grimaced at Fabian, ignoring Kaia's presence. "Alright. How many mage wars were there?"

"Three?" Having Kaia right in front of him only made Fabian more nervous. "Four?" Shayna shook her head again, and a blush crawled up his neck. "Five?"

"Seven," Camdyn said, sounding exasperated.

Kaia laughed. "You're so going to fail." She caught Shayna's angry glare and shrugged. "What else would you expect from three wild mages who only had a month to catch up on everything we soaked up with our mothers' milk?"

"Looks like one of us can keep up perfectly," Shayna said, proudly.

Fabian stared at her, wondering what she was playing at.

When Kaia looked just as clueless, Shayna groaned. "I'm talking about Camdyn. He knows everything."

The boy looked as if he'd been caught stealing. "No, I don't."

Kaia snorted. "Just because he's good at soaking up theory doesn't mean he'll last the year. He might pass today's test, but in terms of practical application, he's even more lost than you two idiots."

Shayna jumped up, pushing her hands into the table. "And you think you'll pass with flying colours, right?" She was right in Kaia's face. Heat wavered in the air.

If anything, though, Kaia looked bored. "I've been honing my earth powers all life long. You guys didn't even know you had magic until a few months ago."

"And how many demons have you defeated?" Fabian asked, imitating her bored tone. It wasn't so much that he enjoyed this stupid stand-off, but after Kaia had cut Camdyn down so recklessly, she deserved a little of her own medicine.

Shayna grinned wildly, looking insanely proud of him. Fabian felt a little flip in his stomach and decided it was high time to get back to learning.

Unfortunately, Professor Terian chose that moment to enter. "Your exam is prepared, if you'll please follow me." He turned and walked out again.

Kaia jumped off the table, now the only one with the big grin. "Good luck, losers."

Camdyn followed quickly, while Fabian rubbed his face in dismay. "They're going to expel me."

"Nonsense." Shayna grabbed his arm and pulled him up. "Professor Terian wouldn't test us if he didn't think we were ready."

"If you say so."

Still depressed, Fabian followed the others. There, the first surprise waited for him. All four tables had been pushed to the side. Instead, a large shimmering portal slowly rotated around its own axis in the middle of the room. Camdyn looked absolutely horrified. Even Kaia didn't quite seem to know what to expect.

Professor Terian's face gave nothing away. "You can put your notes away. You won't be needing them for this test."

Camdyn's fingers tightened around his folder. The skin under his freckles had taken on a greenish tint. Slowly, he let go of the theory he valued so much.

Kaia strutted into the room as if she'd already figured it all out. But Fabian knew better. Her back was a little too straight, the blasé expression too forced.

"The four of you will travel to a magical enclave. This place only exists within the magic and has been crafted specifically around your powers. Your goal is to find the Herb of Heavens. As soon as you've found it, the exam will end and count as passed. For all of you."

Kaia frowned heavily. "For all of us?"

"This is a class test, yes. You have two days."

Fabian coughed heavily. "Wait, what? Two days? Couldn't you have said that earlier?"

"It's perfectly possible to pass the test in a single day. A single hour even." Professor Terian pointed at a pile of travel packs. "Now, take one of those, and enter."

None of them moved for nearly ten seconds. Then Kaia clicked her tongue, grabbed the first backpack, and strode into the portal. Since it neither disintegrated nor pulverised her, Fabian reckoned it was relatively safe. He and Shayna cautiously stepped forward and took a pack each.

"Ophelia will kill me," he muttered.

"Why? Cause you're spending the night with me?"

Shayna might've only been teasing, but Fabian knew it was exactly what Ophelia would think if he failed to come home.

"One day. We'll get it done today." At least, this wasn't a written test.

He waited for the portal to rotate back around, took a deep breath, and stepped through.

Jan

Jan hummed a little melody as he cooked scrambled eggs for breakfast—or in his case, dinner, since he'd just come home from his night shift. Samantha was already awake, studying in the living room. By the sounds of the creaks on the stairs, Matt was getting ready, too.

A few moments later, Matt entered the kitchen and mumbled, "Morning."

"Good morning," Jan said, with a little too much energy. He scraped his eggs onto a plate and dug in.

"You're oddly awake." Matt looked as if he could've used another hour or two of sleep.

"I like the night shift."

Matt grinned lazily. "Might that be because of a certain nurse?"

Jan felt even giddier remembering his late-night chats with Sandra while the rest of the station was quiet. She was a few years older than him, but she had a wicked sense of humour that matched his own.

"Want some scrambled eggs?"

"Sure. Is there coffee?"

Jan nodded to the side. "There's a pot over there." He watched Matt pour himself a cup. "Please tell me she hasn't been sitting there all night."

"Who? Sam?" Matt shrugged and took a sip. "Honestly, I don't know. She was still downstairs when I went to bed and gone already—or still—when I woke up."

That didn't sound like his friends at all. Normally, they couldn't wait to get into bed. "Everything okay with you two?"

"Sure, sure..." Matt bit his lip, the opposite of reassuring. "Actually, can I ask you something?"

"You, me? Uh, why not? Shoot."

Matt took a deep breath. "What are your thoughts on marriage?"

Jan choked on a piece of egg. "Excuse me?" He'd been ready for a lot but not that.

"Marriage. Apparently, it's a human expectation."

After reaching for a glass of water, Jan felt more capable answering Matt's particular brand of half-demon questions. "I guess it is. Though it's not for everyone, you know and..." Slowly, the nature of the request trickled into his brain. "Are you mad? You two are way too young and have barely been together four months."

He got that Samantha and Matt had already been through so much and bought their love with a price much higher than most couples paid, but they weren't even twenty yet.

Matt frowned slightly. "So, what's the right age, then?"

Jan raised an eyebrow. "Are you seriously thinking about marrying Sam? You?"

"What's wrong with me?"

"Oh, I don't know. Maybe the fact you've slept with half of Greenvalley and half of Hell, too?" Matt was truly the last person Jan would ever peg as a happily married man, no matter how much he loved Samantha.

"So, you think it's just temporary?" Matt asked, flatly.

Just then, the door opened and Samantha walked in. "Wonderful. Did you get the back-up you wanted?" She refilled her coffee cup and returned to the living room.

Jan watched her go. It was all coming together now. "Let me guess: for some reason, marriage in general came up and you answered with your typical pragmatism. Right?"

Matt sank against the kitchen counter. "Is that such a problem? I love Samantha more than anything in the world. All worlds. But you're right. We're only nineteen, and I might live hundreds, maybe even thousands, of years." He shrugged. "As you said, I'm not used to monogamy, and though I can't imagine being with anyone else at the moment, eternity is a long time when you can actually live eternally."

It was a surprisingly profound attitude. Reasonable even. "Look, I get it. I just really hope you didn't tell her that."

By the looks of it, Matt absolutely had.

"Did I ruin it again?" Matt asked, his face pure misery.

"I don't know." But then Jan shook his head. "This is Sam we're talking about. Deep down, she knows you're right. It's just that... Girls like their romance, and a realistic outlook is kinda, like, the opposite of that. Everything you said is right, sensible, but you've basically told her your relationship is doomed no matter what. And maybe it is, but... that hurts."

Matt crossed his arms and fixed the floor with a dark stare. Jan let him process his words, sure the half-demon would get there in the end. He'd done the best he could in making him see Samantha's side, but the rest was up to them to figure out. Satisfied, he returned to his scrambled eggs.

With a sigh, Matt unfolded his arms. "Did you hear about the mangled corpse, yet?"

Jan lowered his fork immediately. "Thanks. I was just about to eat." What a masterful change of subject.

"Sorry." Matt winced. "Robert told us—which is kind of remarkable. The corpse was half-eaten."

Jan put his plate aside. "Nice. What kind of monster is it?"

The door swung open again and Samantha entered, her arms crossed. "We've got a siren problem."

Rachel

Rachel was enjoying a blissfully dream-free sleep when she was woken by a terrifying gasp and jostling. Irritated, she opened her eyes, only to see Hugo standing in Adam's chest. Her boyfriend's eyes were bulging and he was clutching at his heart in terror. She was just about to say something when Hugo floated away indignantly.

"Are you crazy, man?" Adam sat up, still holding his chest as he caught his breath.

"It seemed to be the only way to wake you."

"By killing me?"

Rachel put her hand on Adam's arm. "That wasn't nice, Hugo." She knew the ghost was unhappy about Adam's presence, but she wouldn't have thought he'd go so far as trying to harm him. Glowering, she asked, "What's so important?"

"You've received an important group message." Hugo pointed at her phone. "As far as I could see before the screen went dull again, a flock of sirens are nesting in the city. They might've arrived with the good sir here."

"I most definitely didn't bring a flock of sirens," Adam protested.

Hugo raised an eyebrow, as if he doubted Adam's innocence, but was too polite to say anything.

Rachel was still trying to keep up. "And we've got to fight the sirens right now?"

"I didn't read anything about that." When Rachel sighed, Hugo nodded sagely. "But I'm afraid this means the good sir won't be staying for long."

"Why wouldn't I stay?" Adam asked. "I'm a witch, too. I can help with hunting monsters, if necessary."

Hugo let out an ugly laugh. "Oh dear, I suppose coming from those backwaters at the end of the world means you lack the necessary Classic education for this situation: the siren's song is irresistible to the male ear. They will lure you to them and tear you apart. A shame, really." He didn't sound very sorry about it.

Annoyed, Adam threw his blanket off and got up. "I'm gonna get your phone." As usual, it was downstairs.

Rachel crossed her arms and glared at Hugo. "Jealousy doesn't look good on you. Adam's important to me."

"What? That rotting piece of flesh?"

"Well, if he's a rotting piece of flesh, so am I."

Hugo looked utterly horrified. "Miss Rachel, no! He could never compare to you."

She sighed. "Adam's moving in soon. You need to get used to him... and me. Together."

"It's not proper for an unmarried woman and an unmarried man—"

"Get with the times! We're both consenting adults. Besides, you don't care if Lucille does it. She's had a man over." Rachel had been a little surprised to find Matt's friend from Fader in her house, but then again, it was Lucille. She was always looking for love and appreciation. "So, if you really cared about morality..."

Hugo puffed up his chest. "He's not good enough for you."

"He's the man I love, who happens to love me, too. That's not exactly a common experience." In fact, it was the first time—both falling so hard and having her feelings returned.

"I—" Hugo cleared his throat. He paused, listening to something downstairs. "He's taking awfully long for a simple errand."

Rachel thought Adam was just trying to stay away from Hugo, but then worry crept in. "Adam?" She got up and ran downstairs. "Adam!"

Her phone was clearly visible, charging on the dining table, but he was nowhere in sight. A draft hit her and she noticed the front door was open.

Behind her, Lucille was coming down, too. "Hey, Rachel, have you seen Merik? His stuff is still in my room, but... What's going on?"

Hugo floated around. "I swear I had nothing to do with this," he said, with none of his usual pomp.

Rachel tried not to lose her mind. "What did you say about sirens and their irresistible call?"

Twenty minutes later, Rachel and Lucille met Jan, Samantha, Matt, and Ophelia at the Blackstone House. All the windows and doors were closed and magically sealed, which had cut out all sounds from outside, creating a strange silent bubble. If only it hadn't already been too late.

Rachel was on the couch, digging her fingers into her palms, as she tried to remain calm and listen to her friends discuss the new threat. A hot cocoa sat untouched next to her.

"So, there's a flock of sirens in the city," Jan said. "Those creatures Odysseus dealt with?"

"It always amazes me what you've retained from your Latin classes," Lucille said.

Jan snorted. "You mean because I didn't retain anything else?"

"I wasn't going to say it... out loud."

Rachel had no idea how Lucille could be so casual when the man she'd slept with was missing. While her friends joked around, she was losing her mind.

"Our early detection system was very clear about it," Samantha said, taking charge as usual. "Sirens are mixed creatures, half bird, half woman. They lure men in with their intoxicating singing to eat them."

A whimper broke free from Rachel's throat. "Of course, my boyfriend would get eaten first thing." It'd all been too good to believe.

"Not if we go poultry hunting first," Jan declared, enthusiastically.

Lucille cleared her throat, while Samantha winced and said, "Um, I'm sorry, but you and Matt will have to sit this one out."

Matt snorted. "I can withstand a siren's call."

"Are you saying that because you already have experience in that department or—"

"You're the only woman whose call lures me."

Rachel rolled her eyes. Samantha grimaced. "Nice try, but you're staying here."

"Sam—"

"Adam just walked out the door!" Rachel snapped. "You'd have no chance."

"Yeah, but what do you want us to do?" Jan asked, worried. "Sit at home and twiddle our thumbs?"

"Sorry, boys, but this is a women-only job," Lucille said, her smile a little too strained. "We'll deal with them alone. Trust us."

Ophelia put her cell phone away and rose. "I texted Fabian to stay at the Citadel. He has an exam anyway, but it's better if he"—she swallowed—"stays there a bit longer. Let's go."

Rachel detected a surprising amount of hesitance about his safety, which struck her as strange, but she tried not to involve herself too much in their relationship.

"There's a silver lining," Samantha said, trying to sound positive, "you have more time to read Leandres' writings and prepare for your own test."

"Where's the silver lining in that?" Jan said.

"Do you even have a plan on how to kill or chase away a flock of sirens?" Matt asked.

Samantha regarded the girls around her. "I think between the four of us, we're more than capable of dealing with them. Don't worry. Knowing Greenvalley, there'll be a monster for you soon."

"I'm worried about you, not whether I get to kill a monster or not."

Samantha bit her lip, and Rachel suddenly realised the two were fighting. "It'll be alright." Judging by her clenched jaw, she had other things to say, but this wasn't the time for it.

Rachel appreciated it. She wanted to get out there as fast as possible. "I'll grab my crossbow." It seemed the appropriate weapon for a poultry-based monster.

Lucille clapped her hands and forced another smile. "Alright. We'll get armoured up, then we'll pluck some feathers." She still hadn't mentioned Merik. She pointed at Jan and Matt. "You two stay here. Don't even open a window."

"We'll suffocate before following any sirens," Jan said with false earnestness.

"Good boy," Lucille said with a grin. "Matt."

Matt had his arms crossed. He rolled his eyes. "I'll stay here and do nothing. Or write my essay."

Once again, Samantha clearly wanted to say something but swallowed her words. "Okay, let me grab a few potions from upstairs." She never looked back over her shoulder.

Definitely fighting, Rachel thought. But at least they still had each other to fight with.

Shayna

Shayna had never heard of magical enclaves before, but then again, she hadn't heard much about magic anything before. Every day she learnt something new. Yesterday, it'd been talking animals, today, it was another dimension that only existed for the purpose of their exam. And what a dimension it was.

They arrived amid scattered ruins on a hilltop, green land stretching under the blue sky in all directions. Apart from the ruins, there wasn't a single human structure in sight. It was a breathtaking view—and so vast. No wonder they'd been given two days. They'd probably need half of that just to walk to wherever the Herb of Heavens were.

The portal vanished as soon as Camdyn stepped through, leaving them stranded.

"I guess quitting is out of the question," Fabian said, sucking a breath between his teeth. When he noticed Camdyn's offended glare, he immediately apologised, "I didn't mean you. I—"

Camdyn had already turned his back on them, and Fabian took another deep breath. Shayna put her hand on his arm in quiet consolation. He was trying so hard to get along with everyone.

"Alright. Does anyone have an idea what the Herb of Heavens looks like?"

"It's not real," Kaia said, brusquely.

With a sigh, Shayna gave her the stage she so desperately yearned for. "What do you mean?"

Kaia stretched out her arms. "All of this is magic—nothing's real. It's just aesthetics. Similarly, the Herb of Heavens isn't real. It's a hint.

We're looking for a plant, and it's either sky blue or grows high in the air. If you tried to bring it to our world, it'd fall apart immediately."

"I see. So, this is basically a giant virtual reality game?" Fabian asked.

"It's magic," Kaia snapped.

"Magic reality game?" Fabian amended.

Shayna giggled. He wasn't very confrontational, but he had a subtle rebellious humour she appreciated, especially when directed at Kaia.

"But how are we supposed to find it, then?" Camdyn asked. He was ghastly pale, as if the change from theoretical exam to this little adventure had given him vertigo. "This place doesn't look like an enclave. At least not a small one."

Kaia raised her chin. "I suggest we split up."

"But Professor Terian said it's a class test," Fabian protested. "We only pass together."

"Not only—we pass together, yes. Who finds the herb is irrelevant, so splitting up is the most sensible way to get it done quickly. I have an invitation for an alumni dinner tonight, so let's get chopping." And with that, she marched down the hill.

Overwhelmed as ever, Camdyn looked back and forth between her and the other two. Then he took the opposite direction.

Frustrated, Fabian kicked a clump of grass. "I'm pretty sure that's not what Terian meant."

Shayna linked her arm with his. "Who knows what he truly wants? But don't worry, I have no interest in hiking around on my own. We'll stick together. So, shall we go left or right?"

She pointed in the two directions neither Kaia nor Camdyn had taken. The landscape looked the same everywhere—just endless grass and hills.

"Right," Fabian said, with a sigh, and they started walking.

So far, the exam had been pretty boring. The sun was beating down on them, and there wasn't even a hint of any plants other than yellowing grass. Fabian and Shayna climbed yet another hill. As before, there was no mysterious herb. Shayna put down her backpack and sat down, while Fabian held his cell phone up and squinted.

"No signal."

"Do you have to check in with your girlfriend every three hours?" Shayna teased. She grabbed a water bottle from her pack and took a few sips. Real or not real, the hike was exhausting.

Fabian lowered his phone. "No, but I was hoping to call Samantha so she could tell me all she knows about magical enclaves, which seem to be as large as a small country." He put his phone away and sighed. "Why did this exam have to be open world?"

"Is that another gaming reference?" Shayna asked.

"I take it you're not a gamer?" He sat next to her and took out his water bottle.

She laughed. "Not really. I mean, I've played a bit with Alan and Cian on a console, but they usually play war games or car races."

"Of course."

Shayna nudged him and grinned. "I'm not saying computer games are stupid or anything. They're just not my thing. Now, tell me, what have you learnt from your open-world games?"

Fabian's shoulders sank. "To talk to anyone you meet, which is useless, because there's only us, and to pick up everything not bolted to the ground." He tugged on the grass and let the broken blades fall. "That doesn't help, either. Couldn't Terian have given us a map, at least?"

"Sounds like those MR games are a little more complicated."

"If this was a game, it'd be the most boring one I've ever touched."

A scream tore through the landscape.

Fabian jumped up. "Was that Camdyn?"

Shayna stood and looked around. At the bottom of the hill, a black cloud had gathered. "There!"

They left their backpacks and raced down the hill. As they got closer, the cloud dissolved into individual shapes. It was an aggressive flock of birds. Camdyn cowered on the ground, both arms clasped around his head. Thin rivulets of blood flowed down his back.

"Not so boring now," Shayna said, a little out of breath.

She tried to harness the inkling of panic and turn it into heat, the way Professor Terian had taught them. When the ball of fire had grown large enough, she hauled it at the birds. Some broke away, circled the flock, then joined them again.

"Use your wind, Camdyn!"

Next to her, Fabian slid down the slope and landed squarely in front of the boy. His fingers formed a delta, and a stream of water broke from his hands, so powerful, it swept half the flock away. The rest he attacked with thinner, more directed jets. The birds crumpled under the pressure, dissolving into feathers.

Shayna watched in awe as he dealt with the threat confidently and swiftly. In class, he'd often failed to restrain his magic, but here in battle, he was a natural.

When all the birds were gone, Camdyn lowered his arms and looked up at Fabian. Blood ran down his face, pain and misery etched into his features. "Thank you."

Camdyn returned to the top of the hill with them. There, Shayna found a first-aid kit in her backpack and started taking care of his wounds, while Fabian erected two tents. It was only afternoon, but after the birds, none of them had felt like walking anywhere else. There seemed little to no point.

"This is ridiculous," Fabian ranted. "What kind of exam is this? Find the Herb of Heavens. Oh, and try not to die."

"Die?" Camdyn said softly. "You dealt with those birds in seconds."

Fabian grunted. "That's not the point. They were still dangerous. Don't you agree?"

Camdyn only clenched his fists, retreating into himself once more. Shayna tried to coax him from his shell. "Why didn't you defend yourself against the birds and use your powers?"

"If you haven't noticed, I don't have any."

"Of course you do. You're an air mage. That's why you're at the Citadel."

Camdyn shook his head, tears in his eyes. "They only took me because they had to. I don't even want to be here."

Fabian stopped his pacing. "Camdyn—"

But it was too late. Camdyn jumped up. His fists clenched, he shouted, "You belong here! This is your world, your magic. But I don't. I don't want to be here. I don't want to be an elemental mage, and I definitely don't want to use these stupid, weak-ass wind powers!"

Shayna and Fabian exchanged a look but decided to let him continue. It sounded like he'd pent up a lot of emotions and, in Shayna's opinion, it was better if they came out now than when they were in danger.

"All I want is to get this horrible year done with and go back home!" Camdyn continued. "I want to return to my normal school, my normal friends, and my sisters in Ireland." He started shaking, the tears barely held back. "It's easy for you. You get to go home every night and I... and I... I'm not allowed to."

It was all too much. Suddenly, the tears were flowing, his legs gave in, and he collapsed, crying his heart out. He hit his face with the palms of his hands, as if he could somehow push the tears back inside.

Fabian and Shayna looked at each other, full of sympathy for their younger classmate. Shayna had thought he was just a loner, but it turned out there was so much more to Camdyn. He was just as lost as they were. Maybe even more.

Samantha

Though Samantha wanted nothing more than to drown herself in a nice uncomplicated monster hunt, she couldn't stop thinking about Matt. She should've told him to go to Fader or Hell, so she wouldn't have to worry about him. Not that she was worried. In her opinion, he deserved to be nibbled on by a siren.

She sighed. No, he didn't deserve that just because he'd said something stupid. It had just... hurt.

Until last night, she'd full-heartedly believed in them. After everything they'd been through and everything they'd sacrificed, she'd been madly in love. But of course, the honeymoon phase was coming to an end, and it was time to face reality. And the reality was that Matt had never been in a long-term relationship, so why did she expect him to believe in their longevity? A leopard didn't change its spots, not even after tearing up half of Hell to find her.

Samantha stopped at the crossing. Her job was to find the sirens with her magic and lead the rest of the girls there, but her thoughts kept slipping to Matt instead. "Sorry."

"Sorry for what?" Lucille asked, looking worried.

"I'm a little distracted, that's all. I'll find their signature."

She closed her eyes and tried to listen to the hum of the river of magic. If she concentrated hard enough, she could hear the siren song in the murmur, a song so irresistible to the male ear not even Matt would be able to withstand it. He'd be stupid enough to think otherwise. She just knew it. He'd overthink their quarrel and then get all worried about her and come find her, only to fall victim to the sirens.

Rachel groaned. "Alright, spill."

Samantha opened her eyes again. "Spill what?"

"My boyfriend is in danger of being eaten. I need you to lead me to him, but you just said it yourself: you're distracted because of some stupid fight with Matt. So, please, get it all out, so we can comfort you or rant with you, then put it aside to focus on the important stuff."

Lucille raised an eyebrow, her question unspoken but clear.

Samantha's face felt hot. "It's nothing." A glare made her quickly reconsider. "Okay, okay. If you think it'll help." She took a deep breath. "As you already said, it's stupid. We both witnessed that wedding party at university yesterday and he said something silly."

"Oh, that." Lucille nodded sagely. "Yes, that wasn't his finest hour."

"What did he say?" Ophelia asked.

"Oh, he just asked if I wanted that because he clearly doesn't, and basically that he doesn't believe in eternal love. Typical Matt stuff, insensitive as heck, but I should've known. After all, he's still half-demon, and I can't expect him to know how hurtful it is to hear he thinks we're just temporary. And I mean, it's not like I wanted to marry him right there and then." In fact, she hadn't even thought about marriage until then.

Lucille put her hands on her shoulders and looked deep into her eyes. "Sam. Matt loves you. He might not be a big fan of marriage, but he loves you as much as anyone could love someone."

She sighed. "I know. It's just... Sometimes, his pragmatism—or I guess realism—is a bit hard to swallow."

"Because he's not convinced your love is forever?" Rachel asked impatiently. "Most couples don't make it. And they have much shorter lives."

It reminded Samantha of the downfall of her parents' marriage, and suddenly, she felt sad. "So, you think it's not meant to last?"

"Nonsense!" Lucille protested. "You're made for each other. If you don't make it, no one will. But this is all still new and different... especially for Matt. You know he needs a little longer to understand human sensibilities. But that doesn't mean he doesn't love you."

It all made sense to her, but the sting still wouldn't go away. "I guess it really is different when you're basically immortal." Slowly, the words sank in. "Oh god, it's totally different." She pointed at Rachel. "As you said, you can never be sure, but swearing eternal love when you have maybe fifty or sixty years together is much easier. Just look at how much we've evolved in a thousand years." Just thinking about what it meant to be alive for such a long time made Samantha's head swim. "I can't even imagine what that looks like."

"Neither can I," Lucille said, "but while Matt might live that long eventually, he's only nineteen now, just like us. He can't imagine eternity either, no matter how old his siblings are."

"Or eternal love." Samantha rubbed her face. "I have no idea why this suddenly matters. The important thing is we're together now and hopefully will be for a bit longer, unless a siren decides to have him for breakfast."

"Does that mean we're done?" Rachel asked.

Samantha nodded sharply. "Yes, we're done."

She could see a bit clearer now and understood how this must've thrown Matt for a loop. Once she'd dealt with the sirens, she'd sit him down and communicate her feelings to him—and apologise for overreacting.

She filed the thoughts away and listened for the song once more. There was a certain ethereal quality to it, a hint of how intoxicating it could be, but when she listened to it more closely, she recognised the underlying threat like a second, darker melody. The true melody.

"This way, I think."

"You think?" Rachel asked, her voice sharp as a knife.

"There might be more than one nest."

"Yippie," Ophelia said. "Should we split up?"

Samantha shook her head. "Let's not underestimate them."

Lucille nodded. "We'll get them, one by one."

And hopefully, Samantha thought, they'd get through them before Matt lost his mind and came after her.

Fabian

Though there was still plenty of daylight, Fabian and Shayna had decided to pause. They both had the feeling that finding the herb required more thinking and less hiking all over the place. As Kaia had said, there was a hint in there somewhere. But most importantly, they didn't feel like Camdyn was in any state to join them. It was surprising enough he hadn't run away again. Instead, he was sat on a rocky outcrop, watching the countryside—probably homesick for the green hills of his home country. Fabian and Shayna were setting up a fireplace—or rather, Fabian was watching Shayna as she coaxed flames out of a pile of sticks they'd found.

"Do you think I should talk to him?" Fabian asked as his gaze fell on Camdyn yet again. The wind blew through his blond hair, but he didn't seem to feel it. "I didn't want to be an elemental mage either when I first discovered my magic. Knowing I'd have to fight monsters was scary. It's still scary, to be honest."

"And yet you do it." Shayna looked over at Camdyn. "Do you think it's that? Fear?"

Fabian shrugged. "I don't know."

"Talk to him. You're good at that."

"I am?"

"If I remember correctly, you once stopped me from eating my fingers, and you never mocked me for it."

It took Fabian a moment to recall the incident. He'd found Shayna in tears, hiding from the party, losing her mind because of a witch's curse. "That was at Walpurgis, right? You made me swear not to tell anyone."

Shayna smiled. "And you kept your promise." She glanced at Camdyn again. "I think he could use a friend like you. I'm just the bitch who threatened you back then."

"You haven't been a bitch for a long time."

She stared at him, baffled. Then she laughed and shook her head. "Go on."

Fabian got up, stuffed his hands in his pockets, and made his way over to Camdyn. For once, he didn't run away, though he didn't look at him either.

"I didn't know you were from Ireland," Fabian said, hoping to find an easy way into the conversation. "When did you learn German?"

"I didn't." Camdyn's shoulders were stiff, but after a moment it looked like he'd forced himself to relax. "There's a spell on the Citadel that makes all of us able to speak the same language." He finally looked at him. "You know the Citadel is somewhere in Finland?"

"Um, no, I had no idea." He'd suspected it was up north, but since he always travelled via the portal, he hadn't really thought about it. "I mean, I knew it wasn't close-by, so..."

"It's alright. I know you're not a theory guy," Camdyn said. "Or one who reads his student guide." Before Fabian could protest, Camdyn deflated again. "And I'm the one who's not good at magic."

There it was. The thing that made Camdyn so closed-off. "Do you want to tell me why?"

Camdyn just gritted his teeth.

"You know, when I first found out about my water powers, I wanted nothing more than to be rid of them." Now he'd piqued Camdyn's interest. "It scared me... and I... It wasn't just the magic, but the monsters, too. They came with the magic, and my friends... They expected me to use my magic to fight. They were all excited about it, but for me... I was just scared. I didn't want it. The responsibility."

"What changed?" Camdyn asked, hanging on to every word.

"Well, for one, the powers didn't go away, but mostly, I needed them to protect the people I cared about."

To Fabian's horror, Camdyn looked down again, clearly fighting tears.

"Did I say something wrong?"

Camdyn shook his head. "I... I just wish I could protect my sisters with my magic, but... But it makes everything worse. It's the cause of all evil and..." He took a deep breath. "Forget it. Sounds like the people around you were supportive."

"And yours weren't?"

Camdyn took a shaky breath, and Fabian knew he was close to breaking again. He could withdraw now and let him rebuild the wall he'd erected around his heart, or he could push a little further. Carefully.

"Who says you're not allowed home?"

"My grandfather." Camdyn pressed the words out, clearly feeling the sting.

"Your grandfather?"

Camdyn stared ahead as he gave the slightest nod. "He says magic is the tool of the devil. That good people don't play with it." He took another shaky breath. "My mother was a wind mage, a wild mage, just like us. She never learnt how to control it. Bad luck followed her around until..." His breathing accelerated. "She's dead. Because of the magic. And my grandfather says she's burning in Hell because of it."

Fabian was horrified. He realised how lucky he'd been discovering his magic in a town like Greenvalley, surrounded by open-minded friends. It was a privilege not everybody had.

"If it helps, I went to Hell once. It's not exactly my favourite place, but I haven't seen a single soul burning down there." He noticed Camdyn staring wide-eyed. "I'm serious. Hell exists. It's not an afterlife, but the home world of demons. And your mother isn't there, trust me."

For a moment, Camdyn continued to stare. Then the tears welled in his eyes, he grimaced, and suddenly, he started sobbing. Fabian moved a little closer and put his arm around him. At first, Camdyn stiffened, but then he held onto Fabian's shirt and cried and cried.

When it sounded like he was calming down again, Fabian offered him a tissue and let him gather himself.

"He threw me out when the invitation arrived," Camdyn said, after blowing his nose. "He didn't want me to corrupt my sisters."

"Honestly, your grandfather sounds like a real piece of work. I'm so sorry."

The corners of Camdyn's mouth twitched. "It's not your fault."

"So, where are you staying now?"

Camdyn gave a one-shoulder shrug. "At the Citadel. They're taking care of everything, and Professor Terian is supportive and all... but you've seen me in class. I'm not very talented. I haven't progressed at all." Bitterly, he added, "In fact, it doesn't look like I'm a mage at all." Suddenly, his face lit up. "Maybe my grandfather will let me return if they tell him I can't actually do any magic."

Fabian bit his tongue, not wanting to dash his hope, but he didn't believe returning to Ireland would do him any favours. Not like this. "Could it be that you can't do magic because deep down you shun it as much as your grandfather does?"

Eyes full of sorrow, Camdyn turned away again. He never answered and Fabian didn't push. Instead, they sat in silence, watching the sun sinking behind the mountains in the distance.

Jan

One hour in, and Jan was already bored. He'd napped on the couch, but knowing there was a monster in town made it impossible for his brain to settle. He was trying to read through the texts Leandres had left him to study. Apparently, the healer wanted to test him on his herbal knowledge, but Jan already knew he'd fail, and unlike Caspar's books, the pages upon pages of herb descriptions didn't entice him at all.

At the sound of footsteps on the stairs, Jan looked up hopefully as Matt and Crumbs came back down. "Do you want to play something?" He pointed at the TV.

"Just grabbing a snack for Crumbs. I've got plenty of homework to do." Matt pulled a face. "An essay on marriage customs, of all things."

Jan winced. "Ouch. You're probably worrying too much, though."

Matt snorted. "Yeah? Did things look okay to you this morning? She's distancing herself with a monster hunt."

"To avoid the inevitable." Jan nodded sagely. "You should probably think about some big romantic gesture so she'll stop worrying about the future and enjoy the present more."

"She's got nothing to worry about. I'm not going to break up with her. Ever." That didn't mean Samantha wouldn't kick him to the curb if he continued to mess things up.

"Sounds close to eternity for me," Jan said, in a sing-song voice.

Matt snorted again and vanished into the kitchen. After rummaging through the cupboards, he apparently jumped back into his room, avoiding Jan.

Jan laughed softly, feeling invigorated by the brief exchange. He almost felt sorry for Matt, but then he remembered how lacklustre his own love life was. Meg had completely blindsided him when she'd dumped him, and things with Sandra moved at a glacial speed—if they moved at all.

He wondered if she was still on call now.

With a wicked smile, he put his headphones on, grabbed his jacket, and headed to the hospital.

The headphones and heavy hip hop beats in his ears worked perfectly fine, and Jan arrived at the hospital without feeling the urge to follow any strange music. Once safely behind walls again, he took off the headphones, waved to the registration desk attendant, and headed upstairs. He idly wondered how many men the sirens could lure to them. It clearly wasn't the entire city. Maybe they employed a more selective method? A shame they'd gone straight after Rachel's boyfriend. Maybe they preferred magic users, like the banshees had.

Jan took out his phone and dialled his sister's number.

"Jan?" she asked, sounding a little surprised.

"Hey. Um, do you know if Robert is at work today?" Whether he believed it or not, Robert seemed to possess some deep-buried magic.

"I think he only had a half-day."

That made things a little more complicated. "Okay, um, could you let him know—subtly, of course—that he needs to stay inside? There's a bunch of men-eating sirens in town." A nurse walked past, raising an eyebrow. "New movie. It's really good."

Anne giggled on the other side of the line. "I'll tell him. And I assume Finn and Dad should stay inside, too?"

"Finn?" Jan took a moment to remember. "Oh, the boy who replaced me."

"He didn't replace you."

Jan snorted. "Oh, but I'm sure he's a much better son. Well-behaved and all that."

Anne clicked her tongue. "Of course, he's well-behaved. He's terrified they're going to throw him out if he messes up."

Suddenly, Jan felt sorry for the boy. He'd been thrown out before, so the fear wasn't unwarranted. Especially since Finn had simply turned up on their doorstep. "How's he doing?"

"Other than being so damn polite and helpful, alright. He's slowly getting used to everything. And I think it's great having another priest around. I'm learning so much."

"Have you converted to Serathon now?"

Anne laughed. "Switching from the Goddess of Life to the God of Madness? No, thanks. But he can teach me about rituals and what life at the temple was like before they all killed each other. I've got so many questions." Her voice tapered off slightly, as if distracted.

Jan saw Sandra in front of him, sorting pills into trays. "I can only imagine. Look, I've got to go. Take care of everyone."

"I'll tell them—"

Jan had already ended the call. With a lazy grin, he approached the nurse and leant against the wall. "Hey, there."

She gave him one of her brilliant smiles. "Aren't you a bit early for your shift?"

"I was bored."

"I'd ask if you wanted to study for your practical, but knowing you, you're going to ace it."

"Of course, I will. I'm all for the hands-on stuff." When she giggled, Jan felt slightly emboldened. "You know, I was wondering if we could—"

Just then, his classmate André walked past, glaring. "You're off duty. You need to go home and rest."

Irritated, Jan watched him go. Sandra giggled again. "He doesn't like you at all, does he?"

"Well, what can I say? Success breeds envy."

"And admirers." She finished up her pills and started pushing the cart.

Jan followed her. "Is that so? Which are you, then?"

"Wouldn't you like to know?"

She was definitely flirting now. "Maybe you could tell me over dinner. My treat."

Sandra cast her eyes down. "I have to get back to work now."

Jan suppressed a sigh and grabbed two of her trays. "I'll help you." He walked backwards with them. "Because that's what I am. Helpful, caring, hands on…" He winked before turning around and delivering the marked trays to the patients in the room behind.

As he chatted with them and handed them their pills, the most beautiful melody he'd ever heard reached his ears. It came through the open window, beckoning him to follow.

Jan put down the second tray and walked towards the sound. He was on the third floor, but that wouldn't stop him. Within a second, he was on the windowsill, reaching for the rain spout to climb down the side of the building. Alarmed shouts rang in his ears, but the lovely melody soon drowned them out.

Lucille

Lucille felt like they were back at the zoo as they approached a storage unit. She had no idea what was so irresistible to men, but to her, the sirens sounded like screeching harpies. And there was a stench in the air she couldn't quite place. Bird excrement and maybe blood, but also something else, a heavy pungent smell.

"It's compulsion," Samantha whispered, and scrunched up her nose. "The sirens use their song to impose their will on their victims."

Under the mantle of her illusion, they managed to sneak up to a window. Lucille peered through and immediately wished she hadn't. The place was a mess: clumps of flesh and feathers everywhere. She'd thought the men would fight nail and tooth before they'd let themselves be eaten, but instead they prostrated themselves, offering their arms to the sirens with dreamy smiles.

The sirens were the most grotesque creatures Lucille had ever seen. From the navel up, they were beautiful, feathers sticking out of their long hair and their pert breasts bare for all to see. But instead of arms, they had long, multi-coloured wings, and from the hips down, they were fully bird—and not even a pretty bird, but some type of vulture. They ate from the men by tearing pieces of flesh off them with one claw, leaving their mouths smeared with blood.

"There's Merik."

Lucille's heart pounded. She'd hoped he'd just returned to Fader, despite leaving his things behind, but now those hopes were dashed. He was a little further back in the shadows, watching the man in front being eaten in a blissful daze, unaware he was next.

"What's he doing here?" Samantha asked.

"Long story."

Samantha threw her a long look. She sighed. "There are eight sirens, two for each of us. Let's use the illusion to even out those numbers." She quickly pointed to specific sirens to give each a target, picking those hunched over to eat. "Once that's done, we'll deal with the others. Watch each other's backs."

Rachel cocked her crossbow, already laying a bolt into the depression. They hadn't seen Adam among the men, though not everyone had been visible from the window. "Let's go."

Lucille rewove her illusion to mask their steps, and they hurried around the corner. With one last nod, they entered the storage unit and fanned out. She wished she could just set the whole place on fire, but that would've hurt the men, too. Instead, she wove a path through the disgusting lumps on the ground and focused on the siren who was still tearing flesh from her victim. Even though he was bleeding profusely, he kept smiling and proclaiming his undying love.

"Vignec Araca," Lucille whispered, and stretched out her hands.

Vines burst from her palms, cracking through the air like a whip. They wrapped themselves around the siren and tore her from her meal. Shrieking ensued as her friends attacked the others. Lucille trusted them to deal with their targets and sent her fireball racing down her magical vines. The smell of roasted chicken rose in the air.

Bile in her mouth, Lucille ran to Merik. She slapped a hand on his arm and waved the other in front of his eyes, but he stared right through her. "Merik, please. You have to run."

His gaze fell on her, then suddenly, he raised his arms and grabbed her by the throat.

"Me—"

His fingers tightened, and Lucille coughed. Panicked, she kicked and hit him, not sure which spell to use.

Just as suddenly as it started, the attack stopped, and Merik stepped back. "Lucille?"

Still breathing hard, she looked around and saw Samantha had sunk her Thorak into a nearby siren's chest.

"It was her," she said.

Understanding trickled in slowly, just as another siren sneaked up on Samantha. "Sam!"

Her friend reacted a second too late. The siren sunk a claw into her shoulder and jerked her backwards. A bolt flew, hitting a wing, and the siren let go, shrieking. A second bolt ended her.

Lucille ran to Samantha, worried when she saw the blood seeping through the tears in her jacket. Samantha looked like she was still trying to process what had happened, but then the pain set in, and she moaned.

"Are you okay?"

She nodded, inhaling with a hiss. "There's more."

Lucille spun around and saw a siren being swallowed by shadows, while Rachel struck another. Two sirens converged on her, and Lucille threw her fireballs, burning them before the sirens could hurt another of her friends.

"That should be all," Samantha said, breathlessly. She winced again as she tried to move her shoulder.

"What's going on?" Merik asked. He stooped and picked up a feather. Around them, the other men started to stumble around, confused. Some screamed.

"I'm calling an ambulance," Rachel said, ignoring Merik. She checked over Samantha. "Do you need one, too?"

Samantha shook her head. "I'd prefer Jan."

"Good idea," Lucille said, "Let's go back and—"

"Adam isn't here."

Lucille's heart went out to her—she'd been worried sick about Merik, and he was little more than an exciting fling. It must've been so much worse for Rachel. Her boyfriend brought out a side in her Lucille had never seen before, something light and airy. She couldn't allow Adam to slip away so soon.

"We'll find him, but Samantha needs medical assistance."

"It's alright, I can..." Samantha winced again. "If you want, you can go on, and I'll head back."

"No," Lucille said, before Rachel could agree. "We'll all head back to Jan and Matt, regroup, then we'll attack the next nest and the next, until we find Adam."

Rachel looked as if she was going to argue, but then nodded. "Let's make it quick." She called the ambulance as she strode out, Ophelia on her heels.

Lucille sighed and plucked a tissue from her purse, pressing it to Samantha's shoulder. It was soaked in blood instantly. "You sure you don't want to wait?"

Samantha looked a bit strained. "I'm good, I promise. You need to take care of that." She nodded over her shoulder.

"I'm sorry," Lucille said, turning to Merik. "Just another Tuesday in Greenvalley, I'm afraid." More seriously, she added, "You're not safe here, Merik. Go back to Fader. I'll let you know when we've dealt with the sirens."

"You're sending me away?" he asked, one beautifully arched eyebrow raised.

"Unless you want to be eaten?"

He cracked a weary smile. "No, I can't say that was in my plans for today."

"I'll give you my headphones so you'll make it safely to the portal." She stood on her tiptoes and kissed his cheek. "I'll come find you once this is over."

After making sure Merik had made it safely out, the girls returned to the Blackstone House. Crumbs greeted them excitedly, but none of the boys showed or even called out.

"Are they sleeping?" Ophelia asked, sounding bewildered.

"They must be bored out of their minds," Lucille assumed.

A loud noise from the cellar made them all jump. Jan's teacher, Leandres, appeared, patting the snow off his shoulders. "Ah, it's you." He squinted at them and immediately zoned in on Samantha. "Looks bad. Typical. When you need him, the boy's nowhere to be found."

Samantha paled, even taking a step back when Leandres approached. "Jan isn't here?"

"According to the little snow witch, he went to work earlier. Now let me have a—"

Samantha bolted, running upstairs.

Lucille rubbed her face, trying not to curse Jan and his stupidity. "Work? Why would he want to go to work? He's not even on shift."

"Beats me," Leandres grumbled. "The boy's more interested in pulling people out of wrecks and rescuing kittens than true healing."

Samantha came running down again, almost stumbling, looking even paler. "He's gone! We need to leave."

"You're hurt," Lucille pointed out.

"Glad someone else has noticed." Leandres tugged on Samantha's healthy arm and directed her to the couch.

When she tried to resist, he put a hand on her other shoulder. Screaming, she went down like a sack of potatoes.

Lucille winced. "We're going to rescue them all, but first you need to let Leandres do his thing. Besides, are you sure Matt didn't just jump to Hell or Fader? He isn't stupid." Unlike Jan.

"No, no, he left door open." Neve floated through the door, a glistening ice crown on her head.

"Why?" Samantha asked, bewildered. "Why would he do such a thing?"

"Jan gone and Matt forgot warning, and then he forgot everything."

Lucille had no idea what Neve was trying to say, but it didn't matter. "We can't do anything until we've got you patched up, Sam, so please calm down. Take Rachel for example: she also wants nothing more than—Rachel?"

She turned to her friend, but Rachel's eyes were not only staring into nothingness, they were milky white. Ophelia tapped her arm, and suddenly, Rachel swayed, her eyes rolled back, and she fell to the ground, unconscious.

Shayna

The sun was setting over the magical enclave. Fabian had put up all three tents, while Shayna had tended the fire, and Camdyn had cooked a simple porridge for dinner. His earlier chat with Fabian had loosened him and he was even cautiously asking questions.

"What do you think will happen if we don't pass?" Camdyn asked, clearly worried.

Shayna flashed him an encouraging smile. "Oh, you know. Professor Terian will be very disappointed, and in a month, we'll get to try again. Don't worry—they're so excited about having four elemental mages they won't give up on us that quickly." From everything she'd seen, the Citadel was desperate to keep them.

For some reason, the answer left him even more agitated. Fabian put a hand on his back, and he calmed a little. "We still have a full day. Tomorrow, we'll search together, make a proper plan. And if we don't make it, it's not on us, but the lack of clear instructions."

"I'm not surprised," a familiar bitchy voice said. Kaia stomped into their camp as if she owned the place. "If you fail, it's everybody else's fault. Right?"

She sat by the fire, as far from anyone as she could. Despite her haughty behaviour, she looked like she'd had a shit day. Both her clothes and skin were dirty, as if she'd been rolling in the mud, and her usually straight hair was tangled. Shayna lowered her face, so the earth mage wouldn't see her smirk.

"With that kind of attitude," Kaia said, filling a bowl with left-over porridge without asking, "you won't get anywhere in life."

"And where is this supposed to get us?" Fabian asked, sounding a little tired. He was good at comforting angsty little boys, but he had no idea how to handle a bitch like Kaia. "What amazing job opportunities will this education in elemental magic open up for us?"

"You'll be working at the Citadel," Kaia said promptly. "So long as they don't kick you out."

Camdyn looked like he was going to throw up—which Shayna could empathise with. Kaia often had that effect on her. He got up and vanished into his tent.

"You know, you're not making us want to work for the Citadel," Shayna said, pointedly. "If they're all like you, then no, thank you." She'd hate having to learn how to run the bed and breakfast, but she'd rather have her own business than be looked down on her entire life.

"I'm going to bed, too," Fabian said.

Shayna was a little annoyed at him for throwing the towel in so early, forcing her to give in, too, but it was important they stuck together, so she stood as well. "Good idea."

"Please don't sleep with each other tonight, okay?" Kaia said, sounding almost anxious. "The rest of us want to actually sleep."

"We're not a couple," Fabian protested, his face beet-red.

"He's got a girlfriend," Shayna explained.

Kaia's nostrils flared. "Poor girl."

Shayna could see Kaia getting under Fabian's skin. She tugged on his shirt and nodded towards the tents. "Don't react. She's just trying to stir up trouble. She probably doesn't have anyone who can last more than five minutes with her."

He nodded, his thoughts clearly with Ophelia. The little shadow wielder was probably freaking out again, inviting all kinds of thoughts into her head. As much as it saddened Shayna, there was no doubt Fabian loved her. If only his girlfriend wasn't so damn insecure and kept trying to ruin their friendship.

They left Kaia at the fire and went to their separate tents. As Shayna lay in her sleeping bag, trying to get comfortable, she thought about what Kaia had said. Judging by the welcome, she should've guessed their ties with the Citadel wouldn't be snapped after graduation. They hadn't paid any student fees, and everyone had been incredibly accommodating—there had to be a catch. If only she knew enough about the inner workings so she could make a more educated guess.

Once they were back—herb or no herb—Shayna promised herself to dig deeper. Kaia was a dead-end, but surely someone else was willing to talk.

They woke with the sunrise, eager to tackle the second day of their exam. After packing up their tents and eating a quick breakfast, Fabian cleared a patch of dirt and started drawing a map with a stick. It was surprisingly recognisable.

"We need a proper plan. We don't know when our time is up exactly, so let's make the most of it. Shayna and I covered this area yesterday. Camdyn searched here. Kaia?"

Kaia already had her backpack on. "I know where I'm going today."

Fabian took a deep breath. "And if you tell us, maybe we can go together."

"I don't share my secrets with wild mages." Kaia extended her hand and Fabian's earth drawing shook until the map was erased.

"Terian said it's a team task," Shayna snapped. It was one thing to be obnoxious and stubborn, but messing with them was the line she wouldn't let Kaia cross.

The earth mage snorted. "Terian is an idealist. He thinks adding wild mages to the Citadel could be beneficial, even though they're totally ignorant. It'll never work. Your lot are nothing but trouble."

"Is that so?" Fabian said, his voice strained.

"Don't worry," Kaia said, as if they were supposed to be grateful. "I'm going to find the Herb of Heavens for you, because I won't fail." And with that, she marched off towards a stretch of mountains rising in the distance.

As soon as she was out of earshot—or perhaps before—Shayna groaned. "Man, that bitch is so aggravating."

"I think she feels threatened," Camdyn offered quietly.

"Threatened?" Fabian asked.

Camdyn nodded. "As far as I know, she spent all her life with the other Citadel kids. With her parents' position and her being an elemental mage, she's always been at the top of the food chain. But now... now there are three more elemental mages and at least one is much more talented."

"Poor little Queen Bee." Shayna was still too angry after Kaia's morning show to grant her any grace. She grinned at Fabian. "Well, she's right to be afraid of you. Come on, let's show her how threatening a bunch of wild mages can be."

Fabian stared at his destroyed map. "I've always hated petty power struggles. I thought we were supposed to be done with that after school."

"Hardly. But letting her get away with it isn't an option, either. None of us want Cheryl Take Two."

Fabian shuddered. "Oh, please no."

"Who's Cheryl?" Camdyn asked.

"Shayna's best friend," Fabian said sullenly.

Shayna burst out laughing. "Definitely not!" To Camdyn, she said, "Someone who thinks she was the crème de la crème, just like Kaia. And yes, as Fabian will probably tell you, we shared the same friends, so I know how those kind of girls tick, and how to deal with them. Leave Kaia to me."

Camdyn looked back and forth between Fabian and Shayna, clearly overwhelmed. "Okay... what's our plan now?"

Rachel

Rachel had never stepped into the dreamworld while waking before. The experience was abrupt and disjointed. Instead of easing into her meadow of dreams, where she could pick from the flowers around her, she was thrown in without any kind of warning. Worse, it felt unstable, like the deck of a ship rolling on the waves. The edges of her view were tinted black, and if she turned her head she could catch shadows fleeing from her gaze, only to gather at the rim again. The light was odd, too, like a photograph in sepia.

She was in some kind of prison. The cells were filled with young men, all handsome to a degree. They pressed themselves against the bars, not because they wanted to escape, but because they yearned for the attention of the bird women outside. Rachel knew it was the sirens—their song hung heavy in the air—but unlike the ugly creatures of the real world, they looked almost completely human here, with only a hint of feathers here and there. She wondered if that was how the men saw them.

There were dozens of sirens. From time to time, they picked a man from the crowd and led the unlucky chap to a secluded area. Not all were instantly devoured, instead, they served them with glazed-over looks, allowing the sirens to nibble on them if they wanted. Only one of the victims was completely devoured while the others watched on, eager to be next.

Rachel turned away and studied the men, looking for Adam. She couldn't see him anywhere, but she did find Matt and Jan.

"Hey!" She stood right in front of them and snapped her fingers, but they looked right through her, their clouded gazes following the sirens.

A brown-haired beauty opened the cell, and immediately, the crowd of men shifted towards her. Tenderly, she used a feather to stroke their cheeks. Some shuddered and moaned, making Rachel very uncomfortable.

Then she turned her attentions to Matt and said, "You."

The men parted with a groan to let him pass.

"No!" Rachel shouted. "Matt! Don't let her eat you."

The siren smiled at him, then pointed to another, burly guy. "And you." She dragged him out and shut the door with a loud clang. "Fight."

Rachel hadn't expected that and quickly jumped out of the way when Matt and the other guy circled each other, just as eager to draw blood as they were to serve the siren. She winced when Matt landed his first blow. Though his opponent was bulkier, he had little fighting experience and was no match for the half-demon.

More sirens drew nearer to watch the commotion, while the men cheered on their favourites. Some begged to be next. After a few exchanges, Matt had his victim immobilised on the ground.

The siren who'd picked him stepped closer and handed him a dagger. "Kill him," she said, in her seductive sing-song voice.

"No!"

Rachel realised what she was seeing wasn't a dream or vision but what was actually happening. For some reason, the sirens and their nest were connected to the dream world. Which meant... she might be able to fight them.

Matt licked his lips ready to become a killer again.

She ran over and slapped her hands over his ears, willing them to block out the siren song. To her relief, Matt's eyes cleared, and he looked down at his opponent in confusion. What she hadn't accounted for was the fervour the song instilled in its victims.

The other man grabbed the dagger from Matt's limp hand and pointed it at his own throat. "For you, I'll die gladly."

Before Rachel could do anything, he'd sliced his own throat, spraying her and Matt with blood.

Matt's eyelids fluttered in surprise. He got up, trying to assess the situation. The siren stepped forward. Cradling his face, she sang exclusively for him. Though Rachel did her best to block it out, the siren's song was stronger, and Matt's eyes glazed over again. Looking into emptiness, he allowed the siren to lick the blood from his chest.

Frustrated, Rachel turned away, nearly running into a pair of sirens who'd approached Matt.

"I wish I could eat him," the blonde one said, running a finger across Matt's neck. "Just a little bite?"

"He's one of the queen's chosen. She likes the taste of magic in his blood," her friend said.

The blonde snorted. "So do I."

With a sigh, she let go, and they threw themselves on the dying man at their feet instead. Rachel felt her skin crawl and rushed away. From what she'd gathered, Matt was safe for now, and there was a queen. A queen who had a taste for mage blood.

It wasn't hard to find the siren in question. She just had to follow the song down the corridor, past more men and sirens. At last, she reached a separate room. On a throne that looked as if it'd been built from sticks and bones sat a beautiful woman dressed in a feathery robe. A half-naked man knelt at her feet, offering her his arm. His entire back was covered in bite marks that looked almost thoughtfully placed.

"Adam!"

Like Matt and Jan, he didn't hear her, but the queen did. She looked straight at Rachel, letting Adam's hand sink. "What do we have here? A little dreamer?"

Rachel felt overcome with fury. This bird-woman had stolen her boyfriend and fed on him. "I'm the Dreamer. Let him go."

The queen threw her head back and laughed. "Why would I do that? Just because you say so, little girl? You don't have any power here. This is my realm, and I happen to like this specimen of your kind. His magic is," she licked her lips sensually, "delicious."

"That's disgusting."

"It's food." The queen stroked Adam's face with her feathers. "Handsome food."

Rachel shook from fear and anger. "You can't eat him. He's mine."

"You wouldn't be the first woman to die because she couldn't let go of her man. He loves me now. Until his death."

"Or yours," Rachel said with a harsh, unforgiving voice. "This is my world and I make the rules. If you don't want to—"

"You've only just dipped your feather into this realm." The queen spoke with a strange fascination. "The Realm of Dreams is full of false paths and hidden depths. Let me give you a taste of what it is you're asking for when you challenge me."

Her face turned into a frightening grimace, making her almost look as if she had a beak. She opened her mouth and screamed. A storm sprung from her lips, causing the feathers in the room to swirl. It picked Rachel up and threw her not just out of the door, but out of the dreamworld, too.

When Rachel woke, she was lying on the couch at the Blackstone House, surrounded by Samantha, Lucille, and Ophelia, who were watching her with concern.

"Told you she was fine," Leandres grumbled from somewhere behind them.

"What happened?" Lucille asked, agitated.

Rachel sat up slowly, trying to get a feel for the real world again. "I saw it all."

"What?" Ophelia asked, sitting down next to her.

"The sirens. They've got a queen. And I saw the boys." She searched Samantha's gaze. "Matt and Jan don't seem to be on the menu for now. They're just holding them. Unlike Adam. The queen's feasting on him. Apparently, she prefers magical blood. He's alive, and I'm pretty sure she's going to keep him that way a little longer. At least until I come back."

Lucille frowned. "Come back?"

"She has control over the dreamworld somehow. That's where I was, in a dream that's also reality." Rachel was still struggling to understand how that was possible. "Anyway, she said I wasn't strong enough to challenge her, and well, it looks like she was right, because she blasted me right out of there."

Samantha crossed her arms. Apparently, Leandres had finished healing her shoulder. "Were you able to see where they are? If we can't defeat this queen in the dreamworld, we might be able to do it from here."

"I'm pretty sure they're at the prison. I saw lots of cells. No idea what they did to the police, probably put them under a spell too—or ate them."

"Alright, the prison it is, then. Let's go." Despite learning Matt was okay, Samantha didn't seem to want to waste any time getting him back.

"You do that," Rachel said, feeling a sense of clarity. "I think I need to face the siren queen in the dreamworld. Maybe she has to be killed in both. At the very least, I'll distract her." Her gaze fell on Ophelia. "Maybe, if I borrow your powers." She had an idea.

Ophelia's eyes widened. "What do you mean?"

"If you come with me, you can hide us in your shadows. This way, we might be able to sneak up on the queen and pluck her pretty feathers."

"Worth a try," Ophelia said with a grin.

Lucille and Samantha exchanged a look. "Can we hold them down with just the two of us?" Lucille asked.

"We could use your illusions to lure them out one by one or pretend we're sirens."

"Sounds like a plan." Lucille tapped Leandres' shoulder. "Master Leandres?"

He looked up, disgruntled, and pulled a wax clump from his ear. "Huh?"

"Clever. We're going to leave Rachel and Ophelia here. I trust you to take good care of them. We might need your healing powers later," Lucille explained.

Leandres looked even grumpier. "I'm here to teach that lad, not be a convenient healer for daring wannabe heroes." With another grumble he added, "I'll be here."

Lucille smiled warmly. "Thank you." As soon as Leandres put his wax clump back and returned to his reading, she rolled her eyes. "Sometimes I wonder if he missed his calling."

"He's a world-class healer," Samantha said, nodding at her shoulder. "But maybe Jan could teach him something about bedside manner."

Lucille snorted, and they got ready to leave.

Rachel turned to Ophelia and took her hands. "Breathe calmly. Imagine you're floating through space."

She kept talking in a calm, soothing manner until Ophelia's eyelids grew heavy and she fell asleep. Then she closed her eyes and followed her into the dreamworld.

Fabian

After Kaia destroyed his dirt map, Fabian had drawn a traditional paper one to mark their progress. So far, their scouting hadn't proved any more successful than the previous day's. The only difference was there were three of them now, and Camdyn seemed to be warming up. At least, he was answering questions now.

"So, you sleep at the Citadel?" Shayna asked. "What's that like?"

"Quite lonely, to be honest." Camdyn rarely looked up, keeping his eyes trained on the ground instead. Somehow, Fabian doubted it was because he was looking for the herb. "There are all these Citadel mage cliques. They want nothing to do with me."

Fabian knew only too well what that looked like. "Hey, if it gets too much for you, you're always welcome to come to Greenvalley with us. We'll find a bed for you."

"Are you serious?" Camdyn sounded surprised.

"Oh, yes, Fabian's known for picking up strays," Shayna said, the usual humour in her voice.

"If you mean Ophelia—"

"Her and that boy you told me about. Lost and all alone in the world, with no proper home to call their own." The humour vanished, and she said more seriously, "I mean it. Fabian's really good at gathering lost sheep. He just needs to be careful the sheep don't leash on him."

Fabian sighed and rolled his eyes.

"Is Ophelia your girlfriend?" Camdyn asked.

It was so rare to hear him ask a question and show interest, Fabian decided to indulge him. "Yeah. And she can definitely take care of herself."

Shayna raised her hands. "I wasn't contesting that."

"Does she know about your magic?" Camdyn continued, ignoring the jabs.

"Yes, of course. She's a shadow mage, actually."

"And a cultist." Shayna whistled innocently.

"Not anymore," Fabian protested. With a sigh, he let it slide. "Most of my friends back home have some sort of magical power. That's why I was so surprised I received the invitation to study at the Citadel."

Shayna nodded. "Oh, yes, if Kaia ever tries her nonsense against Lucille or Samantha, she'll be in for a surprise. She'll change her tune about untalented wild mages in no time."

Camdyn seemed to be filing every piece of information into his memory. "And your parents?"

"My father has no idea, but my mother's also a witch—not a very strong one, but she runs a magic shop in Greenvalley. She's pretty cool." And more importantly, she was finally getting better, slowly returning to work.

"It must be pretty amazing to have so many supportive people around you who accept you for what you are," Camdyn said, his tone yearning.

On his other side, Shayna sighed. "Definitely."

Curious, Fabian looked at her. "What do you mean?" She'd sounded as if she'd been commiserating with Camdyn there.

"Well, do you think my friends know? Cheryl would have a heart attack if I suddenly told her I could do magic."

"Cheryl, yeah, but Cian knows what's up."

Shayna stopped cold. "What?"

Fabian smiled. "Samantha told him everything a year ago or so."

He couldn't imagine what it'd been like for Shayna having those kinds of destructive powers and trying to hone them all on her own, never able to confide in anyone for fear of ridicule.

She pushed her hands on her hips. "And he never said a thing?"

"He probably thought you'd laugh at him. By the way, he took it well."

For once, Shayna seemed to quiet down, the smile slipping from her face. Fabian left her to her thoughts and told Camdyn, "There are more open-minded people than you think. Maybe not your grandfather, but they exist. There's a place for you. Trust me."

Camdyn gave him a sad little smile. Then he suddenly pointed ahead. "There's a cave!"

"A cave?"

Somehow, they'd reached the mountains. Either distance worked differently in the magical enclave or searching together had put them on the right path. The cave wasn't natural. It probably hadn't even existed this morning. The stone was freshly cut and dust still trickled down.

"Kaia?" Shayna asked.

"Definitely elemental magic," Camdyn confirmed.

To Fabian's annoyance, it seemed there was method behind Kaia's petulance. Together, they entered the freshly hewn cave which soon transformed into a natural cavity. In the distance, they could hear the roar of an underground river. When they finally reached it, they found Kaia at the shore. The earth mage had her arms stretched out, commanding the stone under her feet. With sweat pouring down her brow, she built a narrow bridge from scratch.

Fabian crossed his arms and watched, the other two following suit.

"You could probably part the river," Camdyn whispered.

He nearly snorted. "Do I look like Moses?"

"Just wait. Kaia will show us how it's done," Shayna said, a little too loudly.

The words broke Kaia's concentration, and the tip of her bridge crumbled into the water. "What are you three doing here?"

"Your superiority led us," Shayna answered.

"Go away!" Kaia grunted, concentrating on her bridge again.

Meanwhile, Fabian approached the river and watched the water tumble down the channel, vanishing in the dark. "It's quite fast. If she falls, it'll carry her away." Who knew where the water would wash her out?

"I won't," Kaia said. With great effort, she pushed her bridge over the river. It held.

A delirious smile on her face, Kaia put one foot on her bridge. The stone made a terrible gnashing sound, causing her to use more magic to stabilise it. Then, step by step, she advanced. By the time she reached the middle, small pieces were crumbling into the water. Fabian stretched out his arms, ready to intervene, but she pressed on.

The structure weakening below her, she quickened her steps. But that caused too much strain, and the bridge crumbled under her feet. With a scream, Kaia jumped. Alarmed, Fabian lunged and seized control of the river. Just as Camdyn had mused, the water parted under his command.

Kaia landed on the other side with one foot. Her other leg remained dry, despite hanging off the edge. Surprised, she glanced behind her, finding Fabian's gaze. With a proud jerk of her chin, she pulled up her foot and walked off. He clearly wasn't going to get a thanks. Instead, he was going to have to do something about the water pressure before it flooded. He moved his arms and redirected the river to flow in an arc, reconnecting the stream, but leaving a dry tunnel for them to cross.

"Let's go," Shayna said to Camdyn.

They dropped into the riverbed and walked under the tunnel Fabian had created, clearly in awe. Once they'd made it to the other side, he followed, feeling the strain but far from exhausted.

"That was close," he said, letting the river splash back into its bed.

Kaia snorted. "No, it wasn't. I had it." She turned her back on them and stalked off.

"How about 'thanks'?" Shayna called after her.

While Kaia ignored her, Camdyn whispered a soft, "Thanks."

Fabian smiled, before taking a deep breath, and following Kaia.

Shayna

Shayna was seething. She had so many choice words for Kaia, but for the sake of Fabian and Camdyn, she held back. The last thing anyone needed was a bitch fight. Instead, she channelled all her anger into a little flame, which they used to light up the dark tunnel. Ahead, Kaia was feeling her way through the cave, too stubborn to accept help. Furious about the other girl's behaviour, Shayna walked more slowly, jealously guarding her light. It didn't matter, anyway, because soon they arrived at a giant wall of fire.

"Does anybody else feel like we're being tested individually?" Fabian asked.

"In an exam?" Kaia replied acidly. "Can't be."

"I mean the whole thing. The stone, the river, now fire," Fabian listed, undeterred. "One obstacle for each of us. If we work together—"

The gnashing sound of stone cut him off as Kaia plucked the element from the walls and covered herself in it. As annoying as she was, Shayna had to admit she was resourceful.

"Or you can just do it all alone." It took a lot to anger Fabian, but even he had his limits.

While Kaia stomped through the fire protected by her stone, Shayna approached the flames. She wasn't nearly as strong as the other two. Sure, when she'd been younger, she's caused some quite impressive wildfires, but then she'd learnt to control her element, and ever since, she seemed to be unable to do much more than the flame she'd held in her hand on the way here. This fire wall was intimidating. She could feel the heat blasting her face, both beckoning and threatening her. It wasn't very deep, just enough to dissuade them from simply jumping through. Shayna tried to approach it like Fabian, hoping it would part for her, but she knew deep down her powers didn't compare.

"I'm not sure I can do it."

Fabian had her back, smiling encouragingly. "I'll help. I can't control fire like you, but I can protect us from it."

Knowing he'd be by her side making sure they'd all escaped unscathed gave her the push she'd needed. Using the same motions she'd learnt in class, she slowly lowered the flames. She didn't quite manage to create a tunnel, so Fabian used his water to extinguish it at the bottom. Steam rose, but Shayna felt the fire give and managed to hold it to the sides.

"Quick!"

They ran through and came out unharmed. Giddy with success, Shayna announced, "And that's what teamwork looks like."

Kaia snorted. "Also called 'weakness'. You would've never made it through without him."

Though true, Shayna couldn't bear it. "It's not my first fire!"

"Let's just go," Fabian said, his face tense. "We all want to see Kaia fly on her stones, don't we?"

Kaia wasn't the only one pulling a grimace now. Despite his smarts, it only just seemed to occur to Camdyn he'd be tested, too.

"I..." He swallowed heavily.

With a snort, Kaia marched off.

Shayna put a hand on his shoulder. "You'll show her."

They kept walking, when it slowly got lighter. Shayna extinguished her flame, and they stepped into a wide-open cave with sunlight filtering in from the top. It was a dead-end.

Fabian shaded his eyes and looked up. "I guess it's your turn, Camdyn."

The boy looked as if he was about to keel over.

"Yeah, go on, fly us up," Kaia said. Apparently, she was willing to accept their help now.

"Just remember our lessons," Shayna said, feeling a kinship. Her control over her element hadn't been impressive either. "Focus and find the wind inside yourself."

Camdyn nodded and closed his eyes. He formed a delta with his hands, copying Fabian. A moment later, a gentle breeze swept through the room, ruffling their hair.

"This isn't going to work," Kaia said.

She walked towards the wall closest to the hole and put her hands on the stone. Small mounds formed beneath her touch. Apparently, she was going to climb this time.

Discouraged, Camdyn lowered his arms and stared at the ground. "It's no use."

"Yes, it is. Come on, we'll do it together."

"Together?" Camdyn asked confused. "How's your water going to help?"

Shayna imagined Fabian would create a water column and shoot them up, but instead, he opened his jacket and pulled out a shimmering blue feather.

"Not with water, but I happen to have a little wind aid." He waved his feather, and a strong wind blew through them, nearly picking Kaia off the wall. "Alright, here's the wind. Now you control it, Camdyn, and use it to lift Shayna up."

Shayna winced, not exactly thrilled to be part of the experiment. At least Camdyn seemed more determined now. He planted his feet firmly on the ground and re-assumed his stance.

Shayna felt the feather storm tugging her. Something was working. She tried to relax and let the wind take control, when suddenly, it seized her legs and ripped them out from under her. Her hands took the brunt of the impact, and she let out a scream when pain shot up through her wrists.

"I'm sorry, I'm so sorry." Fabian ran over, fussing over her. "Are you okay?"

She nodded, still a little stunned. Her wrists hurt, but when she rolled them, there was no sharp pain indicating broken bones.

"No, I'm sorry," Camdyn blurted. "I can't control it."

"You did something," Shayna forced herself to say.

"Do you want to try again—?"

Shayna shot Fabian a glare, and he shut up. She felt sorry for Camdyn and wanted him to succeed, but not at the cost of breaking her bones.

Just then, there was a shrill scream. Kaia had reached the ceiling of the cave, but now she was falling. With the hole at least ten metres high and nothing but stone underneath, there was no way she was going to survive.

Fabian jumped up. With one hand, he waved the feather. With the other, he seized control of the air stream. Kaia slowed, then was catapulted back up, right at the hole. She flew through and landed safely on top of the cave, where Shayna could see her crouching close to the ground, her whole body shaking.

"It worked," Fabian said, looking almost as pale as Camdyn.

Stunned, Shayna stood. "It did." Her gaze fell on Fabian. "That was incredible. You just used wind magic. Actual wind magic."

Modest as always, Fabian shook his head. "It's the feather, trust me." He took a deep breath, centring himself. "Do you want to try it?"

Shayna's wrists still hurt, but she nodded. "We all have to get up there, and I trust you more than Kaia." Not that she had much experience with rock climbing.

Inhaling deeply, Shayna stepped into the wind channel. Despite her preparation, she let out a small scream when it picked her up and threw her upwards, much like Kaia before her. To her surprise, she landed in soft snow. The mountain top was right in front of her, the way to it rocky and slippery, but otherwise free from obstacles. Next to her, Kaia shrugged off her jitters.

Shayna leant back over the edge of the hole and shouted down, "Fabian, come up—I think we're almost there."

"Go on without us," he called back. "I have to go after Camdyn."

"What?"

When she looked down, there was no sight of the young wind mage. He must've run away, and now Fabian had gone to work his magic on him. That left her and Kaia alone on the snowy mountain top. She crossed her arms, bracing herself for the task ahead. Kaia looked just as apprehensive.

"I guess it's just you and me now."

Samantha

"So, are we going to talk about Merik?" Samantha asked as she and Lucille headed to the prison. "I suppose he's interesting."

Lucille rubbed her face as though ashamed, but then smiled. "Honestly, he is. It's nothing serious. I like him. He likes me. We get together when he's in town. We're both okay if we don't."

"And you're not starting at zero," Samantha said, remembering Lucille's crisis from a few weeks ago.

"Yes and no. I don't have to keep the part that I'm a witch secret from him until I think he's ready for it or anything like that, but there's so much about him that's new. I mean, he's from an entirely different world. So, in that way, we're starting from zero, but it's an exciting process."

"Yeah, Ashuan's definitely too small for you."

Lucille laughed out loud. "Well, Greenvalley certainly is. You don't think Matt minds, do you? That I'm dating his classmate?"

"Does my boyfriend, a half-demon from the House of Lust, care about who other people invite into their bed?"

"Okay, okay, stupid question." Lucille smiled so happily Samantha knew this was on the edge of becoming more serious for her. She really liked Merik.

"Just be careful, okay? We know almost nothing about these other worlds. Don't want you accidentally committing a capital offence or... getting hurt."

Lucille sobered up and nodded. "I told you: it's nothing. Just a little adventure."

"Well, adventures tend to be dangerous, as we know."

"Are you still mad at Matt?" Lucille asked, eager to change topics.

Samantha snorted. "I'm mad because he opened the damn door and got himself ensnared by a siren. It was probably an accident, but he's supposed to be cleverer than that."

She didn't trust Rachel's assessment that he was safe for now. No men in the company of sirens would ever be safe. She'd just kidded herself he'd be somewhat immune, when he clearly wasn't.

"We're going to get him out of there before any harm comes to him."

The police station looked perfectly normal from the outside, but Samantha could feel the song concentrated behind the walls. They were definitely in the right spot.

They entered, expecting to be stopped, and sure enough, Captain Aster was in the foyer, but his eyes were glazed over and he was swaying slightly.

It took a moment before he looked at them, his movements sluggish. "You're not..." Even his voice was slow and hollow, as if he was half-asleep.

"Yes, we are," Lucille said, confidently, weaving her illusion.

He nodded and stepped aside, looking into space again.

"Let's hope no one needs the police until we're done," Lucille whispered.

Samantha rolled her eyes. "As if they were ever really that helpful." She nodded towards the cells. "Let's hope your illusion works on the sirens as well as it did on Aster."

The plan seemed good at first. Samantha and Lucille were able to slip inside without the police or sirens noticing, wondering if the illusion was even necessary. The station had become a circus—or rather, an illegal fighting ring. Men were packed into the cells, cheering for the combatants, who were wrestling and bashing each other's heads in.

Samantha scanned the corridor but couldn't see a familiar face. The corridor was wide but crowded, making it impossible to sneak past. "Let's take them out one by one."

Under the guise of Lucille's illusion, they approached the nearest siren, a black-feathered beauty who salivated as she watched the men bleed. Samantha wove a quick muting web before stabbing her with her Torakh. They proceeded to kill two more before they came across another siren—only she was already dead, two green marks on her neck, like a poisoned vampire bite.

Samantha looked at Lucille, but then something moved in the shadows. "Lu—"

Suddenly, a woman with slitted golden eyes and scaly skin had Lucille by the neck, ready to sink her snake-like fangs into her neck. Her gaze locked with Samantha's and she paused. Lucille held her breath, her eyes wide, as if she was nothing but a little mouse.

"Your eyes," the woman hissed, though her voice sounded almost normal by the end. "You're her, aren't you?" The slitted eyes became normal and her fangs retracted. The scales on her skin paled. "But why are you a siren?"

Samantha had no idea who this woman was or what she was doing here, only that she was apparently hesitating to kill them. "It's an illusion," she said, following a hunch.

"Impressive," the woman said, and let go of Lucille. "I didn't you know you were an illusionist."

"Um, I... I'm the illusionist," Lucille said. She took a quick step away. "Who are you?"

The woman looked so normal now—breathtaking, but normal, if not for the hint of scales under her skin. "I'm Vydra. I'm studying with your hus—boyfriend. Look, I'd love to chat, but maybe another time. For now, we have some sirens to kill." She looked them up and down once more. "Real ones."

Samantha turned and saw the sirens had discovered the dead bodies and raised the alarm. One pointed at Vydra, and immediately, she slithered into the shadows. A second later, she bit the siren, causing her to drop dead almost immediately. Goosebumps appeared on Samantha's arms. A second too late and Lucille would've been on the floor, too.

"Matt certainly has some interesting classmates," Lucille whispered, still spooked.

But Vydra was right. There was no time to talk. Samantha spotted something silver between the feathers of the siren who'd just been killed. She ran over, ducked, and retrieved the keys to the cells.

Leaving the killing to Vydra, she opened the first one. "You're free!" she told the prisoner, but they just stared at her in confusion. Since she couldn't see Matt, she continued to the next.

"Impostors!" a burly siren called from the end of the corridor. Her wingtip pointed at Lucille and Samantha. "They're no sisters. Kill them." She opened her mouth again and sang, the notes full of aggression.

Movement rippled through the men. Lucille and Samantha stood back-to-back as the sirens' victims burst from the cells, unveiled blood-lust in their eyes.

Rachel

As soon as Rachel entered the dreamworld, she snatched Ophelia from her dreams and took h er along down to the dark corridors of the siren's nest. As before, she saw men eager to be eaten by the sirens, their song heavy in the air.

"Is that what they're hearing?" Ophelia asked. In the dreamworld she was almost a shadow herself, her black hair oozing darkness. "It's nice, I guess, but I wouldn't go crazy for it."

Rachel agreed, but there was more to the music, an unearthly quality that had nothing to do with the sounds in her ears. "It's a magical song, targeted at the male brain, apparently. I wonder if..."

She approached the nearest man and summoned the same kind of waxy ear plugs Leandres had used, forcing them into his ears. His eyes cleared, and he blinked. Then he vanished.

"What happened to him?" Ophelia asked, alarmed.

"He woke up." Rachel strode down the shadowy corridor. "The siren song is connected to the dreamworld. They're basically sleepwalking while under their influence—that's why we can see what's happening in the real world."

Ophelia grinned. "But you woke him up. We can basically free all these men from under their nose."

Rachel winced. "We could, I suppose. But that'd certainly draw their attention. Plus, we don't know how they'll react when the men wake in their presence." She hoped she hadn't just condemned him to be eaten.

"To the queen, then."

"Can you hide us?"

"All I need is a shadow, and there's plenty of those here. Come on."

The shadows flowed towards them, coating them in darkness, like they had in Serathon's temple. Despite knowing it'd happen, Rachel tensed when their tendrils touched her. There was something so utterly finite in the shadows; impenetrable darkness. Anything could be lurking, waiting for its time to pounce. Today, they had to be the thing that pounced.

They entered the throne room. As before, the queen was on her throne. Adam knelt next to her, his head in her feathery lap. She ran her hand through his hair, almost lovingly, but every time she lifted her fingers, she plucked magic from him to eat. Rachel nearly threw up, but she kept her thoughts as dark and empty as the shadows and continued to approach. From the shadows, she drew a crossbow and carefully took aim, about to shoot, when Adam suddenly moved and held his head right in front of the queen's chest. Rachel held her breath.

The queen patted him. "What a good boy you are."

She smacked her wings open. The resulting storm blew the shadows away and left both girls exposed. Ophelia stared at the siren queen, while Rachel kept her crossbow trained on her chest—or rather, Adam's head.

"You brought back-up," the queen said, in her singsong voice. "Very well. I accept your challenge."

She rose, letting Adam sink to his knees, and approached Rachel. Without hesitating, Rachel let her bolt fly. It, loosened, flew through the air and stopped, shaking, right in front of the siren, who swiped it from the air.

A moment later, dozens appeared, all directed at Rachel and Ophelia. It was only thanks to Ophelia's reflexes, who pulled her down at the last second, that they missed piercing their hearts.

"I hope you're aware that if you die in your dreams, you'll also die in the real world." The queen smiled.

It wasn't something Rachel had known, and for a moment, she was too scared to continue. Then her gaze fell on Ophelia.

"Don't listen to her. We'll beat her, and then guess what? She'll die, too."

"I'll do it," Rachel said, making a decision. "You wake up."

Ophelia blinked, and a moment later, she was gone. Though her shadows might prove useful, Rachel couldn't risk a friend, not even one who used to be a cultist. Now she knew the rules, Rachel felt more determined than ever to fight for her place in the dreamworld. She was the Dreamer, after all.

"So, it's a battle of life and death. I won't let you take anything from me, bird brain. Not the dreamworld and not my boyfriend."

The queen laughed. "So brave, little one. Let's see if you have the power to back it up."

Fabian

"Camdyn!" Fabian's steps echoed in the cave as he moved as fast as possible, trying to catch the wind mage. Soon, the sound was drowned out by the hissing and crackling of the fire wall.

He didn't hesitate long, threw up his hands and shot water at it. Steam filled the cave and he dashed through. The impenetrable darkness that followed forced him to go slower, using the side of the wall to guide him. He was just wondering whether he'd accidentally taken another path, one they hadn't seen earlier, when he heard the roar of the nearby river, and the cave got a little lighter. He ran faster, until he came to a skittering stop near the river, where, at last, he found Camdyn.

He was at the edge of the wild river, cooling what looked like a bunch of blisters. He must've just run through the fire. When he heard Fabian, he startled so much, he almost fell into the river. Fabian raised his hands.

"Leave me alone!"

Fabian stood his ground. "Where are you going?"

"Away. I don't belong here." The pain had thickened his voice. "I can't control my magic, I can't even summon it. You're a better wind mage than I'll ever be!"

"Nonsense, I'm a water mage."

Camdyn snorted. "Right."

"The wind came from the feather," Fabian explained, and showed it to him. "It's a powerful magical artefact. Anyone can create wind with it."

"But not everyone can control it."

Fabian swallowed. Camdyn was wrong. He hadn't controlled the wind, he'd just saved Kaia, then picked up Shayna with it. "It's impossible to have two elements."

"Wrong. In the 1830s, Viktoria Pedersen controlled both fire and wind," Camdyn said, in his teacher's pet voice. "Before her death, she was working on controlling the other two elements, but her experiments were cut short during a cholera outbreak. It's possible."

Fabian felt the ground sway under his feet. Two elements? When he'd only just accepted the water as a part of himself? He shook his head. "That doesn't matter. I'm not interested in stealing your magic."

"I don't care," Camdyn said promptly. "You can have it. All I want is to go back to Ireland."

"I know." Every cell of the boy screamed homesickness.

"The Citadel won't need me anymore. It has you now."

Be that as it may—and Fabian was far from convinced—something else was true. "But you need the Citadel."

Camdyn's jaw wobbled. On the verge of breaking, he averted his eyes. Then he pushed himself off and attempted to swim through the river. Immediately, it took him away.

"Camdyn!" Fabian ran towards the shore and dived in without another thought.

The waves dunked him under and whirled him around before he even had a chance to think about seizing their power. For a few precious seconds, Fabian was too busy keeping his head above water to do anything of use, but slowly, he got a feeling for the flow and managed to streamline his movements. He looked up. Camdyn was struggling in front of him. His head vanished as he was swept into the tunnel ahead. Fabian stretched out his hands, feeling through the water until he found him, and pulled him back up. But the cave they were in now was getting smaller and smaller, and the pocket of air above was quickly vanishing.

"Hold your breath, Camdyn. Air..."

Camdyn was trying to hold onto the ceiling but slipped back underwater.

Fabian pushed the water aside, creating a pocket of air, but the space was too limited and the water too fast. The wave crashed over his head, pushing him back under. He no longer knew where up or down was, or if it even mattered. The darkness around him was complete.

Someone grabbed his shoulders and his head popped into an air bubble. He took a shaking breath and pushed panic aside. Then he clutched at the other person's arms, who could only be Camdyn, and held on for dear life.

Just then, the water flow changed, and suddenly, they were tumbling into the deep. A moment later, they plunged back into the water. It was quieter now, more settled. Fabian wrapped an arm around Camdyn and paddled toward the shore he felt nearby. With the last bit of his strength, he pulled them both onto dry land.

They lay there for minutes, doing nothing but breathing the sweet air of survival. Above them, thousands of glowworms illuminated the cave, giving off just enough to light to see each other.

After a while, Fabian turned his head to the side, taking in the younger blond boy. "You did it." Somehow, Camdyn had managed to grab hold of his magic and saved them both.

"But how?" Camdyn whispered.

Fabian laughed. "Emotions."

"Emotions?"

"You know what I mean. Elemental magic reacts to strong emotions. Now that I've read about."

Camdyn almost smiled. "But Professor Terian's been teaching us we need to keep our emotions in check."

Fabian turned on his stomach and propped himself up on his elbows. "And I'm sure he's right, but our power lies in our emotions. Whatever you felt down there, the panic, it broke through the walls inside of you and made you use your magic. Intuitively. Full force. Now you can learn how to control it."

Camdyn looked up at the ceiling and raised a hand, looking at it in wonder. "My magic."

After a much-needed break, Fabian and Camdyn got back to their feet. Fabian sucked the water from their clothes and fed it back to the river, which flowed much more calmly from the underground lake. There was no way back, but they found another path lit by glowworms which, surprisingly, led back to the fire wall.

"I hate this enclave," Fabian muttered. "How is there a shortcut now, but before it tried to drown us?" Just like previously, he used his water to cleave a way through the flames. "Listen, whether we pass this test or not doesn't matter. You've found your magic."

"And you've found more of yours," Camdyn retorted. Unlike before, it no longer sounded bitter.

Fabian was still unsure about that, but he was glad Camdyn was feeling better, so he played along. "See, Professor Terian can't be mad at us."

When they reached the cave with the hole in the ceiling, Camdyn stopped. "Do you know what an elemental circle is?"

"Um, did we cover that in class?"

Camdyn shook his head. "No. Basically, it describes us. A group of elemental mages, one of each element. When I read about it in the library, it said it was one of the strongest mage circles—rather than being four individual mages, they're one cohort. Like a multi-headed beast. There were instructions on how to forge one."

"Forging?" Fabian wasn't sure he liked the idea of being part of a multi-headed beast.

"Yes. It includes training together, trust exercises. Ideally, the elemental mages sleep, eat, and spend every available minute with each other until they trust each other intrinsically and can combine powers effortlessly. I'm pretty sure that's what the Citadel is trying to turn us into."

Fabian didn't like the sound of it. If Professor Terian or anyone had said so at the beginning, maybe, but instead he was hearing it from Camdyn, who in turn had read it in a book.

"Why?"

"To be a tool." Camdyn sighed. "You asked what jobs there are once we've finished our education. Well, the Citadel would like for you—all of us—to work for them. That's why they took in wild mages, and why we have all these special privileges, such as you and Shayna being able to go home each day. I mean, it's not necessarily a bad thing. For people like me, who don't have anything else, it's probably good. At least, I have some kind of future. But you—you have your friends and family. It'll be much harder for you to let go of all that."

"Who says I'm going to?"

"You're so talented. They'll never let you go."

Fabian frowned, liking his insight less with every word. "And I don't get a say?"

"Oh, sure. They won't kidnap you. But wild mage or not, they'll make you an offer you can't refuse."

Fabian tried to see the good in it. Camdyn made it sound as if the Citadel was wrong about trying to build this strong elemental mage circle. He still knew too little about them to properly decide whether they were good, evil, or something in between, but his instincts bristled. There were too many hidden agendas, too much manipulation, and he had the feeling the offer Camdyn was talking about wouldn't just be irresistible money and benefits, but a whole slew of threats if it looked like he wouldn't take it.

Right now, there was little he could do about it, though.

"Thanks for telling me." He held out his hands. "Now, are you ready to put our powers together and fly?"

Camdyn hesitated, but then he nodded. "Together."

Shayna

"I say we wait for the boys." Shayna crossed her arms, ready to stare down Kaia.

The earth mage rolled her eyes. "They could be hours. Until then, our test is over. I don't plan on failing, so I'm going, with or without you. I've gotten this far without help, so suit yourself." She started trudging up the snowy mountain path.

"You got this far without help?" Shayna hurried after her, using her fire to keep herself warm. "Fabian saved your life and was kind enough to help you up here."

Kaia threw a glance over her shoulder, haughty as ever. "And yet you're the one up here with me, while he's gone, looking for lost puppies."

"That's because he's a decent guy, not a cold-hearted bitch like you."

The insult didn't even seem to bother Kaia. If anything, they strengthened her determination. "Maybe but being decent won't help him pass."

"Didn't you listen to Professor Terian? Either we all pass or we all fail."

"And we will pass. When I find the Herb of Heavens." She moved a rock out of the way instead of climbing it. It rolled down the mountain side. "Even Terian will finally realise wild mages have too much to learn to keep up with the rest of us."

"Ugh!" For a moment, Shayna didn't have words for Kaia's infuriating ego, but the snow at her feet was melting. "You're so arrogant. Without Fabian, you wouldn't be even here. Or alive!"

To her surprise, Kaia halted. Hands pushed into her hips, she turned around. "Will you give it a rest? Everyone knows you're into him! Yes, your beloved Fabian probably would've made it, he has just enough talent to warrant his place at the Citadel, but you and Camdyn are just here because the Council would like a complete set."

"A what?"

"One of each element. A full elemental circle has only come together once before, and they built the Citadel. It's pretty obvious we don't measure up to that—not with three wild mages in the mix—but no one listens to me."

"I wonder why that is," Shayna said, but Kaia had already turned away and continued her ascent. Angrily, Shayna followed her. "This precious elemental circle of yours... If they founded the Citadel, doesn't that mean they were all a bunch of wild mages?"

Kaia whirled around, sending a shower of gravel down the mountain side. "They were so much more than you could ever imagine."

"Maybe. But they weren't Citadel-born." Her head held high, Shayna walked past.

The ground rumbled under her, and she lost her footing, knocking her knee on a boulder. Kaia jostled her aside and took the lead.

"Are you mad?" Shayna ignored the throbbing pain and scrambled back up on her feet. "You could've killed me."

"See, that's the thing. We can't die in here," Kaia said, spittle flying. "So, your beloved Fabian didn't save shit. Gosh, I can't wait to be done with this." She huffed and raised her chin. "Ah, there it is. Finally."

She stomped ahead, Shayna on her heels, and climbed the steep incline to the mountain top. There, a sad little plant stood in the snow. If Shayna squinted, she could detect a hint of blue, but for a Herb of Heavens, it was utterly drab and grey.

Kaia stretched out her hands, but flames erupted in front of her. Furious, she turned to Shayna. "What are you doing?"

It took a lot of concentration to project the flames where she did without burning the vital herb, but Shayna was determined to hold her back. "Don't you dare touch it."

"Why the hell not? It's what we're here for."

"We're going to wait for the others."

"Absolutely not." Kaia's face was red. "I will not let their incompetence ruin my exam!"

She reached for the plant again, but Shayna had had enough. Her flames bit Kaia's fingers. Kaia screamed, more in anger than hurt, and hurtled around. The ground shook again. Shayna stumbled and fell on her already sore wrists. She cried out as the pain shot up through her arms again, but the rage inside had grown too large. It was a wild animal, starved and poked with sticks until it lost its mind.

She scrambled up and lunged. The momentum toppled the two girls, and they rolled across the icy rocks. Neither wanted to let go, scratching and kicking. Flames singed Kaia's eyebrows, while she shoved Shayna's face into a rock—or the rock into her face.

Kaia twisted Shayna's right arm and trapped it in stone, making it impossible for her to wield the fire consuming her soul, and she cried out. She tried to yank herself free, but she may as well have tried to rip her arm off.

Kaia stumbled back. The hair had come loose from her ponytail and she was breathing hard. Soot smeared her cheek. "You really are a wild mage."

"And you're an arrogant bitch who only thinks of herself." Tears of anger rolled down Shayna's cheeks, where they sizzled and turned to steam.

With a snort, Kaia turned her back on her and plucked the plant from the ground, only for it to instantly crumble in her hands.

Shayna started laughing, but the sound quickly died out when she, too, realised how hopeless their task was now. She swallowed heavily. "And what now, oh Great Citadel Mage?"

Kaia looked utterly helpless and on the verge of tears. "You ruin everything."

"That bad, huh?" The stone around Shayna's arm crumbled, and she sat up, rubbing her wrist.

"You don't belong here. You..." Kaia swallowed, then glared. "Everyone pities me for having to work with you guys."

"Most of all, you."

Kaia looked away, sniffling. "You know nothing about me."

Shayna remained seated, using her fire to warm herself. "I actually happen to know exactly what it's like to be on top of the pecking order and realise what a horrible human being I've become because of it." Kaia rolled her eyes, but Shayna continued, "There's so much pressure. Your friends expect you to laugh about the same things, you always have to be perfect in their eyes, and never talk to any of the people you all decided were beneath you." Breaking off her friendship with Cheryl last summer had been so freeing, but Shayna was well aware how late she'd come to that conclusion. And how many people she'd hurt before getting there. That wasn't Cheryl's fault, but hers. "So, yeah, I understand you, Kaia. Your Citadel is its own little ecosystem. We're the new ones, and now you're one of us."

"I'm not." Two tears ran down her face.

"Yes, you are. As embarrassing as it might be, you're one of us now. Not a wild mage, but an elemental mage, and that's the only thing that matters. Not your imaginary status, but the talent that unites us." Though Kaia snorted, Shayna smiled. "You want us to match your legendary elemental circle, don't you? Well, we might just pull it off if we stick together. Just like this test."

Kaia rolled her eyes again, but it wasn't nearly as condescending as before. "You sound like Terian."

Shayna giggled. "Well, maybe I'm not as horrible as you think. Even if I am a wild mage."

This time, there was a hint of a smile on Kaia's face. "Maybe."

Samantha

The pure mass of men worked in their favour as Samantha and Lucille defended themselves. The siren victims tripped over each other, held each other back, and just as equally punched their neighbours than they did the girls. But there were so many, and between them were the sirens, who didn't just sing but swung at them with their claws.

Lucille singed feathers, while Samantha ducked under the arms of one of the men, making him crash into another. A protective shield was torn apart within seconds, and the crowd separated them quickly from one another. Samantha weaved in and out, trying to escape the madness. But just as she'd thought there was a chance, someone landed their knee in her stomach and rammed her into the wall.

Gasping, she doubled over. From the corner of her eye, she saw a fist coming towards her and quickly jerked her head to the side. The knuckles hit the wall instead. Some of the stucco crumbled and blood dripped between them, but her assailant didn't seem to care.

That's when she recognised him. "Jan! Jan, it's me—Sam."

Before she could even think of using her magic to free him from the siren's spell, he lunged again. She rotated out of the way, only to come face to face with another man. Startled, she stumbled back. A blow hit her in the neck and she went down.

Jan grabbed her arms, twisted them behind her, and forced her up, onto her knees. "Let me go!" she cried out.

Pain throbbed in her neck, her arms, and her stomach, but Jan was relentless. A side glance told her the men had also taken control of

Lucille, presenting her to the sirens. The bird women took one look at them before throwing their heads back and laughing.

"Kill them both."

Lucille was being held, but she hadn't been gagged, and every man who approached her succumbed to a spell. One was wrapped in vines, the next sank to his knees, screaming, another stumbled back, mushrooms growing on his face. She was doing it. She was going to defeat them, one by one, and free them—but not in time.

The crowd of men parted in front of Samantha and another man approached, confident and lethal.

"Matt."

He ran his hand over Samantha's temple, almost gently, but then his fingers tangled in her hair and he jerked her head back, exposing her throat. Tears ran down her cheek when she saw the black magic gathering in his hand.

Just then, a shadow appeared behind Matt. His hand was pulled down and twisted behind him, just like Samantha's, and long, pointy fingernails wrapped around his throat. Scales spread under the fingers and Vydra's snake-like face appeared, poised to bite him.

"Free yourself and go," she hissed at Samantha. "I won't let him kill you or allow him be killed."

Samantha swallowed, deciding to trust her—not that she had a lot of choice. Frantically, she wove a small explosive web in her mind and set it off, throwing everyone around her—including Jan, Matt, and Vydra—off their feet.

Rachel

Even though Ophelia was gone, Rachel used her shadow magic to cloak herself. Unfortunately, though, the darkness hindered her as much as it did the siren queen, and for a while, she stumbled aimlessly through the shadows.

A song rang out, luring her closer. Rachel let it. It was sweeter than the one used to control the men and spoke as if it knew her soul. The melody was near irresistible. She knew she was walking into a trap, but she couldn't not move in the direction. Instead, she braced herself.

The darkness parted and led her straight into the arms of the queen. Her face had turned half bird. As soon as she saw Rachel, she shrieked, beat her wings, and lunged at her, claws extended. But Rachel was ready. Her crossbow was back in her hand, and she shot the bolt at close proximity. It buried itself in the siren's heart with a loud thud.

The siren looked down and laughed. "Nice try, little one." She pulled the bolt from her chest and crumbled it between her feathers. "But you need to be more creative than that."

She lunged again, and Rachel stumbled back, but the ground beneath her had vanished and she was free-falling. Screaming, she tumbled into the deep. At first, there was nothing but darkness, but then her vision cleared and she saw a stormy sea beneath her... and jagged rocks, waiting to smash her body to smithereens.

"Wings. Wings. I need wings."

Rachel drew inspiration from the Greek coastline to build her own set of wings from wooden boards, wax, and siren feathers. Only a few metres before she hit the rocks, she caught an updraft and soared into the sky, a distant sun peeking through quickly dispersing clouds.

The siren launched herself from one of the rocks further up, and the two met in the air. Rachel tried to evade her, but she had little control over her flight, and the siren clutched her shoulders, digging her claws into her flesh. The next moment, they were going down again, and no amount of beating her make-shift wings helped Rachel stop the momentum. She mirrored the siren and dug her hands into her foe's shoulders, willing her fingernails to become pointy and longer. Blood flowed from both their wounds. The siren let go with a howl. Rachel's fingernails were now several inches long and bloody, and the wings on her back were proper ones now, much like the sirens'. Flying wasn't her thing, though, so she changed the scenery to the place she knew best: her dream meadow.

While Rachel landed softly, the siren queen crashed into the flowers, surprised by her sudden loss of control. Rachel didn't hesitate and forced an old-fashioned, golden bird cage around her.

"Creative enough for you?"

Hissing, the captive siren threw herself against the bars, but Rachel held them together with her will. For a moment longer, the queen raged, then she calmed and sat back, somehow summoning her throne into the cage. Her gaze focused on Rachel, she waved two fingers.

Rachel gasped when Adam entered the dream. Trapped with the queen, he re-assumed his position at her feet, placing his head on her lap. The siren brushed his cheeks with her fingers before grabbing his head with her claws. Adam's gaze never shifted.

"What's that supposed to do?" Rachel asked, trying her hardest not to freak out. "Did you think I'd be jealous because you used your song to make him love you? Or whatever it is your spell does."

The queen didn't answer. "He means a lot to you, doesn't he?"

Rachel didn't deign to answer.

"I could continue savouring his magic, but I've got others in my cells. They'll be just as delicious." She looked at Adam. "Do you know how easy it'd be for me to break his neck? You don't need him anymore, do you?"

Rachel had grown still. The fear of losing Adam was back. Was the siren bluffing or was it true what she'd said before? That Adam would die if he died in the dream? Shaking, she let go of the cage.

The siren watched the bars fall apart without emotion. "Look how weak he makes you. The Dreamer, huh? Let me help you free you from this burden." The claws around Adam's head tightened.

Rachel didn't think. She threw her hand out and shouted, "Scutum Protecto!"

Despite the fact she was no witch, the spell wound itself around Adam, protecting him from the queen.

"Who did you steal that one from?" the queen hissed, and for the first time fear entered her voice.

"Oh, I've got more where that came from." Rachel realised now how truly limitless the dreamworld was. Being creative, as the siren queen had called it, took too much thought and effort. It slowed her down. Drawing inspiration from her friends was much faster. "Sageat negru distrugere!"

Maybe she'd mumbled the words or even misspoke, but the intent was clear, and a crackling black arrow flew straight at the siren.

The queen stood, looking it in the eye and dissolving it before the magic touched her. She smiled, but Rachel had already moved on. She appeared at the queen's back and threw black energy at her, emulating Matt this time. Then she seized the magic like Samantha and wove it into a death web.

Screaming, the siren sank to the ground, her gaze full of fear. The magic struck a final time. She twitched for a moment, before bursting into feathers. At first, Rachel thought it was another trick, but then the feathers turned black and crumbled to dust, and suddenly, there was silence. She hadn't even noticed the song until it was gone. That, and Adam blinking in confusion, assured her she'd won.

"Time to wake you up from this nightmare," Rachel whispered.

She cupped his cheeks and pressed a kiss on his forehead. When she stood back, he faded out of the dream.

Fabian

By combining their wind powers, Fabian and Camdyn made it to the top of the mountain. After so much time alone, Fabian had expected Shayna and Kaia to be at each other's throats. Instead, he found them kneeling over a spot, planting what looked like a seed.

Shayna looked up, her cheeks rosy from the cold. "Finally. We need your help."

"For what, exactly?"

"Kaia found a seed." The two girls shared a look, as if there was a lot more to the story. "If we all use our magic, we might be able to grow the herb from it."

Kaia clicked her tongue in annoyance. "Stop staring and help. We still need water and air."

Fabian looked at Camdyn, confused by the sudden change in demeanour, but the younger boy just shrugged.

They knelt next to the girls and held their hands above the spot, calling their elements. Wind and water mingled, and the ground cracked. A small bud appeared between them. They grinned at each other and continued their efforts until the plant had grown nearly twenty centimetres. Sky-blue blossoms formed and opened.

Shayna bumped Kaia with her elbow. "See? I told you we had to work together."

"Speaking of... When did that happen?" Fabian looked back and forth between Kaia and Shayna. The girls were more at ease now, almost as if they respected each other.

Kaia sighed. "After the old Herb of Heavens... vanished. Arguing killed it. Unity made it blossom."

"Just like the elemental circle," Camdyn whispered. He was still watching the herb in awe.

"You know about that?" Kaia asked surprised. She looked at Shayna. "That's the official name for our complete set."

The idea still didn't sit quite right with Fabian. "Sounds like the Citadel has big plans for us."

"You should feel honoured," Kaia said.

Shayna snorted. "Maybe we would if people actually honoured us a little. Or at least respected us."

Kaia took a deep breath. "I know. I guess, for better or worse, we're a team now."

Team was an improvement from classmates, but when Fabian looked at Camdyn, he knew they needed to be more. "Let's be friends."

Camdyn smiled, perhaps his first proper smile since he'd arrived at the Citadel. Kaia, however, shuddered. A lot must've happened on the mountain top, but apparently, calling them friends was taking things a little too far. At least for today.

She bent over the plant and carefully plucked it from the earth, though it was more as if the ground simply let go. Fabian noticed Shayna hold her breath, then let out a sigh of relief when nothing happened. Instead, a portal opened nearby.

"I assume you'll be presenting the herb to Terian?" Shayna asked Kaia, her voice a little tense.

The earth mage regarded the plant, clearly considering it her Citadel-given right. But then she offered it to Fabian. "You're the strongest of us."

He raised an eyebrow. He hadn't expected an admission like that to come from her mouth. He took the herb but handed it to Camdyn. "Camdyn made the biggest progress. He found his magic, so he gets to do the honours."

The boy's eyes widened. He opened his mouth to protest, but awe washed over him, and he took the plant, gently cradling it in his hands. He stumbled towards the portal, Kaia striding next to him.

Fabian pointed at the dirt on Shayna's face. "What happened there?"

She rubbed her cheek. "Just a small discussion." Laughing, she hooked her arm into his. "So, Camdyn found his magic, huh?"

"Turns out anything's possible with proper motivation."

Together, they stepped through the portal and into the classroom, where Professor Terian was already waiting, beaming proudly.

"Excellent work," he announced, turning the herb in his fingers. Slowly, it dissolved. "You all passed."

"Anything else would've been outrageous," Fabian said. Now they were safely back on Earth, he felt the pain and exhaustion from the last two days. "We almost died in there."

The professor nodded. "You picked a tough path, but you overcame your challenges and came out stronger than before."

"It really would've helped if we'd had a tip about what we were actually looking for," Shayna said, anger rising in her voice.

Kaia pushed her hands on her hips. "And we could've done without raging rivers, burning fire walls, and dangerous chasms."

"Or homicidal birds," Camdyn added, rubbing the scratches on his arms.

Professor Terian only grinned.

"What's so funny?" Fabian blurted. His muscles hurt and he was covered in dozens of bruises from tumbling down the river, never mind almost drowning.

"Well..." Professor Terian stopped laughing and folded his hands. "When I sent you on this test yesterday, you were either eager to show each other up or didn't even want to take it. You had no appreciation for each other and were constantly fighting. And now look at you. Suddenly you're united." His voice became more serious. "It's a risky test, I know, but you left me no choice. Compared to the exams the Citadel ran only a few decades ago, this was child's play. You wouldn't have died in the enclave, but you needed to believe you could so you could reconcile your strong personalities and appreciate each other. You're only strong as a team. Never forget that."

Fabian glanced at Camdyn, but just like his new friend, he swallowed his reservations.

"Very well. You can go home now. Take the rest of the week off, and we'll meet again on Monday."

They exchanged the mission satchels for their backpacks and shuffled out.

"Hey, Camdyn," Fabian called. "If you want to come home with us, you can."

Camdyn's face brightened, but he glanced at Kaia, who'd raised an eyebrow. "Maybe another time. I think I'm ready to give the Citadel another chance."

Kaia slipped an arm around his shoulders. "We need to talk about some unwritten rules if you do that."

Fabian smiled as he watched them heading down the corridor. Grinning, he turned to Shayna. "You need to tell me everything."

"Ditto," Shayna said, linking her arm with his again. "We've got a lot to talk about."

Matt

Screaming filled Matt's ears, making his eyes water. He blinked, and when he saw straight again, he found himself immobilised by a set of scaly arms, blood dripping from his throat. Worse, Samantha was in front of him, the side of her face bruised and lip split. All around, men rose groggily from the ground, looking confused, and Jan stumbled away from Samantha, horrified.

"I'm so sorry, Sam. I didn't mean to—"

Matt's heart plummeted. He remembered approaching Samantha with death on his mind, grabbing her hair, watching her eyes widen.

"Guess you're back," a familiar voice hissed. The scaly arms vanished, along with the pressure on his neck.

Part of him wanted to turn around and find out who'd contained him, but his gaze was locked with Samantha's.

Her eyes were still full of fear and her voice was shaking. "The sirens... You..." She swallowed hard. "Do you still want to kill me?"

Matt shook his head vehemently. The very memory of wanting to kill her burnt him from inside. Samantha inhaled sharply, then threw herself into his arms and sobbed. He held her tight, slowly regaining his bearings.

Bird women shrieked around them. Feathers whirled and claws glinted under the fluorescent light. A man screamed when the monsters drew blood. Jan whirled around and karate chopped one of the sirens, while a fluid shadow felled the others left and right. Some of the men started fighting each other.

Matt pressed Samantha to his side, unwilling to let go, and threw black energy at the sirens. In front of him, Lucille burnt another to a crisp, and Jan had found a dagger, which he sank into another. Two of the sirens had grabbed a man and bitten his neck, when they suddenly froze and dropped him. Behind them, Adam had his arms raised. His skin was covered in bite marks, but he was on his own two feet.

"Adam!" Samantha extracted herself from Matt's grip and ran to him. "You're alive."

His smile was a bit wonky. "And gladly so. Funny how you always know when you're back in Greenvalley."

The slithering shadow killed the two frozen sirens. Then it stood still for long enough to unravel into a beautiful woman. One Matt knew.

"Vydra?" He vaguely remembered her voice cutting through the brain fog, but couldn't fathom what she'd be doing in Greenvalley.

"No time. The law enforcers are waking up."

"The police?" Lucille asked. "Don't worry about them. They're clueless. Just follow my lead."

She closed her eyes for a moment, then started marching purposefully towards the exit, where Captain Aster and a group of policemen were hurrying in and shouting orders. They never even bothered them.

"Illusions," Vydra commented outside. "Handy." She turned to Matt and Samantha. "We need to talk."

The group—minus Lucille who'd gone to inform a friend about the sirens' defeat—returned to the Blackstone House, where they found Rachel waking from a dream. She looked a little worse for wear, but overall fine.

As soon as she saw Adam, she started crying. "You're alive."

"I'd say I'm in one piece, but I'm afraid I'm missing a few bits here and there." He looked at his arms with distaste, barely veiling the pain he must've been in.

"That's my cue," Jan announced. "Let's get you patched up."

But before he could heal him, Leandres stopped him. "Oh no. I'm the healer here. You're still a student."

"I can heal him!" Jan protested.

"We'll see about that." Leandres nodded towards a pile of paper on the dinner table. "You can earn your right to your healing powers by passing your test."

Jan's eyes bulged. "That's one test?"

Matt didn't envy him at all. The pile was big enough to count as a book.

"Oh, no." Samantha looked horrified. "I've got a test tomorrow. Adam, Rachel, Lia… Vydra. It was nice having you over—or maybe not—but I've got to study."

And with that, she hurried upstairs, never even looking back at Matt, who snorted.

Rachel got up and leant into Adam. "I don't have a test, but Adam and I are going to be busy, so if there's a monster…"

"Don't bother," Matt said, with a grin. He had a feeling he knew exactly how they were planning on spending their time.

"Yeah, the next monster is reserved for Matt and me, anyway," Jan said.

"Test. Now," Leandres reminded him. "Do you want to be a healer or not?"

With a groan, Jan sat at the table and stared at the giant test.

Matt clapped him on the shoulder, then followed Vydra onto the terrace where they could talk in private—or near-private, considering Neve was decorating the gutter with icicles.

"What are you doing here?"

"Well, there was something I was hoping to discuss with you, but then I noticed your town was infested with men-killing sirens. They're my tribe's mortal enemies, so I got a bit distracted. I'm glad I did, though, or you might be one girlfriend short."

The memory of Samantha's fearful face had etched itself into Matt's mind, and he felt his throat tighten. "Thanks for stepping in. I wouldn't ever be right again if I caused her harm."

To his surprise, Vydra smiled. "I know. And I have to say, if it weren't for you breaking her flow, she and your other friend might not have even needed my help. She's strong."

Matt found himself beaming. "She is. And smart, too. Patient…" He swallowed. Just before the sirens, he'd caused her harm. Not bodily, but mentally. "I need to make things right with her."

"I trust you will. Never thought I'd see a half-demon madly in love, but I'm rooting for you. Don't let her get away."

He'd do whatever it took to keep her close. "But you didn't come here to tell me that, did you?"

"No." Scales glittered on Vydra's face and, for once, she looked like the lethal killer she was. "I wanted to talk to you about Merik, seeing as you sent him to me."

Matt frowned. "What about him?"

"Do you know why he wanted to talk to me?" When Matt shook his head, she snorted. "Do you know what I am?"

"I don't really care about that kind of stuff."

He'd noticed others in their year had been avoiding Vydra, perhaps even both of them. He'd figured it was because they were both killers.

Vydra smiled wanly. "Charming. I'm an Einin. People approach me or my tribe if they want someone killed. In other words, I'm an assassin."

Slowly, Matt was connecting the dots. "And who did Merik want killed?"

"Now, that's where things get interesting. Normally, I wouldn't question it—he offered more than enough money. However, when the victim is the only Ashuan representative in parliament, and you're friends with the only Ashuan or Hescaryn student at the university, it pays to… ask first."

"Merik wants to kill Adam's father?"

Vydra's eyes sparkled. "I see I made the right decision. In my opinion, Merik doesn't seem to have Ashuan's best interests at heart."

Matt snorted. "So much for his vested interest in my world."

"Do you want me to refuse the job?"

He knew her asking him meant their friendship was true, unlike a certain other. Normally, he wouldn't have gotten involved in other's people's business, much less ask a new acquaintance to refrain from doing their job, but in this case, he had to think like Chay. And as far as he knew, Chay had allied himself with Geoffrey Black.

"Yes. And I might need your help."

Vydra's bright teeth glinted. "Let's talk business."

Lucille

When Merik had told Lucille he was renting an apartment in Fader for his studies, she'd expected a student flat. Maybe a more luxurious student flat, but a small, contained space. What she hadn't expected was a small palace with servants that put even her villa to shame.

The architecture vaguely reminded her of an Indian temple, with big bulbous roofs of white marble and gold accents, but the proportions were off. Purple palm trees had been planted in the garden, apparently kept alive by magic since Fader's climate wouldn't have sustained them for long. It was a little oasis in a town already so colourful and diverse.

Lucille had to walk on a marble walkway across a mirror-like pond with sea lilies to get to the entrance, which was guarded by two men and two women. They didn't bear weapons, but neither did Lucille. One didn't need weapons for defence.

"Hello..." She didn't quite know what to expect. "Is Merik home?"

One of the women gave her the once-over. "State your name and business, and I'll inquire whether the prince will see you."

"The prince?" Lucille swallowed. The guard's brusque demeanour had put her off, but she tried not to hold it against her. Clearly, she was just doing her job... as guard to a prince. "Um, my name's—"

"Lucille!" Merik appeared in the hallway, a beaming smile on his face. "Let her pass, Unara. That woman saved my life." He reached out a hand, and when Lucille stepped forward, he pulled her in and slipped his arm around her. "Have no one bother me."

Merik led her through a marbled hall with several water displays. A servant approached and took her coat, another offered them drinks, but

Merik told them to have them brought to the roof garden, and they stepped onto a plate in the middle of the hall. When it suddenly buckled under them and floated in the air, Lucille startled and held onto Merik.

He laughed. "Don't worry. It's perfectly safe. The magic has been woven immaculately."

"Like everything here," Lucille said, marvelling at the smooth ascent and intricate wall patterns. "By the way, I've finished your translation."

His eyes widened. "You did?" When she showed him the parchment, he laughed and kissed her forehead. "You wonderful, magical woman."

Pleased with herself for translating a language she couldn't even speak, Lucille hugged him tight and enjoyed the ride.

Up and up they went, through several floors, until they arrived in what Merik had called the "roof garden". Again, it wasn't what Lucille had expected. She felt a little stupid for having imagined a flat terrace when the architecture clearly wasn't equipped for that. Instead, the "garden" was in the dome's top, and completely covered. From the inside, the metal was sheer, letting in the outside light. Meanwhile, almost every inch was covered in plants, reminding Lucille of the big glasshouses at botanical gardens she'd visited. Small hangout spaces peeked through the leaves. Lucille saw a table and several chairs and a fountain with benches, but Merik led her to the far end where, hidden by palm fronds, a swinging structure—half-bed, half-couch—looked out over the best view of Fader.

"Wow."

"Pretty good, right?" Merik sat.

Soon, the drinks were delivered, and he ordered a light platter for them to share. It wasn't too different from Lucille's upbringing, though she was sure his was much grander. She took a moment longer to enjoy the view.

Laughing softly, she turned. "So, you're a prince?" She sat next to him and received a glass of liquid. It had a tangy taste that prickled her lips.

Merik snorted. "I thought that was clear from how I introduced myself. Derendi is the Phalesian royal house. If it makes you feel any better, I'm just one of the younger princes, irrelevant in the line of succession."

Lucille's head was swimming, whether from his heritage or the drink, she didn't know. "How many are there?"

"Ahead of me? Four. There used to be more, but ... Phalesian politics." He gave her a wicked smile that did something funny to her stomach.

"Do I want to know more?" Once more, she was amazed at how different this place was, and how many cultures she had yet to learn about.

Merik put a hand on her knee and stroked her thigh with his thumb. "I guess that depends on how this thing between us develops." He leant in for a kiss.

Lucille laughed, leaning back into the pillows. "Slow, I hope. Nice and slow, without too many expectations. For now."

She cupped his face and pulled him in, tasting the tangy drink on his lips, still remembering how it had prickled. The gentle swing of the bed caused some delicious friction, and the pillow covers were impossibly soft, making her feel as if she was lying on a bed of clouds with a gorgeous man who was willing—and able—to fulfil her every wish.

Any thought of the sirens was long forgotten as her head filled with impossible dreams: a faraway world, a prince, cut-throat politics, and fairytale-like opulence. Now that was the excitement she'd been looking for.

Fabian

Fabian felt the magical enclave in every bone of his body when he and Shayna stepped out of the portal. Still, he was glad to see the familiar forest ahead—and for the immediate bars on his phone. As expected, Ophelia had messaged. To his surprise, though, there were only two. One warning him to stay away from Greenvalley because of sirens, and the other telling him the coast was clear. Suddenly, he appreciated the magical enclave so much more.

"Does she still love you?" Shayna commented, dryly.

"Apparently, we missed some men-eating sirens while we were away."

Shayna raised her eyebrows. "Oh, well, it's good you weren't here, then." She bit her lip. "Why didn't you tell Terian about your wind powers?"

Even though he and Camdyn had used their powers together, Fabian was still wary. "Because there's too much agenda for my taste. Did Kaia tell you about the Citadel's plan?"

Judging by the eye-roll, she clearly had. "You mean how the Citadel has only allowed us wild mages to join so they can have a full elemental circle?"

Fabian nodded gravely. "Exactly. Well, you know, I like having a say in my future, but as we know, the Citadel doesn't really care for that. It's bad enough they only invited us for their personal gain. Camdyn said they're going to be really pushy about this."

An offer he couldn't refuse didn't sound like anything he wanted.

Shayna sighed. "You're right, of course."

Fabian cocked his head. "You don't agree?"

"Let's just say I get it. At least to an extent. The Citadel is a safe space, almost like a magical enclave in its own right. It makes sense they're guarding it jealously." Shayna gave him a sad little smile. "Unlike you, I've never had any magical friends. Same with Camdyn. For us, the Citadel opens up pathways and opportunities we wouldn't have otherwise. I'd much rather practise my fire magic than take over my parents' bed and breakfast, because that was my future before the letter arrived."

Fabian mulled her words over. There was still a lot he didn't know about Shayna. She always appeared so strong and confident, but he was starting to see her vulnerable side. He couldn't imagine what it must be like to pretend to be something you're not for so long and hide something as big as her inherent magic. It sounded lonely.

"And they took Camdyn in when he had no one," Fabian added, readjusting his views on the Citadel slightly. "I'm not saying they're bad people or that they don't do good, but they only think about themselves. You say it's a safe space, and I'm asking who's protecting all the struggling wild mages? All the people who have to come to terms with magic on their own, who get attacked by monsters, not knowing why. The Citadel-born mages sit behind their walls in their magical castle, while so many others suffer and even die. That's what I can't get over. They turn their back on so many, and now they want me to be part of them? I just can't."

Shayna linked her arm with his and leant against his shoulder. "And that's why you're so much better than them. You always think of everyone else, while we're all busy with our own little problems."

Fabian didn't know how to reply, so they spent the rest of the walk home in silence, mulling over their own thoughts.

Rachel

The sun was setting when Rachel and Adam departed the Blackstone House and made their way back to her home. His arm was around her, but she still wanted to pinch it now and then to make sure it was real. Leandres' healing had been perfect—not a single bite mark had remained, almost as if it all had been a dream after all.

"You're looking again," Adam teased, gently. "I'm really here. You did it. You defeated the siren queen. In the dreamworld." He sounded in awe. "And you did it with Matt's powers."

"And Lucille's and Ophelia's. It was eye-opening. I've fought monsters in the dreamworld before, but never like this. It's always been about imagination, but this felt more powerful... Which doesn't make any sense, because I was basically just copying other people's skills."

Adam nodded. "What if it's not just about imagination, but faith? Your Emblem of Power is the power of devotion, right? Your friends' skills were stronger because you believed in them. You knew how they worked inside out and their boundaries. You didn't accidentally forget to paint the rest of the sky, if you know what I mean."

Rachel considered his words. The longer she thought about them, the truer they seemed. "I think you're right. They were easy, hardly any effort at all, because I already know them so well." She smiled and kissed his cheek. "Thank you."

"No, no, thank you for making sure I didn't end up siren bait before I had a chance to interview at the hospital."

"Well, the good thing is, after barely escaping with your life, the interview won't even be a challenge." They turned onto the road where her house stood.

Adam snorted softly. "Let's hope you're right." He looked up at the house and sighed. "Now the real question is: what's worse? Being nibbled on by sirens or having your heart stopped by a ghost?"

Rolling her eyes, Rachel unlocked the door and pushed it open. "Hugo doesn't want to kill you. He's not like that."

"Truer words have never been spoken," Hugo said as he floated down the staircase in a dignified manner. "Your death would be a catastrophe. There's only enough space for one ghost at Rachel's side, and that honour belongs to me."

Adam took a deep breath while he slipped out of his shoes. "How fortunate I'm still alive, then."

"A lucky twist of fate. For someone, I suppose."

"Yes, me, for example," Rachel said, annoyed at their spat. "I love Adam. And he won't be going anywhere."

"Well, theoretically, my return flight is next week, but I'll be back," said Adam with a hopeful lilt.

Rachel poked her finger at Hugo, using her no-nonsense voice. "You won't scare him away."

The ghost looked down at her finger, eyebrows drawn deep. "Miss Rachel—"

"Don't force me to exorcise you!"

He sighed, and all the tension went out of him. Slightly deflated, he floated away, straight through a wall. "I apologise."

When he was gone, Rachel shook her head. "Who would've thought ghosts could be so jealous?"

Adam shrugged. "They're dead. Apparently, that doesn't mean they stop having feelings."

"I guess." Still grumpy, she shuddered. "I like him a lot, but not like that." Her annoyance was only fleeting, and one look at Adam had her smiling again. "You're the only one I like that way."

"I know," he said, a little cocky. He stepped forward and grabbed her by the hips. "Now, let me show you how much I like you." Leaning in, his warm breath brushed her ear. "I'm warning you: it might be quite improper."

Laughing, Rachel put her arms around him. She still didn't care much about sex, but Adam managed to make it fun. When he lifted her up, Rachel squealed and wrapped her legs around him, then threw her head back and laughed.

Life before Adam had been so terribly drab. For years, she'd shut her feelings away, protecting herself from all the disappointing turns in her life: her parents' split and mother's rejection, her unrequited and lacklustre feelings for Fabian, and Nico's death. So much had gone wrong—not at all like the books she loved—that she'd found it easier not to feel so deeply, wrapping her heart in shell after shell.

Adam had cracked all that open, unearthing sides of her she'd long forgotten. Instead of being scared of what he might find, she looked forward to every minute.

Samantha

A soft kiss woke Samantha from a distant dream. Her face hurt and was sticking to something. Mortified, she realised she'd fallen asleep on her textbook. "The exam."

"You still have three hours," Matt said, softly. Then he proved to be the best boyfriend in the world by setting a breakfast tray with freshly brewed coffee on the desk. "I thought you may have wanted some extra hours before you go in. And maybe you'd have some time to read my essay." He pointed to a parchment roll on the tray. "But first, coffee."

He poured her a cup and watched her drink it with a gentle smile. What had they been fighting about again?

Her gaze fell on the parchment again. "Your essay about marriage?" Though the coffee gave her life, she set the cup down. "I'm sorry, Matt. I overreacted last night. I didn't want to pressure you, and I've never doubted your love. I know marriage isn't a thing in Hell."

He chuckled softly. "No, you didn't. And I found a handful of demons who've married."

Now, she was intrigued. "For real?" She grabbed the parchment and unrolled it.

"Not many, but a few. Most of them were married to humans and have since lost their loves." He swallowed slightly, reigniting her remorse. "Funny thing is, almost none regretted it. They appreciated it for what it was. A lifetime of love and commitment—just not a demon's lifetime. However, I did find one couple who are still married after nearly three thousand years."

"Wow." She blinked. "When did you have time to ask around?"

"Last night. I didn't want to disturb you and I couldn't sleep, so I went on a field trip. Anyway, if two demons can make it, we'll breeze through."

Samantha felt a tight little knot in her stomach. She didn't know if she was ready for that. "Matt, are you saying—"

He smiled. "Just read."

Still anxious, she dived into his essay. Matt fed her while she read his description of wedding customs around Ashuan compared to those of other worlds. With each, he'd focused on the feelings behind them, comparing them and finding similarities, while slowly building an intelligent thesis about the shift in customs between short- and long-lived species. It opened her eyes. It really wasn't surprising demons didn't get married more often.

When she got to the end, she had tears in her eyes.

...and that's why it doesn't matter how many years have already passed or how many are still in the future. A wedding is a celebration of love—a promise from the present moment to eternity. It's not a prediction nor a guarantee. It only promises one thing: I love you now, in this very moment, and can't imagine that ever changing in my lifetime. Those feelings might change eventually, but in that moment, love is eternal.

Her throat was impossibly tight as tears ran down her cheeks. "Do you really believe that?"

Matt knelt in front of her. "I'd burn the world down for you. All of them."

Samantha laughed, losing some of the tension in her shoulders. "That won't be necessary." She put the parchment back and slung her arms around his neck. "I love you so much it hurts."

"Yeah, what about that? Why does it hurt to love someone?"

She chuckled, then bit her lip. "Because it matters." She drew a shaky breath. "I don't need a wedding. All I need is you, because as you said, right now, I can't imagine ever not loving you."

Matt tightened their embrace. "Good. Because I don't plan on ever letting you go."

Their gazes locked, and she lost herself in his chocolate-brown eyes full of promise, believing every word he'd said.

She'd been scared of the unknown, she realised, of his feelings for her changing eventually. But while the future was unknown, Matt wasn't. The gorgeous man in front of her would burn the world down if it came to saving her—now and forever. He was hers with heart and soul, just as she was his, and nothing would ever change that.

Part 5

Betrayal & Sacrifice

Alecia

The human was back. Alecia watched as he met with the Shadow in one of the back rooms of the residence. It wasn't unusual for human supplicants to visit the residence—they came because their soul was consumed by jealousy and they wished to proposition the Archdemon of Envy. Requests usually went like this: I want more power. Someone stole my power and I want it back. I don't want to share my power, I want it to be mine and mine alone. However, what they didn't realise was nothing would ever be enough. Envy ran deeper.

This human wasn't any different from the others. He was conventionally attractive, in rich clothes, and with overdone manners, indicating he'd been born on the golden side of power with a hunger for more. He was insulted by the rise of those he'd deemed less deserving than him, people who'd come from nothing and had no historical claim to any of what was his.

Alecia had no interest in his sob story—something about a council seat being stolen from his family, now occupied by someone who had no right to it, and an infestation of more of their type. Also, older siblings in his way. What was unusual about the meeting, however, was it wasn't with her master but with this wannabe disciple who'd wormed his way into Pyke's heart. If she could prove the human and the Shadow were colluding against the archdemon, the spot at Pyke's right-hand side would be uncontested once again.

Her ears perked up when the human complained Chay held his hand over these impostors. She knew Chay well. Pyke couldn't stand him, but Pyke couldn't stand anyone. She envied how much the Seven relied on him. As a half-demon, Chay shouldn't have survived more than a decade in Hescaryn's politics, but he'd held out for nearly 150 years already. She'd be failing her position if she dismissed him, especially now he'd made himself indispensable to the new Archdemon of Lust. Between Balthasar's cunning and Chay's unique talent, it wouldn't surprise her to see them running the council in a few years' time.

But there was more. Chay was particularly interested in a group of humans from Ashuan—the Six. And by the sounds of it, so were the Shadow and the golden boy.

"They're talented, I'll give them that," the supplicant said, annoyance thickening his voice, "but they're terribly uneducated. Much like the rest of Ashuan, they know next to nothing about the interglobal community. But of course, they feel entitled to it." He made a hawking sound in his throat, as if he was about to spit, but thought better of it.

The Shadow oozed with excitement. "Have you been able to find out why the Seer thinks they could stop me?"

"Apart from his general obsession with those Ashuanian imbeciles? I would've expected more from a Lukrenian citizen, but then again, he's just a Northman, isn't he?"

Alecia didn't blame the Shadow for hissing impatiently. Humans were always overly concerned about where others originated from, as if location inspired loyalty.

"I've managed to seduce one of the witches," the golden boy continued. Alecia's hairs stood on end. "So much raw power and yet... so gullible." He laughed softly. "She played right into our hands... or, rather, my hands and whatever shadowy appendages you have."

For that alone, Alecia would've relieved him of his precious appendages, but the Shadow was more patient, which meant he needed this pompous fool to do his will. Another weakness for her to exploit.

"I had her translate one of our ancient scrolls of banishment. The monster she's enabled me to free should take out the entire city, which would serve both of us."

Alecia noticed he hadn't answered the Shadow's primary question. The secret of the Six was still hers, but mention of this monster worried her. Were they strong enough to deal with whatever horror the Phalesian was about to unleash on their world? They'd better be, or it wasn't just their world that was doomed, but all of them.

The Shadow slunk around the room, displeased with the report. "Very well," it said, at last. "Go, then. Wipe them out. Hopefully, you're right, and they are Ashuan's last resistance."

From his curled lips, Alecia could tell the golden boy didn't believe they were strong enough. He was underestimating them, just like the Shadow, which would play nicely into Alecia's hands. She couldn't care less about Chay's humans living or dying in the grand scheme of things—not even if they really were the Six. The only thing she cared about was setting the Shadow up to fail. As for the little princeling who'd dared toy with her Lucille? He'd have to die.

Jan

Somehow, Jan managed to pass Leandres' insane test. It had taken a few days, but now they were finally moving on from studying every detail about herbs. Much to his chagrin, they'd started potion brewing.

It hadn't taken much to convince Samantha to join him, providing him not just with company but with her superior knowledge. After several days of brewing, he was no longer able to count how many times she'd saved him from certain disaster. They held lessons in her witch room at the top of the house, using two twin cauldrons in a double fireplace. The room was every bit as witchy as Jan could've imagined: bundles of dried herbs hung from the ceiling, and the shelves were stacked with stained potion books and jars of dubious content. He didn't see any preserved eyes, but there was a jar of scales, and something that looked like a bunch of dried lizard tongues.

"You should be adding the rosemary now," Leandres said, watching them with his hawk-like gaze.

They sprinkled dried rosemary leaves into their cauldrons in near unison, never once stopping to stir.

"Leave it to simmer until the potion turns green. Then I want you to grate one inch of ginger and add the nettles. The potion should be thickening. This will take a while, so shout out once you're done. I'm getting a snack."

As soon as Leandres had shuffled down the spiral staircase, Jan leant over Samantha's cauldron. "Why's yours already blue-green, while mine's still bright red?"

"Bright red?" He didn't like the outraged tone in her voice. "Don't tell me you forgot to add the yarrow earlier."

Jan frowned, trying to remember whether he'd added the flowers when Leandres had asked them to. His gaze fell on the tiny white-pink flowers at the side of his cauldron. "I'm sure I added one spoonful."

"One spoonful? It was supposed to be a handful. Here," she pushed her ladle into Jan's hand, "keep stirring while I try to fix this."

She grabbed a bunch of stuff from the side bench, chopped up a root at chef speed, and added some liquid. After those were incorporated, she sprinkled a generous handful of yarrow flowers into the potion and stirred. Slowly, the potion turned the same colour as hers.

"It probably won't be as effective, but at least you won't poison anyone with too much aconite."

Jan nodded, barely understanding what she was saying. "Knowing Leandres, he'll have us try them later."

"Possibly."

They switched cauldrons again, and Jan watched her grating ginger. Samantha's potion was a nice green now, while his looked a bit murky. "I never thought I'd one day be brewing potions." He snorted. "Maybe I'll start studying Chemistry, too. My parents would lose their minds."

She threw him a pitying look. "Don't make yourself smaller than you are. School wasn't for you, but that doesn't mean you're stupid. You just needed to find your passion."

"You mean healing?" He wasn't quite sure if he'd call it a passion. It wasn't like he'd chosen it, more like it'd chosen him.

"Exactly. I bet your mother would be incredibly proud if she knew."

Jan waved her off. "Nah. She'd just assume I was making it up. Or worse, take drugs again."

Ever since moving out he'd gone low contact with his parents. He wasn't ignoring them, but he wasn't exactly checking in regularly. Neither were they. It worked out for the better if they didn't cross each other's paths much.

"Hmm. How's Anne doing with Finn?"

"Surprisingly well. Finn's enrolled at school. He's struggling a bit, but considering how lacking his previous education was, he's doing fine. No worse than me, for sure." He caught Samantha's glare and laughed.

"Don't worry, I don't mind. As you said, school wasn't my passion. I'm doing perfectly fine at the hospital. Theory's still a bitch, but I'm getting by. And this... As annoying as it, it's fun."

He judged his potion green enough and started grating ginger. Samantha had already added her nettles.

"I'm glad you're enjoying the paramedic training, and it sounds like you're doing more than fine with the whole fast-track programme. Speaking of the hospital..." Samantha frowned slightly. "Robert's doing a voluntary social year there, isn't he?"

"If you're wondering whether he's finally gotten over the fact he accidentally cast a magic spell, then no, he's not. Still avoids me as much as he can, as if I'd drag him back here and make him fight monsters."

He shuddered. Even if Robert turned out to be a secret magic genius, it wouldn't make up for his obnoxious personality.

Samantha continued frowning. "He can do whatever he wants, of course, but I'm curious. I want to know whether he was always able to do that or where it's come from, you know? What if Robert's the one from the prophecy? The one who has to open his eyes?"

"If that's the case, then quite frankly, we're screwed."

Snorting, Samantha whipped her ladle at him. "That's not funny." She peered into his cauldron. "You need to add the nettles or it'll never thicken."

"Yes, ma'am."

Lucille

Though Lucille had moved out of home, she visited often. For one, she had a regular dinner invitation for Friday night—which her father actually managed to attend most weeks, but most of the time, she was actually there to see Pascal, so he could practise his telekinetic powers. They met in one of the mansion's unused rooms, full of trinkets. Lucille pointed them out and Pascal moved them with the power of his mind.

"The step stool to the left."

Though shaky, the stool was pushed to the left, as if by an invisible hand.

"Awesome. How about…" Lucille let her gaze roam the room until she found something suitable. With a wild grin, she said, "That glass bowl. Keep it floating above the podium."

Pascal's eyes widened slightly. "But what if it falls? Isn't it expensive?"

"Probably. But you won't let it, will you?" She raised an eyebrow.

Her brother mirrored her smile and concentrated hard. Slowly, the bowl rose half a metre above the podium it had stood on.

"That was actually quite easy. Don't you have something more challenging?"

Lucille looked around again. She thought about asking him to lift the heavy chest in the back, but then had a different idea. "How about a few things simultaneously? Different heights."

Pascal's concentration deepened. A few smaller items around the glass bowl rose to different heights in the room.

"You're so talented." Lucille was bursting with pride. "Honestly, I don't know what to work on with you anymore. Apart, I guess, from heavier things, and holding them longer each time. But you can build up your endurance on your own." Realising she'd made it sound as if she was going to abandon him, she quickly added, "We'll still hang out. I just don't know what to teach you."

"Well..." Pascal bit his lip. "How about teaching me how to use it in a fight?"

Lucille stared at him. "A fight? Is someone giving you trouble at school?" If so, she had some choice illusions ready.

"No, I meant against monsters."

"Oh." She shook her head almost immediately. "No, absolutely not. You may be the most talented telekinetic in the world, but we're still not taking you monster hunting. You're way too young." He wasn't even a teenager yet.

Pascal rolled his eyes. "What if the monsters start hunting me? Am I too young to defend myself?"

Lucille narrowed her eyes. She leant forward and bopped his nose. "You're too clever for your own good. Let's practise fighting... with pillows." She pointed to the lonely couch in the room. "Throw one of the sofa cushions at me."

With a grin, Pascal turned to the couch. He picked a pillow and made it float, then threw it at Lucille—or rather, moved it towards her. The pillow flew through the air as if pulled along by a ski lift.

Lucille had no trouble plucking it from the air. Then she threw it properly at Pascal. Her aim was off, but he still managed to stop it mid-flight. "Use more energy."

"Momentum," Pascal nodded, deep in thought. "Maybe if I—"

Suddenly, the pillow jerked upwards and smashed past Lucille into the wall next to the door, just as it opened. Albert frowned at it, but a smile split his lips a moment later.

"I see the young master is progressing nicely." He looked at Lucille. "Your date is waiting in the foyer."

"Date?" Pascal said, a hint of disappointment in his voice.

"Sorry. My... boyfriend doesn't live in Greenvalley, so we don't get to see each other much. Next time, I'll stay longer, okay?" She opened her arms and hugged her brother.

Though she felt a little guilty about disappointing Pascal, Lucille was eager to see Merik again. Hopefully this time he wouldn't be kidnapped by sirens or anything else roaming the streets of Greenvalley.

She found him in the foyer, stroking the polished banister with a finger, as if testing for dust. "It's hardly a palace, but it's not too shabby either," Lucille said.

He flashed her a brilliant smile. "Not shabby at all. I just don't understand why you'd move out of here for that small room at Rachel's."

"It's not huge, but there are other advantages."

"There's a certain freedom in moving away from your family. If yours is half as overbearing as mine, I get it." He chuckled softly and held out his arm. "Shall we?"

Lucille took it. "We shall." Laughing, she stepped outside. "To be honest, I often wished my father was a little more overbearing when I was younger."

It had given her so much grief throughout her childhood and teen years, but it no longer hurt the way it did. She knew where it'd come from and had realised how fallible her parents were—and since moved on.

"But quite frankly, it's not so much about getting away from them than about stepping out on my own. You called it 'freedom', and I think that's a beautiful word." Not that she'd ever been constrained much. "I feel like I need to make it in the world on my own, you know? Prove I can do it, even without my daddy paving the way."

Merik pulled a comical face, leaving her to wonder if he felt the same or couldn't imagine shedding any of the privileges he'd grown up with. Maybe it was a little bit of both.

"Anyway, do you want to have dinner or just go back to the house? Or maybe we could—" Her phone vibrated and she pulled it out, her heart sinking. "We could go for a walk by the river."

"By the river?"

"Yeah, apparently, the world is ending. Now."

Twenty minutes later, Lucille met up with her friends at the promenade next to the river. Matt had brought Crumbs, and the dog was happily exploring the riverbank while his owner and the others had their arms crossed, staring down at the water. Up ahead, a news van had arrived, and Lucille saw Philipp taking pictures with his camera. He noticed her and raised his hand in greeting before pointing at the river, fishing for an explanation.

Lucille followed his gaze and nearly did a double take. The water wasn't its usual off-blue or green, but a murky red. And it appeared to be flowing more sluggishly.

"Do we have a bad case of red algae?" Lucille asked, as she joined her friends.

Quietly, Merik wrapped his arms around her middle and rested his chin on her head. Samantha threw a glance at him while Matt snorted.

"If that's red algae, I'll eat Crumbs' food for a week."

"Yeah, that's blood," Samantha said, shivering slightly.

Fabian groaned. "Of course, it is. They're so unimaginative."

Ophelia turned in his arms to look up at him and laughed. "They?"

"The evil forces who want to kill us."

They all laughed at the much-needed levity. Unfortunately, the sight of the bloody river sobered them up quickly.

"I checked the news," Lucille said, getting her phone out to check yet again, "but there are no reports about mysterious deaths or missing people, so where's it all coming from? That must be bucketloads."

"Pig blood?" Jan mused, not sounding very confident. "But that's way more than a few buckets."

"Maybe it's a spell." Samantha had her eyes closed, likely to investigate the magical nature of the phenomenon.

On the other side of the river, a large group of people carrying backpacks and walking sticks paused to watch the river.

"That's a lot of hikers," Anne muttered under her breath.

Apparently, Jan had deemed her old enough to hang with them now. Lucille still thought of her as a young girl, but she was as old as they'd been when they'd started hunting monsters, and the same age as Ophelia.

Fabian frowned. "For this time of year, way too many. But maybe they're from one of the bus tours."

Suddenly, Anne jumped forward and swiped something off her shoulder. All Lucille saw was a small creature hopping into the grass, and her grip on Merik's arm tightened.

Jan, however, started to laugh. "You're such a wimp. It was only a frog, dummy."

"But..." Anne looked up at the cloudy sky. "It came from above."

A moment later, the skies opened, and more frogs fell. Lucille screeched and raised her handbag to protect herself from the croaking creatures.

"It's raining frogs," Rachel noted astutely, not the least bit bothered.

"We're doomed," Fabian said, using his water magic as a shield over himself and Ophelia. "Told you this is the end of the world."

Jan clapped his shoulder. "Well, the end of the world has to wait. My shift's starting."

Samantha sighed. "I'll check what our system's come up with." Her gaze fell on Lucille.

Matt whistled for Crumbs before laying a hand on Merik's arm. "Hey, could I talk to you?" He flashed Lucille an apologetic smile. "You'll have him back in no time. Just need some extra help with my homework."

"Sure. What's bothering you?" Merik let go of Lucille, and the two wandered off, while the others dispersed, leaving just Samantha behind.

Lucille raised her eyebrow. "What was that about?"

Samantha gave her a pained smile and linked her arm with hers. "We need to talk."

Samantha

Samantha wasn't quite sure how to approach the topic—she usually avoided butting into her friends' relationships. In the past, she hadn't always understood Lucille's choices in men, but she'd respected them. This one was even more complicated. Matt had confided in her regarding Merik's true intentions, seeking her advice, and frankly, it'd been a lot, what with Merik apparently trying to hire an assassin to take out Adam's father. The problem was Matt liked Merik, but he also liked Vydra and felt backed into a corner.

Samantha had struggled to advise him on two people who came from very different cultures and belief systems, unlike any on Earth. Merik casually employing an assassin would've made Samantha swallow, but Vydra was an assassin, hardly a preferable option. It'd been a painful journey for Samantha to somewhat come to terms with demonic behaviour, and now this.

As she'd told Matt, she felt completely out of the water. The only thing she knew was she had to make sure Lucille knew.

"How are things with Merik?"

Lucille's eyes were full of doubt, but she answered anyway. "Progressing. It's still very casual due to our distance, but I enjoy it. It feels mature."

"Mature? I didn't know that was important."

"Of course, it's important. We're adults now with adult relationships. I mean, you moved in with Matt."

Samantha swayed her head. "Yeah, maybe my relationship with Matt isn't exactly the benchmark for normal."

As sudden as it might look on paper, Samantha felt like they'd done the work other couples only started when they got together. Officially, they'd been together for five months, but they'd belonged together for much longer. Even when they'd hated each other.

"I'm not judging," Lucille clarified. "If anyone deserves to be happy, it's you two."

"Thanks. And look, I'm not judging you either. If casual is what you want, meaning it's not him avoiding commitment and spinning you some tale about—"

"It's not," Lucille said. Laughing, she put a hand on Samantha's arm. "We're just not there yet. You know, things are a bit more complicated when you live in two different worlds."

Samantha winced. "Speaking of two different worlds. There's something you should know about Merik."

"If you're planning to tell me he's one of the Princes of Phalos, living in a small palace, then, yes, I know."

For a moment, Samantha could only stare. "A prince?" Some of the puzzle pieces in her mind were clicking into place. "Okay…"

"He's just one of the younger princes. He's not really in the line of succession. I mean, he is, but it's highly unlikely he'll ever rule."

Two puzzle pieces, but they wouldn't quite fit. "Well, I didn't know that. I just wanted to tell you something Matt found out after the sirens. You can do with this information what you want, but I will tell Rachel." She had to know—or rather Adam had to know someone was trying to assassinate his father. They'd already informed Chay, who'd promised he'd look into it.

"Rachel? Oh, because we live together, you mean?" Lucille shook her head. "Just tell me what it is. It's still raining frogs, so I'm pretty sure we have more important things to handle."

"Sorry, you're right. Okay, here goes: Matt was told Merik hired an assassin."

As expected, Lucille frowned. "Sounds like a nasty rumour to me."

"He was told by the assassin. Remember that snake woman who saved us when we were fighting the sirens? She's Matt's friend."

"Matt's friends with assassins now?"

Samantha shrugged and rolled her eyes. "He only just found out. Apparently, it's what her tribe does to survive. I mean, you've seen how deadly she was—maybe that's how she pays her student fees. And for the record, no, I'm not okay with it."

Lucille had her eyebrows raised and nodded slowly. "Demons, right?" She shuddered. "So, Merik hired an assassin, and the assassin tattled? Doesn't sound very professional."

"You seem weirdly okay with it."

"About as okay as you are with Matt running around with sexy assassins." Lucille's face softened. "Sorry, that was uncalled for. I wasn't trying to insinuate Matt's got a case of the wandering eye."

"I know he doesn't."

Some other time Samantha might have been insecure about how disconcertingly sensual Matt's classmate was, but Vydra had been so respectful of their relationship, immediately drawing up boundaries Samantha couldn't help but trust her. Most importantly, she trusted Matt.

"And as for Vydra, she came to Matt because there's a connection between us and the proposed victim. Besides, she didn't take the job."

"A connection?" Lucille sounded surprised. "What's that supposed to mean? I figured he'd try kill one of his siblings. Apparently, that's what they do in Phalos."

Samantha was about to question Lucille's judgement, but then she remembered killing siblings was very much a demon thing, too, and Matt had actually killed his half-brother. Maybe Merik's siblings were the same.

"Well, the thing is, he's not going after a Phalesian. The person he wanted assassinated is Geoffrey Black—Adam's father, the parliamentarian."

Stunned, Lucille stopped walking. "I remember him. He was awful."

"Awful enough to be assassinated?"

Samantha pulled a face. She couldn't help wondering if the attack on parliament had also been orchestrated by Phalos. If only she knew more about interglobal politics to properly place her puzzle pieces.

"Of course not," Lucille said, but then her voice faltered. "Then again, we don't know anything about Geoffrey Black. The man abandoned his grieving son. Adam's nice, but his father could be a total jerk. Who knows what he did to get his seat at the parliament? Maybe he's a horrible man spreading anti-Phalesian propaganda or something."

"Chay works with him," Samantha said. It was her only proper argument, considering she didn't know the bigger picture.

Lucille snorted. "Chay also works with Balthasar, and that guy is as ruthless as they come." She shuddered. "And has no sense of common decency. Besides," she said before Samantha could get a word in, "Merik could've just been following orders. Maybe his father told him to hire Vydra. That'd be a royal order he can't refuse."

Her arguments felt like she was grasping at straws and made Samantha dizzy, but she tried to give him the benefit of the doubt. She had to trust Matt would be more successful in getting information out of him. "Well, maybe you could ask him."

"Ask why he wants to assassinate someone?" Lucille huffed. "Wow, yeah, that sounds really romantic."

"Lucille..."

"I'll do it," she said, though she clicked her tongue. "It just feels a bit... intrusive. I don't know if we're at the point in our relationship yet where we can question each other's morality."

"Well, maybe not, but don't you want to know if the guy you're casually seeing is a brutal killer, ruthless strategist, or maybe just wrapped up in some messed up stuff that could affect you? What if Geoffrey retaliates—or one of Merik's siblings?"

Lucille let go of her and rubbed her face. "Is this what you felt like when Matt's family drama spilt over into Greenvalley?"

"You tell me."

"I already said I'll ask him. Just... Just let me do this my way, okay?"

Samantha had to trust she knew what she was doing. "Okay. I'm just trying to look out for you. It felt like something you should know. That's all."

Lucille smiled, but it came across a bit forced. "And I appreciate it, but now I've got a date to ruin, so..."

"Good luck," Samantha said, suppressing a sigh.

This conversation had gone as well as it could've, but she felt like she had more questions than answers. Hopefully, Lucille's instincts were right, and Merik had good reason for his actions.

They met up with the boys, and Samantha watched Lucille and Merik reunite and walk off, looking all lovey-dovey.

With her arms crossed, she turned to Matt. "How was it?"

He winced. "He told me a grand tale about corruption in the Inter-global Parliament, and that I didn't understand the mechanics because I'm not from a world in the fold, which apparently is exactly the problem with Geoffrey Black. Something about 'meddling in affairs he has no business in'. To be honest, I think the main reason is his seat for Ashuan came from the Phalesian section."

Samantha moaned softly as the puzzle pieces finally matched up. "Now it makes sense. From the Phalesian perspective, we stole their seat."

"That's what Merik said."

"And the go-to method for solving conflicts is assassination?"

Matt pulled a face. "Apparently, that's the polite political way." He snorted. "Balthasar would probably agree. Personally, I think you should deal with your own shit, instead of asking other people to kill for you. But Merik pointed out not all people have the innate strength to swiftly take a life like I do."

Samantha could practically taste the bitterness in his words. She put her hands on his face and forced him to look her in the eye. "In my opinion, it makes no difference whether you order a death or deliver it yourself. Merik might call it clean, and demons might call it necessary, but I believe there are better ways to solve a conflict. And so do you. Don't let him use his perception of demon morals against you. What he's doing is wrong."

Matt inhaled sharply, putting his hands on hers. He pulled her in and hugged her tight. "What would I do without you as my moral compass?"

"Kill a lot of people who don't deserve it."

He snorted and chuckled. "Probably." Kissing her forehead, he let go again and took her hand. "Oh, well, maybe Lucille can be his moral compass in the future. I believe we have a mystery to solve."

Samantha flashed him a smile, and they walked back through the pedestrian zone. The rain had stopped, but frogs were still hopping around, their croaks filling the air. Crumbs seemed as confused as they were, sometimes running as if to chase them, then backing away again.

Just then, Samantha saw a familiar face. "Cian?"

Their former classmate turned, his face lighting up. "Samantha. Matt."

"What are you doing here?" Samantha gave him a warm hug. After school, he'd moved to Bielefeld to study Chemistry.

Cian returned the hug and clasped hands with Matt. "My mum's celebrating her fiftieth this weekend, so I'm here to party." He grinned and rolled his eyes. "As much as you can with fifty-year-olds. I'm just waiting for Alan to grab last-minute supplies, but apparently, he's running late." With a frown, he regarded the frogs hopping into the blood-red fountain. "I feel like we should've picked another weekend. Do you know what's going on? I suppose it's monster related."

"We're still investigating," Samantha answered truthfully.

"Could be a monster," Matt mused, "or maybe a spell gone wrong. I mean, blood in the river, frogs falling from the sky—sounds like a spell to me." He and Samantha exchanged a look, wondering if they should've asked Lucille a different question.

Cian pulled a face. "That's a pretty big spell, if you ask me. There's even blood in our pipes, hence the last-minute shopping. My mother nearly had a meltdown earlier."

The thought of blood coming out of the pipes made Samantha queasy. "Disgusting."

"Oh, well, that's Greenvalley for us, right? I so haven't missed it."

"You didn't miss us?" Samantha teased, light-heartedly.

Cian cleared his throat. "Of course I did." Quickly, he smiled again. "Hey, maybe we could get together later. I'm staying until Sunday." He looked at his phone and sighed. "Great. Alan's not coming. I'd better get those water bottles, and then I'm off to see Shayna. Apparently, she has big news or something."

"Oh... Yes, big news."

Cian cocked his head. "You know? Are you... friends now?"

"Um… her and Fabian are, I think." It really wasn't her place to tell him about Fabian and Shayna's surprising connection.

Cian's eyes widened. "Are they now?" He laughed softly. "Okay, I'm intrigued. This is going to be good." Pointing a finger at her, he grinned. "We definitely need to catch up before I leave. Keep me posted, okay?" With a last laugh, he strode towards the supermarket.

Matt put his arm around Samantha's shoulders and pulled her close. "I think he might still be in love with you."

"Nonsense."

After their last class trip, Samantha and Cian had ended their friends with benefits arrangement. It'd always just been a refuge for her, and Cian had seemed to understand, despite developing more feelings. But five months later and after two months of university life, surely he'd set his sights elsewhere.

Though Matt didn't protest, he slipped his arm down to her waist and held it tight, making her think his motivations stemmed more from jealousy than astute observation. Not that she was complaining.

Shayna

Shayna had been looking forward to Cian's visit ever since she'd come back from the test. The thought that one of her oldest friends could be open-minded about magic filled her with giddiness. At last, she could share her secret with someone she loved without risking ridicule. Now, they were behind the reception desk at her parents' bed and breakfast, while she showed him her flame-creating ability under the table.

The light flickered across Cian's face. "Incredible. Why didn't you ever say anything?"

Shayna closed her fingers and extinguished the flame. With a bitter taste in her mouth, she snorted. "In front of Cheryl and the others? When they were constantly complaining about how ridiculous magic was, and making fun of Samantha?"

"You could've told Alan and me."

The three of them had been something of a separate entity within the bigger group, just like Cheryl and Ani were.

"You took part as well, and so did I. It was embarrassing, and I didn't want to be one of the weirdos. It was only in the last few years I realised being weird wasn't necessarily a bad thing. But by then, the lines were drawn."

Cian snorted. "I can't believe we let that happen." He shook his head. "It seems so ridiculous and childish now." He nudged her, a twinkle in his eye. "But I heard you and Fabian are friends now?"

"We are," Shayna blurted out, unable to stop the heat rising in her cheeks. "It's crazy. We're both students at the Citadel of Magic, studying

Elemental Magic. Compared to me, though, he's a genius. Have you seen him wield water?"

"I don't think so, but he's one of the Six, so I assume he must be powerful."

Shayna frowned. "The Six? Is that what we're calling their clique now?"

Cian shook his head. "Hasn't he told you? I suppose Fabian's never been one to brag. There's this big prophecy involving the six of them."

"You mean the one about our world ending and some dude with wings being our only hope?" Shayna narrowed her eyes. Prophecies were one aspect of magical life she hadn't quite adjusted to yet. How was it possible to tell the future?

"Um, what?"

Shayna told him what Fabian had said about his adventure to Yl-vadin.

Cian rubbed his neck in discomfort. "The end of the world? Damn. Um..." He seemed a little perplexed, which Shayna didn't blame him for. "No, this one is... bigger." He shook his head, as if to clear the cobwebs. "I know it sounds ridiculous, but apparently, the fate of all worlds is on the line, and the only ones who can save us from it are those six. They're reborn heroes or something, and they each have a magical item that's a slice of true power."

"The feather." Shayna saw it herself: a large feather, shimmering in all shades of blue. "He can call the wind with it."

"And draw anything to life for an hour or so," Cian said.

Shayna raised an eyebrow. That sounded like an impossibly powerful artefact. If the Citadel found out... "And they're destined to save the world?"

"All worlds." Cian nodded. "Crazy, I know. Just imagine, in a few years you can say you went to school with the heroes of legend." He chuckled. "I mean, if you ask me, they're already plenty heroic."

She nudged him. "Especially Samantha, huh?"

By the way a secret little smile slipped on his lips, Shayna could tell he was still head over heels for the witch. Too bad she and Matt were as close to a package deal as they could be.

Flustered, Cian cleared his throat. "So, you and Fabian are at magic school now?"

"Crazy, huh? Cheryl would throw a fit. She thinks I'm at hospitality school so I can take over this place." She sighed heavily. As proud as she was of her parents' business, the reality of it—endless blanket washing, room cleaning, and dealing with idiots—was painful. "I couldn't imagine anything more boring. Magic school, however, is fun. Especially with Fabian."

"I see. So, you're getting along well now."

Shayna couldn't stop grinning. "More than well."

"Is he still with Ophelia?"

The grin slipped off her face faster than warm butter off a breakfast plate. "Yes, he is. And he loves her so much, but... they're not perfect. They've got their problems." Mostly, it was Ophelia being insecure as heck.

"Let me tell you from experience: don't hope for more than there is."

Shayna pouted. "It's not that serious, Cian. Just an innocent flirt." And Fabian was certainly flirting back, whether he realised it or not. "I'm not like you, who won't ever love anyone else." She rolled her eyes for good measure.

Cian scoffed at her. "You're exaggerating. I'm over Sam. She has Matt now and they're happy. They're, like, destined for each other, so no wonder I never had a chance." He quickly changed the topic, telling Shayna everything she needed to know. "But are you just toying with Fabian, or what?"

"Of course! I just adore how flustered he gets. I've always loved how quickly he blushes, like he wears his heart on his sleeve. It's refreshing, and pretty cute. And I guess I do have an effect on him."

She could tell Cian only half-believed her. "You're playing with fire, Shayna. But apparently, that's your thing."

She boxed him in the arm.

"Ouch. I'm just saying." He leant back, still frowning. "You always pretend you don't care and just want to have fun, but I know you. You hide your true feelings behind this mask of—"

Before he could dig any deeper, the door slammed open and a group of people tumbled in, frantically batting the air.

Shayna and Cian exchanged a look, and she stood. "May I help you?"

"Do you have something for gnats?" the woman closest asked, panting.

"Gnats?" Shayna looked outside. A dark cloud of insects covered the windows, blocking out the light, their hum so loud it sounded like rolling thunder. Her breathing choppy, she searched blindly for Cian's hand. When he took hers, she whispered, "I'm scared."

Cian swallowed. "Me, too."

Anne

The sight of the bloody river and frogs falling from the sky had filled Anne with foreboding. She knew the end of the world was coming to Ashuan. She just hadn't expected it so soon. Or to be so biblical.

Everything had been going wrong since the banshees had shown up and Robert had banished them. He was usually the sweetest, kindest guy in existence, and delightfully goofy. He made her laugh, and to top it off, seemed to worship the ground she walked on. And then, he'd accidentally cast a powerful spell. Now, he'd been avoiding her, and if she ever dared bring up the topic of his surprising magic abilities, he pretended not to hear or shut down completely.

It wasn't just his abilities. He also didn't want to hear about hers. Anne wanted to support him and she wanted to be supported, because so far, her journey as a priestess had been built on bits and pieces, with none fitting well enough to build a strong base. The only silver lining from the last few weeks was she now had Finn, whose entire life had been built on priesthood. They supported and learnt from each other, but it wasn't the same as hanging out with Robert.

And then she'd made the mistake of reading the "Circle of Magic" book Chay had penned, with its frightening prophecy, the long—and incredibly exciting—history of the Twelve Heroes, all the information about the six Emblems of Power, and its endless lists of reincarnations. She'd spent many hours fantasising about the names on the list and looking for patterns, and had found out six of the previous reincarnations—one for each of the Six—had all died within days of each other in the same place. Of course, their counterparts had died around that time, too, but they'd been scattered across many different worlds. The fact half of them had gathered was a sign of divine power. Something had started pulling the souls closer.

Each of the Twelve Heroes had a list of names, but there was also a thirteenth, one none of the others had paid much attention to, because he wasn't one of the Heroes, in fact, quite the opposite. Roric Drakenson—the first proper demon in existence, son of the most powerful mage who'd ever lived. Draken's soul was the only one who hadn't regenerated, sealed in the Land of the Dead, but Roric's had. And throughout the aeons, he'd always stayed close to at least one of the others—most of the time, it was Kairos', sometimes Hanna's. This time, it was her brother, and the one who carried Roric's tainted soul was none other than Robert.

Anne was nearly bursting with the weight of her secret. She'd told Finn, but he knew too little of the prophecy and her brother's friends—much less Robert—to truly appreciate how important it was. She hadn't told the others yet, afraid of what they might do to Robert if they found out he carried the soul of Draken's son. And she hadn't told Robert, because he was already freaking out enough about his powers. Roric's powers.

Roric had been an accomplished mage, specialising in banishing circles and other darker arts, like compulsion. Throughout the War that broke the Old World, he'd mainly fought for his father, but he'd developed a soft spot for young Kairos and nearly succeeded in corrupting him, almost derailing the entire war. It was Anne's goddess, Hanne, who'd killed him back then, opening the way for Kairos to take down Draken.

Roric certainly wasn't someone Anne cared to meet. But how much of him was inside of Robert? Was his soul truly wiped clean, as the reincarnation suggested? Or had some dark part of him survived? Would Robert remain Robert or would he slowly turn into Roric? And what role would he play in the grand schemes of things? Chay wouldn't have included him if he wasn't important, but there was no part of the prophecy that hinted at a seventh person being involved.

Since Chay wasn't available to answer her questions, and she could neither talk to Robert or her brother and his friends, the only one Anne could turn to was the goddess she was still trying to understand.

Anne and Finn often visited the Spring of Magic. Greenvalley didn't have a temple for either of their gods, but this place felt right, especially for Anne, who saw Hanna's hand in the growth around the clearing. Even now, as winter approached, the clearing was still green and flourishing.

She had her hands folded and was mentally telling Hanna about the weird occurrences in town, asking for her help and guidance in the coming challenges, when she heard a ruckus behind her. She opened her eyes and glanced around, surprised to see the same group of wanderers she'd seen at the river. The clearing was off the main hiking paths, but the people seemed determined to come this way. When they saw the clearing, their eyes lit up, and Anne watched their faces transform, as if they'd shed weeks of deprivation and exertion. Then they noticed the two teenagers bowed in prayer.

A middle-aged woman with a heavy, grey-streaked braid bowed her head in front of Anne. "Greetings be with you, Priestess of Life."

Anne's eyes widened as she froze. No one had ever addressed her like that, and she felt a weight settle on her shoulders.

"They're pilgrims," Finn whispered.

"Pilgrims?"

The woman smiled warmly. "That's right. The Goddess led us to you."

"Me?" Anne repeated.

"Her chosen one."

Anne's mouth felt dry, but the only question that came to her lips was: "You believe in Hanna?"

The pilgrim laughed. "Of course we do." Her face sobered quickly, and she frowned. "The Goddess worries death and decay will enter our beautiful world. If no one stops him, many will die."

Finn paled. "Not again," he whispered.

"I don't think—"

Anne's thoughts were interrupted when she heard the aggressive buzz of gnats. It became louder and louder until an entire cloud descended on the clearing. Two small children began to cry, and the pilgrims looked worried.

"It's begun," the woman said. She sank to her feet and pressed her forehead into the moss. "Help us, Goddess."

The gnats attacked and people screamed. Anne batted the air, trying to shoo them away, but there were too many, and she quickly felt their stings.

Finn grabbed her arm. "Quick! Call to Hanna."

"I..." Anne forced herself to breathe, ignoring the buzzing insects and their increasingly itching stings. She closed her eyes, trying to find the motherly warmth inside. "Hanna, please, if you can hear me, if you chose me... help me protect this land and the life around me."

One moment, her skin was throbbing, the next it had stopped. Just like a mother who'd applied cooling salve, the touch of her goddess was comforting and undeniable. The sensation calmed her racing heart. When the clearing quieted alongside her, Anne dared open her eyes. All around her, the pilgrims were staring. Then, one by one, they sank to their knees. There was no sight of the gnats—not even a single buzz. Instead, a shimmering cupola was protecting the clearing, Anne at its centre.

The woman who'd spoken was the last to bow. She smiled. "Blessed be the Goddess of Life and her chosen one."

Anne turned to Finn, but he just grinned. "Your goddess loves you."

Truth be told, Anne felt loved and protected in the soft warmth of the divine, but she also felt an immense responsibility, as if all these strangers were hers to protect now. What was she supposed to do with a good dozen pilgrims during the end of the world?

Fabian

At the weekends, Fabian still helped out at the Magic Circle. They were usually the busiest days of the week with tourists washing into the shop after a hike, but the hiking season was as good as over and the ski season hadn't started, so the going was slow enough to restock the shelves while Ophelia sat at the counter, scrolling on her smartphone.

According to reports, the phenomenon they'd encountered had been spreading across the country: bloody rivers, frogs, gnats, and flies. Fabian didn't need to look at a map to know where the centre of activity was.

"Blood-like, my ass," Ophelia snorted. "How about just blood?"

"Put it away," Fabian said, his nerves already frayed.

They'd been warned the end was near, and now supernatural phenomena of biblical proportions had been occurring. It was only a matter of time until the first volcano blew up, and they had no idea where this supposed saviour was. They hadn't even had time looking for or preparing likely candidates, such as Camdyn or Finn.

"At least it's not just happening in Greenvalley," Ophelia said.

"That doesn't really improve the situation."

It was kind of the point of a world-ending catastrophe. Soon, it wouldn't just be in the Harz region or contained to Germany, but sweep across the entire world.

Fabian pulled out his phone. "I wonder if they're monitoring the situation at the Citadel."

Ophelia's face fell. "Oh, no!"

"No?"

"You will not bugger off again to the Citadel with her." She pushed her hands on her hips and blinked. There was no doubt who she was talking about.

Fabian scrunched up his nose. "I didn't say I was going with Shayna. Or at all." He shook his head. "Now I've forgotten what I wanted to do."

"Well, maybe you understand how I feel, then?"

"What?"

Ophelia crossed her arms. "You say you love me, but you're also interested in her."

Fabian's eyes widened. "What? No!"

Unimpressed, she raised her eyebrow. "You sure?"

"Of course, I am! Are we going to have the same argument every week? Shayna and I are friends. You're seeing things that aren't real."

Maybe if he weren't already in a relationship, it would be different, but Fabian loved Ophelia, and he had no plans to risk that.

"Yes, yes, I'm being silly again." There were definitely tears in Ophelia's eyes now.

Fabian softened his voice. "I didn't say that. I—"

The door opened, nearly crashing into the wall, as a man stormed into the shop, looking as if he'd run a marathon.

"May I help you?" Fabian asked.

"I need a healing potion. Or a protective amulet. Or... I don't know. But I've already been to the vet, and he said my little Flakey had to be euthanised. This morning, she was healthy as a bean, and I thought with everything else happening... Please help me."

Fabian and Ophelia stared at each other.

Matt

"Hey, Crumbs."

Matt held out his hand, but Crumbs only looked at him wearily. An hour ago, he'd been running around, pulling on his leash, and hunting frogs. Now he was in front of Matt's and Samantha's bed, too tired to play, eat, or drink.

"What's wrong?"

Matt scratched him between his ears, which usually delighted him, but the dog only huffed sadly. With increasing worry, he pulled him onto his lap.

Samantha's steps sounded from the stairs. "Our system's going crazy. According to the readings, there are hundreds of monsters in the city. But nothing definite—" Her gaze fell on him. "What's wrong?"

"Crumbs is sick." There was no other explanation.

Samantha's face fell. She quickly approached them and checked Crumbs all over. In a minute, she'd tell him he was being silly, and Crumbs was just exhausted or had eaten too much or—

She gasped.

"What is it?"

He didn't like the way she'd pressed her lips together and swallowed. "Do you remember that magical plague we had?"

Did he remember? Samantha had almost died in his arms, trying to save the city. He'd carried her through half of Hell to save her life. "Crumbs has the plague? But... you... you brewed a healing potion. I mean, Elda did..."

"Yes, with a plant that no longer—"

Matt felt the blood drain from his face. "Don't you dare end that sentence."

There was no way Adrianes had regrown the saplings already. Carefully, he peered at Crumbs' fur. Through the golden fluff, black boils were showing. Matt felt like throwing up.

"I'm sure it's something else," Samantha said quickly. "Why don't you bring him to the vet while I work on a way to clean the river so we don't all to die from thirst?"

Spurred into action, Matt lifted Crumbs in his arms and hurried downstairs, Samantha on his heels.

At the foot, Leandres was looking up at him. "Have you seen the boy anywhere?"

"Jan with Anne," Neve declared happily. "She asked for help." She floated over to Matt. "Oh, no, no. What's wrong with Crumby? Does he need ice pack?"

Matt gave her a tortured smile. "I don't think ice is going to help." He buried his face in Crumbs' face. "You can't die, okay? It's not allowed." He was barely two. When he raised his head again, he was looking straight into Chay's eyes. The half-demon was at the bottom of the stairs, his face dead serious. To Matt's surprise, he was accompanied by Vydra. "What are you two doing here?"

"Warning you. I've managed to interpret a part of your prophecy."

Matt rolled his eyes. "Too late. The world's already ending." Slowly, his flippant words sank into his mind and he swallowed. "Do we need to evacuate?"

Chay frowned. "This isn't—"

Without thinking, Matt reached out and touched Chay, forcing his immediate future on the Seer. Chay's eyes widened, and he nearly bent in half, reeling. As soon as he'd recovered, his gaze grew even more intense.

"Matt, you need to sit down."

Not the answer he'd wanted to hear. "I can't. Crumbs might be dying."

"The vet won't be able to help him."

Matt's knees buckled, and he stumbled against the railing. The big dog in his arms felt so heavy, yet he was still just a pup in his eyes. Crumbs couldn't possibly be taken from him.

Chay glanced past him at Samantha. "I've found out who the Dark One is. Pyke has a new disciple. It's not a demon or a human, but a dark entity that calls himself the Shadow."

"Pyke wants to destroy Ashuan?" Matt asked, still breathless, before explaining to Samantha, "He's the Archdemon of Envy, petty as heck, but mostly harmless."

"No archdemon is ever harmless," Chay warned.

Though he was likely right, Matt found it hard to respect an archdemon who envied what others had. He didn't scheme and didn't attack, he just whined and demanded.

"What does Pyke want with Ashuan?"

If this was some hare-brained perceived sleight because someone had mentioned working with Ashuan, Matt was going to give him something to be envious about. They'd dealt with enough archdemon shit from his mother and his uncle already.

"My source says the Shadow has Pyke's ear and commands most of the residence. Pyke might not care about Ashuan, but the Shadow does. He's the one behind the banshees and the sirens, and whatever monstrosity is plaguing you right now. This is all part of his scheme to eliminate potential enemies before he comes for Ashuan's light."

Vydra looked as if she wanted to say something, but then thought better of it.

"Are you saying this is not the end of the world?" Samantha asked, her voice lifting. "Just another monster we can defeat?"

Chay nodded sharply. "According to my source—" His gaze suddenly fell on Matt. "Matt, you should really sit—"

Matt gasped when a sharp pain in his stomach brought him to his knees. In an enormous effort of will, he managed to lower Crumbs before dropping him, then the cramps overwhelmed him and he gritted his teeth, trying not to scream out.

"Matt!" Samantha dropped to her knees at his side. "What's wrong?"

"I..." The pain was almost too strong to speak. "Don't know... it just..." He bowled over, digging his fingers into his stomach, as if he could rip whatever was ailing him out of his intestines. "Hurts."

Pounding steps announced Leandres' approach, but before the healer could even touch him, Matt's head hit the floor and he passed out.

Samantha

Samantha didn't know what to do with herself while Leandres looked after Matt. She didn't want to get in the way, but she didn't want to leave his side, either. He was never sick, and if he was hurt, he healed, but this time was different. An hour after his collapse he was still flitting in and out of consciousness, constantly in pain, and now feverish.

In the meantime, Rachel and Lucille had arrived. Rachel had Crumbs on her lap, gently stroking the sick dog's fur, while Lucille had arrived with Merik—still on her date. Thankfully, Chay had stepped in and, citing the lack of space and sensitive situation, had asked him to stay downstairs. Even Lucille had agreed, showing nothing but concern for Matt. Unlike Merik, Vydra had stayed, though she'd withdrawn to the back of the room, standing so still Samantha doubted Lucille and Rachel had even noticed her.

After the twelfth healing regimen, Leandres sat back and rubbed his forehead.

Samantha pounced on him. "And?"

"It's some type of growth, but one that's resistant to healing or potions." He stared at Matt, lost deep in thought. "We might have to start focusing on managing his pain."

Samantha whimpered, clutching her belly to prevent herself from losing her mind. Lucille jumped up and hugged her tight. "Matt will be fine. He's resilient."

"Not if this is the end of the world," Rachel mumbled.

"It's not." Chay shook his head and focused on Lucille. "Isn't any of this familiar to you?"

Lucille let go of Samantha. "Familiar? To me?"

Chay spoke in a language Samantha didn't understand, but she heard Lucille gasp and saw her eyes widen.

"What did you do?" Rachel asked, a little harsher than necessary.

"I didn't... I... What did I do?" she asked.

He got up, making sure the door was closed. "You were tricked."

Samantha looked back and forth between them. "Can someone tell me what's going on?" If it had anything to do with why Matt had fallen ill, she had a right to know.

Chay sighed. "A week ago, Lucille used her magic to translate a scroll for the Phalesian prince, not knowing Phalos used to be famed for their banishing magic. In the past, they made a name for themselves by banishing a great number of monsters and creatures not just in their own world, but other worlds, too. It brought them a huge reputation and made them assume an unofficial 'world police' position, until a couple generations back, when their talent waned—I don't know the specifics of how, but the result was fewer and fewer banishers were born. Which brings us to today, where it's considered a lost talent. Over the same time period, the Phalesian language evolved, and much of their creature library became unreadable. Apart from the librarian and a few select scholars, no one could read the older scrolls, which is necessary to release them."

"Release them?" Rachel said. "Why would anyone want to do that?"

"Several reasons. What seems like a monster to you might be a holy creature to someone else. Phalos likes to stylise themselves as grand monster hunters, making the worlds safer, but they're not above a little blackmail. Diplomatic relationships change, and sometimes, they gave a monster back, or used especially nasty ones against their enemies."

"And their enemy is Ashuan?" Samantha asked, incredulous.

From what she'd gathered, Ashuan's seat in the Interglobal Parliament was brand-new, while the world itself wasn't even part of the conglomerate.

Chay glanced at Matt as if considering whether there was enough time to school them in interglobal politics. "Ashuan has been known to the Interglobal Parliament for hundreds of years—there've been ties since before its initiation. Likewise, mages in Ashuan have always known about other worlds. And don't believe for one minute those mages never had any influence on global politics. Yet despite its strong position, the Citadel and other organisations never reached out. Until recently. And the reason for that is Phalos."

He checked the door again. "Phalos kept Ashuan small on purpose, whether through deals or threats, or by redirecting diplomatic efforts from other worlds. Why? Well, long ago, it was prophesied that Phalos' star would dim as Ashuan's rose. For thousands of years, they managed to hold that prophecy at bay, but now Geoffrey Black sits in the Interglobal Parliament, on a seat that used to belong to the Phalos delegation. And while many of their issues are homemade, they, of course, blame Ashuan for their waning powers." He rolled his eyes. "Nowhere in the prophecy does it say that Ashuan will be the cause of Phalos' downfall, but—"

"Correlation isn't cause," Rachel said, wisely. "It's a mistake as old as time."

"One could also say a self-fulfilling prophecy." Chay's gaze landed on Lucille. "Merik released the banshees and the sirens. Both were offerings he brought to the Shadow when he turned to the Archdemon of Envy for support. They were recently banned monsters, written in New Phalesian."

Lucille sucked in a breath, swaying slightly. "But I translated something much older?"

Chay nodded grimly. "Blood in the water, frogs, gnats, flies," his gaze fell on Crumbs, "sickness among the animals... and people."

"That's the ten plagues," Rachel said, her eyes widening. "Phalos banned those?"

"Long, long ago, yes."

Lucille whimpered and stumbled back until she could lean on the wardrobe. "And I freed them?"

"You translated the text. Merik freed them. He must have that much magic left in him."

"But if those are the ten plagues," Samantha said, her voice shaky, "we're still missing four."

Rachel was quick to supply the rest. "Hail, locusts, darkness, and death of the male firstborns."

Samantha felt her knees weakening. She looked back at Matt and whimpered. "And is that counted from the father or the mother?" One kept him safe, the other doomed him to death.

"He won't die," Lucille declared, tears in her eyes. "And Crumbs won't either."

"I could take care of Merik," Vydra said, stepping out of the shadows. "That way it won't fall back on Ashuan. Especially if Chay contracted me."

Lucille startled. "What is she doing—No! I'm not just... I'm going to talk to him. Make him see sense and banish the plague before the rest unfold." She pushed off the wardrobe and rushed towards the door. "No assassination necessary."

Samantha reached out for her. "Lucille..."

Her friend stopped, gaze fixed on Matt, then on her. "Don't worry. After all, I'm good with words, aren't I?" Her voice shook, and a tear rolled down her face. She opened the door and ran downstairs, letting the door shut behind her.

Uncomfortable silence spread in the room. Samantha felt sorry for her. If Merik was truly behind everything—and Chay wouldn't lie—he'd already proven how easily he could wrap anyone around his finger. Even Matt had considered him a friend, and now he was in bed, struck down by a biblical sickness.

Rachel cleared her throat, breaking the spell. "Do we trust Lucille to talk this prince out of destroying our world?"

Vydra's snake-like gaze moved through the room. It fell on Matt, then Samantha. She raised an eyebrow, as if to ask her to hire her. Thankfully, she turned to Chay. "My offer still stands."

He narrowed his eyes, as if to gauge how much he could trust her. Samantha held her breath. To her, condemning anyone to death was unthinkable. Even more so, asking someone else to kill them. But with Matt lying here, dying, immune to any healing... They had to do something.

Chay nodded, his eyes uncharacteristically harsh. "Yes, I'll pay the fee. Find Merik and kill him."

"Find him?" Vydra raised an eyebrow.

"Did you think he'd stick around while we discussed his depravity?"

"But if you knew he'd bolt, why didn't you stop him?"

Samantha didn't understand what was going on. While they'd had some arbitrary history lesson, Merik had been given every opportunity to leave the world and hide in Fader or worse, at home in Phalos. They'd never find him and convince him to reverse the spell in time.

Chay didn't meet her eyes, and she noticed his hands shaking. Whether wilful decision or stupid mistake, he was afraid. "Because the future weaves as the future weaves, and no path is ever as direct as we wish." At last, he raised his gaze. "There's a plan, trust me. I hope."

His last half-swallowed words nearly shattered her hope.

Chay had been right, of course. Left to his own devices, Merik had snooped around a bit, wiped the whiteboard with their prophecy leads, and high-tailed it out of there. Both Lucille and Vydra had gone looking for him, while Rachel stuck around, silently taking care of Samantha while she tried to ease Matt's pain.

None of the healing Leandres had applied seemed to be having any effect. Samantha had half a mind to run to Hell and ask Adrianes for help, but she knew better than anyone that the flower that'd saved them before was no longer in existence. They'd made that deal, and now she was suffering the consequences.

In her despair, she and Rachel wandered over to the pharmacy to buy non-magical painkillers, only to find a long queue outside. Matt wasn't the only one who'd fallen sick.

"Sam?" a familiar voice said. Cian stepped out of the pharmacy and came towards them. He took one look at her tear-stained face and pulled her out of the queue. "Come with me. I've got enough for both of us." He opened the package he'd just bought and gave her half.

"Don't you need them?"

"I've still got enough for ten dosages. I got lucky, you know—after me, they started opening them up and selling them separately." He sighed. "My mother's sick. It's not looking good. But you probably know exactly what I'm talking about. It's Matt, isn't it? He's not healing as usual?"

Tears welled in her eyes and she shook her head. "He hasn't opened his eyes since he collapsed."

Cian pulled her into his arms. "He'll be fine, Sam. This will pass. The six of you will find what caused it and save us all." He gave her a hopeful smile that nearly tore her heart out.

Next to her, Rachel winced. "We're working on it. You haven't seen Robert anywhere?"

"Robert?"

At first, Samantha was just as confused, but then she understood what Rachel was onto. "Oh... Yes, if you see Robert, can you please tell him to call me? It's important. Like life-and-death important."

Robert had banished the banshees—somehow, he carried the old magic of Phalos in him. If Merik couldn't be brought to heel, Robert could be their only chance of getting control over the situation.

Cian nodded slowly. "I'll tell him if I see him, sure."

"Thanks for the painkillers. I hope your mum improves quickly."

"Same with Matt. I mean, I know he will. You deserve to be happy after everything."

Samantha tried to smile, but the feelings welled up quickly and fresh tears tumbled down her face.

Cian pulled her back into a hug. "You've got this. You're the Six, right? Destiny has big plans for you."

If destiny could only be trusted. "We'll try our best."

"Take care." Cian let go and gave Rachel a quick wave.

"You, too."

She watched Cian go, before finding the strength to wipe her tears, take a deep breath, and head home to her dying boyfriend.

Lucille

It had started to rain. The rain had washed away the gnats and flies, but the frogs flourished in the weather, croaking in all corners of the town. For two hours, Lucille had tried to find Merik. She'd walked through the streets and gone all the way out to the Spring of Magic, which had turned into some kind of shelter. She'd met Anne there, who'd told her she hadn't seen anyone use the portal all day. Either Merik really was working with demons from the House of Envy who'd whisked him away, or he was still in Greenvalley. But where?

The task provided only minor distraction from her thoughts. Part of her still insisted they'd gotten Merik wrong, despite knowing as soon as Chay had spoken the words she'd translated it was true. While she'd translated the text, she hadn't really understood it. The magic had taken over, unravelling the letters from one Phalesian language to another. She'd felt the power behind the words and a sense of foreboding, but had thought it was just the magic working through her, nothing more. Because why would Merik give her such a terrible scroll to translate?

She closed her eyes and took a shaky breath. Chay had said he'd used her. That all of it had been a lie. Lucille slung her arms around herself, shivering in the rain. If it was true, he must've felt some perverse glee, not just using her for his translation but her body, too. The thought nearly made her double over. It couldn't be true. There must've been another explanation. She just needed to talk to him. If she could find him. But now she was cold and fresh out of ideas.

She called Albert to pick her up and take her home, where most of her magic books still were.

"Ah, Miss Lucille," the butler greeted her. "I was wondering when you'd call. Your boyfriend is already here, waiting for you. Master Pascal is entertaining—"

"Do not leave them alone!" Lucille snapped. She wiped the water from her face. "Please ask Tobias to pick me up at the west end of the pedestrian zone. I'm coming as soon as possible, just... don't leave him alone with Pascal."

Her heart pounded against her chest. Just a few hours ago, she would've been charmed to find Merik spending time with her little brother, but if Chay was right—and damn him, he probably was—this was no innocent get-together.

The car arrived shortly after Lucille had reached the end of the pedestrian zone. As she drove, they were passed by three ambulances, sirens blaring. Countless people were braving the rain, lining up in front of doctor's offices and pharmacies. More than one collapsed as they waited for help that wouldn't come. It truly felt like the end of times. And it was all her fault.

As soon as she reached the villa, she dropped her shoes and coat and ran upstairs, nearly taking Linda out.

"Where are you going so fast?" Linda asked.

"Where's Pascal?"

"He's in the library, showing your boyfriend around." Linda smiled. "What a good-looking and well-mannered man. And the fashion. Can you ask him which designer he's wearing? It's unlike anything I've seen."

Lucille had no patience for this. "Yes, yes, I'll ask." Then she sprinted on to the library.

With bated breath, she cracked open the door and almost immediately found herself faced with Albert, who'd taken up position near the door. "All is well, Miss Lucille."

She released her breath and pushed the door open. Merik and Pascal were at the far end of the room. Her brother was pointing out which classic novels he liked most, while Merik listened with a wistful smile and all the patience in the world. How could this kind and considerate man do something as cruel as releasing the ten plagues on their world? Chay must've made a mistake. Still, Lucille's heart wouldn't stop pounding.

"There you are."

Why was he here instead of the Blackstone House if he was innocent? Why cross the entire unfamiliar city when frogs were falling from the sky?

Merik turned and smiled at her. "Were you looking for me?" He put a hand on Pascal's shoulder. "Your brother gave me a tour of the library."

"Thank you, Pascal. Why don't you go with Albert and get yourself some jelly from the kitchen?"

Pascal made a step forward, but Merik's grip tightened, holding the boy back. Immediately, the mood shifted. Albert leant forward, ready to step in, while Pascal's eyes widened and his shoulders tensed. Lucille's gaze was locked with Merik's in a silent battle of wills.

"Did you have a pleasant chat with Chay?" Merik said, the left side of his face twitching. "It's not fair, you know? That kind of favouritism. He's not even from Ashuan."

Lucille broke eye contact to check on Pascal. "You've got this."

The boy nodded. A moment later, several books fell onto Merik's head and he went down with a groan. Pascal bolted straight into Lucille's arms. She hugged him tight for a moment before handing him off to Albert.

"Take him. I'll handle this." Five seconds later, she was alone with Merik.

Merik shoved the books aside and straightened, wincing when he touched his head. "Aren't you full of surprises?" he said, with a sneer she'd never seen on him, forcing the truth down her throat.

"Not as surprising as you." Her stomach tightened. There was tension in her eyes. "Why?"

She had the big Chay explanation, the politics and history, but she wanted to hear from the man she'd thought she'd known.

"You need to be stopped."

Lucille barked a mirthless laughter. "Me, specifically?" Or was she really just a means to his ends?

Merik shrugged, still wincing slightly. "Absolutely. I mean, look at you. First day in Fader, you get an exclusive tour of the parliament and manage to destroy a carefully planned intervention."

"Intervention? That was a terrorist attack."

He snorted. "No, my dear. This, right here, is a terrorist attack." Annoyed, he shook his head. "You have no idea about the precarious balance in the interglobal community. A balance your world is trying to upset. There are a lot of factors at play, but you barge in here with your Ashuan ignorance, pick a side without the slightest knowledge of anything beyond your world, and interfere with interglobal matters, all sanctioned by the Seer. Are you really blaming me for taking retaliatory action?"

At first, Lucille felt a little ashamed. She had travelled to Fader with preconceived notions, trusting Chay's assessment without doubt. It wasn't until Ylvadin that she'd learnt what a masterful chess player he was, and how he'd absolutely sacrifice a few pieces for the greater good. Only his good was to assure everyone's survival, and using Lucille as a pawn had been to guide her into helping him save all worlds.

She could've seen Merik's point, emphasised by his world apparently being thrown under the bus, but he'd lost her at the end. Ignorant she might be, but ignorance could've been met with education, diplomacy, and bargaining. Instead, he'd chosen violence.

"Actually, yes. I don't know how you do things in Phalos, but in Ashuan we talk."

"And that's why Ashuan isn't part of the interglobal community and never will be."

Lucille inhaled sharply. Maybe the signs had been all there. The way he'd talked about his siblings, how some had already perished on their way to the throne. He might've told her he stood no chance, but he clearly had ambition—and no scruples.

Though her veins burnt with fury, Lucille tried to take her own advice. Answering violence with violence wouldn't stop the world from ending.

"I've heard about the prophecy," she said, softly. "Have you ever stopped and asked yourself whether you're bringing about your own downfall? Maybe the only reason Ashuan will rise, and it will," she added defiantly, deciding here and now that they wouldn't succumb to whatever he'd unleashed, "is because you're leaving a vacuum of your own design. Ashuan never did anything to you. It's all you."

"Spoken like the ignorant little witch you are," Merik drawled. "You never did anything to us? Then why is your representative sitting in our seat?" he hissed the last words. "Why has he taken what's rightfully ours when he doesn't even represent a world, just some mage faction in it?"

Lucille's eyebrows crawled up. Who was Geoffrey Black representing if not Ashuan as a whole? And how had he got his seat?

"How many seats does Phalos have?"

"Thirty-one."

Her mind boggled. "Thirty-one? And you're making a fuss over one seat? One tiny, single vote that's not even worth a coalition?"

Merik's eyes flared. "You have no idea what you're speaking of. It was ours. You don't deserve it."

"You know you sound a lot like—" she stopped. She'd wanted to say Malcolm, but this came from a slightly different angle. "You sound jealous."

"Jealous of what?" he said, laughing sharply. "Your lack of knowledge? Magic? Political acumen?"

Lucille crossed her arms, unimpressed. "For starters, you're jealous of Chay's attention. You're jealous he's so focused on our stupid little world, when you're right there. That our world will play a bigger role in the future, even though we lack your rich history."

"Your stupid little world will end." Merik's voice shook, his lips undecided between a snarl and a manic grin. "Your town, probably your entire country, will be so severely damaged by what I've unleashed, you'll take decades to recover. Only you don't have them. The Shadow will swallow you up before you've completed another rotation around the sun."

Less than a year. That was all the time they'd left. Not that it mattered if they all died tonight. Lucille closed her eyes and took a deep breath, trying to push all the indignation and hurt away to do what she had to do.

"You sold your soul to Pyke, didn't you?"

She had to remember this: Merik was under the influence of Envy. While his motivation had been to aid Phalos in regaining their lost glory, he was doing the bidding of another. Phalos didn't want to destroy Ashuan; the Shadow did.

Merik shrugged. "What's it to you?"

"I'm offering you a bargain. Right now, you're nothing but a glorified servant to the Shadow."

"You dare call me a servant?" Merik bristled, nostrils flaring.

Lucille tried not to smile. She'd hoped to provoke his pride. "Well, hasn't he got you running errands for him? You've already sacrificed banshees and sirens, both of which were destroyed, now this disaster. Is this how he's going to end our world? By depleting Phalos' Creature Library? Why not take Ashuan for yourself?"

"You spoke of a bargain, woman," Merik said.

Taken aback, Lucille caught her breath. That was all she was to him? Just some random woman? It took everything inside her to swallow the insult along with the rest and push on.

"I'll help you break the bond and regain your soul. In return, I want you to re-banish the plagues."

By now, she knew he was one of the very few surviving banishers. And instead of using his abilities for the good of all worlds, he'd brought pain and death.

"You plan on taking it up with an archdemon?"

"Wouldn't be the first time."

Merik blinked. "It wouldn't?"

Lucille checked her nails. "A little over a year ago, we killed the Archdemon of Greed. A few months ago, we orchestrated the death of the Archdemon of Lust. We can make Envy next."

It seemed the only logical solution, though Lucille had no interest in facing yet another demon. But with the Shadow a disciple of Envy, and Merik under his influence, it seemed the only option. For better or worse, Pyke was waging war on them and needed to be stopped.

If she'd wanted to impress Merik, she was sorely disappointed when he started laughing. "Did you now? Some little witch in a backwater town of a backwater world defeated not one but two archdemons?"

Her temper flared again, and she nearly threw a fireball at him. "I'm not just some little witch. I'm one of the Six."

The laughter stuck in Merik's throat. His eyes widened, and he snarled, "No!"

She huffed. "Well, why do you think Chay favours us? We're the Six, born in this backwater town, in this backwater world."

The snarl only grew more vicious. "No! The Six are not some ignorant, bumbling fools from Ashuan. They're true heroes, and they'll be born in places who appreciate them."

Lucille narrowed her eyes. "Are you seriously jealous of that, too?" Pyke must've dug his claws deeper into Merik than she'd realised.

"You don't deserve this honour!"

"Do we have a bargain?" Lucille snapped, losing her patience. So much for the magic of words.

Merik snorted. "Absolutely not. I'll take my chances with the demons over whatever pitiful alliance you can offer. I hope your male friends aren't firstborn." When the realisation hit Lucille, Merik smirked. "Guess the Six will have to be reborn another time."

Matt might be safe—if he wasn't already struck down by the sickness—but Fabian and Jan had no older siblings to take the fall. And what about Pascal? Did their new familial bonds protect him, or would the curse strike him, too?

"Goodbye, Lucille."

She blinked. Merik was already halfway across the room. "Oh no, you're not going—"

A litany of Phalesian burst from his lips, and suddenly, she found herself faced with a double-winged, husk-like creature that jumped at her, shrieking.

"Scutum Protecto!" Lucille shouted, barely managing to get her shield up in time.

The creature clung to her magic and opened its mouth to shriek again, exposing thin, circular rows of needle-like teeth. Beating its wings, it launched itself off her shield, only to circle back and come for her again.

"Globus Igneus!"

She let the shield fall and threw green fire into the creature's face. The flames engulfed it and it let out one last ear-shattering shriek before it burnt to cinders. Nothing but a pile of ash remained on the carpet.

Lucille held her side, wheezing. The fight had been short but intense—and it had given Merik just enough time to barrel past and take flight. She took a deep breath and raced after him.

"Merik!" she shouted, hoping to snare him back into a conversation.

Linda would have a heart attack if she found Lucille sprinting through the villa like this, but her family was nowhere to be seen, hopefully whisked to safety by Albert. Or maybe Merik had decided he needed a few more hostages. She was about to turn and search the house, when she saw the front door flapping in the wind.

"Merik!"

Racing down the stairs as fast as she could, Lucille reached the door, only to stumble back immediately when ping-pong ball-sized ice thundered from the sky. Hail.

"Lucille?"

Pascal was at the foot of the stairs. He ran to her and threw his arms around her. "You're okay."

She suppressed a whimper as she pulled him into an embrace. She might be okay, but how long would Pascal remain so?

Jan

Jan had just finished the longest shift of his brief career. At least it'd felt like that. As soon as they'd delivered one patient, they'd been called out again to pick up another. Or rather, a whole bunch of them. The hospital was completely overworked and waiting room filled to the brim, forcing the emergency room to shut down. Jan would've stayed to help, but then Anne had called, so he'd finished up, hopped into his rusty old car, and driven to his parents' apartment.

As he walked up the stairs, he could hear a hum, as if Anne were having a party. Sure enough, the door was slightly ajar and he saw people moving inside.

"Excuse me. Coming through." He pushed through the throng of strangers with their big backpacks until he finally saw a familiar face. "Finn!"

The boy looked up, balancing a pitcher of water and stack of cups. "Jan. Anne's in the living room."

"Who are all these people?" Jan muttered, threading his way towards the living room.

More strangers filled the room, most of them bleeding from superficial wounds. Anne was in front of the couch, which was apparently serving as her clinic as she and an older woman applied first aid.

As soon as she saw Jan, her eyes lit up. "Jan. You're here, thank Hanna." She clapped her hands. "Make some space for my brother, please. He's a healer."

"What's going on?" Jan hissed, while he quickly assessed her current patient. Without thinking, he applied his healing powers, barely registering the sharp bite of pain.

"Um, these are pilgrims. They came to Greenvalley to find me. I met them at the Spring of Magic, but then it started hailing, and I brought them here. It's not safe outside."

"You can't just invite a bunch of strangers into your home." Jan waved the pilgrim away, so the next could take a seat.

Anne shrugged helplessly. "They came to me for help."

"Ever heard of the word 'no'?" He healed another woman and sent her on her way. "What if Dad and Mum come home? Shouldn't they be back soon?"

"That's why I called you," Anne said, shyly. "I was hoping you'd help me tell them about... well, everything."

Jan nearly doubled over—and not from the pain. "You want to tell Mum and Dad about Hanna?"

"And magic, the monsters—I can't keep sneaking around."

"Obviously not," Jan said with a snort. "They're going to have a heart attack when they get home." He quickly thought of an alternative. "Get me something to write with."

The woman next to Anne wordlessly handed him a pen and notebook from her backpack.

Jan started writing. "This is my address. I own the house and there's another healer there. It's much bigger than this place." To Anne, he said, "We'll send everyone on their way, then we'll wait for Mum and Dad."

Just then, he heard the distinctive heavy fall of his father's boots in the hallway. "Anne? Finn? Who are all these people?"

Jan rolled his eyes and handed the woman the notebook. "Get everyone out. I'll meet you there as soon as possible."

As the pilgrims shuffled around, grabbing their bags, Jan went out to greet his father—and his mother, who must've come home with him.

Stefan's scornful look found him immediately. "You."

"Me, yeah." He jerked his head towards the living room. "Come on in. Everyone's just about to leave."

"What are you doing here?" Ida asked, more confused than angry. "Is this a party?"

"Nope, a triage centre, apparently. Don't worry, we're moving it. Anne has something to tell you. I'm just here for support."

There was a bit more shuffling until the last of the pilgrims had left and there was enough space for Jan's parents to sit. Anne kneaded her hands together while Finn tried to melt into the background.

"Are we going to get an answer to what the hell is going on here?" Stefan barked. Ida put her hand on his thigh, a silent reminder to soften his tone. This was Anne, after all.

Jan crossed his arms and nodded at Anne. "Let's get it over with."

After years of telling his parents about magic and monsters, he doubted today was the day they were going to see the light.

"Okay..." Anne took a deep breath. "I'm going to tell you a bunch of stuff that will probably sound pretty out there, but it's an explanation for what's currently happening, and I want you to listen. Can you do that for me?"

"Of course, darling," Ida said. Jan rolled his eyes. The Anne Effect was unfolding already.

"A month ago, I gave you a pretty weak explanation about Finn needing a place to stay. He's not a friend from school who needs a temporary roof over his head until his home life improves." She took another deep breath. "Finn's from another world, one that no longer exists."

Jan stared while Finn shrank even smaller. That was where she wanted to start?

Unsurprisingly, his father barked at him instead of Anne. "Did you get her on drugs?"

"Of course not!" Jan hissed. "Can't you just shut your mouth and listen?"

"Boy, if you—"

Ida increased the pressure of her hand. "Stefan, please. We promised Anne we'd listen." While she sounded more amiable, it was clear from the tension in her voice she didn't believe her either.

"Sorry, that was probably the worst way to broach the subject." Anne threw a nervous glance at Jan, who barely managed to repress another eye-roll. "What I actually wanted to say was there are things happening in Greenvalley which can only be explained by magic. That's because we actually have a so-called spring of magic, deep in the forest."

A vein pulsed in Stefan's temple, but he managed to keep his act together and listen.

"Those people you saw here were pilgrims on their way to the spring. They were looking for help and they found me. I often go there, because it's the only place I feel close to Hanna. Who is the Goddess of Life. Who chose me to be her priestess."

Stefan took a very deep breath, the Anne Effect reaching its limits. "Sweetheart," he said, in an effort to keep his voice down, "Don't get me wrong," the tension in his voice was practically palpable, "but I thought we'd been through this obsession with the occult with your brother."

"It's a wicca thing, right?" Ida said, equally shaky. "One of those new-age religions?"

Jan rolled his eyes and groaned. "Everything but actual magic, right?"

"There is no such thing as magic," Stefan bellowed. Furiously, he pointed a finger at Jan. "You! You put that nonsense into her head. It's not enough for you to ruin your own life, now you need to drag Anne down, too."

"Stefan!" Ida warned.

Jan couldn't believe how much animosity his father still bore him, just because he was too stubborn to accept the truth. Before he could fight back and defend Anne, he felt a tug on his arm. Finn had come out of his corner and was holding out his hand.

"Why don't you prove it to them?"

"You sure?" He didn't want to hurt Finn just to prove a point.

Finn nodded and produced a small knife from his pocket. "I'll do it myself."

"Oh my god, what are you doing?" Ida had jumped up, eyes wide. But before she could intervene, Finn had drawn the blade across his palm. Blood welled up from a cut deep enough to turn Jan's stomach. "Put the knife away and hold up your hand. I'm going to get some bandages."

"Mum, stay," Anne said, suddenly confident. "Jan's got this. He'll heal Finn. With magic."

Meanwhile, Jan turned Finn's hand to him and inspected it. He held his fingers above the cut and pressed the sides together, slowly healing them, as well as the deeper parts Finn had hurt. The pain was strong enough to make his mouth twitch, but it was over in under a minute.

By then, Anne had come over and wiped Finn's blood away to show her parents the unmarred hand. "You see? Magic."

Ida dropped back on the couch while Stefan rubbed his eyes, stared, and rubbed his eyes again.

"How," his mum's voice was a whisper, "how did you do it?"

"It's not so different from what you do. I push the torn skin together and reattach the sides. Just instead of needle and thread, I use magic."

"And that was only a minor injury," Anne announced, proudly. "When I was in the hospital with the plague, he snuck in every day to heal me."

Jan drew a sharp breath. "And infected myself." He sighed. "I can't heal everything. The larger the wound, the more it hurts me, but I'm trying. I'm actually learning how to do more, not just as a first responder. I have a mentor living with me." He locked his gaze with his father's. "I'm really trying."

Stefan just nodded weakly.

"My powers don't even compare to his," Anne said, sounding awfully delighted. "I'm sort of dependent on how my goddess decides to work through me. Sometimes, she lets a plant grow faster. Or today, she blessed me with a shield to protect me and others against danger... or monster hail."

"Speaking of the hail," Jan had kept tabs on the group chat throughout the day, though he'd barely had time to process, "that and the other plagues were released by... some idiot." He'd almost said prince and blown the rest of his father's fuse.

"Robert?" Anne asked stunned.

He frowned. "Why would Robert do that? He doesn't even... No, it was Merik. Matt's friend from another world." Something had obviously gone wrong and suddenly, Jan found himself itching to go check it out. "I guess you're good here. I'll head home to help Leandres set up a triage station and find out what the hell we're going to do about this."

"A triage station?" Ida asked. "Let me get the first-aid box from the car. I'll come with you."

"Ida." Stefan sounded outraged.

"What? Whether this is made-up bullshit or not doesn't really matter. You've seen what it's like outside. If I can help, I will."

Jan found himself actually impressed. "Didn't you just finish a shift?"

"Didn't you?"

"Touché."

If she didn't come with him, she'd just go back to the hospital. At least at the Blackstone House, Jan could keep an eye on her. And maybe... Maybe, when this had all blown over, she'd actually believe him.

Fabian

Fabian had just finished boarding up the Magic Circle to protect against the hail, while Ophelia kept serving customers. Ever since the weather had turned, there'd been an endless stream of people who'd been looking for anything remotely protective: charms, potion, even novelty vampire stakes. It was the best day of sales in the history of the Magic Circle. Fabian hadn't been comfortable with profiting from the desperate, but Ophelia had convinced him they were selling the real deal, and if it could help people, they should.

"We're running out of stock," Ophelia called. "Could you check if we have anything out back?" She smiled at a customer. "Won't be long."

With a sigh, Fabian went to the storage, grabbing what little was still there. It would take his mum weeks to replenish. He heaved the box onto the counter. Ophelia practically ripped its contents out.

"Woah."

"It's not enough," she snapped, processing the payments as fast as she could. "Think! What else could we sell? Books? Some of them have spells in them."

"None of these people can do magic."

"What if we sold them Lucille's or Samantha's services?"

"They're not even here." Clearly, the doomsday frenzy didn't agree with her temper.

She stared, then suddenly, she was grinning. "Water. We can sell your water." Before he could stop her, she shouted, "We have water! Fresh water!"

Fabian gritted his teeth as she ushered him towards the café. He pretended to pretend to fill glasses at the sink, using his power. The actual water was running bloody like everywhere else, but his magic remained unaltered. The rumours spread, and soon more and more people were coming to the shop, bottles in tow.

During a rare moment of peace, Fabian hissed at Ophelia, "I can't believe you're making me sell my water magic."

The effort was draining him, and it was already way past closing time.

Ophelia cashed in another sale and frowned. "Are you too good to help the people in town now? Or is your water reserved for the Citadel only?"

"Is that another dig at Shayna?" he asked, seething. The emotion filled up the next two bottles with ease.

"Don't be silly," Ophelia said, with a huff. "You're the one who's always telling me not to conflate the Citadel with Shayna."

It was absolutely another dig. While the world was ending. "I can't believe you." Fabian nearly threw the bottle on the counter. It spilt and flooded half the surface. "You can deal with this crap on your own."

He stomped out, leaving wet footprints on the wooden boards. He was so angry, even the hail bent away from him. He enjoyed helping, but that had been nothing short of extortion, and now Ophelia had the audacity to drag Shayna back into it?

"Fabian?" a familiar voice called out.

Fabian stopped. The water bent slightly less around him than before. On the other side of the street, Cian was holding a jacket over his head to protect himself from the hail.

"Cian."

"Speak of the devil," he said, then crossed the street. "Neat trick."

"I'm the devil now?" Fabian asked, not in the mood for any Elite Clique antics.

"I visited Shayna earlier." When Fabian groaned, Cian laughed softly. "I see you're well aware of the situation."

Fabian rolled his eyes. "I wish I wasn't." He fell into step beside him, extending his water bending umbrella to cover them both. "The world's coming to an end. I don't have the capacity to deal with Shayna's games or Lia's jealousy." It felt good saying it out loud.

"Two girls are absolutely crazy about you. My condolences."

It was such a typical guy answer. "Well, what am I supposed to do? It's not like I can be with both of them, can I?"

Cian's eyes widened. "Wait. Does that mean you're interested in Shayna?"

Fabian stopped. Why had he just said that? Was he interested in Shayna?

Before he could come to a conclusion, a deep hum reached his ears, like a train approaching. "What's that?"

Cian leant forward, squinting against the dark sky. "I think it's a cloud."

The hum grew louder, vibrating in their bones. Then Fabian saw it: a cloud of insects was coming at them. "Are those grasshoppers?"

"Locusts," Cian said, paling at the sight. "It's the eighth plague."

"Plague?" Fabian had barely had time to look at his phone while working, but he remembered seeing the word 'plague' here and there. He'd thought they'd been referring to all the sick animals and humans.

Cian swallowed. "The ten plagues of Egypt. Samantha said... She told me to find Robert."

"Well, Robert can wait. Let me deal with these first."

Fabian stretched out his arms and the water parted the cloud of locusts, forcing them to fly around them. The hum was incredibly loud, as if they were standing next to a jackhammer. He gritted his teeth as the vibrations went straight to his stomach, struggling to keep the water up until the swarm had passed. At last, the cloud parted—only to reveal even bigger locusts, the size of his lower arm.

"What the hell?" Cian gasped.

"Hell sounds about right." These monster locusts definitely didn't belong to Ashuan. "Run?"

"Run!"

Rachel

More and more people came to the Blackstone House, searching for protection and healing. Leandres had opened a triage centre, dealing with the injured as they came in, while Samantha had woven a protective web over the garden that kept those who were healthy safe from gnats, hail, and the recently arrived locusts. Rachel had tried to help, but she was quickly overwhelmed by all the people moaning, muttering, or crying out in pain.

Her phone buzzed with another message from Adam. Rachel had told him all about the developing drama. It was her only lifeline in the chaos.

Adam: Please tell me you're leaving for Fader any minute.

Oh, how she wished just leaving all this mess behind and living a blissfully ignorant life in a far-away world was a possibility,.

Adam: I'm coming for you.

Rachel: NO!!!

Her brain hadn't even stopped to think before her answer had gone out. As much as she appreciated Adam's support, he was not allowed to set a foot in Greenvalley. Not without an older brother to keep him safe.

She was relieved when Lucille's car arrived with Albert and Pascal in tow.

"I failed," Lucille said the moment she stepped inside, tears welling up in her eyes. "I tried to make him see sense or at least bargain with him, but he's so under Envy's thumb, he wouldn't have any of it."

"So, then you apprehended him?" Rachel asked. Unfortunately, no one was dragging Merik out of the car.

"I tried but he escaped," Lucille admitted, taking a shaky breath. "He threw a monster at me. I killed that one, at least."

Rachel tried to be more sympathetic. If Merik had thrown some random monster at her, she probably would've been toast. But then again, she would've never tried to reason with a psychopath in the first place.

Lucille put her hands on Pascal's shoulder as she turned to Chay. "You're still here, good. I... I need a favour. I think you owe me one."

The half-demon raised his eyebrows. "I do? What do you want me to do?"

"Take Pascal and Albert and bring them somewhere safe. Somewhere the curse won't affect Pascal."

"The curse?" Rachel said. "Did Merik curse him?"

Chay stepped forward and brushed his thumb against Pascal's cheek. "I don't usually do this, but he'll be fine. The curse doesn't apply to him."

Lucille let out a shaky breath of relief. "He's going to be fine?"

"Wait," Pascal piped up. "Does that mean I'm not a firstborn? I've got an older brother?"

It finally clicked for Rachel. Lucille was worried her brother would be struck down by the deaths of the male firstborns. But that meant...

"What about Fabian? And Jan? And likely half the town? Plus, everyone who'll die regardless of biblical sexism. We can't evacuate all of them, which means we need to stop Merik. Now."

"I know. That's why I'm dropping Pascal off," Lucille said. "I've already got a tracking spell ready and a dozen others. He's not going to get away a third time."

"Let me grab my crossbow. I'm coming along."

"Me, too." Chay looked at the injured. "I can't do anything here, so I might as well stick with you. Besides, I'd love to have a chat with Merik about the Shadow."

Rachel thought the time for chatting was over, but a skilled half-demon surely wouldn't be amiss. With Pascal and Albert settled safely in the library, they stepped back outside… and were met with complete darkness.

"That wasn't there before," Lucille said.

"Cutting it close, as usual," Rachel muttered, taking out her smartphone. Another message had come in, but the letters were all jumbled and scattered and there was no bar. The flashlight was still working, however, even though it only lit up a small circle in front of them. "You have a tracking spell?"

Instead, Lucille said, "Erit Lux!"

Light blinded them for a few seconds, but then it fizzled out, eaten up by shadows, until they were left with nothing but a slight halo around them.

"That bodes well," Rachel muttered.

Lucille did her tracking spell, and they set off in the darkness. If there was a visual cue, the darkness had swallowed it. "I can feel a pull. Just stick close."

A pull it might've been, but the magic knew nothing of the street layout. Before too long, Rachel couldn't count the times they'd nearly run into someone's fence or had to circle a whole block to find the right direction again. The air was alive with the buzz of gnats and flies, the whirring of locusts, and croaking of frogs. Occasionally, they heard screaming or moaning, but the streets were emptying fast.

Limited by the extent of their light, Rachel stumbled. Chay steadied her, wincing through it, and let go quickly. Rachel turned around to shine a light on the obstacle and immediately wished she hadn't. It was a woman, her face nearly unrecognisable beneath ghastly wounds. A foot-long locust was still gnawing on her cheek. Chay blasted it away with his energy.

"Thank you," Lucille said, sounding as if she'd vomited.

Rachel shuddered, wondering what kind of monster locusts these were, her ears straining to pick up the hum in the darkness. She could only hope Lucille's shield spell would protect them from a similar fate if one chose to attack.

There were hurried steps in front of them. They tensed. No one walked this fast in complete darkness. Not without a purpose.

"Erit Lux," Lucille whispered again, blinding them once more.

The person in front let out a yelp and a groan, their voice distinctively female and familiar. "Lucille?"

Rachel recognised her immediately. "Ophelia." Now it made sense how she could move so fast. Shadows were practically her element. "Are you lost?"

"No, I'm looking for Fabian. He..." She sounded as if she was about to cry. "We had a fight and he stormed off, leaving me alone with all those crazies who wouldn't understand we were sold out! Anyway, I can't reach him on the phone and he's not at home. And..." She swallowed. "He's probably with Shayna."

"Shayna?" Lucille asked.

"We don't have time for this," Rachel reminded them sharply. "It doesn't matter whether he's with Shayna or got lost in the forest. He'll be dead if we don't find Merik. You command the shadows, Lia. Can't you make this darkness go away?"

She snorted. "Shadows never go away. You just need to accept... No, I can't, but the shadows won't hurt us."

"It's not that," Lucille said. "We're trying to find Merik to stop this madness. I've got a spell, but we can't see anything."

Ophelia grinned, looking rather ghastly. "That I can do. Let me see what the shadows have to say about your spell." She seemed to listen to something within and nodded. "Follow me."

She was gone so quickly they had trouble following. The shadows seemed to whisper as they parted in front of them, revealing a unique path. The best part of it was that the shadows wrapped around them, hiding them from all the creatures. Normally, Rachel found Ophelia's powers a little creepy, but today it had its merits.

Soon, they heard some intense noises ahead: grunting and hissing, a loud thud, and screeching, like nails on a chalkboard. They ran and their light revealed Merik—and a small horde of monsters—attacking Vydra.

Matt's assassin classmate was holding her own, as evidenced by the dead bodies around her, but her right arm hung from its socket, and blood ran down her face. As the dim light engulfed them, Vydra's movements became faster, and she dispatched two creatures at the same time. But a third was about to jump on her back.

"Down!" Rachel bellowed, cocking her crossbow.

Vydra ducked moments before the bolt sailed past her head and buried itself in the creature's neck. It screeched and fell backwards. Two more were strangled by shadows.

Merik, who'd backed up against a fence, scrambled up and bolted just as Lucille shouted, "Frigar!"

It was almost comical how the spell froze him mid-movement, defying gravity with his locked limbs. Only his eyes were still able to move.

Meanwhile, Chay had mowed down three more creatures, while Vydra struck down the last, then swiftly moved and held her knife to Merik's neck.

"Wait!" Chay shouted, a heartbeat before it would've been too late. "I want a word."

Lucille crossed her arms, staring down on Merik's motionless form. "Not so bad for an Ashuan backwater witch, huh?"

Chay cleared his throat and strode over. "Could you unlock his mouth? I want to—" Suddenly, he bowled over and vomited blood.

"Chay!" Rachel ran to his side. "What—Oh. You're a firstborn, too, right?"

Instead of answering, Chay spat up more blood and collapsed.

Jan

"I'm back!" Jan called, stepping into the Blackstone House.

It was so dark outside, he was glad he'd even managed to find the house, though the darkness was trying to creep inside, too. An armada of electronic lights and candles had created a dusky atmosphere. Just like at his parent's, countless people had gathered, awaiting medical attention.

Samantha came past, a bowl of water in her hands and her flower stuck under her arm. "Great. We can use all the help we can get."

"How's Matt?"

"Unchanged. I don't think he's..." Samantha took a shaky breath, then forced a smile. "Mrs Kerscher. Are you here to help?"

His mother, still shaken by all that had happened, looked around the overflowing living room with big eyes. But then her nurse training snapped into place. "Where do you need me?"

"Everywhere. We've got a sort of triage going. Everyone uninjured is in the garden—I've made the whole place safe from any creatures. Leandres is taking the worst cases in the guest room upstairs, I'm taking care of minor injuries as they come in, and Mildred," Samantha pointed at the same pilgrim who'd been helping Anne before, "is overseeing the triage. She could use help, for sure, and I need a moment to check on Matt and—"

Ida put her hand on Samantha's arm, then took the water basin from her. "Go check on your boyfriend. I've got this."

Jan rolled up his sleeves. "If Leandres is in the guest room, I'll set up in my room. Send anyone with severe injuries to me."

"Oh, one more thing," Samantha said, already halfway up the stairs, "could you try to call Robert? My phone's dead. We need him to do his thing again and banish the plagues. I don't care if he's scared or ashamed or whatever, we need him."

"Robert's in this, too?" Ida asked surprised.

Jan winced. "We wish. Heal people, call Robert—got it."

Samantha ran up the stairs. Jan was about to follow her when someone crashed through the door behind him.

"My arm," a strangled voice cried out. The young man was drenched and covered in blood, cradling a mangled arm. "A grasshopper ate my arm."

"Robert?"

Jan took Robert to his room, where he carefully rinsed off the blood around the wound and applied a quick and dirty healing job. As soon as the golden shimmer erupted from his fingers, Robert averted his gaze.

"Still running from it, huh?" The pain from Robert's healing hit Jan much more intensely than he expected and he let out a loud hiss. "How deep is—"

His hands were shaking and sweat rolled down his forehead, but he forced himself to keep pushing until tendons snapped back into place, muscles reformed, and veins were repaired. By the time he got to the skin, he was breathing as if he'd run all the way from his old flat to here, instead of taking the car. He could feel the asthma taking hold in his chest.

"Damn."

"Sorry," Robert muttered, quickly pushing down the torn arm of his jumper.

Jan leant back, his chest heaving. "No worries. I... Um, we need to talk—"

"I'll send the next person up. Unless you want a break?" Robert didn't wait for an answer and shuffled to the door.

Despite his condition, Jan jumped up and slammed a hand against the door before Robert could open it. "This is—important." His head was swimming from the sudden movement and no amount of blinking would clear it.

"There are others injured," Robert muttered, looking dejectedly at the ground.

"And there'll be more if you don't get your head out of your ass and take responsibility!" Jan hung his head, desperate to catch his breath, black spots dancing in his vision.

"You don't understand."

"I really don't." Unable to hold himself upright any longer, Jan leant back against the wall next to the door. Closing his eyes, he tried to take nice deep breaths.

Robert shuffled his feet. "The problem is... the responsible thing would be to walk away, so that's what I need to do."

Jan could hear Robert reaching for the handle, but he couldn't bring his body to react. To his surprise, the door didn't open. Robert gave it a shove and jerked the handle, to no avail.

"Did you lock the door?"

"Don't be ridiculous. I don't even have a key." If there'd ever been one, it'd been long lost with Jonathan Blackstone.

"Someone must've blocked it outside."

"It opens inward," Jan said. He heard Robert pulling again and opened his eyes. "Here, let me."

Jan's fingers closed around the handle, but the door wouldn't budge. "What the hell? Neve!" he called out, his vision hazy again. "Did you freeze the door?"

"Freeze the door?" Robert asked incredulously.

"It's a thing," Jan said vaguely. "Old house..." He waved aimlessly with his hand. He bent over, hanging his head, hoping it would lead to more air.

"I don't think it's frozen." Robert peered through the slit. "And it's not locked either. It just... it just won't open."

"That's ridiculous." Jan groaned, straightening again. "I'll break it down."

Robert raised an eyebrow. "You don't look like you should even be upright."

"It'll pass."

In truth, Jan had no idea what was going on. Healing hurt, but it didn't come with nasty aftereffects that far surpassed the initial pain. He gritted his teeth and trudged away from the door. If there was actual speed in his run-up, it fizzled out the moment he slumped against the wood, knees buckling and head swimming.

In a valiant effort, Robert caught him and carefully lowered him to the ground. "You've got asthma, right? Do you have your inhaler?"

Jan managed to raise his arm, hoping he was pointing at his bedside table. His chest was so tight. His breaths didn't just lack depth—they felt like needles.

Robert rummaged through the drawer and quickly returned, forcing the inhaler between Jan's lips. "Should I push or—"

Jan grabbed the inhaler, pushed down on it, and took two deep breaths. Normally, he repeated the procedure once, but this time, it took five puffs until he felt his chest ease. Exhausted, he let the hand with the inhaler drop and leant his head against the door.

"So much for healing people."

Robert sat next to him and sighed. "At least you can do good."

"So can you. You can banish this shit." He didn't have enough breath to make a huge argument, but he turned his head and saw Robert locking his jaw.

"You wouldn't understand."

Jan closed his eyes again, waiting for his chest to expand and the pain to ease. Slowly, the reality of the situation sank in. The door that wouldn't open. The hefty price he'd paid for healing. The lack of efficiency in his medication.

"Hey Robert?"

"Hm?"

"Are you an only child?"

"I have two older brothers and a sister."

Jan snorted, half laughing, half crying. An older brother would be nice just about now. "Aren't you lucky?"

Fabian

The darkness had completely messed with Fabian's sense of place. The sun had already set when he'd left the Magic Circle and met Cian, but nighttime wasn't supposed to be this dark. The lack of stars made sense since it was still hailing outside of his watery shield, but where was the light in the houses? Where were the streetlamps? The darkness reminded him of the Dûr Lôrac, but even there they'd had glowing algae demons or sylver shimmering in the walls.

"Are you still there?" he called out.

The answer came in the form of a hand on his shoulder, startling him. "I'm still here, yes. My smartphone torch isn't working properly," Cian said.

Fabian looked over and saw a dim light. "This is bad."

"You don't say. Samantha said it's the ten plagues. This is the ninth."

"What's the tenth?" Fabian asked. Cian's silence said everything he needed to know. "Death, of course."

"Of all male firstborns," Cian confirmed softly, his voice tightening at the end.

Fabian laughed. How many times had he thought he was going to die in the last two years? How many times had his friends ridiculed him? He'd been wrong every single time, but now it was all but guaranteed.

"Did Sam say how she's planning on stopping this?"

"All she said was—"

The earth rumbled beneath them. A jolt went through Fabian's feet, and then they were falling. He grabbed Cian's arm and let out a yelp as he tumbled down what felt like a steep mountain slope. Had they somehow walked into the forest and missed a step?

The landing was rough, but Fabian walked away without any broken bones. "Are you hurt?"

Cian moaned. "No. You?"

"Just bruised."

Just then, the ground began to vibrate again, and they heard a loud humming.

"Ouch!" Cian bumped into him. "Something bit me!"

Fabian grabbed his arm again and put his other hand on the slope behind them. Dragging Cian along, he walked and walked, only to realise they were going in a circle. "Damn it! I think we're in a sinkhole or something."

Behind him, Cian was breathing erratically. "With murderous monster locusts."

Something flew at Fabian's face, and he batted it away. His arm made contact with something rough and surprisingly big. "Monster, indeed."

"This is when the tenth plague starts, right?" Cian's voice was cracking. "Where we're both going to die?"

"Absolutely not!"

Fabian couldn't see, but that didn't stop him from bending the hail to his will and using it to take down locusts left and right. Though he heard the bodies crashing to the ground, the hum grew louder and louder. Locusts swatted their wings against his head and shoulders, and suddenly, he felt a sharp bite on his hip.

"Fuck!" Fighting appeared to be fruitless, and they were definitely in a hole. "We need to climb up."

"Good idea."

"You go first. I'll hold them back."

Fabian concentrated on all the water in the air, then threw it outwards. For a moment, the hum ceded. Behind him, he could hear gravel slide under Cian's feet. A larger slab broke off, and Cian fell backwards, nearly taking Fabian out in the process. The locusts rose again.

"Change of plans," Cian said, panting. "You go. I'll steady and push you up. I think if you stand on my shoulders, I can push you up the rest of the way."

Fabian stared in the direction of Cian's voice. "But if you push me up, how will you get up? And who will defend us against the monsters?"

Cian whimpered softly. "I don't matter."

"What?"

"You're one of the Six, Fabian. Samantha told me all about it. The world needs you. All the worlds. So, we have to make sure you survive this shit." His voice shook, but it gained strength at the end. "I don't know what this is, but it's not the end of all worlds. So, get on my shoulders. Now!"

Fabian stumbled back against the wall. "I can't pull you up."

"Don't you think I know?" Cian shouted, before letting out a yelp as a locust bit him. "Go! Just go!"

Stunned, Fabian found himself nodding. "I... I... I'm sorry."

He faced the wall and searched for something to hold onto while Cian used his hands to vault him up. Locusts swarmed them and tears streamed down Fabian's face as he grappled for purchase. He felt like the worst person in the world as he stepped onto the other boy's shoulders, his fingertips just reaching the top.

"I..."

"Just go," Cian whispered, his voice choked by tears. "Just go and save yourself."

Samantha

People were dying. Despite all the care, mundane or magical, people kept dying on them, almost all boys or men. Everyone was trying their best, but things had progressed so quickly it was impossible to get on top of it. And there was so little Samantha could do. She'd run out of potions hours ago and her flower's healing pollen had barely enough to ease the pain and close superficial wounds. She was brewing new potions, but the process was slow, and she was exhausted.

She and Ida tried to help a boy of thirteen who just kept vomiting, then started choking. No amount of Heimlich manoeuvres and other procedures did him any good, and he passed away just before midnight. Covered in vomit and blood, Samantha stumbled back and pressed the heels of her hands against eyes.

Ida put a hand on her shoulder. "You did everything you could. Go upstairs, take a shower, and some deep breaths. Sit with Matt."

"What about everyone else?"

She couldn't take a break and abandon the misery in her home. Not when so many people needed her. Besides, if she went up to Matt now, she'd never leave his side again.

Ida made sure to look deep into her eyes. "You need to take care of yourself. That's Healthcare 101. Go."

Samantha nodded and trudged upstairs, past the rooms where Jan and Leandres were working their asses off to save those who could be. The entire house was filled with cries and moans. It all quieted down when she made it to the top floor and closed the door behind her. For a moment, she leant against the door and took one shaky breath after the other.

"Sam?" a quiet voice called out.

Her eyes flew open, and she rushed to Matt's bedside, taking his hand. Beads of sweat covered his forehead, while his skin was sunken and pale. His other hand was buried in Crumbs' fur. The dog looked at her with glassy eyes, his breathing too shallow to detect.

"I'm here," she said, fresh tears falling.

She pulled out the flowers which she'd kept yellow all day, and blew some pollen on Crumbs and Matt. It was the only thing that'd kept them alive for so long.

Matt's breathing eased, and he let out a soft sigh. The grip of his hand grew a little stronger. "How—"

"Shh. It's going to be okay."

But it wasn't. There was no end in sight to this misery, and Samantha had begun to believe nothing would stop until the plagues had run their course, killing half of Greenvalley and countless others in the surrounding areas.

Matt pulled a face. "It hurts."

"I know. You just need to hold on a little longer. Try to sleep, darling." Silently, she wove her flowers from yellow to pink. "I love you." She blew the sleeping pollen onto Matt's face.

He fell asleep, the lines of pain easing, and his breathing slowing as the dreamworld pulled him away from the waking world. She doubted he'd ever wake again.

She stared at Matt, her throat raw with emotion. It wasn't fair. He wasn't a first-born, and he was young and had an eternal future ahead of him. Instead, he was lying at death's feet. Four months. That's all they'd had with each other. How she was expected to keep going, she didn't know. Losing Daniel had nearly broken her. Losing Matt would shatter her into a million pieces, unable to ever be whole again.

Sobbing, she threw herself on his chest and begged the night not to take him.

Lucille

"Chay, go!" Lucille shouted as she grabbed his shoulder and held him back. "We'll deal with Merik. Just go and save yourself."

"Don't," he sputtered, fresh blood bubbling across his lips. He bent over again, coughing half his lungs out.

Another gurgling sound made Lucille whip her head around. Vydra had sunk her fangs into Merik's neck and dropped him on the ground. Merik's hand flew to the puncture wound, but it was the poison he needed to worry about, not the blood loss. He sank to his knees, eyes wide, as first his neck then face swelled. His gaze found Lucille, just before his eyes rolled in his head and he keeled over, hitting the pavement with a sickening crunch.

"Finally," Rachel said, her crossbow still trained on him. "If you didn't do it, I would've."

"I always keep my contracts," Vydra said. "It's over now, right?"

Lucille looked back at Chay. He was still bent over, hands splayed on the concrete, spitting blood. "Is it getting better?" Lucille asked, her voice shaking. He didn't look any better, but perhaps the end of the curse wouldn't be so sudden. Still, he was a half-demon and should've shown some improvement by now.

"It's still dark," Ophelia whispered. "The shadows don't feel any different."

And there was still the buzz and hum from all the insects.

Lucille staggered backwards. "It didn't stop."

"Banish," Chay croaked, then winked out of existence, at last saving himself.

Lucille fell on her bottom, her gaze flicking to Merik's unmoving form. "Please tell me he's just paralysed."

Vydra nudged him with her boot. "Oh, he's dead."

Overcome with despair, Lucille slapped her hands to her face. "No, no, no. He's the only one who can undo this. He—"

"I thought killing him would solve it," Rachel said, but doubt laced her voice.

"Why would it?" Lucille sobbed and took a moment to catch her breath. "The plagues were released from a scroll. They need to be banished back into a scroll."

"Can you do it?" Ophelia asked, arms crossed. "Like, you know the text, right?"

Lucille stared at her. "I just translated it, and no, I don't know the exact words and... I don't have that kind of power."

Ophelia bolted, and immediately, the shadows pressed back in.

"Lia!"

"She's off to find Fabian," Rachel said, her voice meek. "They're all going to die now."

Lucille sank to her knees, hope leaving her body like air from a popped balloon. She wanted to scream, only to realise she already was.

Shayna

Shayna stumbled through the darkness, her flames barely enough to light the ground beneath her feet and stave off the monster locusts roaming the streets. All around her, people were crying out in fear or pain. She wanted to help but couldn't find them in the dark. Her mind was racing, with only one thought clear enough to hold onto: she had to find her way to the Blackstone House. The others would be there, ready with a plan that she could help with.

For years, Shayna had sat back and let the others save the town over and over again, rationalising with herself that her help was neither wanted nor needed. Now Fabian's voice was stuck in her head.

You should've said something. You could've helped us.

Immense guilt flooded her. Her own cowardice, her fear of being on the receiving end of Cheryl's mocking and losing her reputation had held her back. They hadn't seemed like they'd needed her, and what good was her meagre, barely controlled fire anyway?

It didn't matter. The others had fought even when their powers had barely blossomed. Fabian had fought monsters despite being deadly afraid of both his powers and the creatures. And what had she done? Sat back and kept her mouth shut when Cheryl took another jab at Samantha, or Alan pushed Fabian into a door. Disgust filled her, but Shayna dismissed it. She could dissect the regret later. Now, she had to find a way to help. Any way.

She bumped into a familiar figure. "Ophelia?"

"You!" Ophelia hissed, immediately followed by sniffing noises, as if she was on the verge of a breakdown.

"Have you been crying?" Shayna asked. "Is Fabian okay?" Her heart fluttered at the thought of something happening to him.

Ophelia shook her head. "I don't know. I can't find him. But he's doomed. He's an only child."

Shayna had no idea what that had to do with anything. Nevertheless, she took Ophelia's arm and pulled her along with her. "Let's find him."

"How? You got a tracking spell or something?" Ophelia asked, her tone a little confrontational.

With a sigh, Shayna let go again. "He's probably at the Blackstone House. Or if not, we'll find out where he went. He's probably somewhere fighting this thing."

"You don't get it!" Ophelia shouted. "He can't. He's a male firstborn."

"You keep saying that, but—"

"It's the ten plagues. Every male firstborn in this area is doomed to die! And we just killed the only person who could stop this." Ophelia burst into tears.

Shayna staggered back in horror. "Every male firstborn?" she whispered. There would be so many. Her father was at risk, and so were Alan and Cian. And Fabian.

"That's why I need to find him," Ophelia cried. "We need to find him and drag him to the portal to send him away before... before..."

Shayna didn't hesitate. She stepped forward and pulled Ophelia into a hug, stroking the younger girl's back until she'd calmed a little. "We'll find him." Shayna reached out a hand. "Together."

Ophelia drew back. She stared at her hand as if it was a poisonous frog, but then she sniffled and took it. "The Blackstone House is that way. I know my path in the shadows."

"That's amazing," Shayna said.

She knew all about Ophelia's shadow magic, of course, but mostly from Fabian's perspective, who was simply too pure for shadowy magic and snake whispering, Goody Two-Shoes that he was. Or maybe he wasn't, since he was head over heels for Ophelia. Maybe the darkness in her had attracted him.

They walked down the streets until they heard someone grunting in front of them. Shayna sent her flames ahead, wary of what other horrors the night held. The fire lit up a dirt-streaked, bloody face under a mop of red hair.

"Fabian!" Ophelia ran towards what looked like the rim of a sinkhole, which Fabian was struggling to climb out of.

"I'm going to push you up," Shayna heard a familiar voice say from the dark.

Fabian's body lurched upwards suddenly and he grappled for more purchase. Ophelia was already at his side and pulled. Her heart pounding in her chest, Shayna dropped everything and ran forward to help drag him over the edge. When he was finally safe, he rolled onto his back and lay there panting, Ophelia fussing over him.

Meanwhile, Shayna looked over the edge, lighting another fire. "Cian?"

About four metres below her was Cian, smiling in a seriously deranged way, tears streaming down his face. "I got him out for you. Can you tell Sam—" He jerked back, screaming loudly, and Shayna saw a flurry of shadowy creatures descend on his body. Monster locusts.

"Get off of him!" Shayna cried, throwing balls of fire at them. A few fluttered away, only to return with friends.

Next to her, Fabian had rolled over and was half hanging down, trying to reach for Cian. "Grab my hand!"

Cian managed to free himself from a particularly nasty locust that had taken a bite out of his shoulder and ran for the wall. His feet hit the incline at the bottom, and he jumped. His fingertips brushed Fabian's, then he fell again, scraping his body raw on the wall, before crumpling under a cloud of locusts.

Shayna was too scared to use her fire this close to him. Instead, Ophelia commanded her shadows to tear the creatures off, and Fabian poured a massive shower of water over him, washing the rest away. He emerged, stumbling and crawling, only to collapse on his face, bleeding from countless bites.

"Get up!" Shayna screamed, throwing her flames at the returning locusts. "Cian, get up. You can do this! Get up and jump. Cian, please!" Tears mixed with snot as she mirrored Fabian's pose, reaching as low as she could, nearly tumbling into the hole herself. "Cian!"

He tried. Cian scraped himself up from the ground and attempted to stand, but a locust broke through, flying at his face. As he batted it away, he stumbled backwards, hit the wall, and sank back down.

"I'm going in," Fabian announced, but Ophelia threw herself on his back and slung her arms around him, holding him down with her whole body.

"You can't!" she cried.

Though she knew Ophelia was right, Shayna hated her. Fabian was much stronger than Cian. He had his magic and experience, none of which would help him against the curse of the firstborn. The truth was Fabian was as much at risk, and Cian had done everything in his power to help Fabian claw his way out of the hole.

For a moment, it looked as if the locusts had withdrawn, eager to find new, less protected blood but it was only for a short break.

Cian stopped trying. Hunched over, arms over his head, he cowered on the ground as the swarm descended. Water and fire shot down, partially negating each other. Not that it would've mattered. They were exhausted, the night dark, and the enemy endless.

Shayna's sight blurred, and her throat seized up. "Cian... don't... just don't..."

Jan

The asthma had returned, and no amount of medicine from his inhaler was doing anything for Jan. It'd never been this bad before, more annoying than life-threatening, but nothing was normal anymore.

What a life, he thought bitterly. Just as he was finally turning things around and finding his feet, the ground had been ripped out from under him. Had he done enough to wipe out the stains of his teenage years? Had he saved enough people to forget those he'd failed?

He looked at his blood-stained hands, wondering if they were those of a healer or a fighter. If anyone had told him two years ago that he'd be dedicating his life to the healthcare industry, he would've laughed in their face. Doing the soul-sucking job that left his mother tired and drained day after day? That made her miss half the holidays and birthdays, and saw her spat on, assaulted, and in tears from all the misery she witnessed? Never.

He'd always thought he'd end up in the coal mine like his father, working day in day out, without anything ever changing. A boring, physically exhausting job, but one he could clock out of every day at the same time, then down a few beers and not have to think about until the next morning. It wasn't fulfilling by far, but jobs weren't meant to be. They were just a means to the end, a necessary evil to enjoy what little was left of life.

That's what he'd thought two years ago, though it felt like a lifetime. And now, where had he ended up? As a magical healer and first responder, the first to arrive on someone's worst day of their life. Sometimes, their last. So much life had trickled through his fingers, yet he went out there again and again. To try. To do good. To save those he could. But who would save him now?

He let out a laugh that quickly turned into a cough. He was going to die locked in his own room with no one but Robert by his side.

Robert was panicking. He'd fussed over Jan, asking a million times how he could make him more comfortable—by shutting up. Then he'd tried to run into the door—to no avail. He didn't have the strength. He'd tried prying the window open, but the darkness had pressed in, and he couldn't even break the glass. Back to the door it was, banging and shouting for help—from those on their deathbeds themselves.

At last, he'd slid down the door and sat, exhausted, and for a few blissful seconds, there'd been silence. As silent as it could be when Jan's breath rattled and wheezed, his airways constricting further and further with each inhale.

"What do I do?" Robert asked, in a thin voice.

"I don't know," Jan muttered. "Watch me die, I suppose." He was so very tired of breathing.

Robert shoved his elbow into Jan's side. "I mean the magic. What do I do? How do I stop this? How do I save you?"

Jan forced his chin up, squinting. "I don't know. How did you do it last time?" He wouldn't have been able to explain the process on a good day, much less with his airways shutting down. Closing his eyes, he leant back. Somehow, he landed on Robert's shoulder. "Just... let it... happen."

Robert sat for a moment, stewing. Then he pushed Jan back and stood. Jan pried his eyes open and saw him rummaging through his stuff. His head soon drooped on his chest again. His lungs hurt, but every time he took a breath, it was never enough. He gasped, black stars dancing in front of his eyes. This was it. His next inhale would be his last.

Suddenly, the pressure around his chest was gone, and he nearly choked on the first deep breath he'd taken in a while. It took him a couple of minutes to get control over his residual asthma, but then a wonderful realisation hit him: he was alive. And there was light.

Jan scrambled up. Robert was in front of him, one of Jan's workbooks in his hands. Only, instead of medical notes, it was filled with strange letters that resembled no language he'd ever seen. Jan could only assume it meant the plagues had been banished. Being alive was all the proof he needed.

Robert looked up at him, his brown eyes full of fear, but Jan didn't care. He grabbed his face with both hands and pressed his lips on his forehead. "You wonderful, wonderful boy. You did it."

His magic had ended the plagues.

Fabian

The darkness was lifting. The hail had stopped, and the sky was clearing. Stars popped up and a grey shimmer on the horizon announced the sun's return. Fabian didn't notice how loud it'd been until the hum and buzz of insects had died down and the last frog hopped off, croaking.

"It's over," Ophelia said. She slid off his back and looked at the horizon, which bore the faintest trace of pink now.

"It's over," Shayna shouted on his other side, her voice tear stricken. "Do you hear that, Cian? It's over."

Fabian peered at the blond boy below them. The only locusts left were the ones he'd drowned or Shayna had burnt. Nothing moved—least of all Cian.

"No... no."

Tears shot into his eyes and he blinked hastily, trying to tell himself Cian was simply too exhausted to move a muscle. From above, it looked as if he'd fallen asleep with his head on his knees. But his arms had fallen to the ground and his blond hair was coated with blood.

"CIAN!" Shayna shouted.

She scrambled up and would've thrown herself into the sinkhole if it weren't for Fabian wrapping his arms around her waist and holding her back. She fought, hitting and shoving him, heat erupting in his arms, but his grip remained steadfast until her fury broke, and she burst into tears.

"It can't be real," she sobbed. "He's not dead. He's tired, exhausted—"

Fabian pressed her against his chest, one hand on her back, the other stroking her hair. The survivor's guilt and Shayna's grief was tearing him apart. It should've been him. It should've been him.

Distraught, he sought Ophelia, a soft whimper escaping his lips. She looked at him like a deer in the headlights. She inhaled sharply and threw herself around his neck, burying her nose in his hair, the only comfort she could offer.

Fabian stared at the reddening horizon, trying to understand how he'd got here. How was he alive when someone else was dead? Wasn't he supposed to be the hero? The one who kept everyone else safe? Instead, Cian had given his life for him. Even though he'd been terribly scared, he'd had this idea in his head of Fabian's apparent importance and had decided it'd be a cause worth dying for.

Recalling his words filled Fabian's mouth with ash. He didn't deserve this sacrifice. His life wasn't worth more than anyone else's. And yet he was here, left behind with all the weight of sacrifice forced on him. The one who'd survived.

Matt

When Matt woke, sunlight was filtering through the blinds. He had a massive headache and a blurry recollection of what had happened in the last twenty-four hours. His body felt heavy. It took a minute before he realised it was the two bodies on him: Crumbs and his beautiful girlfriend. The dog was waking up, too. As soon as he saw Matt, he licked his face, then jumped off the bed and ran for the door, wagging his tail.

Matt wasn't quite so quick to leave his sick bed—that's what it was. He'd fallen sick last night... or had it been two nights ago?

He reached out to Samantha and gently stroked her hair, her curls spread across his abdomen. She was still dressed and at his bedside, rather than next to him. Slowly, he noticed details, such as the blood on her clothes and yellow of her magical flowers.

"Hey," he said, immediately clearing his throat. His voice was so hoarse and quiet.

Samantha startled, looking around wildly, as if she wasn't allowed to sleep. Crumbs barked and her gaze fell on him first, but it took less than a moment for her to comprehend what she was seeing.

"Crumbs?" She turned to Matt. The redness of her eyes and the sticky shimmer of tears on her face told him how she'd spent the hours at his bedside.

"Hey," he repeated, sheepishly.

With a stifled cry, Samantha threw herself into his arms and started sobbing again. "You're alive. You're alive."

Stunned, Matt wrapped his arms around her and held her as close as he could, burying his left hand in her hair. "Of course, I'm alive. I went to Hell and back for you. Do you really think I'd leave you that quickly?" He was still trying to piece together what had happened after Crumbs had fallen sick and he'd collapsed on the stairs. Hadn't Chay been there at some point?

"You have no idea what we've been through," Samantha cried, her words muffled by her tears.

"I'm sorry," he whispered. Whatever had happened had clearly shaken her to the core.

A lot had happened it seemed. When Matt came downstairs, Crumbs bounding ahead, the rooms were still filled with people. Though many had recovered, the atmosphere was sombre, and Matt saw several bodies covered with blankets. Slowly, the house cleared out, officials taking care of the bodies, while he, Samantha, and Jan spent all day cleaning and tidying the house.

Later that evening, they came together in the living room. Chay had returned from Hescaryn, after barely managing to jump there. Matt was surprised to see Vydra, despite having a vague recollection of her standing at the bottom of the stairs. Rachel hung her crossbow, while Lucille immediately curled up on the couch and hugged herself.

To Matt's surprise, Robert had stayed. He'd heard from Jan that Robert had ultimately saved them all, something else to wrap his head around. Anne was staying, too. She and Robert helped make a quick but nurturing meal. When Fabian and Ophelia arrived, Fabian immediately went to Samantha and vanished with her into the study next to the stairs.

Ophelia looked at the others. "Cian died."

Within seconds, Matt was also in the study, catching the tail end of Fabian's confession. "...gave his life because of that damn prophecy. Like he truly believed our lives were more important than his. I tried saving him, too, but... there were just too many..." Fabian's voice petered off, as if he'd simply run out of words.

Samantha's face had fallen, but it looked like she'd already cried all her tears. Nevertheless, Matt stepped forward and enclosed her in his arms.

Fabian shuffled his feet, unable to meet his gaze, and muttered, "I'd better leave you alone." He stepped out before Matt or Samantha could stop him.

"I'm sorry," Matt whispered.

He hadn't always been the greatest fan of Cian—his jealousy getting the better of him—but in the end, they'd become something close to friends, and Matt mourned the relationship that could've been, the one they'd both been denied because of the friends they'd attached themselves to. Their one—and only—chance had withered before it could blossom.

But mostly, his heart went out to Samantha. While she'd never loved Cian, she'd been fond of him. He'd helped her through a dark time—a time when Matt hadn't been able to, had even been the cause of. Cian had been the one who'd put her back together, and for that, Matt was eternally grateful.

Samantha shuddered in his arms, then looked up, blinking rapidly despite not having shed any tears. A sad little smile popped up on her lips. "This day sucks."

"Tell me about it."

She wrapped her arms around his waist and snuggled against his chest. Matt buried his chin in her hair and watched the sun set outside. It felt like the night had fallen on their youth. There was no going back now.

Lucille

Lucille barely ate anything or joined in the cautious chatter of compared notes, shedding the nightmare they'd just lived through. A nightmare that was worming its way deeper and deeper into Lucille's heart. She'd been responsible for this. Tricked or not, she'd given Merik the tools to cast such devastation over her hometown. So many were dead or traumatised, all because she'd been blinded by a pretty face, charming words, and a challenge like no other.

As soon as dinner was over, Robert took his leave. "Listen, I… I'll help you as much as I can. I'll take over the shop, make up excuses for why you're not there, or… whatever. But I don't want to do magic. I… It's better if I don't, you know. It's just… that's your thing."

"Dude, you saved us all," Jan protested. "What are you talking about? Look, we get it. Magic is scary, and monsters are even scarier. We've all been through it." His gaze fell on Fabian, who quickly averted his eyes and stared at the ground. "You just need time or—"

"I don't want time," Robert snapped, in a rare show of anger. "If there's really no other way, then sure, but you can't rely on me. Ever."

Before anyone could stop him, he grabbed his jacket and walked out. Anne threw them an apologetic look before hurrying after him.

Jan shook his head. "Did anyone else think that was weird?"

"He has his reasons," Chay said, in his calm and rational voice, and Lucille knew another puzzle piece had fallen into place.

Something snapped. "Just like you had your reasons?" She wished she could take the words back as soon as they were out of her mouth but then thought better of it. "If you knew everything that was going to happen—"

"Not everything."

"—why did you let Merik escape? Why didn't we catch him straightaway and... and...?" Her throat tightened as she found herself unable to put into words what Vydra had done to Merik. What she should've done to him right away.

Chay regarded her with unbearable pity. "As you know, killing him didn't stop what he'd already unleashed, but he had to be stopped. Now, if I'd killed him straightaway, Robert never would've risen to the challenge, and Greenvalley would've fared even worse. And though he might be in denial, the boulder is rolling down the hill and can't be stopped. He's important to the prophecy, though I don't quite know how yet."

Lucille let out a helpless laugh, tears filling her eyes. "Really? Important enough to let all this happen? Why... why did you let me start anything with him? Why did you let him use me?"

The words tasted like acid as they cut straight to the core of what she was feeling. All of this could've been avoided if Chay had just stopped her going down this road from the start.

"You want me to tell you who to date?" he asked, sounding a little incredulous.

She knew she was being ridiculous. The last thing she wanted to do was run her relationships by him, but... "If they're a psychopath."

Chay's face softened. "I can't protect you from your choices, Lucille. Or anyone really." He huffed softly. "If I could, I'd wrap you all in cotton until Draken makes his way here. But then you'd die. You wouldn't be the ones who can beat him. You wouldn't be experienced, brave, or confident enough." He was looking at them one after the other. "You wouldn't have the connections you need to help you win that battle. The support. If I protect you now, I only doom you later, and everyone else, along with you."

There was a stunned silence while the words sunk in.

"Sounds good to me," Vydra said, breaking the spell.

Lucille shot her an evil glare. No one she knew had died. Her city hadn't been laid to waste. And she hadn't been chosen for some larger-than-life battle with crushing stakes.

Samantha reached out and put her hand on Lucille's knee. The little gesture eased some of her pain. Cian was among those who'd died because of her actions, but Samantha didn't blame her. Maybe Chay was right and even this experience had been unavoidable.

"Besides, there was one thing that played into my hands precisely because of your relationship with the Phalesian prince."

"Does it have to do with the Interglobal Parliament?" Lucille asked, sulking.

Chay shook his head. "No, that's a different matter, complex and... not of importance. Not now. This is about your prophecy for Ashuan. As I tried to tell you when I first arrived, Merik was working with the Archdemon of Envy. Or rather with the Shadow, the Dark One mentioned in the prophecy and one of Envy's new disciples. I only received this information because of a leak in Pyke's residence, and that was due to you, Lucille. Do you remember Alecia, Pyke's first disciple?"

It took her a moment, but then she remembered the honey-haired envy demon who'd help her fight her way through Melaney's residence. "What about her?"

"Well, she doesn't like the Shadow. She also didn't like Merik." Chay gave her a pointed look.

Matt caught on before her. "She likes Lucille?"

"Apparently so. Enough to go behind Pyke's back and reach out to me. It's still a very tentative alliance, and I had to promise I'd do my best to keep Pyke alive. In return, she'll try to find out as much as she can about the Shadow's origins, his weaknesses, and his plans. As for now, assume she's watching you."

"Does it even matter what we do?" Fabian asked, arms crossed. "That particular prophecy is about one guy saving us all, not six. And unless we find them, we're screwed. Wait! Could it be Robert?"

Jan massaged his temples. "If it is, we'll have to punch his eyes open. He just declared we're on our own here."

"I'll put him on the list anyway," Samantha said, only to find her whiteboard wiped. "Fine, we'll start a new list. Robert, Finn—"

"Camdyn," Fabian added.

"Your classmate?"

"He's a wind mage, very insecure about his powers, but slowly learning to embrace them. Definitely not in a position to be a hero yet, but with some confidence..." Fabian smiled softly. "He could fly, at least."

Lucille watched Chay as her friends discussed the likely identity of their would-be saviour. If she had to take a stab at it, he seemed pleased. As if they were moving in the right direction at least.

"Very well, you work on that Camdyn boy. Jan will work his magic on Robert."

"Me?" Jan stared at her.

"You're close."

"Since when?"

"He's dating your sister. Or maybe we'll just leave it to Anne, since she's living with Finn, too."

Finn seemed eager to help and didn't need any convincing. Plus, he knew his way around prophecies. All he needed was some direction and a deeper purpose, but he was lacking one thing that the other two had: powerful magic.

The moment it looked like Anne was about to be burdened with the task, Jan stepped up. "I'll wear Robert down."

"Either way, the Shadow will continue to attack you," Chay said.

"Why?" Fabian asked. "We're not the ones he wants."

"In a way, you are. Listen. The Shadow knows about the prophecy. He knows there's someone in Ashuan who could unravel his entire plan. He wants to eliminate this adversary and all others who could pose a danger to him. That means you, prophecy or not. So, he's going to keep coming for you."

Lucille glared at no one in particular. "Well, he's not the first who's tried that. Let him come. We'll stop him." If no winged boy stepped up, she'd go down to Hell herself and tear this shadow apart.

Samantha grimaced. "But how many people will die in our place while we fight this abomination?" She quickly glanced at Fabian. "You know I'm beyond glad you're still with us."

Fabian gave her a sad little smile. "Same."

Meanwhile, Matt put his arms around her. "I think the question is less about how many will die, and more about how many we can save."

At that, Chay cracked a rare smile, his eyes brimming with pride. "That's exactly what this is all about."

As much as Lucille appreciated the idea of concentrating on those who lived instead of those who died as a philosophical concept, the reality was the number of deaths kept haunting her. Sixty-two people had lost their lives in Greenvalley, with a further eighty afield, a disproportionate number of them male. The news stations were scrambling for an explanation.

In her stupor, Lucille's feet had led her to her parents' home, finding Philipp on her doorstep. He must've missed the memo that she wasn't living there anymore. All she wanted was to lie down and never get up, not paint a pretty picture for the newspapers. But then she noticed his red eyes and her stomach dropped.

"Your brother?" Philipp had once told her he was the younger of two.

Philipp nodded, unable to speak, and Lucille wished Vydra had poisoned her instead.

"I'm sorry," she blurted out. Blinking rapidly, she took him up to her room. Closing the door behind her, Lucille confessed. "It's all my fault."

Philipp cocked his head in confusion. "What do you mean?"

"I caused this."

Bit by bit, it broke out of her. The plagues. The scroll she'd translated. Merik. How stupid she'd been. How gullible, blinded, not by love but by the flutter of excitement her entanglement with the Phalesian prince had brought. Fresh tears ran down her face. Instead of wiping her cheeks, she let them grow sticky under the weight, denying herself even that small comfort.

Suddenly, Philipp was there. He cupped her face, peered into her eyes, then wrapped his arms around her and held her tight, his own tears dropping into her hair.

Lucille held onto him, clawing at his back as the sobs ravaged her throat. "I'm so sorry. So, so sorry."

"It wasn't your fault," Philipp said, his voice coarse, clearly not entirely honest. "You were tricked and dragged into something much bigger than you."

"Isn't that the truth?" Lucille muttered bitterly.

Philipp took a step back and rubbed his face. "Are you saying this is just the beginning?"

"There are prophecies, and all that shit." Lucille swallowed.

If this was just a preview of the heartbreak to come, she didn't want any of it. Why did it have to be her and her friends? And why did they have to go through so much pain just to be strong enough for yet another devastating battle, one they might not even survive?

She gasped, new tears springing to her eyes. Suddenly, she felt like she was drowning, the weight of the prophecy and her failure pushing her under. Philipp reached out once more, but she batted his hand away.

"I can't. This is... I'm sorry about your brother. I really am. I just... I need some space."

He nodded. "Thank you for taking the time to explain everything to me. I'll... see you around." He raised his hand, but let it fall, stepping out of the room.

The door closed, and Lucille choked back a sob. She heard Pascal in the corridor, asking Philipp for a favour that broke her heart all over again, "I know it's a long shot, but I figured a journalist like you would have access to files I don't. The curse of the firstborn didn't hit me, so I gathered—"

"You have an older brother," Philipp surmised, his voice laced with pain.

"I need to know."

Philipp sighed. "Of course. I'll see what I can do."

His kindness was like a dagger in her guts. Despite losing his older brother just hours ago, he was willing to go out of his way to help his ex's little brother find his.

Lucille leant her back against her door, slowly sinking to the ground and wrapping her arms around her knees. The guilt was eating her alive, while the shame wormed itself deeper into her flesh. Merik had merely toyed with her. With sweet words and amazing sex and an irresistible task, he'd coerced her into aiding him with his terrible vendetta. She felt used, abused, and violated, but none of that was enough to stave off the guilt: she'd fallen for him and been blind to all his faults. Her actions had killed over a hundred people.

If she never crawled out of bed again, it would still be too early.

Her phone buzzed with a message from Rachel that managed to cut straight through her pain and bring out a sad little smile, but a smile nonetheless.

Rachel: Come home.

Jan

Slowly, the town recovered. They buried their victims and held a huge memorial in the town square. With the first snow, life went on, a little too soon for Jan's taste. But not everything returned to normal.

The plagues had left their mark on Greenvalley. The Magic Circle was booming like it never had before, as more and more people turned to supernatural solutions for supernatural problems. Philipp's column had been moved to the front page, too, as Greenvalley fully embraced its witchy heritage, and people were moving into the town to take the deceased's places. People who believed in magic.

However, the biggest changes Jan saw were in his parents. His mother frequently stopped him in the hospital's hallways to learn about his magical brand of healing, growing more intrigued by the day. As for his father... He'd agreed to build Anne and Finn a temple in the forest.

The hail had knocked down a whole lot of trees, which he and his team cleared, preparing the site for a simple temple, as per Anne and Finn's design. They'd put a lot of thought into making the temple as versatile as possible. While it would be dedicated to Hanna, there would be smaller altars to leave an offering for other gods, such as Serathon. It would officially open in spring, when Anne was planning some life-affirming ceremony to consecrate the temple with the pilgrim woman, Mildred. Jan loved her enthusiasm, and he selfishly hoped a bit of divine protection would come along with the temple. The town surely needed it.

Jan found Anne walking the perimeter with his father, explaining her grand vision. To his credit, Stefan was listening patiently, though he still had the steep crease on his forehead Jan had always associated with disbelief.

"This won't interfere with your schoolwork, will it?" he asked, as if school was the most important thing in the world when they were facing almost certain doom.

Always the ever-dutiful daughter, Anne shook her head. "No, of course not. School comes first. But don't tell Hanna."

Jan snorted, drawing their attention. A sigh escaped his father, and he braced himself for the inevitable accusations about dragging Anne into his mess.

"Don't you believe in this Hanna?"

"Honest answer? I still struggle with all the gods and goddesses and reincarnated souls, but I've seen Anne's prayers answered, and I do believe in her."

Anne beamed. Stefan scratched his chin. "I guess you're right. This is all a bit strange, but... I mean, if it makes her happy..."

"It does."

"I don't see any harm in it."

Jan very nearly snorted again. Of course, Anne's magic was harmless and nice and socially agreeable. "Awesome."

Stefan shot him a tortured look. "I... You have to agree all of this is quite hard to believe, right? Magic and monsters... It's a lot."

"Sure," Jan said, with a non-committal shrug.

He knew he'd never get an apology from his father. Men like him didn't apologise, and Jan didn't care if he ever did—it wouldn't change anything. He was glad his father was changing his tune for Anne, though.

His father looked relieved. "Good. For what it's worth... your mother's been telling me about all the good you do with your healing... skill. I'm proud of you."

Jan's eyebrows shot up. He opened his mouth, then shut it again before he could question it and gave a sharp nod.

Stefan took a deep breath, as if he'd shed a huge weight, before clapping Anne's shoulder. "Alright. Let me see what else we can get done today."

Jan crossed his arms and watched him leave. "He's getting sappy with age, isn't he?"

Anne giggled. "Dad? Never." She studied his profile. "How's everyone holding up?"

He winced. "Not so good. Especially not with this other prophecy hanging over our heads. Speaking of the other prophecy: we think it might be Robert."

Anne gasped, her eyes wide. Jan had expected a range of emotion, but not outright shock, as if he'd told Anne he was planning to kill him.

"It can't be," she whispered.

"Look, I don't like it either. Robert our saviour? He's a bumbling idiot on his good days, and on his bad days, he's—"

"Roric."

"Come again?"

Anne sighed. "Do you know who Roric is?"

The name rang a vague bell.

"He's part of your prophecy. The big one. Roric is Draken's son."

"Draken as in 'the Greedy One who'll bring upon the end of all worlds'? That guy had a son?"

"I know you hate reading, but you should at least get the CliffsNotes for your own history." Anne shook her head. "Yes, he had a son. Roric used to be Hanna's fiancé, but as soon as he met Kairos, he was more interested in him, eventually kidnapping and tempting him to the dark side. He almost ruined it all. Roric is evil, and a pretty strong mage who specialises in banishing magic and several other dark arts."

"Wait. Are you saying Robert is—"

"Roric's reincarnation, yes. And he can feel it. He's used his powers twice now, and every time he said it feels like something is taking over him. That's not him. That's Roric."

Jan frowned. "Are you sure? Because souls get cleansed, or something." He'd already forgotten Chay's explanation—or had it been Matt's? "They lose all their memories. I certainly don't feel like Vesta's taking over me when I heal." As for Herne, his other soul, he'd never felt an inkling of his particular talent—some sort of mystical travel magic.

"Maybe it's different for him." Anne shrugged. "Look, I don't know. All I know is Chay confirmed the reincarnation in the book, and

Robert's scared to death that this dark presence inside will take over one day and hurt the people he loves. I highly doubt he's the one the prophecy spoke of."

"Who knows? The prophecy never said our saviour had to be a good guy."

Alecia

A delicious shriek echoed through the residence as the Shadow discovered the failure of his servant. Alecia pretended not to hear the frustration and continued serving Pyke his special tea, though she did it with a smug little smile that didn't escape the archdemon.

"You're happy about this development?"

"Very," she answered truthfully.

She knew Pyke had no personal stake in his servant's vendetta. All he cared about was the envy it produced, which strengthened his seat.

"Would you like me to check on the Shadow?" Alecia asked, setting the delicate pot down.

Pyke nodded. "Please, my dear."

Alecia slipped out of the throne room and hurried towards the quarters the Shadow had claimed. He was surrounded by his mirrors, hissing at them in anger. It only took Alecia a couple of seconds to recognise the people the mirror showed, her gaze landing on Lucille almost immediately.

She looked sad as she sat in her lecture, her red eyes a telltale sign she'd been crying herself to sleep. Alecia felt a surge of anger towards Merik. Even though his soul had already left his body, she wished she'd been the one to deal the death blow or, failing that, was able to travel to the Land of the Dead so she could make him regret every choice during his short, puny life.

"Is anything the matter?" Alecia said, announcing her presence to distract herself from Lucille's grief.

The shadows flowed around her. Others would've found it disconcerting, but Alecia was bored.

"They destroyed my tool," the Shadow hissed.

"Who did?" She snorted and laughed. "Not those meagre humans you're so obsessed with." Shrugging, she turned to a different mirror, this one showing the little witch Melaney's son had forsaken his birthright for. She wondered if he was happy with his choice. He'd been so close to the crown. "You use a human tool, you get human results. They're just so very fragile."

The Shadow hissed again. "These are special humans. They're the Seer's pets."

Alecia held her breath at the mention of Chay. Had the Shadow found out about her betrayal already? If so, how? "What would the Seer want with a bunch of humans?" she asked, using a particularly derisive tone.

The Shadow smiled. She didn't know how she could tell, since he had no mouth or face to speak of, but she felt his glee. He'd lost something important, but he'd gained something even more valuable: information.

"They're no mere humans, my dear. Those are the Six."

"The Six?"

Alecia tried to sound incredulous despite the pounding of her heart echoing in her ears. How had he found out about it? That was her information, hers alone. But just like her place at Pyke's side, he'd stolen it. That dirty little thief.

"You know exactly what I'm talking about," the Shadow said, his voice smug. "But don't worry, they won't be the Six for much longer, because I'll crush them, one by one. And then who will stop me? You?"

Alecia was seething. "I will stop you." She leant forward, unafraid of his shadowy tendrils. "Because you came from nothing and you'll return to nothing once Pyke's through with you. If they're the Six, you don't stand a chance."

The Shadow chuckled as she withdrew, not cowed in the slightest. "We shall see."

In a huff, Alecia left and nearly barrelled into her master. Quickly, she attempted to smooth her features and hide her feelings about the

Shadow's intrusion, lest Pyke call her out. But of course, he saw right through her.

With a smile, the archdemon raised his hand and gently cupped her cheek. "Isn't it invigorating?" Pyke asked, his eyes alight with fervour. "I haven't seen you jealous like this in a long time, my dear. Drink it in. Let the envy fill you, then wreak as much chaos as you can."

Thank you for reading The Element of Surprise. The adventure will continue in The Element of Jealousy (Ashuan Envy 2).

Please review! Authors depend on reviews to get the word out about their books. If you enjoyed The Element of Surprise, consider reviewing it on your favourite retailer, review site or your personal blog.

Dramatis Personae

Family de Cerque

Lucille – 19, one of the Six, a witch and illusionist, studies History in Greenvalley

    Bastien – Lucille's absentee father, a busy man

    Linda – Lucille's stepmother, a designer

    Pascal – 11, Lucille's adoptive brother, a telekinetic

    Cecille – dead, Lucille's witch grandmother, killed by the Archdemon of Wrath

    Alena – dead, Lucille's mother, died in a car crash

    Albert – the de Cerque butler, a mind reader

    Tobias – the de Cerque chauffeur

Family Kollmer

Samantha – 19, one of the Six, a witch and potion maker, studies Chemistry in Greenvalley

    Meg – 17, Samantha's little sister and Jan's girlfriend, best friend of Anne

    Ben – Samantha's father, runs a car workshop with Joachim Bendtfeld

    Juliane – Samantha's mother, an aspiring actor

Elda – Samantha's grandmother, the Greenvalley Witch, lives in the forest
   Erich – dead, Samantha's grandfather, a demon hunter

Family Bendtfeld

Fabian – 19, one of the Six, a water elemental mage, studies Elemental Magic at the Citadel of Magic
   Joachim – Fabian's father, runs a car workshop with Ben Kollmer
   Caroline – Fabian's mother, runs the Magic Circle, a magic shop
   Merle – the family cat

Family Hadden

Rachel – 19, one of the Six, a dreamwalker, studies Mathematics in Greenvalley
   Nico – dead, Rachel's twin brother, appears in her dreams
   Annette – Rachel's mother, a hair stylist with an alcohol problem
   Mick – Rachel's father, a Maths professor, lives in LA

Family Kerscher

Jan – 21, one of the Six, a healer, in paramedic training
   Anne – 17, Jan's little sister
   Stefan – Jan's father, a coal miner
   Ida – Jan's mother, a nurse

Family Traidous and Matt's demon relatives

Matt/Melchior – 19, one of the Six, a half-demon of the House of Lust, studies World Studies in Fader

René– Matt's father, a former demon hunter and elementary school teacher

Crumbs – the family dog

Melaney – dead, Matt's mother, a demon, the former Archdemon of Lust, killed by Balthasar

Balthasar – Matt's oldest brother, the Archdemon of Lust, leader of the Small Council

Caspar – dead, Matt's older brother, a demon of the Houses of Wrath and Lust, Menuha's twin brother, killed by Matt

Menuha – dead, Matt's older sister, a demon of the Houses of Wrath and Lust, Caspar's twin sister, killed by Melaney

Greenvalley

Adam Black – 22, hospital technician

André – 20, paramedic trainee

Antonia – 22, 3rd-year Chemistry, TA

Cian – 19, former classmate, studies Chemistry in Bielefeld

Dennis – 22, 3rd-year History

Ellie – fellow paramedic trainee

Finn – 15, originally from Ylvadin, a priest of Serathon

Hugo von Hohenstetten – an old-fashioned ghost

Jakob – 23, 3rd-year History

Mr. Kinzel – paramedic teacher

Mildred – pilgrim woman

Neve – a snow witch, occupies Blackstone House

Ophelia de la Vega – 17, Fabian's girlfriend, can speak to snakes and command shadows

Philipp Vendenberg – Lucille's boyfriend, a reporter for the Greenvalley View

Robert – 19, a friendly guy who follows the Six around, in nurse training

Shayna – 19, studies Elemental Magic at the Citadel of Magic
Timothy – fellow paramedic trainee

Demons

Adrianes – Matt's nephew, Balthasar's son, Chief Gardener of Hell's Gardens
    Alecia – First Devotee of Pyke
    Chay – "The Seer" a half-demon, Matt's best friend, can see the future
    Hel – the Archdemon of Pride
    Iyaga – the new Archdemon of Greed
    Malcolm – dead, Melaney's brother, the former Archdemon of Greed
    Moloch – the Archdemon of Gluttony
    Pyke – the Archdemon of Envy
    Volac – the Archdemon of Wrath
    Yash – the Archdemon Sloth

Citadel of Magic

Camdyn Winter – 16, an elemental mage of air
    Clio – an undead cat woman
    Elisabeth Takuna – first councillor of the Citadel, Kaia's mother
    Kaia Takuna – 20, an elemental mage of earth
    Professor Takuna – director of studies, Kaia's father
    Professor Terian – teacher for Elemental Magic

Fader

Geoffrey Black – an Ashuan parliamentarian, Adam's father
    Merik an Derendi – Phalesian prince, 3rd-year in World Studies

Vydra – an Einin assassin, 1st-year in World Studies

JANNA RUTH

THE ELEMENT OF JEALOUSY

ASHUAN ENVY BOOK 2

JANNA RUTH

A FORCE OF NATURE

SPIRIT SEEKER BOOK 1

JANNA RUTH

GHOSTS OF THE CATACOMBS

About Janna Ruth

About Janna Ruth

Once upon a time, Janna Ruth studied the plate boundaries of this world. Now, she's creating her own worlds. Born in Berlin, Germany, Janna lives in Wellington, New Zealand, writing both English and German books.

Janna's writing career kicked off when she won a writing competition for German publisher Ueberreuter. Her first self-published novel "Im Bann der zertanzten Schuhe" (Melody of Curse, coming in June 2022) went on to win the 2018 SERAPH for "Best Independent Title". She debuted in English with her witchy novella "Witching with Dolphins" in 2020 and has since published urban fantasy, YA sci-fi, and contemporary coming-of-age novels and series.

When Janna isn't writing, she has a plethora of hobbies, such as aerial acrobatics, cake decorating, drawing, reading, and anything crafty you can throw her way.

Find out more about Janna and her books here: